New York Times be

Nora Roberts

has published over a hundred and forty novels, and has been translated into over twenty-five different languages and published all over the world.

With over 200 million copies of her books in print worldwide, she is truly a publishing phenomenon.

Also available from Mills & Boon® and
Nora Roberts

Blithe Images
Courting Catherine
Dance of Dreams
Dance to the Piper
Enchanted
Entranced
First Impressions
For Now, Forever
Gabriel's Angel
Her Mother's Keeper
Home for Christmas
In from the Cold
Lawless
Less of a Stranger
Local Hero
Loving Jack
Mind Over Matter
Night Shadow
Night Shift
Night Smoke
Nightshade
Partners
Rules of the Game
Search for Love
Skin Deep
Song of the West
Storm Warning
Temptation
Tempting Fate
The Heart's Victory
The Last Honest Woman
The Name of the Game
The Right Path
Treasures Lost, Treasures Found
Unfinished Business
Without a Trace

Nora Roberts

Against All Odds

Mills & Boon™

> DID YOU PURCHASE THIS BOOK WITHOUT A COVER?
> If you did, you should be aware it is **stolen property** as it was
> reported 'unsold and destroyed' by a retailer.
> Neither the author nor the publisher has received any payment
> for this book.

First Published 1991
First Australian Paperback Edition 2010
ISBN 978 1 742 55560 7

First Published 1991
First Australian Paperback Edition 2010
ISBN 978 1 742 55560 7

AGAINST ALL ODDS © 2010 by Harlequin Books S.A.

A MAN FOR AMANDA
© 1991 by Nora Roberts
Philippine Copyright 1991
Australian Copyright 1991
New Zealand Copyright 1991

SUZANNA'S SURRENDER
© 1991 by Nora Roberts
Philippine Copyright 1991
Australian Copyright 1991
New Zealand Copyright 1991

Except for use in any review, the reproduction or utilisation of this work in whole or in part in any form by any electronic, mechanical or other means, now known or hereafter invented, including xerography, photocopying and recording, or in any information storage or retrieval system, is forbidden without the permission of the publisher, Harlequin Mills & Boon®, Locked Bag 7002, Chatswood D.C. N.S.W., Australia 2067.

This book is sold subject to the condition that it shall not, by way of trade or otherwise, be lent, resold, hired out or otherwise circulated without the prior consent of the publisher in any form of binding or cover other than that in which it is published and without a similar condition including this condition being imposed on the subsequent purchaser.

All rights reserved including the right of reproduction in whole or in part in any form. This edition is published in arrangement with Harlequin Books S.A..

This is a work of fiction. Names, characters, places, and incidents are either the product of the author's imagination or are used fictitiously, and any resemblance to actual persons, living or dead, business establishments, events, or locales is entirely coincidental.

Published by
Harlequin Mills & Boon®
Level 5
15 Help Street
CHATSWOOD NSW 2067
AUSTRALIA

® and ™ are trademarks owned by Harlequin Enterprises Limited or its corporate affiliates and used by others under licence. Trademarks marked with an ® are registered in Australia and in other countries. Contact admin_legal@Harlequin.ca for details.

Printed and bound in Australia by
McPherson's Printing Group

CONTENTS

A MAN FOR AMANDA   7

SUZANNA'S SURRENDER   179

A Man For Amanda

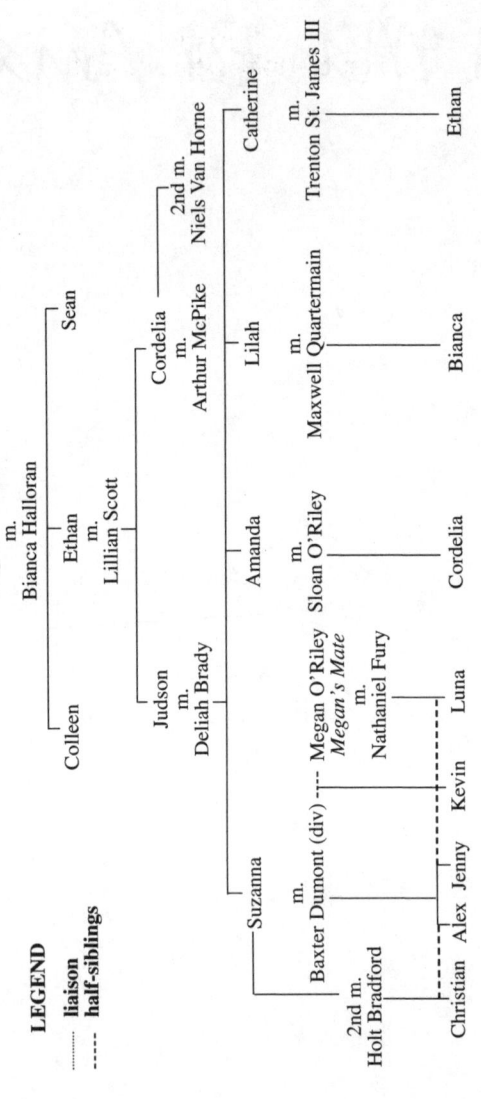

To Joyce,
from one baby sister to another

Prologue

Bar Harbor
June 8, 1913

In the afternoon, I walked to the cliffs. The day, our first day back in The Towers, was bright and warm. The rumble of the sea was as I had left it ten long months ago. There was a fishing boat chugging over the blue-green water, and a neat sloop gliding cheerfully along. So much was the same, and yet, one vital change dimmed the day for me.

He was not there.

It was wrong of me to wish to find him waiting where I had left him so many months ago. To find him painting as he always did, slicing the brush against canvas like a dueler in the heat of battle. It was wrong of me to wish to see him turn, look at me with those intense gray eyes—to see him smile, to hear him say my name.

Yet I did wish it.

My heart was dancing in my breast as I rushed from the

house to race across the lawn, past the gardens and down the slope.

The cliffs were there, so high and proud, jutting up to the pure summer sky. The sea, almost calm today, mirrored the color so that it seemed I stood cupped in a lovely blue ball. The rocks tumbled down before me, down and down to where the waves slapped and hissed. Behind me, the towers of my summer home, my husband's home, speared up, arrogant and beautiful.

How strange that I should love the house when I have known such unhappiness inside it.

I reminded myself that I am Bianca Calhoun, wife of Fergus Calhoun, mother to Colleen and Ethan and Sean. I am a respected woman, a dutiful wife, a devoted mother. My marriage is not a warm one, but that does not alter the vows I took. There is no place in my life for romantic fancies and sinful dreams.

Still, I stood and I waited. But he did not come. Christian, the lover I have taken only with my heart, did not come. He may not even be on the island any longer. Perhaps he has packed up his canvases and brushes, moved from his cottage and gone on to paint some other sea, some other sky.

It would be best. I know it would be best. Since I met him last summer, I have hardly gone an hour without thinking of him. Yet I have a husband I respect, three children I love more than my life. It is to them I must be faithful, not to the memory of something that never was. And never could be.

The sun is setting as I sit and write by the window of my tower. In a short time I must go down and help Nanny put my babies to bed. Little Sean has grown so, and is already beginning to toddle. Soon he will be as quick as Ethan. Colleen, quite the young lady at four, wants a new pink dress.

It is of them I must think, my children, my precious loves, and not of Christian.

It will be a quiet night, one of very few we will have during our summer on Mount Desert Island. Fergus has already talked of giving a dinner dance next week. I must...

He is there. Down below on the cliffs. He is hardly more than a shadow with the distance and the dimming light. Yet I know it is he. Just as I knew, as I stood and pressed my hand to the glass, that he was looking up, looking for me. However impossible it is, I would swear I could hear him call my name. So softly.

Bianca.

Chapter 1

He was a solid wall of denim and muscle. Ramming into him knocked the wind out of her lungs and the packages out of her hands. In her rush to get from one place to the next, she didn't even bother to glance at him but dove to save the flying boxes.

If he'd been looking where he'd been going, she wouldn't have run into him. Amanda managed to bite her tongue before she snapped out the thought, and scowled instead at the run-down heels of his boots. In a hurry, as usual, she knelt on the sidewalk outside the boutique where she'd been shopping, to gather up her scattered packages.

"Let me give you a hand, honey."

The slow southwestern drawl grated on her nerves. She had a million things to do, and scrambling on the sidewalk with a tourist wasn't on her schedule. "I've got it," she muttered, leaning over so that her chin-length hair drifted down to curtain her face. Everything was grating on her nerves today, she thought as she hurried to restack bags and boxes. This little irritation was the last in a long line.

"It's an awful lot for one person to carry."

"I can manage, thanks." She reached for a box just as her persistent helper did the same. The brief tug-of-war had the top slipping off and the contents spilling onto the sidewalk.

"Now, that's mighty pretty." There was amused, masculine approval in the voice as he scooped up a scrap of thin red silk that pretended to be a nightie.

Amanda snatched it from him and stuffed it into one of the bags. "Do you mind?"

"No, ma'am. I sure don't."

Amanda pushed back her tumbled hair and took her first good look at him. So far, all she'd seen were a pair of cowboy boots and the line of faded denim from knee to ankle. There was a great deal more of him. Even crouched down beside her he looked big. Shoulders, hands. Mouth, she thought nastily. Right now he was using it to grin at her. It might, under different circumstances, have been an engaging enough grin. But at the moment it was stuck in the middle of a face she'd decided to dislike on sight.

Not that it wasn't a good one, with its slashing warrior's cheekbones, velvet green eyes and deep tan. The curl of his reddish-blond hair over the collar of his denim shirt might have been charming. If he hadn't been in her way.

"I'm in a hurry," she told him.

"I noticed." He flipped a long finger through her hair to tuck it behind her ear. "Looked like you were on the way to a fire when you plowed into me."

"If you'd moved," she began, then shook her head. Arguing would take time she simply didn't have. "Never mind." Grabbing at packages, she rose. "Excuse me."

"Hold on."

He unfolded himself as she tapped her foot and waited. Disconcerted, she frowned up at him. At five feet ten inches, she was accustomed to meeting most men almost eye to eye. With this one she had several extra inches to go. "What?"

"I can give you a ride to that fire if you need it."

Her brow arched in her frostiest look. "That won't be necessary."

Using a fingertip, he pushed a box back in place before it could slide out of her grip. "You look like you could use a little help."

"I'm perfectly capable of getting where I'm going, thank you."

He didn't doubt it for a minute. "Then maybe you can help me." He liked the way her hair kept falling into her eyes, and the impatient way she kept blowing it away again. "I just got into town this morning." His gaze lazily skimmed her face. "I thought maybe you could make some suggestions about...what I should do with myself."

At the moment, she had a pocketful of them. "Try the chamber of commerce." She started by him, then whirled when his hand came down on her arm. "Look, buster, I don't know how they do things back in Tucson—"

"Oklahoma City," he corrected.

"Wherever, but around here, cops take a dim view of men who hassle women on the streets."

"That so?"

"You bet it's so."

"Well then, I'll have to watch my step since I plan to be around awhile."

"I'll hang out a bulletin. Now, excuse me."

"Just one more thing." He held up a pair of brief black panties embroidered with red roses. "I think you forgot this."

She grabbed the bikinis, then stalked off as she balled them into her pocket.

"Nice meeting you," he called after her, and laughed when she doubled her already hurried pace.

Twenty minutes later, Amanda gathered up her packages from the back seat of her car. Balancing some under her chin, she kicked the door closed with her foot. She'd nearly forgotten about the encounter already. There was too much on her mind. Behind her, the house rose up into the sky, its gray stones staid, its towers and peaks fanciful and its porches sagging. Next to her family, there was nothing Amanda loved more than The Towers.

She raced up the steps, avoided a rotting board then struggled to free a hand enough to open the towering front door. "Aunt Coco!" The moment she stepped into the hall, an oversize black puppy raced down the stairs. On the third from the bottom, he tripped, rolled and went sprawling onto the gleaming chestnut floor. "Almost made it that time, Fred."

Pleased with himself, Fred danced around Amanda's legs as she continued to call for her aunt.

"Coming. I'm coming." Tall and stately, Cordelia Calhoun McPike hurried in from the rear of the house. She wore peach linen slacks under a splattered white apron. "I was in the kitchen. We're going to try my new recipe for cannelloni tonight."

"Is C.C. home?"

"Oh, no, dear." Coco patted the hair she'd tinted the day before to Moonlit Blonde. In an old habit, she peeked into the hall mirror to make certain the shade suited her—for the moment. "She's down at her garage. Something about rocker arms, I think—though what rocking chairs have to do with cars and engines, I can't say."

"Great. Come upstairs, I want to show you what I got."

"Looks like you bought out the shops. Here, let me help you." Coco managed to grab two bags before Amanda dashed up the stairs.

"I had the best time."

"But you hate to shop."

"For myself. This was different. Still, everything took longer than I thought it would, so I was afraid I wouldn't get back and be able to stash it all before C.C. got home." She rushed into her room to dump everything onto the big four-poster bed. "Then this stupid man got in my way and knocked everything all over the sidewalk." Amanda stripped off her jacket, folded it, then laid it neatly over the back of a chair. "Then he had the nerve to try to pick me up."

"Really?" Always interested in liaisons, romances and assignations, Coco tilted her head. "Was he attractive?"

"If you go for the Wild Bill Hickok type. Anyway, I made it—no thanks to him."

As Amanda sorted through the bags, Fred tried twice, unsuccessfully, to leap onto the bed. He ended by sitting on the rug to watch.

"I found some wonderful decorations for the bridal shower." She began to pull out white-and-silver bells, crepe paper swans, balloons. "I love this frilly parasol," she went on. "Not C.C.'s style maybe, but I thought if we hung it up over…Aunt Coco." With a sigh, Amanda sat on the bed. "Don't start crying again."

"I can't help it." Already sniffling, Coco took an embroidered hankie from her apron pocket and dabbed carefully at her eyes. "She's the baby, after all. The youngest of my four little girls."

"There's not one of the Calhoun women who could be called little," Amanda pointed out.

"You're still my babies, and have been ever since your mother and father died." Coco used the hankie expertly. She didn't want to smear her mascara. "Every time I think of her being married—and in only a matter of days, really—I just fill up. I adore Trenton, you know." Thinking of her future nephew, she blew delicately into the hankie. "He's a wonderful man, and I knew they'd be perfect together right from the start, but it's all so fast."

"You're telling me." Amanda combed a hand through her sleek cap of hair. "I've barely had time to organize. How anyone expects to put on a wedding with barely three weeks notice—or why they'd want to try—is beyond me. They'd be better off eloping."

"Don't say that." Scandalized, Coco stuck her hankie back into her pocket. "Why, I'd be furious if they cheated me out of this wedding. And if you think you can when your time comes, think again."

"My time isn't going to come for years, if ever." Meticulously Amanda tidied the decorations again. "Men are as far down on my list of priorities as they can get."

"You and your lists." Coco clucked her tongue. "Let me tell you, Mandy, the one thing you can't plan in this life is falling in love. Your sister certainly didn't plan it, and look at her. Squeezing fittings for a wedding dress in between her carburetors and transmissions. Your time may come sooner than you think. Why just this morning when I was reading my tea leaves—"

"Oh, Aunt Coco, not the tea leaves."

Grandly Coco drew herself up to her considerable height. "I've read some very fascinating things in the tea leaves. After our last séance, I'd think you'd be a bit less cynical."

"Maybe something happened at the séance, but—"

"Maybe?"

"All right, something did happen." Letting out a deep breath, Amanda shrugged. "I know C.C. got an image—"

"A vision."

"Whatever—of Great-Grandmama Bianca's emerald necklace." And it had been spooky, she admitted to herself, the way C.C. had been able to describe it, though no one had seen the two tiers of emeralds and diamonds in decades. "And no one who's lived in this house could deny that they've felt some—some presence or something up in Bianca's tower."

"Aha!"

"But that doesn't mean I'm going to start gazing into crystal balls."

"You're just too literal minded, Mandy. I can't think where you get it from. Perhaps from my Aunt Colleen. Fred, we must not chew on the Irish lace," Coco cautioned as Fred began to gnaw on Amanda's bedspread. "In any case, we were speaking of tea leaves. When I took a reading this morning, I saw a man."

Amanda rose to hide the decorations in her closet. "You saw a man in your teacup."

"You know very well it doesn't work precisely like that. I saw a man, and I had the strongest feeling that he's very close."

"Maybe it's the plumber. He's been underfoot for days."

"No, it's not the plumber. This man—he's close, but he's not from the island." She let her eyes unfocus as she did when she practiced looking psychic. "In fact he's from some distance away. He's going to be an important part of our lives. And—I'm quite sure of this—he's going to be vitally important to one of you girls."

"Lilah can have him," Amanda decided, thinking of her free-spirited older sister. "Where is she anyway?"

"Oh, she was meeting someone after work. Rod or Tod or Dominick."

"Damn it." Amanda scooped up her jacket to hang it neatly in the closet. "We were supposed to go through more of the papers. She knew I was counting on her. We have to find some lead as to where the emeralds are hidden."

"We'll find them, dear." Distracted, Coco poked through the other packages. "When the time is right. Bianca wants us to. I believe she'll show us the next step very soon."

"We need more than blind faith and mystic visions. Bianca could have hidden them anywhere." Scowling, she plopped down onto the bed again.

She didn't care about the money—though the Calhoun emeralds were reputed to be worth a fortune. It was the publicity that had resulted when Trent, her sister's fiancé, had contracted to buy The Towers, and the old legend had become public knowledge. Amanda's idea of an ordered existence had been thrown into chaos since the first story had hit.

It certainly made good print, Amanda mused as her aunt oohed and aahed over the lingerie she had bought for her sister's shower.

Early in the second decade of the century, when the resort of Bar Harbor was in its elegant heyday, Fergus Calhoun had built The Towers as an opulent summer home. There on the cliffs overlooking Frenchman Bay, he and his wife, Bianca, and their three children had vacationed, giving elaborate parties for other members of the well-heeled society.

And there, Bianca had met a young artist. They had fallen in love. It was said that Bianca had been torn between duty and her heart. Her marriage, which had been firmly supported by her parents, had been a cold one. With her heart leading her, she had planned to leave her husband and had packed away a treasure box that had contained the emeralds

Fergus had given her on the birth of their second child and first son. The whereabouts of the necklace was a mystery as, according to legend, she had thrown herself from the tower window, overwhelmed with guilt and despair.

Now, eighty years later, interest in the necklace had been revived. Even as the remaining Calhouns searched through decades of papers and ledgers for a clue, reporters and hopeful fortune hunters had become a daily nuisance.

Amanda took it personally. The legend, and the people in it, belonged to her family. The sooner the necklace was located, the better. Once a mystery was solved, interest faded quickly.

"When is Trent coming back?" she asked her aunt.

"Soon." Sighing, Coco stroked the silky red chemise. "As soon as he ties things up in Boston, he'll be on his way. He can't stand being away from C.C. There will barely be enough time to begin the renovations on the west wing before they'll be off on their honeymoon." Tears filled her eyes again. "Their honeymoon."

"Don't start, Aunt Coco. Think of what a fabulous job you'll do catering the reception. It's going to be great practice for you. This time next year you'll be starting your new career as chef for The Towers Retreat, the most intimate of the St. James hotels."

"Imagine it." Coco patted her hand at her breast.

At the knock on the front door, Fred was up and howling.

"You stay here and imagine it, Aunt Coco. I'll go answer the door."

In a race with Fred, she clattered down the steps. When the dog's four legs tangled, sending him somersaulting, she laughed and gathered him up. She was snuggling the dog against her cheek when she opened the door.

"You!"

The tone of her voice had Fred quaking. Not so the man who stood at the threshold, grinning at her. "Small world," he said in the same slow drawl he'd used when they'd knelt on the sidewalk. "I'm liking it better all the time."

"You followed me."

"No, ma'am. Though it would've been a damn good idea. The name's O'Riley. Sloan O'Riley."

"I don't care what your name is, you can turn around and start walking." She started to slam the door in his face, but he slapped a hand against it and held it wide.

"I don't think that's such a good idea. I've come a long way to get a look at the house."

Her dark blue eyes narrowed. "Oh, have you? Well, let me tell you something, this is a home, a private home. I don't care what you've read in the papers and how badly you want a shot at looking under loose stones for the emeralds. This isn't Treasure Island, and I've had my fill of people like you who think they can just come knocking at the door, or sneaking into the garden at night with a pick and shovel."

She looked just fine, Sloan thought as he waited out the tirade. Every furious inch of her. She was tall for a woman and lean with it—but not too lean. She curved out nicely in all the right places. She looked as though she could ride hard all day and still have the energy to kick up her heels at night. Stubborn chin, he decided, and approved. When she jutted it out, her warm brown hair swayed with the movement. Big blue eyes. Even while they spit fire they reminded him of cornflowers. When it wasn't scowling or swearing, he imagined her full, shapely mouth would be soft.

Soft and tasty.

"You run down yet?" he asked when she stopped to take a breath.

"No, and if you don't leave right now, I'm going to let my dog loose on you."

Taking his cue, Fred leaped out of her arms. With neck fur bristling, he bared his teeth in a growl.

"Looks pretty fierce," Sloan commented, then hunkered down to hold out the back of his hand. Fred sniffed it, then his tail began to wag joyously as Sloan scratched his ears. "Yep, pretty fierce animal you got here."

"That's it." Amanda set her hands on her hips. "I'm getting the gun."

Before she could turn inside to look for the fictitious weapon, Coco came downstairs.

"Who is it, Amanda?"

"Dead meat."

"I beg your pardon?" She stepped up to the door. The moment she spotted Sloan her ingrained vanity took over. In the blink of an eye she whipped her apron off. "Hello." Her smile was warm and feminine as she extended a hand. "I'm Cordelia McPike."

"A pleasure, ma'am." Sloan brought her fingertips to his mouth. "As I was just telling your sister here—"

"Oh, my." Coco let out a trill of delighted laughter. "Amanda's not my sister. She's my niece. The third daughter of my late brother—my much older brother."

"My mistake."

"Aunt Coco, this jerk knocked me down outside of the boutique, then followed me home. He just wants to wheedle his way into the house because of the necklace."

"Now, Mandy, you mustn't be so harsh."

"That's partially true, Mrs. McPike." Sloan gave Amanda a slow nod. "Your niece and I did have a run-in. Guess I didn't get out of her way in time. And I am trying to get into the house."

"I see." Torn between hope and doubt, Coco sighed. "I'm terribly sorry, but I don't think it would be possible to let you in. You see we have so much to do with the wedding—"

Sloan's eyes whipped back to Amanda. "You getting married?"

"My sister," she said tightly. "Not that it's any of your business. Now if you'll excuse us?"

"I wouldn't want to intrude, so I'll just be on my way. If you'll tell Trent that O'Riley was by, I'd appreciate it."

"O'Riley?" Coco repeated, then fluttered her hands. "Goodness, are you Mr. O'Riley? Please come in. Oh, I do apologize."

"Aunt Coco—"

"This is Mr. O'Riley, Amanda."

"I realize that. Why the devil have you let him in the house?"

"*The* Mr. O'Riley," Coco continued. "The one Trenton called about this morning. Don't you remember—of course you don't remember, because I didn't tell you." She patted her hands to her cheeks. "I'm afraid I'm just so flustered after keeping you standing outside that way."

"Don't you worry about it," he said to Coco. "It's an honest mistake."

"Aunt Coco." Amanda stood with her hand on the doorknob, ready to pitch the intruder out bodily if necessary. "Who is this O'Riley and why did Trent tell you to expect him?"

"Mr. O'Riley's the architect," Coco said, beaming.

Eyes narrowing, Amanda studied him from the tip of his boots to his wavy, disordered hair. "This is an architect?"

"Our architect. Mr. O'Riley will be in charge of the renovations for the retreat, and our living quarters. We'll all be working with Mr. O'Riley—"

"Sloan," he said.

"Sloan." Coco fluttered her lashes. "For quite some time."

"Terrific." Amanda let the door slam.

Sloan hooked his thumbs in his jean pockets and gave her a slow smile. "My thoughts exactly."

Chapter 2

"Where are our manners?" Coco said. "Here we are keeping you standing in the hall. Please, come in and sit down. What can I offer you? Coffee, tea?"

"Beer in a long-necked bottle," Amanda muttered.

Sloan merely smiled at her. "There you go."

"Beer?" Coco ushered him into the parlor, wishing she'd had a moment to freshen the flowers in the vase and plump the pillows. "I have some very nice beer in the kitchen that I use for my spiced shrimp. Amanda, you'll entertain Sloan, won't you?"

"Sure. Why not?" Though she wasn't feeling particularly gracious, Amanda gestured to a chair, then took one across from him in front of the fireplace. "I suppose I should apologize."

Sloan reached down to pet Fred, who had followed them in. "What for?"

"I wouldn't have been so rude if I'd realized why you were here."

"Is that so?" As Fred settled down on the rug between them, Sloan eased back in his chair to study his unwilling hostess.

After a humming ten seconds, she struggled not to fidget. "It was a natural enough mistake."

"If you say so. What exactly are these emeralds you figured I was here to dig up?"

"The Calhoun emeralds." When he only lifted a brow, she shook her head. "My great-grandmother's emerald necklace. It's been in all the papers."

"I haven't had much time to read the papers. I've been in Budapest." He reached into his pocket and pulled out a long, slim cigar. "Mind?"

"Go ahead." Automatically she rose to fetch an ashtray from across the room. Sloan considered it a pleasure to watch that out-of-my-way walk of hers. "I'm surprised Trent didn't mention it."

Sloan struck a match and took his sweet time lighting the cigar. He took an appreciative drag, then blew out a lazy stream of smoke. All the while, he was taking stock of the room, with its sagging sofa, the glistening Baccarat, the elegant old wainscoting and the peeling paint.

"I got a cable from Trent telling me about the house and his plans, and asking me to take it on."

"You agreed to take a job like this without even seeing the property first?"

"Seemed like the thing to do at the time." She sure had pretty eyes, Sloan thought. Suspicious, but pretty. He wondered how they'd look if he ever managed to get a smile out of her. "Besides, Trent wouldn't have asked if he didn't think I'd get a kick out of it."

Her foot began to tap as it did when she had sat in one place too long. "You know Trent well then?"

"We go back a few years. We were at Harvard together."

"Harvard?" Her foot stopped tapping as she gaped at him. "You went to Harvard?"

Another man might have been insulted. Sloan was amused. "Why, shucks, ma'am," he murmured, exaggerating his drawl, then watching her cheeks flush.

"I didn't mean to…it's just that you don't really seem—"

"The Ivy League type?" he suggested before he took another pull on the cigar. "Guess appearances can be deceiving. Take the house here for instance."

"The house?"

"You take your first look at it from the outside and it's hard to figure if it's supposed to be a fortress, a castle or an architect's nightmare. But you take the time to look again, and you see it's not supposed to be anything but what it is. A timeless piece of work, on the arrogant side, strong, maybe stubborn enough to hold its own, but with just enough fancy to add some charm." He grinned at her. "Some people believe that a house reflects the personality of the people who live in it."

He rose when Coco came back in wheeling a tray. "Oh, sit down, please. It's such a treat to have a man in the house. Isn't it, Mandy?"

"I'm all aflutter."

"I hope the beer's all right." She lifted a brimming pilsner glass from the tray.

"I'm sure it's fine."

"Do try some of these canapés. Mandy, I've brought us some wine." Delighted with the chance to socialize, she smiled at Sloan over the rim of her glass. "Has Amanda been telling you about the house?"

"We were just getting to it." Sloan took a long swallow of beer. "Trent wrote that it's been in the family since the early part of the century."

"Oh, yes. With Suzanna's children—Suzanna's my eldest niece—we've had five generations of Calhouns at The Towers. Fergus—" she gestured to the portrait of a dour-faced man over the mantel "—my grandfather, built The Towers in 1904, as a summer home. He and his wife, Bianca, had three children before she threw herself out of the tower window." As always, the idea of dying for love had her sighing. "I don't believe Grandpapa was ever quite right after that. He went insane later in life, but we kept him in a very nice institution."

"Aunt Coco, I'm sure Mr. O'Riley isn't interested in the family history."

"Not interested," Sloan agreed as he tapped out his cigar. "Fascinated. Don't stop now, Mrs. McPike."

"Oh, call me Coco. Everyone does." She fluffed her hair. "The house passed along to my father, Ethan. He was their second child, but the first son. Grandpapa was very adamant about the Calhoun line. His—Ethan's—elder sister, Colleen, was miffed about the arrangement. She rarely speaks to any of us to this day."

"For which we're all eternally grateful," Amanda put in.

"Well, yes. She can be a bit—overwhelming. That left Uncle Sean, my father's younger brother. He had a spot of trouble with a woman and sailed off to the West Indies before I was born. When my father was killed, the house passed to my brother, Judson. After his marriage he and his wife decided to live here year-round. They adored the place." She glanced around the parlor with its cracked walls and faded curtains. "Judson had wonderful plans for revamping the house, but tragically he and Deliah were killed before he could begin to implement them. Then I came here to care for Amanda and her three sisters. Have another canapé."

"Thanks. Can I ask why you decided to convert part of your home into a hotel?"

"That was Trent's idea. We're all so grateful to him, aren't we, Amanda?"

Since she accepted the fact that there would be no winding down Aunt Coco, Amanda smiled. "Yes, we are."

Coco sipped delicately from her glass. "To be frank, we were in some financial distress. Do you believe in fate, Sloan?"

"I'm Irish and Cherokee." He spread his long fingers. "That doesn't give me any other choice."

"Well then, you'll understand. It was fated that Trent's father would see The Towers while he was sailing in Frenchman Bay, and seeing it, develop a deep desire for it. When the St. James's corporation offered to buy the house and turn it into a resort hotel, we were torn. It was our home after all, the only home my girls have ever known, but the upkeep…"

"I understand."

"Things happen for the best," Coco put in. "And it was really very exciting and romantic. We were on the brink, the very brink, of being forced to sell, when Trent fell in love with C.C. Of course he understood how much the house meant to her, and came up with this marvelous plan of converting the west wing into hotel suites. That way we can keep the house, and overcome the financial difficulty of maintaining it."

"Everyone gets what they want," Sloan agreed.

"Exactly." Coco leaned forward. "With your heritage, I imagine you also believe in spirits."

"Aunt Coco—"

"Now, Mandy, I know how practical minded you are. It baffles me," she said to Sloan. "All that Celtic blood and not a mystical bone in her body."

Amanda gestured with her glass. "I leave that for you and Lilah."

"Lilah's my other niece," Coco told Sloan. "She's very fey. But we were talking about the supernatural. Do you have an opinion?"

Sloan set his glass aside. "I don't think you could have a house like this without a ghost or two."

"There." Coco clapped her hands together. "I knew as soon as I saw you we'd be kindred spirits. Bianca's still here, you see. Why at our last séance I felt her so strongly." She ignored Amanda's groan. "C.C. did, too, and she's nearly as practical minded as Amanda. Bianca wants us to find the necklace."

"The Calhoun emeralds?" Sloan asked.

"Yes. We've been searching for clues, but the clutter of eight decades is daunting. And the publicity has been a bother."

"That's a mild word for it." Amanda scowled into her glass.

"It might turn up during the renovation," Sloan suggested.

"We're hoping." Coco tapped one carefully manicured finger against her lips. "I think another séance might be in order. I'm sure you're very sensitive."

Amanda choked on her wine. "Aunt Coco, Mr. O'Riley has come here to work, not to play ghosts and goblins."

"I like mixing business and pleasure." He toasted Amanda with his glass. "In fact, I make a habit of it."

A new thought jumped into Coco's mind. "You're not from the island, Sloan."

"No, Oklahoma."

"Really? That's quite a distance." She slid her gaze smugly toward Amanda. "As architect for the renovations, you'll be very important to all of us."

"I'd like to think so," he said, baffled by the arched look Coco sent her niece.

"Tea leaves," Coco murmured, then rose. "I must go check on dinner. You will join us, won't you?"

He'd planned on taking a quick look at the house then going back to the hotel to sleep for ten hours. The annoyed look on Amanda's face changed his mind. An evening with her might be a better cure for jet lag. "I'd be mighty pleased to."

"Wonderful. Mandy, why don't you show Sloan the west wing while I finish things up?"

"Tea leaves?" Sloan asked when Coco glided from the room.

"You're better off in the dark." Resigned, she rose and gestured to the doorway. "Shall we get started?"

"That's a fine idea." He followed her into the hall and up the curving staircase. "Which do you like, Amanda or Mandy?"

She shrugged. "I answer to either."

"Different images. Amanda's cool and composed. Mandy's...softer." She smelled cool, he thought. Like a quiet breeze on a hot, dusty day.

At the top of the stairs she stopped to face him. "What kind of image is Sloan?"

He stayed one step below her so that they were eye to eye. Instinct told him they'd both prefer it that way. "You tell me."

He had the cockiest grin she'd ever seen. Whenever he used it on her she felt a tremor that she was certain was annoyance. "Dodge City?" she said sweetly. "We don't get many cowboys this far east." She turned and was halfway down the hall when he took her arm.

"Are you always in such a hurry?"

"I don't like to waste time."

He kept his hand on her arm as they continued to walk. "I'll keep that in mind."

My God, the place was fabulous, Sloan thought as they started up a pie-shaped set of steps. Coffered ceilings, carved lintels, thick mahogany paneling. He stopped at an arched window to touch the wavy glass. It had to be original, he thought, like the chestnut floor and the fancy plaster work.

True, there were cracks in the walls—some of them big enough that he could slide his finger in to the first knuckle. Here and there the ceiling had given way to fist-sized holes, and portions of the molding were rotted.

It would be a challenge to bring it back to its former glory. And it would be a joy.

"We haven't used this part of the house in years." Amanda opened a carved oak door and brushed away a spider web. "It hasn't been practical to heat it during the winter."

Sloan stepped inside. The sloping floor creaked ominously as he walked across it. Somewhere along the line heavy furniture had been dragged in or out, scarring the floor with deep, jagged grooves. Two of the panes on the narrow terrace doors had been broken and replaced with plywood. Mice had had a field day with the baseboard. Above his head was a faded mural of chubby cherubs.

"This was the best guest room," Amanda explained. "Fergus kept it for people he wanted to impress. Supposedly some of the Rockefellers stayed here. It has its own bath and dressing room." She pushed open a broken door.

Ignoring her, Sloan walked to the black marble fireplace. The wall above it was papered in silk and stained from old smoke. The chip off the corner of the mantel broke his heart.

"You ought to be shot."

"I beg your pardon?"

"You ought to be shot for letting the place go like this." The look he aimed at her wasn't lazy and amused, but hot and quick as a bullet. "A mantelpiece like this is irreplaceable."

Flustered, she stared guiltily at the chipped Italian marble. "Well, I certainly didn't break it."

"And look at these walls. Plasterwork of this caliber is an art, the same way a Rembrandt is art. You'd take care of a Rembrandt, wouldn't you?"

"Of course, but—"

"At least you had the sense not to paint the molding." Moving past her, he peered into the adjoining bath. And began to swear. "These are handmade tiles, for God's sake. Look at these chips. They haven't been grouted since World War I."

"I don't see what that's—"

"No, you don't see." He turned back to her. "You haven't got a clue to what you've got here. This place is a monument to early-twentieth-century craftsmanship, and you're letting it fall apart around your ears. Those are authentic gaslight fixtures."

"I know very well what they are," Amanda snapped back. "This may be a monument to you, but to me it's home. We've done everything we could to keep the roof on. If the plaster's cracked it's because we've had to concentrate on keeping the furnace running. And if we didn't worry about regrouting tiles in a room no one uses, it's because we had to repair the plumbing in another one. You've been hired to renovate, not to philosophize."

"You get both for the same price." When he reached out toward her, she rammed back into the wall.

"What are you doing?"

"Take it easy, honey. You've got cobwebs in your hair."

"I can do it," she said, then stiffened when he combed his fingers through her hair. "And don't call me 'honey.'"

"You sure fire up quick. I had a mustang filly once that did the same thing."

She knocked his hand aside. "I'm not a horse."

"No, ma'am." In an abrupt change of mood, he smiled

again. "You sure aren't. Why don't you show me what else you've got?"

Wary, she eased to the side until she felt safe again. "I don't see the point. You haven't got a notebook."

"Some things stick in your mind." His gaze lowered to her mouth, lingered, then returned to her eyes. "I like to get the lay of the land first before I start worrying about...details."

"Why don't I draw you a map?"

He grinned then. "You always so prickly?"

"No." She inclined her head. It was true, she wasn't. She could hardly have made a success in her career as assistant manager in one of the resort's better hotels if she was. "Obviously you don't bring out the best in me."

"I'll settle for what I've got." He curled a hand around her arm. "Let's keep going."

She took him through the wing, doing her best to keep her distance. But he had a tendency to close in, blocking her in a doorway, maneuvering her into a corner, shifting unexpectedly to put them face-to-face. He had a slow and economical way of moving, wasting no gestures that would tip her off as to which way he was going to turn.

They were in the west tower the third time Amanda bumped into him. Every nerve was on edge when she stepped back. "I wish you wouldn't do that."

"Do what?"

"Be there." Annoyed, she shoved aside a cardboard box. "In my way."

"It seems to me you're in too much of a hurry to get someplace else to watch where you are."

"More homespun philosophy," she muttered, and paced to the curved window that overlooked the gardens. He bothered her, she was forced to admit, on some deep, elemental level. Maybe it was his size—those broad shoulders and wide-palmed hands. His sheer height. She was accustomed to being on a more even level with most men.

Maybe it was that drawl of his, slow and lazy and every bit as cocky as his grin. Or the way his eyes lingered on her face, persistent, with a half-amused gleam. Whatever it was, Amanda thought with a little shake, she would have to learn how to handle it.

"This is the last stop," she told him. "Trent's idea is to convert this tower into a dining room, more intimate than the one he wants on the lower level. It should fit five tables for two comfortably, with views of the garden or the bay."

She turned as she spoke, and an early evening sunbeam shot through the window to halo her hair and pool lustrously around her. Her hands gestured with her words, a graceful flow of movement underlined by nerves. She lifted one hand to her hair to push it back. The light streamed through the honey-brown tresses, tipping them with gold. In the single shaft of light, dust motes danced around her like minute flakes of silver.

His mind wiped clean as new glass, Sloan stood and stared.

"Is something wrong?"

"No." He took a step closer. "You sure are easy on the eyes, Amanda."

She took a step back. There wasn't amusement in his eyes now, or the quick flaring anger she had seen briefly earlier. What was there was a great deal more dangerous. "If you, ah, have any questions about the tower, or the rest of the wing—"

"That was a compliment. Maybe not as smooth as you're used to, but a compliment just the same."

"Thank you." Her eyes darted around the room for a means of dignified escape as she retreated another step. "I think we could—" She ended on a gasp as his arm snaked around her waist to draw her tight against him. "What the hell do you think you're doing?"

"Keeping you from taking the same jump as your great-grandma." He nodded toward the window at her back. "If you'd kept dancing backward, you might have gone right through the glass. Those panes don't look very strong."

"I wasn't dancing anywhere." But her heart was pounding as if she had just finished a fast rumba. "Let go."

"You're a real nice armful." He leaned closer to take a sniff of her hair. "Even with all those thorns." Enjoying himself, he kept his arm where it was. "You could've said thanks, Calhoun. I probably just saved your life."

Her pulse might have been jumping, but she refused to let herself be intimidated by some slow-talking cowboy with an attitude. "If you don't let me go, now, someone's going to have to save yours."

He laughed, delighted with her, and was tempted to scoop her up there and then. The next thing he knew, he was landing on his butt five feet away. With a smug smile, Amanda inclined her head.

"That concludes our tour for this evening. Now, if you'll excuse me." When she started by him, his hand snaked out and snagged her ankle. Amanda barely had time to shriek before she landed on the floor beside him. "Why, you—oaf," she decided, and tossed the hair out of her eyes.

"What's good for the goose is good for the gander." He tipped a fingertip under her chin. "More homespun philosophy. You've got quick moves, Calhoun, but you've got to remember to keep your eye on the target."

"If I were a man—"

"This wouldn't be half as much fun." Chuckling, he gave her a quick, hard kiss, then tilted his head back to stare at her while she gaped. "Well, now," he said softly while lightning bolts went off inside his chest. "I think we'd better try that again."

She would have shoved him away. She knew she would have. Despite the heat trembling along her spine. Regardless of the thick syrupy longing that seemed to have replaced the blood churning in her veins. She would have shoved him away, had even lifted a hand to do so—certainly not to bring him closer—when footsteps clattered on the iron steps that led to the tower.

Sloan glanced up to see a tall, curvy woman in the doorway. She wore jeans that were ripped through at the knee with a plain white T-shirt tucked in the waist. Her hair was short and straight, offset by a fringe of sassy bangs. Below them her eyes registered surprise, then amusement.

"Hi." She looked at Amanda, grinning as she noted her sister's flushed face and tousled hair. The one place you didn't expect to see business-first Amanda Calhoun was on the floor with a strange and very attractive man. "What's going on?"

"We were going for the best two out of three," Sloan told her. He rose, then hauled Amanda up by the arm. With what sounded like a snarl, Amanda jerked out of his hold, then busied herself brushing the dust from her slacks.

"This is my sister, C.C."

"And you must be Sloan." C.C. walked in, offering her hand. "Trent's told me about you." Green eyes dancing, she flicked a glance at her sister, then back again. "I guess he didn't exaggerate."

Sloan held the offered hand a moment. C. C. Calhoun was exactly the opposite of the kind of woman he'd expected his old friend to be involved with. And because Trent was his friend, Sloan couldn't have been more delighted. "I can see why Trent's got himself roped and corralled."

"That's one of Sloan's whimsical compliments," Amanda pointed out.

With a laugh, C.C. threw an arm around Amanda's shoulders. "I think I figured that out. I'm glad to meet you, Sloan. Really glad. When I went up to Boston with Trent a couple of weeks ago, everyone I met was so..."

"Stuffy?" He grinned.

"Well." A little embarrassed, she moved her shoulders. "I guess it's hard for some of them to accept that Trent's going to marry a mechanic who knows more about engines than opera."

"Looks to me like Trent's getting one hell of a deal."

"We'll see." She knew with the least encouragement she would get mushy and embarrass herself. "Aunt Coco said you were staying for dinner. I was hoping you'd take one of the guest rooms here while you're on the island."

Sloan couldn't see it, but he'd have bet the pot that Amanda bit her tongue. The idea of ruffling her feathers made it tempting to change his plans. "Thanks, but I'm all taken care of. Besides..." Now he grinned at Amanda. "I'm going to be underfoot enough as it is."

"However you're most comfortable," C.C. told him. "Just so that you know you're welcome here at The Towers."

"I'll go down and see if Aunt Coco needs any help." Amanda sent Sloan a cool nod. "C.C. will show you down when you're ready."

He winked at her. "Thanks for the tour, honey."

He could almost hear her grinding her teeth as she walked away.

"That's some sister you've got there."

"Yes, she is." C.C.'s smile was warm, and warning. "Trent tells me you're quite the ladies' man."

"He's still mad because I stole a woman out from under

his nose when we were both still young and foolish." Sloan took C.C.'s hand as they walked through the doorway. "You sure you're stuck on him?"

She had to laugh. "Now I see why he told me to lock up my sisters."

"If they're anything like that one, I expect they can take care of themselves."

"Oh, they can. The Calhoun women are as tough as they come." She paused at the top of the iron circular stairs. "I'd better warn you. Aunt Coco claims she saw you in the tea leaves this morning."

"In the...aah."

She gave a half apologetic, half amused shrug. "It's kind of a hobby of hers. Anyway, she might start to try to manipulate, especially if she decides the fates have linked you with one of my sisters. She means well, but..."

"O'Rileys are pretty good at handling themselves, too."

It only took one long look at him to have her believing it. C.C. tapped his shoulder. "Okay then. You're on your own."

Sloan started down behind her. "C.C., are there any men Amanda's involved with who I'm going to have to hoist out of the way?"

C.C. stopped, studying him through the opposite side of the open stairs. "No," she said after a moment. "Amanda's done all the hoisting herself."

"That's fine." He was smiling to himself as he descended the winding stairs. When they reached the second floor, he heard an echo of high-pitched screams and the frantic yapping of the dog.

"My sister Suzanna's kids," C.C. explained before he could ask. "Alex and Jenny are your typical quiet, retiring children."

"I can hear that."

A sturdy pale-haired missile zoomed up the steps. In reflex, Sloan caught it and found himself staring into a curious little face with a pouty mouth and big blue eyes.

"You're big," Jenny said.

"Nah. You're just short."

At five, she was just beginning to learn the wiles of womanhood and sent him a beaming smile. "Can I have a piggyback ride?"

"Got a quarter?" Giggling, she shook her head. "Okay," he said, "the first one's free then." When she squirmed around to his back, he started down again. At the base of the steps, Amanda had a dark-haired little boy in a headlock.

"Suzanna?" C.C. asked.

"In the kitchen. I was drafted to watch these two." She narrowed her eyes at Jenny. "The little pig-nosed one got away from me."

"Oink, oink." From the tower of Sloan's back, Jenny giggled and snorted.

"Who's he?" Alex wanted to know.

"Sloan O'Riley." Sloan offered a hand, man to man, which Alex eyed dubiously before accepting it.

"You talk funny. Are you from Texas?"

"Oklahoma."

After a moment's consideration, Alex nodded. "That's almost as good. Did you ever shoot anybody dead?"

"Not lately."

"That's enough, you ghoul." C.C. took charge. "Come on, let's go get cleaned up for dinner." She swung Jenny from Sloan's back.

"Cute kids," Sloan commented when C.C. hauled them up the stairs.

"We like them." Amanda offered him a genuine smile. Seeing him with Jenny riding his back had softened her.

"They'll be in school most of the day, so they shouldn't bother you while you're working."

"I don't figure they'd be a bother one way or the other. I've got a nephew of my own back home. He's a pistol."

"Those two can be shotguns, I'm afraid." But the affection came through. "It's nice for them to be around a man now and again."

"Your sister's husband?"

The smile faded. "They're divorced. You might know him. Baxter Dumont?"

A shutter seemed to come down over Sloan's eyes. "I've heard of him."

"Well, that's history. Dinner's nearly ready. Why don't I show you where to wash up?"

"Thanks." Distracted, Sloan followed her. He was thinking that there were some points of history that had an unfortunate habit of overlapping.

Chapter 3

Anticipating the shock, Amanda dove into the cold water of the pool. She surfaced with a delicious shiver then began the first of her usual fifty laps.

There was nothing she liked better than beginning a day with a vigorous workout. It ate away the old tension to make room for the new that would develop before the workday was done.

Not that she didn't enjoy her job as assistant manager of the BayWatch Hotel. Particularly since it gave her the privilege of using the hotel pool before the guests began to crowd in. It was the end of May and the season had begun to swing. Of course it was nothing compared to what it would be by midsummer, but most of the rooms in the hotel were occupied, which meant she had her hands full. This hour, which she gave herself whenever weather permitted, was prized.

As she approached one end of the pool, she curled, tucked and pushed off.

In another year, she thought as she sent beads of water flying, she would be manager of The Towers Retreat. A St. James hotel. The goal that she had worked and struggled for since she'd taken her first part-time job as a desk clerk at sixteen was about to be realized.

It nagged at her from time to time that she would have the job only because Trent was marrying her sister. Whenever it did, she became only more determined to prove that she deserved it, that she had earned it.

She would be managing an exclusive hotel for one of the top chains in the country. And not just any hotel, she thought, cutting cleanly through the water, but The Towers. A part of her own heritage, her own history, her own family.

The ten luxurious suites Trent intended to create out of the crumbling west wing would be her responsibility. If he was right, the St. James name and the legend of The Towers would keep those suites filled year-round.

She would do a good job. An exceptional one. Every guest who traveled home from The Towers would remember the excellent service, the soothing ambience, the silky smooth organization.

It was going to happen. There would be no more slaving for a demanding and unappreciative supervisor, no more frustration at doing the work and handing over the credit. At last the credit, and the failure, would be hers alone.

It was only a matter of waiting until the remodeling was done.

And that brought her thoughts ramming headfirst into Sloan O'Riley.

She certainly hoped Trent knew what he was doing. What baffled her most was how such a smooth and polished man such as Trenton St. James III had ever become friends with a throwback like O'Riley. The man had actually knocked her down. Of course, she'd knocked him down first, but that was entirely beside the point.

Amanda kicked off again. Her leanly muscled arms sliced through the water, her long legs scissored. She didn't regret, not for a minute, that she'd had the wit and the strength to get the best of him first. He'd been pushy and overfamiliar and too full of himself from the moment she'd met him. And he'd kissed her.

She turned her head up for air then slid her face into the water again.

She hadn't given him the least bit of encouragement. In fact, just the opposite. But he'd sat there, grinning like a fool, and had kissed her. The memory of it had her gasping for air again.

Not that she'd liked it, Amanda assured herself. If C.C. hadn't walked in, she would have given the arrogant Mr. O'Riley a piece of her mind. Except that she hadn't had one left.

Because she'd been angry, that's all. She wasn't a bit attracted to the rough, outdoorsy type with callused hands and dusty boots. She wasn't fool enough to fall for a pair of dark green eyes that crinkled at the corners when they smiled. Her image of the ideal man included a certain sophistication, smooth manners, culture, a quiet aura of success. If and when she became interested in a relationship, those would be her requirements. Slow-talking cowboys need not apply.

Maybe there had been something sweet about him when he'd talked to the children, but it wasn't enough to overcome the rest of the deficits in his personality.

She remembered the way he'd flirted and charmed Aunt Coco at dinner. He'd kept C.C. amused with stories of Trent's college days and had been tolerant and easy with Alex's and Jenny's questions about horses and Indians and six-shooters.

But he'd watched Suzanna a little too closely, a little too carefully for Amanda's liking. A woman chaser, Amanda decided. If Lilah had been at dinner, he probably would have flirted with her, as well. But Lilah could take care of herself where men were concerned.

Suzanna was different. She was beautiful, sensitive and vulnerable. Her ex-husband had hurt her deeply, and no one, not even the cocky Sloan O'Riley was going to get the chance to hurt Suzanna again. Amanda would make sure of it.

When she reached the edge of the pool this time, she gripped the coping and dipped her head back into the water to slick her hair out of her eyes. Surfacing, she found herself staring up into a watery image that was entirely too familiar.

"Morning." Sloan grinned down at her. The sun was at his back, bringing out the reddish tones in his untidy hair. "You got a nice form there, Calhoun."

She blinked her eyes clear. "What the hell are you doing here?"

"Here?" He glanced over his shoulder at the whitewashed hotel. "You could say I'm hanging my hat here." Watching her, he jerked a thumb up and back. "Room 320."

"You're a guest at the BayWatch?" Amanda propped her elbows on the coping. "It figures."

Agreeable, Sloan crouched down. She had the clear creamy Calhoun skin, he noted, particularly striking, and vulnerable, now washed clean of any cosmetics. "Nice way to start the day."

Her full damp mouth turned down in a frown. "It was."

"Since we're asking, what are you doing here?"

"I work here."

Things were becoming more and more interesting, he thought. "No fooling?"

"No fooling," she said dryly. "I'm assistant manager."

"Well, now." He dipped an experimental finger into the water. "Checking out the water temperature for the guests? That's dedication."

"The pool doesn't open until ten."

"Don't worry." He hooked his thumbs in the front pockets of his jeans. "I wasn't planning on taking a dip just yet." What he had been planning was to take a walk, a long solitary one. But that was before he'd spotted her doing laps. "So, I guess if I have any questions about the place, you're the one I talk to."

"That's right." Amanda moved over to the steps to climb out. The one-piece sapphire-colored suit clung like a second skin as water slid from her. "Is your room satisfactory?"

"Hmm?" She had legs designed to make a man sweat, he thought, slim and shapely and a yard long.

"Your room," she repeated as she reached for her towel. "It suits you?"

"It suits me fine. Just fine." He skimmed his gaze up those damp calves and thighs, over the slim hips on a lazy journey to her face. "The view's worth the price of admission."

Amanda hooked the towel around her neck. "The view of the bay's free—like the continental breakfast now being served in The Galley. You'll want to take advantage of it."

"I've found that a couple of croissants and a cup of coffee don't do much to stanch the appetite." Because he wasn't ready for her to walk away, he reached out to take both ends of the towel in a light grip. "Why don't you join me for a real breakfast?"

"Sorry." Her heart was beginning to thud uncomfortably. "Employees are discouraged from socializing with the guests."

"I reckon we could make an exception in this case, seeing as we're...old friends."

"We're not even new friends."

There was that smile again, slow, insistent and all too knowing. And then he said, "That's something we can fix over breakfast."

"Sorry. Not interested." She started to turn away, but he tightened his grip on the towel and held her in place.

"Where I come from people are a mite more friendly."

Since he wasn't giving her a choice, she held her ground. "Where I come from people are a great deal more polite. If you have any problems with the service during your stay at the BayWatch, I'll be more than happy to accommodate you. If you have any questions about The Towers, I'll make myself available to answer them. Other than that, we have nothing to discuss."

He watched her patiently, admiring the way she could coat her husky voice with frost even while her eyes glinted. This was a woman with plenty of control. And, though he was certain she'd snarl at the term, plenty of spunk.

"What time do you go on the clock here?"

She let out a hiss of breath. Obviously the man's head was as thick as his accent. "Nine o'clock, so if you'll excuse me, I'd like to go get dressed."

Sloan squinted up at the sun. "Looks to me like you've got about an hour before you punch in. The way you move, it won't take you half that to get yourself together."

Amanda shut her eyes briefly on a prayer for patience. "Sloan, are you trying to irritate me?"

"Don't figure I have to. It seems to come natural." Casually he wound the ends of the towel around his fists and had her jerking closer. He grinned as her chin shot up. "See?"

She resented bitterly the way her pulse was dancing, and the tight, clutching sensation deep in her stomach. "What's the matter with you, O'Riley?" she demanded. "I've made it absolutely plain that I'm not interested."

"I'll tell you how it is, Calhoun." He flipped his wrists again, shortening the towel farther. The humor she was used to seeing in his eyes changed into something else in the space of a heartbeat. And that something else was dark and dangerous. And exciting. "You're one long, cool drink of water," he murmured. "Every time I'm around you I get this powerful thirst." With a last jerk, he had her tumbling against him, her hands trapped tight between their bodies. "That little sip I had yesterday wasn't nearly enough." Bending down, he nipped at her bottom lip.

He felt her tremor, but as he kept his eyes on hers, he could see it wasn't from fear. A trace of panic maybe, but not fear. Still he waited to see if she would give him a flat-out no. That was something he would have to respect, however much the need churned through him.

But she said nothing, only stared at him with those wide wary eyes. Softly he brushed his lips over hers and watched the thick lashes flutter down. "I want more," he murmured. And took.

Her hands curled into fists between them, but she didn't use them to push him away. The struggle was all inside her, a wild and violent combat that jolted her system even as he bombarded her senses. Caught in the crossfire, her mind simply shut down.

His mouth wasn't lazy now. Nor were his hands slow. Hard and hot, his lips took from hers while his fingers pressed against her damp back. The scrape of his teeth had her gasping, then moaning when his tongue slid seductively over hers.

Her fingers uncurled to clutch at his shirt, then to claw their way up to his shoulder, into his hair. The desperation was new, terrifying, wonderful. It drove her to strain against him while her mouth burned with an urgency that matched his.

The change rocked him. He was used to having his senses clouded by a woman, to having his body throb and his blood burn. But not like this. In the instant she went from dazed surrender to fevered urgency, he knew a need so sharp, so jagged that it seemed to slice through his soul.

Then all he knew was her. All he could feel was the cool slick silk of her skin. All he could taste was the honeyed heat of her mouth. All he could want was more.

She was certain her heart would pound its way out of her breast. It seemed the heat from his body turned the water on her skin to steam, and the vapors floated through her brain. Nor did they clear when he eased her gently away.

"Amanda." He drew in a deep gulp of air but wasn't sure he'd ever get his breath back again. One look at her as she stood heavy eyed, her swollen lips parted, had the edgy desire cutting through him again. "Come up to my room."

"Your room?" She touched unsteady fingers to her lips, then her temple. "Your room?"

Lord, that throaty voice and those dazed eyes were going to have him on his knees. One thing he'd yet to do was beg for a woman. With her, he was afraid begging was inevitable.

"Come with me." Possessively he ran his hands over her shoulders. Somewhere along the line the towel had slid to the concrete. "We need to finish this in private."

"Finish this?"

On a groan, he brought his lips back to hers again in a last, long, greedy kiss. "Woman, I think you're going to be late for work."

He had her arm and had pulled her toward the gate before she shook her head clear. His room? she thought fussily. Finish this? Oh, Lord, what had she done? What was she about to do? "No." She jerked away and took a deep, cleansing breath that did nothing to stop the tremors. "I'm not going anywhere."

He tried to steady himself and failed. "It's a little late to play games." His hand snaked out to cup the back of her neck. "I want you. And there's no way in hell you're going to convince me you don't want me right back. Not after that."

"I don't play games," she said evenly, and wondered if he could hear her over the riot of her heartbeat. She was cold, so terribly cold. "I don't intend to start now." She was the sensible one, she reminded herself. She wasn't the kind of woman who raced into a hotel room to make love with a man she barely knew. "I want you to leave me alone."

"Not a chance." He struggled to keep his fingers light as temper and need warred inside him. "I always finish what I start."

"You can consider this finished. It had no business starting."

"Why?"

She turned away to snatch up her wrap. The thin terry cloth wasn't nearly enough to warm her again. "I know your type, O'Riley."

He reached deep for calm and rocked back on his heels. "Do you?"

Clumsy with temper, she fought to push her arms through the sleeves. "You swagger from town to town and fill a few free hours with an available woman having a quick roll between the sheets." She pulled the tie on the wrap tight. "Well, I'm not available."

"You figure you got me pegged, huh?" He didn't touch her, but the look in his eyes was enough to have her bracing. He didn't bother to explain that it was different with her. He hadn't yet explained it to himself. "You can take this as a warning, Calhoun. This isn't finished between us. I'm going to have you."

"Have me? *Have* me." Propelled by pride and fury, she took one long stride toward him. "Why you conceited self-absorbed sonofabitch—"

"You can save the flattery for later," he interrupted. "There will be a later, Amanda, when it's just you and me. And I promise you, it won't be quick." Because the idea appealed to him, he smiled. "No sir, when I make love with you, I'm going to take my time." He ran a finger down the collar of her wrap. "And I'm going to drive you crazy."

She slapped his hand away. "You already are."

"Thanks." He gave her a friendly nod. "I think I'll go see about that breakfast. You have a good day."

She would, she thought as he walked off whistling. She'd have a fine day if he was out of it.

It was bad enough that she had to work late, Amanda thought, without having to listen to one of Mr. Stenerson's droning lectures on efficiency. As manager of the BayWatch, Stenerson ruled his staff with fussy hands and whines. His preferred method of supervision was to delegate. In that way he could dole out blame when things went wrong, and gather in credit when things went right.

Amanda stood in his airy pastel office, staring at the top of his balding head as he ran through his weekly list of complaints.

"Housekeeping has been running behind by twenty minutes. In my spot check of the third floor, I discovered this cellophane wrapper under the bed of 302." He waved the tiny clear paper like a flag. "I expect you to have a better handle on things, Miss Calhoun."

"Yes, sir." *You officious little wienie.* "I'll speak to the housekeeping staff personally."

"See that you do." He lifted his ever-present clipboard.

"Room service speed is off by eight percent. At this rate of deterioration, it will lower to twelve percent by the height of the season."

Unlike Stenerson, Amanda had done time in the kitchen during the breakfast and dinner rush. "Perhaps if we hired another waiter or two," she began.

"The solution is not in adding more staff, but in culling more efficiency from those we have." He tapped a finger on the clipboard. "I expect to see room service up to maximum by the end of next week."

"Yes, sir." *You supercilious windbag.*

"I'll expect you to roll up your sleeves and pitch in whenever necessary, Miss Calhoun." He folded his soft white hands and leaned back. Before he'd opened his mouth again, Amanda knew what was coming. She could have recited the speech by rote.

"Twenty-five years ago, I was delivering trays to guests in this very hotel. It was through sheer determination and a positive outlook that I worked my way up to the position I hold today. If you expect to succeed, perhaps even take over in this office after my retirement, you must eat, sleep and drink the BayWatch. The efficiency of the staff directly reflects your efficiency, Miss Calhoun."

"Yes, sir." She wanted to tell him that in another year she would have her own staff, her own office and he could kiss his whipping boy goodbye. But she didn't tell him. Until that time, she needed the job and the weekly paycheck. "I'll have a meeting with the kitchen staff right away."

"Good, good. Now, I'll want you on call this evening, as I'll be incommunicado."

As always, she thought but murmured her agreement.

"Oh, and check the August reservations. I want a report on the ratio of Escape Weekends to Seven-Day Indulgences.

Oh, and speak with the pool boy about missing towels. We're five short already this month."

"Yes, sir." Anything else? she wondered. Shine your shoes, wash your car?

"That'll be all."

Amanda opened the door and struggled to keep her unflappable professional mask in place. All she really wanted to do was knock her head against the wall for a few indulgent minutes. Before she could retreat to some private, quiet place to do so, she was called to the front desk.

Sloan took a seat in the lobby just to watch her. He was surprised to see that she was still working. He'd put in a full day at The Towers, and the scarred briefcase beside the chair was bulging with notes, measurements and sketches. He was ready for a tall beer and a rare steak.

But here she was, soothing guests, instructing desk clerks, signing papers. And looking just as cool and fresh as spring water. He watched her pull off an earring, jiggling it in her palm as she took a phone call.

It was one of life's small pleasures to watch her, he decided. All that drive and energy, the effortless control. Almost effortless, he thought with a grin. There was a line between her brows—frustration, he thought. Annoyance. Or just plain stubbornness. He had a powerful urge to go up to her and smooth it away. Instead, he gestured to a bellman.

"Yes, sir."

"Is there a florist around here?"

"Yes, sir, just down the street."

Still watching Amanda, Sloan dug out his wallet and pulled out a twenty. "Would you run down there and get me a red rose? A long-stemmed one that's still closed. And keep the change."

"Yes, *sir.* Thank you, sir."

While he waited, Sloan ordered a beer from the lobby bar and lighted a cigar. Stretching out his booted feet, he settled back to enjoy.

Amanda clipped on her earring then pressed a hand to her stomach. At least when she went down to give the kitchen staff a pep talk she could grab something to eat. A glance at her watch told her that she wouldn't have time to take her evening shift going through the paperwork, looking for a clue to the necklace. If there was any bright side to the enforced overtime, it was that Sloan wouldn't be at The Towers when she returned.

"Excuse me."

Amanda glanced up to see a trim, attractive man in a bone-colored suit. His dark hair was brushed back from a high forehead. Pale blue eyes smiled pleasantly as they looked into hers. The faint British accent added charm to his voice.

"Yes, sir. May I help you?"

"I'd like to speak with the manager."

Amanda felt her heart sink a little. "I'm sorry, Mr. Stenerson is unavailable. If there's a problem, I'll be glad to handle it for you."

"No problem, Miss—" his eyes flicked down to her name tag "—Calhoun. I'll be checking in for a few weeks. I believe I have the Island Suite."

"Of course. Mr. Livingston. We're expecting you." Quick and competent, she tapped the information into the computer herself. "Have you stayed with us before?"

"No." He smiled again. "Regrettably."

"I'm sure you'll find the suite very comfortable." She passed him a registration form as she spoke. "If there's anything we can do to make your stay more pleasant, don't hesitate to ask."

"I'm already certain it will be pleasant." He gave her another lingering look as he filled out the form. "Unfortunately, it must also be productive. I wanted to inquire about the possibility of renting a fax machine during my stay."

"We offer fax service for our guests' convenience," she said.

"I'll require my own." The diamond on his pinky winked as he slid the form across the counter. "I'm afraid I wasn't able to clear up all my business, as I had hoped. It simply wouldn't be practical for me to run down here every time I need to send or receive a document. Naturally, I'll be willing to pay whatever necessary for the convenience. If renting isn't feasible, perhaps I can purchase one."

"I'll see what I can arrange."

"I'd appreciate that." He offered her his credit card for an imprint. "Also, I'll be using the parlor in the suite as an office. I'd prefer if housekeeping left my papers and disarray undisturbed."

"Of course."

"Might I ask if you're familiar with the island?"

Smiling, she handed him his card and his keys. "I'm a native."

"Wonderful." His eyes on hers, he held her hand lightly. "Then I'll know to come to you if I have any questions. You've been very helpful, Miss Calhoun." He glanced at her name tag again. "Amanda. Thank you."

"You're quite welcome." Her pulse gave a quick jitter as she slid her hand from his to signal a bellman. "Enjoy your stay, Mr. Livingston."

"I already am."

As he walked away, the young desk clerk beside Amanda gave a low feminine sigh. "Who was that?"

"William Livingston." Amanda caught herself staring after him and pulled herself back to file the imprint.

"Gorgeous. If he had looked at me the way he looked at you, I'd have melted on the spot."

"Melting's not part of the job description, Karen."

"No." Dreamy eyed, Karen put her hand on a ringing phone. "But it sure is part of being a woman. Front desk, Karen speaking. May I help you?"

William Livingston, Amanda thought, tapping his registration form against her palm. New York, New York. If he could afford a couple of weeks in the Island Suite, that meant he had money as well as charm, good looks and impeccable taste in clothes. If she'd been looking for a man, he would have fit the bill nicely.

Opening up the phone book, Amanda reminded herself she was looking for a fax machine, not a man.

"Hey, Calhoun."

With her finger on Office Supplies in the business section, she glanced up. Sloan, his chambray shirt rolled up to the elbows, his hair curling untidily over its collar, leaned on the counter.

"I'm busy," she said dismissively.

"Working late?"

"Good guess."

"You sure look pretty in that little suit." He reached over the counter to rub a thumb and finger down the crisp red lapel of her jacket. "Kinda prim and proper."

Unlike the little bounce her pulse had given when William Livingstone had taken her hand, it went haywire at Sloan's touch. Annoyed, she brushed it away. "Do you have a problem with your room?"

"Nope. It's pretty as a picture."

"With the service?"

"Slick as a wet rock."

"Then if you'll excuse me, I've got work to do."

"Oh, I figured that. I've been watching you tow the mark here for the last half hour."

The line appeared between her brows. "You've been watching me?"

His gaze lingered on her mouth as he remembered just how it tasted. "It made the beer go down easy."

"It must be nice to have so much free time. Now—"

"It's not how much, it's what you do with it. Since you were...tied up for breakfast, why don't we have dinner?"

Well aware that her co-workers had their ears pricked, Amanda leaned closer and kept her voice low. "Can't you get it through your head that I'm not interested?"

"No." He grinned, then sent a wink toward Karen, who was hovering as close as discretion allowed. "You said you didn't like to waste time. So I figured we could have a little supper and pick up where we left off this morning."

In his arms, she thought, lost for a moment. With her mind fuddled and her blood racing. She was staring at his mouth when it curved and snapped her back to reality. "I'm busy, and I have no desire—"

"You've got plenty of that, Amanda."

She set her teeth, wishing with all her heart she could call him a liar and mean it. "I don't want to have dinner with you. Clear?"

"As glass." He flicked a finger down her nose. "I'll be upstairs if you get hungry. Three-twenty, remember?" He lifted the rose from behind the counter and put it into her hand. "Don't work too hard."

"Two winners in one night," Karen murmured, and watched Sloan walk away. "Lord, he sure knows how to wear jeans, doesn't he?"

Indeed he did, Amanda thought, then cursed herself. "He's crude, annoying and intolerable." But she brushed the rosebud against her cheek.

"Okay, I'll take bachelor number two. You can concentrate on Mister Beautiful from New York."

Damn it, why was she so breathless? "I'm going to concentrate on my job," Amanda corrected. "And so are you. Stenerson's on the warpath, and the last thing I need is some cowboy stud interrupting my routine."

"I wish he'd offer to interrupt mine," Karen murmured, then bent over her terminal.

She wasn't going to think about him, Amanda promised herself. She set the rose aside, then picked it up again. It wasn't the flower's fault, after all. It deserved to be put in water and appreciated for what it was. Softening a bit, she sniffed at it and smiled. And it had been sweet of him to give it to her. No matter how annoying he might be, she should have thanked him.

Absently she lifted the phone as it rang. "Front desk, Amanda speaking. May I help you?"

"I just wanted to hear you say that." Sloan chuckled into the phone. "Good night, Calhoun."

Biting back an oath, Amanda banged down the receiver. For the life of her she couldn't understand why she was laughing when she took the rose back into her office to find a vase.

I ran to him. It was as if another woman burst out into the twilight to race over the lawn, down the slope, over the rocks. In that moment there was no right or wrong, no duty but to my own heart. Indeed, it was my heart that guided my legs, my eyes, my voice.

He had turned back to the sea. The first time I had seen

him he had been facing the sea, fighting his own personal war with paint and canvas. Now he only stared out at the water.

When I called to him, he spun around. In his face I could see the mirror of my own joy. There was laughter, mine and his, as he rushed toward me.

His arms went around me, so tightly. My dreams had known what it would be like to finally be held by them. His mouth fitted truly to mine, so sweet, so urgent.

Time does not stop. As I sit here and write this, I know that. But then, oh then, it did. There was only the wind and the sound of the sea and the sheer and simple glory of being in his arms. It was as if I had waited my entire life, sleeping, eating, breathing, all for the purpose of that single precious window of time. If I have another hundred years left to me, I will never forget an instant of it.

He drew away, his hands sliding down my arms to grip mine, then to bring them to his lips. His eyes were so dark, like gray smoke.

"I'd packed," he said. "I'd made arrangements to sail to England. Staying here without you was hell. Thinking you would come back, and that I'd never be able to touch you nearly drove me mad. Every day, every night, Bianca, I've ached for you."

My hands moved over his face, tracing it as I'd often longed to. "I thought I'd never see you again. I tried to pray that I wouldn't." As shame crept through my joy, I tried to turn away. "Oh, what you must think of me. I'm another man's wife, the mother of his children."

"Not here." His voice was rough, even as his hands were gentle. "Here you belong to me. Here, where I first saw you a year ago. Don't think of him."

He kissed me again, and I could not think, could not care.

"I've waited for you, Bianca, through the chill of winter, the warmth of spring. When I tried to paint, it was your image that haunted me. I could see you standing here, with the wind in your hair, the sunlight turning it copper, then gold, then flame. I tried to forget you." His hands were on my shoulders, holding me back while his eyes seemed to devour my face. *"I tried to tell myself it was wrong, that for your sake if not my own, I should leave here. I would think of you, with him, dancing at a ball, attending the theater, taking him into your bed."* His fingers tightened on my shoulders. *"She is his wife, I would tell myself. You have no right to want her, to wish that she would come to you. That she could belong to you."*

I lifted my fingers to his lips. His pain was my pain. I think it will always be so. "I have come to you," I told him. "I do belong to you."

He turned away from me, the struggle between conscience and love as strong in him as it was in me. "I have nothing to offer you."

"Your love. There is nothing else I want."

"It's already yours, has been yours from the first moment I looked at you." He came back to me to touch my cheek. I could see the regret, and the longing, in those beautiful eyes. *"Bianca, there is no future for us. I cannot and will not ask you to give up what you have."*

"Christian—"

"No. Whatever wrongs I do, I will not do that. I know you would give me what I ask, what I have no right to ask, then come to hate me for it."

"No." Tears came to my eyes then, bitter in the cooling wind. *"I could never hate you."*

"Then I would hate myself." He crushed my fingers against his lips again. *"But I'll ask you for the summer, for*

a few hours when you can come here and we can pretend winter will never be." He smiled and kissed me softly. *"Come here and meet me, Bianca, in the sunlight. Let me paint you. I'll be content with that."*

And so tomorrow, and every day during this sweet, endless summer I will go to him. On the cliffs above the sea we will take what happiness we can.

Chapter 4

"Well, hello."

At the husky greeting, Sloan looked up from his notes on the billiard room to see a willowy gypsy in a flowing flowered robe. Long cables of red hair streamed down her shoulders and back. Dreamy green eyes assessed him before she glided into the room like a woman who had all the time in the world and was willing to spend it generously.

"Hi." Sloan caught the elusive scent—like crushed wildflowers—before she offered a hand.

"I'm Lilah." Her voice was as lazily flirtatious as her eyes. "We've missed each other the past couple of days."

If there was a man who didn't get a jolt from this one, Sloan thought, he was dead and buried. "I'm real sorry about that."

She laughed then gave his hand a companionable squeeze. First impressions ranked high with Lilah, and she'd already decided to like him. "Me, too. Especially now. What have you been up to?"

"Getting a feel for the place, and the people in it. How about you?"

"I've been busy trying to figure out if I was in love."

"And?"

"Nope." She moved her shoulders gently, but he caught the wistful look in her eyes before she turned to move around the room. "So, what's the plan here, Sloan O'Riley?"

"Elegant dining in a turn-of-the-century atmosphere." He kicked back in the Windsor armchair he'd been using and gestured toward the papers spread over the library table. "We take out part of that wall there, open up into the adjoining study, add a couple of glass pocket doors, and we've got a lounge."

"Just like that?"

"Just like that—after we deal with the structural hassles. I'll have some preliminary sketches for your family and Trent to look over in a couple of days."

"It seems strange," she murmured, running a finger along the old, dusty chair rail. "Thinking about this place being fresh and new again, having people in it." But if she closed her eyes, she could see it perfectly, the way it had once been. "They used to give huge parties, very elaborate, very chic. I can imagine my great-grandfather standing here beside a billiard table sipping Scotch, and wheeling and dealing." She turned back to Sloan. "Do you think about those things when you make your sketches and calculate stress and space?"

"As a matter of fact, I do. There's a burn mark on the floor right over there." He tipped his pencil toward the spot. "I imagine some fat guy in a dinner suit dropped his cigar while he was discussing the war in Europe. A couple of others were standing by the window, stripped down to their shirtsleeves and swirling brandy while they talked about the stock market."

Laughing, Lilah crossed back to him. "And the ladies were down in the parlor."

"Listening to piano music and gossiping about the latest fashions from Paris."

Lilah tilted her head. "Or discussing the possibility of being given the vote."

"There you go."

"I think you're just what The Towers needs," she decided. "Can I take a look at your drawings, or are you temperamental?"

"I make it a policy never to turn down a beautiful woman."

"Astute and clever." She went to lean over his shoulder and push through his papers. "Why, it's the Emperor's Room."

"The what?"

"The Emperor's Room, that's what I call the best guest room. Must be the harps and cherubs on the ceiling." Sliding her hair behind her shoulder, she leaned closer. "This is great."

The dressing room would be a cozy parlor, she noted, complete with a wet bar and an entertainment center that would be hidden behind the original paneling. The bath would remain almost as it was, with the addition of a private whirlpool tucked away in what had been an old storage closet.

"Both ends of one century," Lilah murmured. "You've hardly changed any of the original layout."

"Trent indicated he wanted to keep the luxury and convenience without altering the mood. We'll save most of the original materials, duplicate what's beyond hope."

"You're going to do it." And because she could see that as well, quite clearly, her eyes filled as she laid a hand on his shoulder. "My father wanted to. My mother and he used to talk about it all the time. I wish they could have seen this."

Touched, Sloan laid his hand over hers. Their fingers had linked when Amanda came to the door. Her first reaction was shock at seeing her sister with her cheek all but brushing Sloan's. Then came the spear of jealousy. There was no denying there was something private, even intimate passing between them. On the heels of that sharp green shaft, pride stepped in.

Hadn't she told herself he was a woman chaser?

"Excuse me." Her voice was a thin sheet of ice as she stepped into the room. "I've been looking for you, Lilah."

"You found me." She blinked back the tears but didn't bother to straighten. "I thought I'd come by and meet Sloan."

"I see you have." Determined to be casual if it killed her, Amanda jammed her hands into the pockets of her sweats. "It's your turn for a shift in the storeroom."

"That's what I get for having the day off." She wrinkled her nose, then sent Sloan a smile. "The Calhouns have become detectives, searching for clues to the hiding place of the elusive emeralds."

"So I've heard."

"Maybe you'll take a hack at one of the walls, and they'll fall out, looking as fabulous and glittery as the day Bianca hid them." With a sigh, she drew away. "Well, since duty calls, I'd better get dressed for it. Mandy, you ought to take a look at some of Sloan's sketches. They're great."

"I'll bet."

The tone would have been a direct tip-off, even if Lilah hadn't known her sister so well. So, Lilah thought with a lifted brow. That's the way it was. Since she'd never been able to resist teasing her sister, she leaned down to kiss Sloan's cheek. "Welcome to The Towers."

He didn't have a doubt as to what she was up to. The eyes might be dreamy, he thought, but there was a shrewd and devilish brain behind them. "Thanks. I'm feeling more at home every day."

"I'll meet you in the sweatshop in fifteen minutes," she said to Amanda, then grinned to herself as she went out.

"Is that your new uniform?" he asked Amanda as she stood scowling in the center of the room, her hands still fisted in the pockets of baggy gray sweats.

"I don't go in until two today."

"That's nice." He crossed his outstretched legs at the ankles. "I like your sister."

"That was obvious."

He only grinned. "What does she do, anyway?"

"If you mean professionally, she's a naturalist at Acadia National Park."

"Wildflowers and stuff. It suits."

As if the admiration in his voice didn't bother her in the least, she shrugged and walked to the terrace doors. "I thought you'd be taking measurements or something." Glancing over her shoulder, she shot him a narrow look. "Of the rooms, that is."

This time he laughed outright. "You're mighty cute when you're jealous, Calhoun."

Now she turned to look deliberately down her nose. "I don't know what you're talking about."

"Sure you do, but you can relax. I've already set my sights on you."

Did he expect her to be flattered? she wondered. The hell of it was that, in a odd way, she was. "Do I look like a target?"

"I'd say more like the grand prize." In a gesture of peace, he held up a hand as she sucked in her breath to swear at him. "Before you get more fired up, why don't we deal with business?"

"I am not fired up," she lied. "And I don't see what business we could have."

"Trent said you were the one I should...collaborate with, until he got back. Seeing as you're the one who handles most of the family business, and you've got a firsthand knowledge of hotels."

Because it was logical, she calmed enough to consider it. "What do you want to know?"

How long it's going to take me to knock down that wall around you, he thought. "I figured you'd want to take a look at what I've started. I'd like to get to the drawing board soon."

Actually she was dying to see, but kept her agreement grudgingly cool. "All right, but I only have a few minutes."

"I'll take what I can get."

He waited as she crossed the room. She didn't trust him worth spit, Sloan decided. And that was just fine for now.

"I've got two of the suites mapped out," he told her, shuffling papers. "Plus the tower and most of the dining room here."

She leaned closer, squinting a bit to focus without her reading glasses. As Lilah had been, she was impressed with the sketches. Not only were they competent, but they showed a quick understanding of mood, tone and the practicality necessary for smooth service.

"You work fast," she said, surprised.

"When it's called for." He enjoyed watching the way she lifted a hand to tuck back the swing of hair, not with the sinuous movements of her redheaded sister, but with a quick, absent flick. She smelled of soap and some cool sprinkle of scent.

"What's this?"

"What's what?" He was too busy with the way the

sunlight showered on her hair to pay attention to anything else.

"This." She tapped a finger on a sketch.

"Hmm. That's an old servants' stairway. We bring this wall out here, to box it in." He took her finger to slide it along the sketch, the rough side of his palm fitting over the smooth skin of her hand. "It makes this suite two levels, the sitting room and bath down here, two bedrooms and a master bath up here. Since the stairs are already open, it gives us a separation of functions without closing off the flow of space."

"It's nice." Vaguely uneasy with the contact, she flexed her hand but only succeeded in tangling her fingers with his. "I suppose you're going to get estimates and bids."

"I've made some calls."

Something seemed to be happening to her legs from the knees down. They'd gone weak on her, as if she'd run a very long, very fast race. "Well, you…" She braced and turned her head to face him. His eyes were very close, very quiet, very calm. "Obviously you know what you're doing."

"Yeah, I do."

Oh, yeah, he did, she thought as she felt herself pulled toward him—not by his hand, but by something soft and warm and needy inside her. She had only to give in to it, to lean a little closer. Her mouth could be on his, and she would know, as she had known the day before, a kind of whippy excitement and dazzling pleasure. He was waiting, watching her, with those dark green eyes going from calm to intense, willing her to make that slight and significant move. As she began to slide toward him, she heard herself sigh.

Then she remembered.

He had been in almost this same position with Lilah just moments before. Faces close, fingers linked. Only a fool let herself be manipulated by a man who was that casual with a woman's feelings. And Amanda Kelly Calhoun was no fool.

She jerked back, tugging her hand from under his. Sloan felt the knots already winding through his stomach yank tighter.

"Did I miss something?" he asked with a casualness that cost him dearly.

"I don't know what you mean."

"The hell you don't. You were a hair's breadth away from kissing me, Mandy. Your eyes were full of it. Now you've got them frosted up again."

She wished it was as easy to put the ice back into her blood. "You're letting your ego get the best of you. But then, that's probably typical. If you want to take time out to flirt and snuggle with a woman, try Lilah again."

He was used to holding on to his temper. When a man had a dangerous one, he learned early to keep it chained down. But it wasn't easy, not with her, not with the way she so consistently racked his system. "Are you telling me that Lilah's available to any man who asks?"

She went from frost to fire so quickly he could only stare in amazed appreciation. "You don't know anything about my sister, O'Riley. Watch what you say or you'll find yourself on your butt again."

"I was asking what you said," he reminded her.

"I can say what I like, you can't. Lilah has a warm, generous heart. If you do anything to hurt her, I'll—"

"Hold on." Chuckling, he threw up both hands, palms out. "I don't mind you taking a chunk out of me, Calhoun, but I'd rather it be for something I did—or was at least planning to do. First, I'm not quite the tomcat you seem to think I am. And second, I'm not interested in—what was it—snuggling with Lilah."

Amanda's chin lifted a fraction higher. "What's the matter with her?"

Exasperated, he let his hands fall again. "Not a damn thing. Tell me, has your great-grandaddy's insanity trickled down or are you just being plain obstinate?"

"Take your pick." Now she was as embarrassed as she was angry and stalked over to the window to stare out. Whether he was a tomcat—as he'd put it—or not, it was no concerns of hers. It was her problem that she had overreacted to his meeting with Lilah. She was getting herself wound up over nothing, Amanda told herself. If she kept snapping at him every time they spent five minutes together, their business relationship would suffer. And business was, after all, her strongest suit. She gave herself another moment to be sure she'd regained some balance, then turned back.

"We seem to have gotten offtrack. Let's put this back on a professional level, and keep it there."

"You do that real well," he observed.

"What?"

"Pull yourself in. It can't be easy if being around me churns you up half as much as I get being around you." Then he grinned and recrossed his ankles. "Go ahead, be professional. I got real admiration for that side of you."

She wasn't sure whether to scream or laugh or just throw her hands up in defeat. Instead she shook her head and tried again. "I like your work."

"Thanks."

"Trent and I have discussed the budget for the project. He and C.C. may still be on their honeymoon when the bids start coming in. If that's the case, you and I will have to go over them. As far as the hotel section goes, you have a free hand. As to the other part of the house, the family part, we're only interested in essential repairs."

"Why? The place deserves a decent face-lift."

"Because the hotel is a business, and the Calhouns and St. Jameses will be partners. We have the property, he has the funds. We've all agreed that we won't take advantage of his generosity, or the fact that he's marrying C.C."

Sloan considered a moment. "Trent seems to have other ideas. And I've never known him to let anyone take advantage."

The smile softened her face. "I know, and we, all of us, appreciate that he's willing to help, but we feel strongly about this. The Towers, our part of it, is a Calhoun problem. Our position is that we'll accept the needed repairs to the plumbing, the wiring and other immediate necessities, then we'll pay him back from our share of the retreat. If business is good, we'll be able to take care of the rest ourselves within the next few years."

There was pride at stake here, he noted. And more, integrity. He nodded. "You work things out with Trent. Meanwhile, I'll concentrate on the west wing."

"Fine. If your schedule allows, you can take a look at the rest. It would be helpful if we had an idea what the budget will be on the family areas."

He started to point out that he was an architect not a contractor, then shrugged. It wouldn't hurt him to take a look. "Sure. I'll work up an estimate."

"I'd appreciate it. Once you do, I'd prefer if you gave it to me. Just me."

"You're the boss."

She lifted a brow. Odd, but she hadn't thought about it quite that way before. Her lips curved as she digested it. "Then we understand each other. One more thing."

He linked his hands behind his head. "We can have as many things as you want."

"Only one," she said, though her lips quivered. "When I was finalizing some of the wedding plans, I realized you were down as best man. I left your list with Aunt Coco."

"My list?"

"Yes, of the timetable, the duties you're responsible for, that sort of thing. There's also a copy of the necessary information—the name and phone number of the photographer, the contact for the musicians, the bartender we hired...oh, and I jotted down the names of three shops where you can rent a tux." Once again she took in the sheer size of him. "You really should get in for a fitting right away."

"I've got it covered." Impressed, he shook his head. "You're damn efficient, Calhoun."

"Yes, I am. Well then, I'll let you get back to work. I'll be in the third-floor storeroom in the other wing until about one. After that you can reach me at the BayWatch if you have any questions."

"Oh, I know where to find you, Calhoun. Good hunting."

He watched her walk away, and thought of her sitting in the storeroom, surrounded by dusty boxes and mounds of yellowing papers. She'd probably already found a way to put things in their tidy place, he thought with a grin. He wondered if she realized what a sweet contrast it was. She would stack and catalogue and file in the most practical way possible, while she searched through pieces of the past for an old dream.

Amanda found no dreams that morning. By the time she arrived at the BayWatch, she had already put in a five-hour day. When she had started the quest for the necklace weeks before, she had promised herself she wouldn't become discouraged, no matter how long it took or how little she found.

Thus far, they had come across the original receipt for the emeralds, and a date book where Bianca had mentioned them. It was enough, Amanda had decided, to prove the necklace had indeed existed, and to keep hope alive that it would be found again.

She often wondered about it, about what it had meant to Bianca Calhoun and why she had secreted it away. If indeed she had. Another old rumor was that Fergus had tossed the necklace into the sea. After all the stories Amanda had heard about Fergus Calhoun's abiding love of a dollar, it was hard to believe that he had willfully thrown away a quarter of a million in jewels.

Besides, she didn't want to believe it, Amanda admitted as she pinned on her name tag. Though she wouldn't have cared for anyone to know it, she had a strong streak of the romantic, and that part of her held tight to the notion that Bianca had hidden away the emeralds, like a gift or promise, waiting for the time they would be needed again.

It embarrassed her a little to know she felt that way. Amanda preferred the outward, and the logical, routine of sorting through papers and organizing them in the practical pursuit of a valuable heirloom.

Bianca herself remained as much a mystery to Amanda as the necklace. Her ingrained pragmatism made it impossible to understand a woman who had risked everything for, and ultimately had died for, love. Feelings that intense and that desperate seemed unlikely to her, unless they were in the pages of a book.

What would it be like to love that strongly? she wondered. To feel as though your life were so completely bound to another's that it was impossible to survive without him. Inconvenient, she decided. Uncomfortable and unwise. She could only be grateful that she hadn't inherited that dangerous kind of passion. Feeling smug about her own unbattered heart, she settled down to work.

"Amanda?"

She was halfway through the August reservations and held up a hand. "Minute," she murmured, and totaled her calculations to that point. "What is it, Karen? Wow." She pushed her glasses back up her nose and studied the luxurious spray of roses in the desk clerk's arms. "What did you do, win a beauty pageant?"

"They're not mine." Karen buried her face in them. "Don't I wish. They just came in, for you."

"Me?"

"You're still Amanda Calhoun," Karen pointed out as she offered the florist's card. "Though if you want to trade places until these three dozen long-stemmed beauties fade, I'm game."

"Three dozen?"

"I counted." Grinning, Karen laid them on the desk. "Three dozen and one," she added, nodded toward the single rose that stood beside them.

Sloan, Amanda thought, and felt her heart give a quick, catchy sigh. How was she supposed to get a handle on a man who did sweet, unexpected things every time she thought she'd made up her mind about him? How could he have known about her secret weakness for red roses? She hadn't even thanked him for the first one.

"Aren't you going to read the card?" Karen demanded. "If I have to go back to the desk without knowing who sent them, I'll be distracted and my work will suffer. The evil Albert Stenerson'll fire me, and it'll be your fault."

"I already know who they're from," she began, unaware of the softness in her eyes. "It was really so sweet of him to—oh." Baffled, she studied the name on the card. Not Sloan, she realized, with a cutting edge of disappointment that surprised her. They weren't from Sloan.

"Well? Do you want me to beg?"

Still puzzled, Amanda handed the card over.

"*With my appreciation. William Livingston.* Whew." Karen tossed back her long, dark hair. "What did you have to do to deserve this kind of gratitude?"

"I got him a fax machine."

"You got him a fax machine," Karen repeated, handing the card back to Amanda. "Last Sunday I cooked a pot roast with all the trimmings and all I got was a bottle of cheap wine."

Amanda continued to frown and tapped the card on the edge of her desk. "I guess I'd better thank him."

"I guess you'd better." Karen picked up one of the roses and sniffed. "Unless you'd rather delegate. I'd be glad to go up and express your appreciation to Mr. Eyes-To-Die-For Livingston."

"Thanks, but I'll handle it." She picked up the phone, then sent Karen an arched look. "Scram."

"Spoilsport." Laughing, she went out, discreetly shutting the door at her back as Amanda dialed the extension for the Island Suite.

"Livingston."

"Mr. Livingston, this is Amanda Calhoun."

"Ah, the efficient Miss Calhoun." There was a laugh in his voice, a pleasant and flattering one. "What can I do for you?"

"I wanted to thank you for the flowers. They're beautiful. It was very thoughtful of you."

"Just a small way of showing you that I appreciate your help, and the quick work."

"That's my job. Please let me know if I can be of any further assistance during your stay."

"As a matter of fact, there is something you could help me with."

"Of course." Automatically she picked up a pen and prepared to write.

"I'd like you to have dinner with me."

"Excuse me?"

"I'd like to take you to dinner. Eating alone is unappetizing."

"I'm sorry, Mr. Livingston, it's against hotel policy for the staff to socialize with the guests. It's kind of you to ask."

"Kindness has nothing to do with it. Can I ask if you'd consider it if hotel policy could be…bent?"

There was no chance of that, Amanda thought. Not with Stenerson. "I'd be happy to consider it," she said tactfully. "Unfortunately, as long as you're a guest at the BayWatch—"

"Yes, yes. I'll get back to you shortly."

Amanda blinked at the dead receiver, shrugged, then replaced it to get back to work. Ten minutes later, Stenerson was opening her door.

"Miss Calhoun, Mr. Livingston would like to have dinner with you." His mouth primed up even more than usual. "You're free to go. Naturally, I'll expect you to conduct yourself in a manner that will reflect properly on the hotel."

"But—"

"Don't make a habit of it."

"I—" But he was already shutting the door. Amanda was still staring at it when her phone rang. "Miss Calhoun."

"Shall we say eight o'clock?"

On a long breath, she sat back in her chair. She was on the point of refusing when she caught herself stroking the single rosebud Sloan had given her. Amanda snatched back her hand and balled it in her lap.

"I'm sorry, I'm on until ten tonight."

"Tomorrow then. Where shall I pick you up?"

"Tomorrow's fine," she said on impulse. "Let me give you directions."

Chapter 5

Sloan knew the minute Trent returned to The Towers. Even in the library at the end of a long corridor he could hear the high happy yaps of the dog, the shouts of children and the mix of laughter. Setting aside his notebook, he strolled out to see his old friend.

Trent had gotten no further than the foyer. Jenny was hanging on his legs as Fred circled and danced. Alex was jumping up and down in a bid for attention while Coco, Suzanna and Lilah all fired questions at once. C.C. only stood beaming, held snug against Trent's side. At a shout from above, Sloan looked up to see Amanda bolting down the stairs. Her laughter glowed in her face as he'd never seen it before. Squeezing through her sisters, she took her turn at a hug.

"If you hadn't come back today, I was sending out a team of mercenaries," she told Trent. "Four days before the wedding and you're down in Boston."

"I knew you could handle the details."

"She has miles of lists," Coco put in. "It's frightening."

"There, you see?" Trent gave Amanda a quick kiss.

"What did you bring me? What did you bring me?" Jenny demanded.

"Talk about mercenary." Laughing, Suzanna scooped her daughter up. When she spotted Sloan in the hallway, her easy smile faded. She tried to tell herself that it was her imagination that his eyes changed whenever he looked at her. It had to be. What possible reason would he have for disliking her on sight?

Sloan studied her another moment, a tall, slender woman with pale blond hair pulled back in a ponytail, a face blessed with classical beauty and sad blue eyes. Dismissing her, he looked back at Trent. His smile came naturally again.

"I hate to interrupt when you're surrounded by beautiful women, but time's wasting."

"Sloan." His arm still around C.C., Trent stepped forward to grip Sloan's hand. In all of his varied groups of acquaintances, associates and colleagues, this was the only man he considered a genuine friend. "On the job already?"

"Getting started."

"You look like you've just gotten back from a long vacation in the tropics instead of six weeks in Budapest. It's good to see you."

"Same here." Sloan sent a quick wink at C.C. "It's really good to see that you're finally developing some taste."

"I like him," C.C. said.

"Women tend to," Trent said. "How's your family?"

Sloan's gaze flicked to Suzanna again. "They're fine."

"You two must have a lot to catch up on." Feeling awkward, Suzanna took her son's hand. "We're going to take a walk before dinner."

Amanda waited until Coco had urged everyone along toward the parlor before she put a hand on Sloan's arm. "Wait."

He grinned at her. "I've been waiting, Calhoun."

She wasn't even tempted to rise to the bait. "I want to know why you look at Suzanna that way."

The humor faded from his eyes. "What way is that?"

"Like you detest her."

It annoyed him that those particular and very private feelings showed so clearly. "You've got more imagination than I gave you credit for."

"It's not my imagination." Baffled, she shook her head. "What could you possibly have against Suzanna? She's the kindest, most good-hearted person I know."

It was difficult not to sneer, but he kept his face bland. "I didn't say I had anything against her. You did."

"You didn't have to say it. Obviously I can't make you talk about it, but—"

"Maybe that's because I'd rather talk about us." Casually he set both hands on the banister behind her, caging her between.

"There is no us."

"Sure there is. There's you and there's me. That makes us. That's real basic grammar."

"If you're trying to change the subject—"

"You're getting that line between your eyebrows again." He lifted a thumb to rub at it. "That Calhoun line. How come you never smile at me the way you smiled at Trent?"

"Because I like Trent."

"It's funny, most people figure I'm an amiable sort of guy."

"Not from where I'm standing."

"Why don't you stand a little closer?"

She had to laugh. If there had been a contest for persistence, Sloan O'Riley would have won hands down. "This is close enough, thanks." More than close enough, she added silently when she had to fight back an urge to run her fingers through that untidy mane of reddish-blond hair. "*Amiable* isn't the word I would use. Now, *cocky, annoying, tenacious,* those might suit."

"I kind of like tenacious." He leaned closer to breathe in her scent. "A man doesn't get very far if he caves in every time he runs into a wall. You climb over, tunnel under, or just knock the whole damn thing down."

She put a hand to his chest before he could close that last inch of distance. "Or he keeps beating his head against it until he has a concussion."

"That's a calculated risk, and worth it if there's a woman behind the wall looking at him the way you look at me."

"I don't look at you any particular way."

"When you forget that you want to be professional, you look at me with those big blue eyes of yours all soft, and a little scared. A lot curious. Makes me want to scoop you up right there and carry you off to someplace real quiet so I can satisfy that curiosity."

She could imagine it all too clearly, feel it all too sharply. There was only one solution. Escape. "Well, this has been fun, but I've got to go change."

"Are you going back to work?"

"No." Agile, she swooped under his arm and swung up the steps. "I've got a date."

"A date?" he repeated, but she was already racing across the second floor.

He told himself he wasn't waiting for her, though he'd been pacing the foyer for a good twenty minutes. He wasn't going to hang around like an idiot and watch her go strolling off with some other man—after she'd tied him into knots by just standing there and looking at him. There was plenty for him to do, including enjoying the dinner Coco had invited him to, talking over old times and new plans with Trent, even sitting down at his drawing board. He wasn't about to spend the evening mooning over the fact that some obstinate woman preferred someone else's company to his.

After all, Sloan reminded himself as he paced the foyer, she was free to come and go as she pleased. The same as he was. Neither one of them was branded. Just because he had a hankering for her didn't mean he was going to get riled up when she spent a couple of hours with another man.

The hell it didn't.

Turning, he took the steps two at a time.

"Calhoun?" He strode down the corridor, banging on doors. "Damn it, Calhoun, I want to talk to you." He was at the far end of the hall and starting back when Amanda opened her door.

"What's going on?" she demanded.

He stared a moment as she stood in the stream of light that spilled out of the room behind her. She'd done something fancy to her hair, he noted, so that it looked sexily rumpled. Played with her face, too, in that damnably sultry way some women have a talent for. Her dress was a pale icy blue, full at the skirt, nipped at the waist with two skinny straps slinking over her shoulders. Chunky stones in a deeper blue glittered at her ears and throat.

She didn't look efficient, he thought furiously. She didn't look competent. She looked as delectable as a pretty white cake on a fancy tray. And he was damned if any other man was going to take even one small nibble.

Her foot was already tapping when he started toward her.

Amiable? she thought, and had to resist the urge to bolt

back into her room and lock the door. No one would call him amiable now. He looked as though he'd just finished chewing a mountain of glass and was raring for the second course.

"What kind of date?" he snapped at her, and found himself further incensed by the fact that her skin smelled like glory.

Amanda inclined her head slowly. The hands she had fisted on her hips slid carefully to her sides. When you were facing a raging bull you didn't wave a red flag but tried to ease yourself over the fence. "The usual kind."

"Is that the way you dress for the usual kind?"

Irked, she glanced down and smoothed her skirts. "What's wrong with the way I'm dressed?"

For an answer, he took her arm and swung her around. He'd been right, he thought as his stomach clutched up. Those two little straps were all that were covering her back. Right down to the waist. "Where's the rest of it?"

"Rest of what?"

"The dress."

She turned back, still cautious, and examined his face. "Sloan, I think you've gone around the bend."

She didn't know how right she was, he thought. "I've got as much sense as any man can hang on to after ten minutes with you. Cancel."

"Cancel?" she repeated.

"The date, damn it." He nudged her none too gently toward her bedroom. "Go in and call him up and tell him you can't make it. Ever."

"You really are crazy." She forgot about bulls and red flags and cut loose. "I go where I please and with whom I please. If you think I'm going to break a date with an attractive, charming and intelligent man because some overbearing baboon tells me to, then think again."

"It's the date," he warned, "or that pretty stiff neck of yours."

Her eyes narrowed down to two slits of righteous blue fire. "Don't you threaten me, you pinhead. I have a dinner date with your antithesis. A gentleman." She elbowed him aside. "Now get out of my way."

"I'll get out of your way," he promised. "After I give you something to think about."

He had her back against the wall with his mouth covering hers before she could blink. She could taste the anger. That, she would have fought against to the last breath. But she could also taste the need, and that, she surrendered to. It was such a perfect echo of her own.

He didn't care if it was unreasonable. He didn't care if it was wrong or stupid or any of the other terms that could so easily apply to his actions. He wanted to curse her for making him behave like some reckless teenager. But he could only taste her, drowning in the flavor that he was coming to understand he would always crave. He could only pull her closer against him so that he could feel the instant heat that pumped from her body into his.

He could sense each change as it flowed through her.

First the anger that kept her rigid and aloof. Then the surrender, reluctant then melting so that her bones seemed to dissolve. And the passion overlapping so quickly it stole his breath. It was that he understood he couldn't live without.

Her arms went around him as if they belonged there. Strained against his, her body throbbed until it was one sweet ache. This was an ache that once felt could never be forgotten, would always be craved. Eager, she nipped at his mouth, knowing in another moment delirium could overtake her. Wanting it, wanting that liberating mindless whirl of desire only he could ignite inside her.

Only he.

In one long possessive stroke his hands ran from her

shoulders to her wrists, holding there a moment while her pulse scrambled under his palms. When he lifted his head, she leaned back limply against the wall, watching him while she struggled to catch her breath. While she fought to break through the torrent of sensations and understand the feelings beneath them.

The thought of another man touching her, of looking into her face and seeing it flushed with passion as it was now, of seeing her eyes clouded with it, terrified him. Because he preferred good clean anger to fear, he gripped her shoulders again, all but lifting her off her feet.

"Think about that," he told her in a low dangerous voice. "You think about that good and hard."

What had he done to her to make her need so terribly? He had to know, just by looking at her, that he had only to pull her inside her room to take everything he claimed to want. He had only to touch her again to have her desperate to give. He wouldn't even have to ask. It shamed her to realize it, destroyed her to understand that anyone would have such complete power over her pride and her will.

"You made your point," she said unsteadily, infuriated that tears were stinging the back of her eyes and throat. "Do you want to hear me say that you can make me want you? Fine. You can."

The sparkle of tears in her eyes did what her fury couldn't. It beat him soundly. There was regret in his voice when he lifted a hand to her face. "Amanda—"

She stiffened and shut her eyes. If he was gentle—she knew if he showed her even a scrap of tenderness, she would crumble. "You've got your conquest, Sloan. Now I'd appreciate it if you'd let me go."

He let his hand slide to his side before he stepped back. "I'm not going to tell you I'm sorry." But the way she looked at him made him feel as though he had just shattered something small and fragile.

"That's all right. I'm sorry enough for both of us."

"Amanda." Lilah stood at the top of the stairs, watching them both with her sleepy-eyed curiosity. "Your date's here."

"Thanks." Frantic for escape, she turned into her room to grab her jacket and purse. Being careful not to look at Sloan, she hurried out again to rush downstairs. Lilah glanced after her, then walked down the hall to rest her hands on Sloan's shoulders.

"You know, big guy, you look like you could use a friend."

He couldn't begin to put a name to any of the emotions currently running riot through him. "Maybe I'll just go downstairs and throw him out a window."

"You could," Lilah agreed after a moment, "but Mandy's always been a sucker for the underdog."

Sloan swore then decided to work off some of the frustration by pacing the corridor. "So, who is he anyway?"

"I've never met him before. His name's William Livingston."

"And?"

Lilah gave a gentle shrug. "Tall, dark and handsome as the saying goes. Very faint, very charming British accent, Italian suit, upper-class manners. That patina of wealth and breeding without being ostentatious."

Sloan swore and considered punching a hole in the wall. "He sounds just dandy."

"Sounds," she agreed, but her look was troubled.

"What is it?"

"Bad vibes." Absently she ran a hand up and down her arm. "And he had a very muddy aura."

"Give me a break, Lilah."

With a little smile, she glanced back at him. "Don't knock

it, Sloan. Remember, I'm on your side. I happen to think you're just what my take-it-all-too-seriously sister needs." In her easy way, she hooked a friendly arm through his. "Relax, Mr. William Livingston doesn't have a chance. Not her type." She laughed as she walked with him to the steps. "She thinks he is, but he's not. So let's go eat. There's nothing like Aunt Coco's Trout Amandine to put you in a good mood."

Pretending she had an appetite, Amanda studied her menu. The restaurant William had chosen was a lovely little place overlooking Frenchman Bay. Since the night was warm, they could enjoy the terrace service with candlelight flickering in the gentle sea breeze, and the fragile scent of spring flowers.

Amanda left the choice of wine up to him and tried to convince herself that she was about to have a delightful evening.

"Are you enjoying Bar Harbor?" she asked.

"Very much. I'm hoping to get some sailing in soon, but in the meantime, I've been content to enjoy the scenery."

"Have you been to the park?"

"Not yet." He glanced over at the bottle the waiter offered, perused the label, then nodded.

"You shouldn't miss it. The view from Cadillac Mountain is stupendous."

"So I'm told." He tasted the wine, approved, then waited for Amanda's to be poured. "Perhaps you'll find some time and act as my guide."

"I don't think—"

"Hotel policy's already been bent," he interrupted, and touched his glass lightly to hers.

"I wanted to ask you how you managed it."

"Very simply. I gave your Mr. Stenerson a choice. Either

he could make an exception to his policy, or I could move to another hotel where it wouldn't be an issue."

"I see." She took a thoughtful sip of wine. "That seems a bit drastic just for a dinner."

"A very delightful dinner. I wanted to get to know you better. I hope you don't mind."

What woman could? she asked herself, and only smiled.

It was impossible not to relax, not to be charmed by his stories, flattered by his attentiveness. He did not, as so many successful men did, talk constantly of his business. As an antique dealer he'd traveled all over the world and, throughout the meal, gave Amanda glimpses of Paris and Rome, London and Rio.

When her thoughts drifted now and again to another man, she doubled her determination to enjoy herself where she was, and with whom.

"The rosewood chiffonier in your foyer," he commented as they lingered over coffee and dessert. "It's a beautiful piece."

"Thank you. It's Regency period—I think."

He smiled. "You think correctly. If I had run into it at an auction, I would have considered myself very fortunate."

"My great-grandfather had it shipped over from England when he built the house."

"Ah, the house." William's lips curved as he lifted his cup. "Very imposing. I half expected to see medieval maidens drifting about on the lawn."

"Or bats swooping out of the tower."

On a delighted laugh, he squeezed her hand. "No, but perhaps Rapunzel letting down her hair."

The image appealed and made her smile. "We love it, and always have. Maybe the next time you visit the island you'll stay at The Towers Retreat."

"The Towers Retreat," he murmured, tapping a finger thoughtfully against his lips. "Where have I heard that before?"

"A projected St. James hotel?"

His eyes cleared. "Of course. I read something a few weeks ago. You don't mean to say that your home is The Towers?"

"Yes, it is. We hope to have the retreat ready for occupancy in about a year."

"That is fascinating. But wasn't there some legend attached to the place? Something about ghosts and missing jewelry?"

"The Calhoun emeralds. They were my great-grandmother's."

With a half smile, he tilted his head. "They're real? I thought it was just a clever publicity gimmick. Stay in a haunted house and search for missing treasure. That sort of thing."

"No, in fact we're not at all pleased that the whole business leaked out." Even thinking about it annoyed her so that she began to drum her fingers on the table. "The necklace is real—was real in any event. We don't know where it might have been hidden. In the meantime we're forever bothered by reporters or having to chase erstwhile treasure hunters off the grounds."

"I'm sorry. That's very intrusive."

"We hope to find it soon, and put an end to all the nonsense. Once renovations start, it might turn up under a floorboard."

"Or behind the ubiquitous secret panel," he offered with a smile and made her laugh.

"We don't have any of those—at least that I know of."

"Then your ancestor was remiss. A place like that deserves at least one secret panel." He laid a hand over hers again. "Perhaps you'll let me help you look for it…or at least let me use it as an excuse to see you again."

"I'm sorry, but at least for the next few days I'm tied up. My sister's getting married on Saturday."

He smiled over their joined hands. "There's always Sunday. I would like to see you again, Amanda. Very much." He let the subject, and her hand slip gently away.

On the drive home he kept the topics general. No pressure, Amanda thought, grateful. No arrogant assumptions or cocky grins. This was the kind of man who knew how to treat a woman with the proper respect and attention. William wouldn't knock her to the ground and laugh in her face. He wouldn't stalk her down like a gunslinger and fire out demands.

So why was she so let down when they stopped in front of the house and Sloan's car was nowhere in sight? Shaking off the mood, she waited for William to come around and open her door.

"Thank you for tonight," she told him. "It was lovely."

"Yes, it was. And so are you." Very gently he placed his hands on her shoulders before touching his lips to hers. The kiss was very warm, very soft—an expert caress of lips and hands. And to her disappointment, it left her completely unmoved.

"Are you really going to make me wait until Sunday to see you again?"

His eyes told her that he had not been unmoved. Amanda waited for the banked desire in them to strike some chord. But there was nothing.

"William, I—"

"Lunch," he said, adding a charming smile. "Something very casual at the hotel. You can tell me more about the house."

"All right. If I can swing it." She eased away before he could kiss her again. "Thanks again."

"My pleasure, Amanda." He waited, as was proper, for

her to go inside. As the door shut behind her, his smile changed ever so slightly, hardened, cooled. "Believe me, it will be my pleasure."

He walked back to his car. He would drive it well out of sight of The Towers. And then he would come back to do a quick and quiet tour of the grounds, to note down the most practical entrances.

If Amanda Calhoun could be his entryway into The Towers, that was all well and good—with the side benefit of romancing a beautiful woman. If she didn't provide him with a way in, he would simply find a different route.

One way or the other, he didn't intend to leave Mount Desert Island without the Calhoun emeralds.

"Did you have a good time?" Suzanna asked when Amanda came in the front door.

"Suze." Amused but not surprised, Amanda shook her head. "You waited up again."

"No, I didn't." To prove it, Suzanna gestured with the mug in her hand. "I just came down to make myself some tea."

Amanda laughed as she walked over to rest her hands on her sister's shoulders. "Why is it that we Irish-as-Paddy's-pig Calhouns can't tell a decent lie?"

Suzanna gave up. "I don't know. We should practice more."

"Honey, you look tired."

"Mmm." Exhausted was the word, but she didn't care for it. Suzanna sipped the tea as they started up the stairs together. "Springtime. Everybody wants their flowers done yesterday. I'm not complaining. It looks like the business is finally going to turn a real profit."

"I still think you should hire on some more help. Between the business and the kids you run yourself ragged."

"Now who's playing mama? Anyway, Island Gardens needs one more good season before I can afford anything but one part-time helper. Plus I like to be busy." Even though fatigue was dragging at her, she paused outside of Amanda's door. "Mandy, can I talk to you for a minute before you go to bed?"

"Sure. Come on in." Amanda left the door slightly ajar as she slipped out of her shoes. "Is something wrong?"

"No. At least nothing I can put my finger on. Can I ask you what you think of Sloan?"

"Think of him?" Stalling, Amanda set her shoes neatly in the closet.

"Impressions, I guess. He seems like a very nice man. Both kids are already crazy about him, and that's an almost foolproof barometer for me."

"He's good with them." Amanda took off her earrings to replace them in her jewelry box.

"I know." Troubled, she wandered the room. "Aunt Coco's set to adopt him. He's slipped right into an easy relationship with Lilah. C.C.'s already fond of him, and not just because he's a friend of Trent's."

Pouting a little, Amanda unclasped her necklace. "His type always gets along beautifully with women."

Distracted, Suzanna merely shook her head. "No, it's not a man-woman kind of thing at all. Just a kind of innate relaxation."

Amanda had no comment for that as she recalled the fevered tension in him a few hours earlier.

"He seems like an easygoing, friendly man."

"But?"

"It's probably my imagination, but whenever he looks at me, I get this wave of hostility." With a half laugh, she shrugged. "Now I sound like Lilah."

Amanda's eyes met her sister's in the mirror. "No, I sensed something myself. I can't explain it. I even called him on it."

"Did he say anything? I don't expect everyone to like me, but when I feel a dislike this strong, at least I want to know why."

"He denied it. I don't know what to say, Suzanna, except that I don't think he's the kind of man who would react that way to someone he doesn't even know." She made a helpless gesture with her hands. "He can certainly be annoying, but I don't think he's a man to be deliberately unfair. Maybe we're both being oversensitive."

"Maybe." Suzanna pushed the uncomfortable feelings away. "We're all a little crazed with C.C.'s wedding, and the renovations. Well, I won't lose any sleep over him." She kissed Amanda's cheek. "Good night."

"Night." As she eased down onto the bed, Amanda let out a long sigh. It was unfortunate, she thought. It was infuriating. But she already knew she'd be losing sleep over him.

Chapter 6

She was right on schedule. If there was one thing you could count on about Amanda Calhoun, Sloan thought, it was that she'd be on time. She was moving fast—typically—so he lengthened his stride and crossed the hotel patio to waylay her by the gate leading to the pool. His hand covered hers on the latch.

She jerked away, which was no less than he'd expected. "Don't you have anything better to do?" she asked.

"I want to talk to you."

"This is my time." She shoved open the gate, strode through then whirled around. "My personal time. I don't have to talk to you." To prove it, she slammed the gate smartly in his face.

Sloan took a long, slow breath, then opened the gate. "Okay, you can just listen." He caught up with her as she heaved her towel onto a deck chair.

"I'm not going to talk, and I'm not going to listen.

There's absolutely nothing you have to say that could interest me." She stripped off her terry wrap, tossed it aside, then dove into the pool.

Sloan watched her through the first lap. She was mad enough to spit, he thought, then moved his shoulders. So, they'd do it the hard way.

With each kick and stroke, Amanda cursed him. She'd spent half the night replaying their last scene together over and over in her mind. It had made her miserable. It had made her furious. When she'd awakened that morning, she'd promised herself that he would never get the chance to touch her again. Certainly he would never get the chance to make her feel helpless and needy again.

Her life was just beginning to move along as she wanted. There was no way, no way in hell that Sloan O'Riley or anyone else was going to block her path.

She ran straight into him, a dud torpedo into a battleship. Sputtering, she surfaced to see him standing chest high in the water. Bare-chest high.

"What are you doing?"

"I figured I'd have a better chance of getting you to listen in here than I would if I stood on the side and yelled at you."

Eyes narrowed, she slicked the hair back from her face. There was a laugh bubbling in her throat that she refused to acknowledge. "The pool isn't open to guests until ten."

"Yeah, I think you mentioned that. What you didn't mention is that this water is freezing."

"Yeah." Now she did smile, and there was as much humor as smugness in the curve of her lips. "I know. That's why I like to keep moving."

She started off, slicing cleanly through the water. Less than a foot away, he was matching her stroke for stroke. He'd stripped off more than his shirt, she noted. The only thing covering that very long body was a pair of brief navy briefs. Each time her face went into the water, her eyes slid over to take another look.

His broad shoulders and chest tapered down to a narrow waist and hips. The skin was stretched taut over the bones there, without an ounce of excess flesh. His stomach was board flat, and…oh my. When she nearly sucked in water instead of air, Amanda forced her gaze to skip down several strategic inches to the hard, muscled thighs and calves.

The tough, weathered tan was over every inch of exposed flesh. His skin gleamed like wet copper. And what would it feel like to run her hands over it now? To feel those sleek, smooth muscles under her fingers? How could their bodies fit together now, if slick as otters, they slid against each other through the chill water?

Chill? she thought. The pool was beginning to feel like a sauna. Deliberately she pushed off hard and increased her pace. If she could outrace him, maybe she could outrace her own wayward thoughts.

He was still beside her, matching speed and stroke so that they crossed the pool in a kind of unstudied and effortless harmony. It was lovely, almost sensuous, the way their arms lifted and pulled at the same moment, the way their legs scissored and their bodies stretched…like making love, she thought dreamily, then shook herself to knock that hot image from her brain.

Amanda kicked in and put all that frustrated passion into speed. Still, their hands slapped the wall in unison. She began to enjoy it for what it was, an unstated competition between two people who were evenly matched. She'd lost track of the laps and didn't care. When her lungs were straining and her muscles weak, she gripped the edge of the pool to surface, laughing.

He knew she'd never looked more beautiful, with her hair and face drenched with water and her eyes filled with delight. More than anything he'd ever wanted, he wanted to pull her against him then, just to hold her while her laughter danced on the morning air. But he'd made a promise to himself sometime during his own sleepless night. He intended to keep it.

He sent her a friendly grin. "That warmed things up."

"You're pretty good. For an Okie."

"You're not bad yourself, for a female."

She laughed again and rested her head on the side of the pool to look at him. His hair was dark with water, curling over his brow and neck in a way that had her fingers itching to play with it. "I like to race."

"Race? Is that what we were doing? I thought we were just taking a nice, leisurely swim."

She tossed water into his eyes, then stood. "I have to get in."

"Are you going to let me talk to you now?"

The laughter faded from her eyes. "Let's just leave it," she suggested, and hitched herself up on the side of the pool.

He laid a hand on her leg. "Mandy—"

"I don't want to argue with you again. Since we've actually managed to get along for five minutes, why can't we just leave it at that?"

"Because I want to apologize."

"If you'd just—" She broke off to stare at him. "You what?"

"I want to apologize." He stood to put his hands lightly on her arms just beneath her shoulders. "I was out of line last night, way out, and I'm sorry."

"Oh." Disconcerted, she looked down and began to rub at the beads of water on her thigh.

"Now you're supposed to say, all right, Sloan, I accept your apology."

She looked up through wet, spiky lashes, then smiled. Things were suddenly too comfortable to cling to anger. "I guess I do. You acted like such a jerk."

He grimaced. "Thanks a lot."

"You did. Spouting off threats and orders. Then there was all that steam coming out of your ears."

"Want to know why?"

She shook her head and started to rise, but he held her in place. "You brought it up," he pointed out. "I couldn't stand the idea of you being with someone else. Look at me." Gently he cupped her chin, turning her face back to his. "You triggered something in me right off. I can't shake it. I don't much want to."

"I don't think—"

"Thinking has nothing to do with it. I know how I feel when I look at you."

She was losing fast. The quick skip of panic couldn't compete with the flood of pleasure. "I have to think," she murmured. "I'm made that way."

"Okay, well here's something new for you to think about. I'm falling in love with you."

Panic was more than a skip now, but a hard slap. It darted into her eyes as she stared at him. "You don't mean that."

"Yes, I do. And you know it or you wouldn't be sitting there looking like a rabbit caught in the high beams."

"I don't—"

"I'm not asking how you feel," he cut in. "I'm giving you my side of it, so you can get used to it."

She didn't think she would, ever, any more than she would get used to him. Certainly it would be impossible to get used to the feelings shooting off inside her. Is this what love was? she wondered. This edgy and bright sensation that could turn warm and soft without warning? "I don't—I'm not sure how…" She let out a huff of breath. "Did you do this just to make me crazy?"

It helped to be able to smile. "Yep. Give me a kiss, Calhoun."

She twisted and slid wetly out of his hold. "I'm not kissing you again, because it erases every intelligent thought from my head."

Now he grinned. "Honey, that's the nicest thing you've ever said to me." When he rose smoothly from the pool, Amanda snatched up her towel. She snapped it once, hard enough to make the air crack.

"Keep back. I mean it. You either give me time to figure all this out or I aim and fire. And I aim below the belt." There was both amusement and challenge in her eyes when she tilted her chin. "You don't have a lot of protection at the moment."

He ran his tongue around his teeth. "You've got me there. How about a drive after you get off work?"

It would be nice, she thought, to go driving with him up into the hills, with the windows open and the air streaming. But, regretfully, duty came first.

"I can't. C.C.'s shower's tonight. We're surprising her when she gets home from work." She frowned a little. "It's on your list."

"Guess it slipped my mind. Tomorrow then."

"I have the final meeting with the photographer, then I have to help Suzanna with the flowers. Not the next night, either," she said before he could ask. "Most of the out-of-town guests will be arriving, plus we've got the rehearsal dinner."

"Then the wedding," he said with a nod. "After the wedding, Calhoun."

"After the wedding, I'll…" She smiled, realizing she was

enjoying herself. "I'll let you know." Grabbing her wrap, she headed for the gate.

"Hey. I haven't got a towel."

She tossed a laugh over her shoulder. "I know."

Late that afternoon, Sloan stood out on the lower terrace, making sketches of the exterior of The Towers. He wanted to add another outside stairway without disturbing the integrity of the building. He stopped when Suzanna came out carrying two wicker baskets pregnant with spring flowers.

"I'm sorry." She hesitated, then tried a smile. "I didn't know you were out here. I'm going to set things up for the shower."

"I'll be out of your way in a minute."

"That's all right." She set the basket down and went back inside.

Over the next few minutes, she went back and forth, carrying out chairs and paper decorations. They passed the time in nerve-racking silence until she finally set aside one of Amanda's swans and looked at him.

"Mr. O'Riley, have we met before?"

He kept right on sketching. "No."

"I wondered because you seemed to know me, and have a poor opinion of me."

His gaze lifted coldly to hers. "I don't know you—Mrs. Dumont."

"Then why—" She broke off. She hated confrontations, the way they tightened up her stomach muscles. Turning away, she started back inside. She could feel his eyes on her, icy and resentful. After bracing a hand on the jamb, she forced herself to turn back. "No, I'm not going to do this. You're in my home, Mr. O'Riley, and I refuse to walk on eggshells in my own home ever again. Now I want to know what your problem is."

He tossed his sketch pad onto a small glass-topped table. "The name doesn't ring any bells with you, Mrs. Dumont? O'Riley doesn't strike a chord?"

"No, why should it?"

His mouth tightened. "Maybe if I add a name to it. Megan. Megan O'Riley. Hear any bells now?"

"No." Frustrated, she pushed a hand through her hair. "Will you get to the point?"

"I guess it's easy for someone like you to forget. She wasn't anyone to you but a slight inconvenience."

"Who?"

"Megan. My sister, Megan."

Completely lost, Suzanna shook her head. "I don't know your sister."

The fact that the name meant nothing to her only infuriated him. Sloan stepped toward her, ignoring the quick fear in her eyes. "No, you never met her face-to-face. Why bother? You managed to see that she was pushed aside easily enough. Not that you ended up with any prize. Baxter Dumont was always a bastard, but she loved him."

"Your sister?" Suzanna lifted an unsteady hand to rub at her temple. "Your sister and Bax."

"Starting to get through?" When she started to turn away, he grabbed her arm and whirled her back. "Was it for love or money?" he demanded. "Either way, you could have shown some compassion. Damn it, she was seventeen and pregnant. Couldn't you have stood back far enough to let the spineless sonofabitch see his son?"

She'd gone a translucent shade of white. Under his hand, her arm seemed to turn to water. "Son," she whispered.

"She was just a kid, a terrified kid who'd believed every

lie he'd told her. I wanted to kill him, but it would only have made it worse for Meg. But you, you couldn't even find it in your heart to give her the scraps from the table. You went right ahead with your fancy life as if she and the boy didn't exist. And when she called and begged you just to let him see the boy once or twice a year, you called her a whore and threatened to have her son taken away if she ever contacted your precious husband again."

She couldn't get her breath. Not since her last hideous argument with Bax had she found it so difficult to breathe. Weakly she batted at the hand that held her arm. "Please. Please, I need to sit down."

But he was staring at her. As the impetus of his own rage ebbed he could see that it wasn't shame in her eyes, it wasn't derision or even anger. It was pure shock. "My God," he said quietly, "you didn't know."

All she could do was shake her head. When his grip loosened, she turned and bolted into the house. Sloan stood for a moment, pressing his fingers against his eyes. All the disgust he had felt for Suzanna turned sharply on himself. He started after her and ran into a furious Amanda in the doorway.

"What did you do to her?" With both hands she shoved him back. "What the hell did you say to her to make her cry like that?"

The fist in his stomach squeezed tighter. "Where did she go?"

"You're not getting near her again. When I think that I'd begun to believe I could—damn you, O'Riley."

"There's nothing you can say to me that's worse than what I'm already thinking about myself. Now where is she?"

"You go to hell." She slammed the terrace door and flipped the lock.

Sloan gave brief thought to kicking it in then, swearing,

went around to the stone steps on the side of the house. He found Suzanna standing on the second-floor balcony, looking out at the cliffs. He'd taken his first step toward her when Amanda burst out of the doors.

"You keep away from her." She already had a protective arm around her sister. "Just turn around and start walking. Don't stop until you get back to Oklahoma."

"This isn't any of your concern," Sloan told her, and Suzanna had to grab hold before Amanda sprang at him.

"It's all right." Suzanna squeezed Amanda's hand. "I need to talk to him, Mandy. Alone."

"But—"

"Please. It's important. Go down and finish setting up, will you?"

Reluctant, Amanda stepped back. "If it's what you want." She aimed a killing look at Sloan. "Watch your step."

When they were alone, Sloan struggled for the right words. "Mrs. Dumont. Suzanna—"

"What's his name?" she asked.

"What?"

"The boy. What's his name?"

"I don't—"

"Damn it, what's his name?" She whirled away from the wall. Shock had been replaced by angry tears. "He's half brother to my children. I want to know his name."

"Kevin. Kevin O'Riley."

"How old is he?"

"Seven."

Turning back to the sea, she shut her eyes. Seven years before she had been a new bride, full of hope and dreams and blind love. "And Baxter knew? He knew that she'd had his child?"

"Yes, he knew. Megan wouldn't tell anyone at first who

the father was. But after she'd called and spoken to you…but she didn't speak to you, did she?"

"No." Suzanna continued to stare straight ahead. "Baxter's mother perhaps."

"I want to apologize."

"There's no need. If it had been one of my sisters, I would have struck out with more than a few hard words." To warm herself she cupped her elbows with her hands. "Go on."

She was tougher than she looked, Sloan thought, but it didn't ease his conscience. "After she'd called, she fell apart. That's when she finally told me everything. How she'd met Dumont when she'd gone to New York to visit some friends. He was there on some business and he started showing her around. She'd never been to New York before, and it—and he dazzled her. She was just a kid."

"Seventeen," Suzanna murmured.

"And naive with it. Well, she got over that quick enough." The bitterness came though. "He gave her all the usual bull about getting married, about how he'd come out to Oklahoma and meet her family. Once she got home, he never contacted her. She got through to him on the phone once or twice. He made excuses and more promises. Then she found out she was pregnant."

He steadied himself, trying not to remember how angry and frightened he'd been when he'd learned his baby sister was going to have a baby of her own.

"When she told him, he changed tactics fast. He said some pretty awful things to her, and she grew up fast. Too fast."

Suzanna understood that, more than he could know. "It must have been terribly difficult for her, having the child without having the father."

"She handled herself. I have a very supportive family. Well, you'd know about that."

"Yes."

"Luckily, money wasn't a problem, either, so she could get all the care she and the baby needed. She never wanted his money, Suzanna."

"No, I understand that, too."

He nodded slowly, seeing that she did. "And when Kevin was born...well, Meg was great. It was for his sake that she tried to contact Dumont again, and eventually decided to appeal to his wife. All she wanted was for her son to have some contact with his father."

"I understand." Steadier, she turned around to look at him. "Sloan, if I had any influence with Bax I'd use it." She lifted her hands and let them fall. "But I don't, not even when it concerns the children he's chosen to acknowledge."

"I figure Kevin's better off the way things are. Suzanna—" he dragged a hand through his disordered hair "—how the hell did a woman like you end up with Dumont?"

She smiled a little. "Once I was a young, naive girl who believed in happy ever after."

He wanted to take her hand but wasn't certain she'd accept it. "I know you said you didn't want an apology, but I'd feel a hell of a lot better if you'd take it just the same."

It was she who offered her hand. "It's easy to do when it's family. I guess in an odd way, that's what we are." She pressed her free hand to their joined ones. Later, she promised herself, she would find a few minutes alone to let the grief come. And to let it go. "I want to ask you a favor. I'd like for my children to know about Kevin, and unless it would upset your sister, for them to have a chance to meet each other."

"When I take a wrong turn, I take it big. It would mean a lot to her."

"Jenny and Alex are going to be thrilled." She looked at her watch. "Speaking of which, they're probably already home from school and driving Aunt Coco crazy. I'd better go."

He looked down the steps toward the terrace. And thought of Amanda. "Me, too. I've got other fences to mend."

Suzanna lifted a brow. "Good luck."

He had a feeling he was going to need it. By the time he'd reached the terrace, he was sure of it. Amanda was there, fastening streamers while Lilah leisurely tied balloons to the back of chairs. A long table was already covered with a frilly white cloth.

Amanda heard the scrape of boot heels on stone and turned to aim one deadly glare. Lilah didn't need another hint.

"Well." She flicked a balloon with a fingertip to send it dancing. "I think I'll go see if Aunt Coco's got any of those chocolate pastries ready." As she walked by Sloan, she paused. Unlike Amanda's, her eyes were cool, but the meaning was clear. "I'd hate to think I was wrong about you." She walked through the terrace doors and, after a brief hesitation, shut them to give her sister privacy.

Amanda didn't wait to pounce. "You've got a nerve, or maybe you're just plain stupid, showing your face here after what you did."

"You don't know anything about it. Suzanna and I worked it out."

"Oh, you think so?" Ready to joust, she slammed down a package of pretty pink-and-silver plates. "Not by a long shot. When I think that just a few hours ago you'd nearly convinced me you were the kind of man I could care about, then I come home and find my sister running away from you looking devastated. I want to know what you did."

"I ran with the wrong information. And I'm sorry about it."

"That's not good enough."

His own emotions were a bit too raw for reason. "Well, it's going to have to be. If you want to know more, you're just going to have to ask Suzanna."

"I'm asking you."

"And I'm telling you that what happened was between her and me. It doesn't have anything to do with you."

"That's where you're wrong." She crossed the terrace until they were toe to toe. "You mess with one Calhoun, you mess with them all. I may have to put up with you until after the wedding, since you're supposed to be best man. But when it's over, I'm going to do whatever I have to do to see to it that you go back where you came from."

Pushed to the end of his chain, he took her by the lapels. "I told you before, I finish what I start."

"You are finished, O'Riley. The Towers doesn't need you, and neither do I."

He was just about to prove her wrong when Trent opened the terrace doors. Trent took one look at his friend and future sister-in-law glaring daggers at each other and cleared his throat.

"Looks like I'm going to have to work on my timing."

"Your timing's perfect." Amanda rammed an elbow into Sloan's stomach before she pulled away. "We've got no time for men around here tonight. Why don't you take this jerk you've sicced on us and go do something manly." She shoved by Trent and stalked into the house.

"Well." Trent let out a long breath. "I don't think I mentioned the Calhoun temperament when I asked you to take on the job."

"No, you didn't." Scowling at the empty doorway, Sloan rubbed his stomach. "Is there a dark, noisy bar anywhere in this town?"

"I guess we could find one."

"Good. Let's go get drunk."

* * *

He found the bar, and he found the bottle. Sloan slumped in the corner booth and hissed through his teeth as the whiskey stung his throat. Over the first drink, and the second, he told Trent about his altercation with Suzanna.

"Baxter Dumont is Kevin's father? You never told me."

"I gave Meg my word I wouldn't tell anybody. Even our folks don't know."

Trent was silent a moment, sipping thoughtfully at his club soda. "It's hard to figure out how such a selfish bastard managed to father three terrific kids."

"It's a puzzle, all right." Sloan signaled for another round. "Then I go off and unload both barrels on Suzanna." He broke off and swore. "Damn it, Trent, I'm never going to forget the way she looked when I cut loose on her."

"She'll handle it. From what C.C.'s told me, she's dealt with worse."

"Yeah, maybe. Maybe. But I don't care much for slapping down women. I was already feeling like something you scrape off your shoe when Amanda lit into me."

"These women stick together."

"Yeah." Scowling, Sloan drank again. "Like a dirt clod."

"Why didn't you explain things to her?"

Sloan shrugged and knocked back more whiskey. He had his own share of pride. "It wasn't any of her business."

"You just explained it to me."

"That's different."

"Okay. Do you want some pretzels to go with that?"

"No."

They sat for a moment, nursing drinks, two dynamically different men, one in battered jeans, the other in tailored slacks; one slumped comfortably, the other comfortably alert. They'd both come from money—Trent from real estate, Sloan from oil, but their backgrounds and family lives had been opposites. Trent's first experience with real family ties had come through the Calhouns, and Sloan had known them always. They had almost nothing in common, and yet in their first semester in college they had become friends and had remained so for more than ten years.

Because he was feeling sorry for himself, Sloan enjoyed the sensation of getting steadily drunk. Because he recognized the symptoms, Trent stayed meticulously sober.

Over yet another drink, Sloan eyed his friend. "When'd you start wearing basketball shoes?"

Trent glanced down at his own feet and grinned to himself. They were a symbol of sorts of the way one hot-tempered brunette had changed his life. "They're not basketball shoes, they're running shoes."

"What's the difference?" Sloan narrowed his eyes. "And you're not wearing a tie. How come you're not wearing a tie?"

"Because I'm in love."

"Yeah." With a short oath, Sloan sat back. "See what it's doing to you? It makes you nuts."

"You hate ties."

"Exactly. Damn woman's been driving me crazy since the first time I saw her."

"C.C.?"

"No, damn it. We were talking about Amanda."

"Right." Settling back in the seat, Trent smiled. "Well, some woman's always driving you crazy. I've never seen anyone with a more...admirable affection for the gentler sex."

"Gentler my ass. First she runs into me, then she knocks me on my butt. I can hardly say two words without having her claw at me." After calling for another drink, he leaned across the table. "You've known me for over ten years.

Wouldn't y'say that I was a kind of even-tempered, affable sort of man?"

"Absolutely." Trent grinned. "Except when you're not."

Sloan slapped a hand on the table. "There you go." Nodding agreement, he pulled out a cigar. "So what the hell's wrong with her?"

"You tell me."

"I'll tell you." He jabbed the cigar toward Trent's face. "She's got the devil's own temper and a mule's stubbornness to go with it. If a man can keep his eyes off her legs, it's plain enough to see." He picked up his fresh whiskey and scowled into it. "She sure enough has first-class legs."

"I've noticed. They run in the family." As Sloan downed the liquor, Trent winced. "Am I going to have to carry you home?"

"More'n likely." He settled back to let the whiskey spin in his head. "What you want to go and get yourself married for, Trent? We'd both be better off hightailing it outta here."

"Because I love her."

"Yeah." On a sigh, Sloan let out a lazy stream of smoke. "That's how they get you. They get you all tangled up so you can't think straight. Used to be I thought women were God's own pleasure, but I know better now. They've only got one reason for being here, and that's to make a man's life misery." He squinted over at Trent. "Have you seen the way her skirt jiggles when she walks—especially when she's in a hurry, like she always is."

On a chuckle, Trent lifted his glass again. "I take the Fifth on that one."

"And the sassy way her hair moves when she's yelling at you. Her eyes get all snappy. Then you grab ahold of her to shut her up, and God Almighty." He took another quick slug of whiskey, but it did nothing to put out the fire. "You ever missed your step and gone down on an electric fence?"

"Can't say I have."

"It burns," Sloan murmured. "Burns like fire and knocks you senseless for a minute. When you get your senses back, you're kind of numb and shaky."

Carefully Trent set down his drink and leaned closer to study his friend. "Sloan, is this leading where I think it's leading, or are you just drunk?"

"Not drunk enough." Annoyed, he shoved the glass aside. "I haven't had a decent night's sleep since I set eyes on her. And since I set eyes on her it's like there was never anyone else. Like there's never going to be anyone else." With his elbows propped on the table, he rubbed his hands over his face. "I'm crazy in love with her, Trent, and if I could get my hands on her right now, I'd strangle her."

"Calhoun women have a talent for that." He grinned at Sloan. "Welcome to the club."

It rained all day so I could not go down to the cliffs to see Christian. For most of the morning I played games with the children to keep them from becoming fussy about being kept indoors. They squabbled, of course, but Nanny distracted them with cookies. Even the boys enjoyed the tea party we had with Colleen's little china dishes. For me, it was one of those sweet, insular days that a mother always remembers—the way her children laugh, the funny questions they ask, the way they lay their heads on your lap when nap time approaches.

The memory of this single day is as precious to me as any I have had, or will have. They will not be my babies very long. Already Colleen is talking about balls and dresses.

It makes me wonder what my life would be like if it could be Christian who would stroll into the parlor. He would not nod absently as he opened the brandy decanter. He would not forget to ask about his children.

No, my Christian would come to me first, his hands outstretched to meet mine as I rose to kiss him. He would laugh, as I hear him laugh during our stolen hours at the cliff.

And I would be happy. Without this bittersweet pain in my heart. Without this guilt. There would be no need then for me to seek the quiet and solitude of my tower, or to sit alone watching the gray rain as I write my dreams in this book.

I would be living my dreams.

But it is all just a fancy, like one of the stories I tell the children at bedtime. A happy-ever-after story with handsome princes and beautiful maidens. My life is not a fairy tale. But perhaps, someday someone will open these pages and read my story. I hope they will have a kind and generous heart, condemn me not for my disloyalty to a husband I have never loved, but rejoice for me in my joy in those few short hours with a man I will love even after death.

Chapter 7

Sloan's head was filled with tiny little men wielding pick axes. To quiet them, he tried rolling over. A definite mistake, he realized, as the slight movement sent a signal to the army-navy band waiting in the wings to punch up the percussions. Gingerly he pulled a pillow over his face, hoping to smother the sound or—if that didn't work—himself.

But the noise kept booming until his abused system told him it was the door, not just the hangover. Giving up, he stumbled out of bed, grateful there was no one around to hear him whimper. With the road gang working away inside his temples, he turned the air between the bedroom and the parlor door a ribald shade of blue.

When he wrenched it open, Amanda took one look, noting the bloodshot eyes, night stubble and curled lip. He was wearing the jeans, unclasped, that he'd fallen asleep in, and nothing else.

"Well," she said primly, "you look like you had a delightful time last night."

And she looked as neat and crisp as a freshly starched shirt. It was, he was sure, reason enough for homicide. "If you came up here to ruin my day, you're too late." He started to swing the door shut, but she held it open and stepped inside.

"I have something to say to you."

"You've said it." Instantly he regretted turning sharply away. As his head throbbed nastily, he vowed to hold on to what was left of his dignity. He would not crawl away, but walk.

Because he looked so pitiful, she decided to help him out. "I guess you feel pretty lousy."

"Lousy?" He narrowed his eyes to keep them from dropping out of his head. "No, I feel dandy. Just dandy. I live for hangovers."

"What you need is a cold shower, a couple of aspirin and a decent breakfast."

After making an inarticulate sound in his throat, he groped his way toward the bedroom. "Calhoun, you're on dangerous ground."

"I won't be in your way long." Determined to accomplish her mission, she followed him. "I just want to talk to you about—" She broke off when he slammed the bathroom door in her face. "Well." Blowing out a huffy breath, she set her hands on her hips.

Inside, Sloan stripped off his jeans then stepped into the shower. With one hand braced on the tile, he turned the water on full cold. His single vicious curse bounced along the walls then slammed right back into his head. Still, he was a little steadier when he stepped out again, fought with the cap on the aspirin bottle and downed three.

His hangover hadn't gone away, he thought, but at least he was now fully awake to enjoy it. Wrapping a towel around his waist, he walked back into the parlor.

He'd thought she would have gotten the message, but there she was, hunched over his drawing board with glasses perched on her nose. She'd tidied up, too, he noted, emptying ashtrays, piling cups on the room service tray, picking up discarded clothes. In fact, she had her hands full of his clothes while she studied his drawings.

"What the hell are you doing?"

She glanced up and, determined to be cheerful, smiled. "Oh, you're back." The sight of him in nothing but a damp towel had her careful to keep her eyes strictly on his face. "I was just taking a look at your work."

"I don't mean that, I mean what are you doing picking up after me? It's not part of your job to play Sally Domestic."

"I didn't see how you could work in a sty," she shot back, "so I straightened up a little while I was waiting for you."

"I like working in a sty. If I didn't, I would've picked the damn stuff up myself."

"Fine." Incensed, she hurled his clothes into the air so that they scattered over the room. "Better?"

Slowly he pulled off the T-shirt that had landed on his head. "Calhoun, do you know what's more dangerous than a man with a hangover?"

"No."

"Nothing." He took one measured step toward her when there was another knock at the door.

"That's your breakfast." Amanda's voice was clipped as she strode toward the door. "I had them put a rush on it."

Defeated, Sloan sank onto the couch and put his head in his hands so that he could catch it easily when it fell off. "I don't want any damn breakfast."

"Well, you'll eat it and stop feeling sorry for yourself." She signed the check, then took the tray herself to place it on the table in front of him. "Whole wheat toast, black coffee and a Virgin Mary, heavy on the hot sauce. It'll take the edge off."

"An electric planer couldn't take the edge off." But he reached for the coffee.

Satisfied that she had made a good start, Amanda took off her glasses and slipped them into her pocket. He really did look pathetic, she thought. His wet hair was dripping down his face. She had a strong urge to kneel down beside him and stroke those damp curls back. But he'd probably have snapped her hand off at the wrist, and she had an equally strong urge to survive.

"Trent mentioned that you did quite a bit of drinking last night."

After trying the spiced-up tomato juice, he eyed her narrowly. "So you came by to see the morning-after in person."

"Not exactly." Her fingers toyed with her name tag, then the top button on her jacket. "I thought since it was my fault you got into this condition, I should—"

"Hold it. If I get drunk, it's because my hand reaches for the bottle."

"Yes, but—"

"I don't want your sympathy, Calhoun, or your guilt any more than I want your maid service."

"Fine." Pride and temper went to war. Pride won. "I merely came by this morning to apologize."

He bit off another piece of toast. It did soothing things to the rocky sea of his belly. "What for?"

"For what I said, and the way I acted yesterday." Unable to stand still, she walked over to the window and pulled the shades open, ignoring Sloan's quick hiss of pain. "Although I still think I was perfectly justified. After all, I only knew that you'd said something to hurt Suzanna badly." But there was regret in her eyes when she turned back. "When she told me about your sister—about Bax—I realized how you must have been feeling. Damn it, Sloan, you could have told me yourself."

"Maybe. Maybe you could have trusted me."

She took her glasses out again, playing with the earpieces to keep her hands busy. "It wasn't really a matter of trust, but of automatic reflex. You don't know what Suzanna went through, how deeply she was hurt. Or if you do, because of your own sister, then you should understand why I couldn't bear to see her look like that again." She shoved the glasses away. When she looked at him, her eyes were damp. "And it was worse, because I have feelings for you."

If there was one thing he had no defense against, it was tears. Wanting to ward them off as much as he wanted to make peace, he rose to take her hands. "I made my share of mistakes yesterday." Smiling, he rubbed her knuckles over his cheek. It felt good—damn good. "I guess it's as hard for you to apologize as it is for me."

"If you mean it's like swallowing a lump of coal, then you're right."

"Why don't we call it even, all around?" But when he lowered his head to kiss her, she stepped back.

"I really need to think straight for a while."

He caught her hand again. "I really need to make love with you."

Her heart took a quick leap into her throat. For someone who moved so slowly, how did he get from one point to the next so fast? "I'm, ah, on duty. I'm already over my break, and Stenerson—"

"Why don't I give him a call?" Still smiling, he began to kiss her fingers. The hangover was down to a dull ache, not nearly as noticeable as another, more pleasant one in the pit of his stomach. "Tell him I need the assistant manager for a couple hours."

"I think—"

"There you go again," he murmured, brushing his lips lightly over hers.

"No, really, I have to..." Her mind clouded as he trailed those lips down her throat. "I really have to get back to my desk. And I—" She took a big, shuddering gasp of air. "I need to be sure." Scrambling for survival, she pulled away. "I have to know what I'm doing."

Sloan pressed a hand to the familiar burn that spread inside his gut. He had a feeling he was just going to have to live with it for a while longer. "Tell you what, Calhoun. You think about it, and think hard, until after the wedding. Like we said before." Before she could relax, he had her chin cupped firmly in his hand. "And after the wedding, if you don't come to me, you'd better run fast."

The line appeared between her brows. "That sounds like an ultimatum."

"No, that's a fact. If I were you, I'd get out that door now, while I still had the chance."

All dignity, she marched to it before turning back with a smile that should have tipped him off. "Enjoy your breakfast," she told him, then slammed the door with a vengeance. She could almost see him holding his battered head.

"I didn't think I'd be nervous." C.C. stared at the wedding dress of snowy silk and lace that hung on the back of her closet door. "Maybe it'd be better if I just wore regular clothes."

"Don't be ridiculous. And stop fidgeting." Amanda bent close to her sister to add a bit more blusher to her cheeks. "You're supposed to be nervous."

"Why?" Annoyed with herself, C.C. pressed a hand to her

fluttery stomach. "I love Trent and want to get married. Why should I be nervous now that it's going to happen?" She looked back at the dress and swallowed. "Less than an hour from now."

Amanda grinned. "Maybe I should call Aunt Coco and have her give you a booster-shot course on the birds and the bees."

"Very funny." But the idea did amuse her enough to make her smile. "When's Suzanna coming back?"

"I told you, as soon as she has the kids dressed. Jenny might love the idea of being flower girl, but Alex is a most reluctant ring bearer. He'd rather be carrying a machine gun down the aisle than a satin pillow. And before you ask, again, Lilah is supposed to be downstairs making sure all the last-minute details go off properly. Though why we think we can trust her is beyond me."

"She'll be fine. She always handles things when it's important." C.C. laid a hand on Amanda's. "And it is important, Mandy."

"I know, honey. It's the most important day of your life." Misty-eyed, she laid her cheek against C.C.'s. "Oh, I feel as though I should say something profound, but I can only say be happy."

"I will be, and it's not as if I'll be really going away. We'll be living here most of the time, except when...when we're in Boston." Her throat filled up.

"Don't start," Amanda warned. "I mean it. After all the work I put in making you beautiful, you're not going out in the garden with red eyes and a runny nose." Blowing her own, she stepped back. "Now, let me help you get dressed."

When Suzanna came in a short time later, a child's hand in each of hers, she had to struggle with her own tears. "Oh, C.C., you look wonderful."

"Are you sure?" Fretting, she plucked at the lace at her throat. The dress was a slim column, elegantly simple with only that whisper of lace at the neck, and another whisper at the hem to adorn it. "Maybe I should have gone for something less formal."

"No, it's perfect." Suzanna bent down to her son, her own dress rustling with the movement. "Alex, stand still for five minutes, please."

He tried out the sneer he'd been practicing in the mirror. "I hate cummerbunds."

"I know, but if you don't want me to strap it around your mouth, you'll stand still." Tweeking his nose, she straightened. "I have something for you." She offered C.C. a small box. Inside was a single teardrop sapphire on a braided gold chain.

"Mama's necklace," C.C. whispered.

"Aunt Coco gave it to me when I—on my wedding day." She took it out to fasten around her sister's neck. "I want you to have it and wear it on yours."

C.C. lifted a hand to it, closing her fingers around the stone. "I'm not nervous anymore."

"Then that's my cue to panic." Afraid to say more, Amanda gave her a quick kiss. "I'll run downstairs and make sure everything's on schedule."

"Mandy—"

Amanda smiled over her shoulder. "Yes, I'll send Lilah up." She went out, hurrying downstairs while she ticked off duties in her mind. Taking a moment, she stopped by the hall mirror to adjust the spray of baby's breath over her ear.

"You look great." She glanced over and saw Sloan. "Just great."

"Thanks." They stood awkwardly a moment, a man in a tuxedo and a woman in a tea-length gown the color of ripe peaches. "I, uh, where's Trent?"

"He needed a couple of minutes to himself. His father came by with some advice." Relaxing slowly, Sloan grinned. "When a man's been married as many times as Mr. S.J., he comes up with some interesting viewpoints." He had to laugh at the expression on Amanda's face. "Don't worry, I nudged him along outside with a glass of champagne and Coco. Seems like they're old friends."

"I think she met him a long time ago." When Sloan took a step toward her, she began to talk rapidly. "You look terrific. I didn't expect you to look good in a tuxedo." Before he'd finished laughing, she was rambling on. "What I mean is I didn't expect it to suit you. I mean—"

"You're cute when you're flustered."

She ended up smiling at him. As far as she could recall, he was the only person who had ever accused her of being cute. "I really have to go." Before she gave in to the urge to fuss with his tie or something equally mushy. "We'll be starting in a few minutes. Guests need to be seen to."

"Most everybody's already in the garden."

"The photographer."

"All set up."

"The champagne."

"On ice." He took the last step toward her and tilted up her chin with a fingertip. "Weddings make you nervous, Calhoun?"

"This one does."

"Going to save a dance for me?"

"Of course."

He toyed with the flowers in her hair. "And later?"

"I..."

"C.C.'s ready!" Alex bellowed from the top of the stairs. "Can we get this dumb thing over with."

With a laugh, Sloan kissed her fingers. "Don't worry, I'll make sure the groom's in place."

"All right, and—damn!" She swore, then snatched up the ringing phone. "Hello? Oh, William, I really can't talk. We're about to start the wedding…. Tomorrow?" She lifted a distracted hand to her hair. "No, of course. Umm…yes, that's fine. Late afternoon would be best. Three o'clock? I'll see you then." Still off balance, she turned to find Sloan watching her with very cool, measuring green eyes.

"You take big chances, Calhoun."

"That wasn't what it sounded like." She caught herself trying to explain and frowned. "What do you mean, 'chances'?"

"That's something we'd better discuss later. We've got a wedding to get to."

"You're absolutely right." They strode off in opposite directions.

Moments later, the Calhoun women took their turns walking down the garden path. First Suzanna, then Lilah, then Amanda, followed by a beaming Jenny and a thoroughly embarrassed Alex. They took their places with Amanda doing her best not to glance in Sloan's direction. Then she forgot everything as she watched C.C. come forward, a wispy veil over her hair. Beside her, prepared to give her youngest niece away, Coco held her arm and wept.

She watched her sister marry under an arbor of delicately fragrant wisteria. Through a mist of tears she looked on as the man who was now her brother-in-law slipped the circle of emeralds onto C.C.'s finger. The look that passed between them spoke more eloquently of promises than any of the vows exchanged. With her hands clasped with her sisters', she saw C.C.'s face lift to Trent's as they shared their first kiss as husband and wife.

"Is it finally over?" Alex wanted to know.

"No," Amanda heard herself say as her gaze drifted to Sloan's. "It's just beginning."

* * *

"Beautiful wedding." After Amanda was thoroughly kissed by Trent's father, she managed to nod in agreement. "Trent tells me you put most of it together."

"I'm good with details," she said, and offered him a plate for the buffet.

"So I hear." Trim, tanned and expansive, St. James smiled at her. "I've also heard that all of the Calhoun sisters are lovely. I can now corroborate that myself."

He was quite the elegant old flirt, Amanda mused but smiled back as he arranged food on his plate. "We're delighted to welcome you to the family."

"It's odd the way things have worked out," he said. "A year ago I looked up from my boat in the bay and saw this house. I simply had to have it. Now, not only is part of it a portion of my business, but it's a part of my family." He glanced over to see Trent and C.C. dancing on the terrace. "She's made him happy," he said quietly. "I never quite had the knack for that myself." With a vague movement of his shoulders, he brushed the thought aside. "Would you care to dance?"

"I'd love to."

They'd hardly taken three steps on the dance floor, when Sloan swung Coco around and smoothly switched partners.

"You might have asked," Amanda muttered as his arms slid around her.

"I did, before. Anyway, she'll flirt with him the way he wants instead of treating him like a distant relation."

"He is a distant relation." But she glanced over and saw that Coco already had St. James laughing. "Everything's going well, I think."

"Smooth as glass." Just as smoothly, he noted, as she fit into his arms. "You did a good job."

"Thanks, but I hope it's the last wedding I have to plan for quite a while."

"Don't you think about getting married yourself?"

She missed a step and nearly stumbled over his feet. "No—that is, yes, but not really."

"That's a definitive answer."

"What I mean is it's not in my short-range plans." No matter what longings had tugged at her when her gaze had locked with Sloan's under the arbor. "I'm going to be busy over the next few years with the retreat. I've always wanted to manage a first-class hotel, to make policy instead of just carrying it out. It's what I've been working for, and now that Trent's giving me the chance, I can't afford to divide my loyalties."

"An interesting way of seeing it. With me it's always been a matter of getting tied down with one person in one place, then finding out I made a mistake."

"There's that, too." Relieved that they weren't arguing, she smiled. "I never asked, but I guess you do a lot of traveling."

"Here and there. A drawing board's portable. You might like to do some traveling yourself, check out the hotel competition. Why don't we go somewhere quiet and talk about it?"

"Sorry, I'm on call. And if you want to be helpful, you'll play best man and go get a few more bottles of champagne from the kitchen." She tucked her arm through his. "I've got to run up and get the streamers anyway."

"Streamers?"

"To decorate the car. They're up in my room."

"Tell you what," Sloan began when they reached the kitchen. "Why don't I come up to your room and help you get the streamers?"

"Because I want to decorate the car before they get back from their honeymoon." With a laugh, she dashed away. Amanda was halfway down the hall on the second floor when the creak of a board overhead had her stopping. Tuned to the moans and groans of the old house, she frowned. Footsteps, she realized. Definitely footsteps. Wondering if one of the wedding guests had decided to take an impromptu tour, she started back toward the stairway. On the third-floor landing, she spotted Fred, curled up and sleeping.

"Fine watchdog," she muttered, bending down to shake him. He only rolled over with a groggy snore. "Fred?" Alarmed, she shook him again, but instead of bouncing up, ready to play, he lay still. When she picked him up, his head lolled onto her hand. Even as she gathered him up, someone shoved her from behind and sent her headfirst into the wall.

Stunned and sprawled on the dog, she struggled up to her knees. Someone was running down the stairs. With the wrath of the Calhouns filling her, she jumped up, Fred tucked under her arm like a furry football, and gave chase. She turned sharply on the second-floor landing, ears straining. On an oath she headed down to the main floor, heels clattering on wood. Sloan caught her as she stumbled on the last step.

"Whoa. What's the hurry?" Grinning, he scanned her tumbled hair and the spray of baby's breath now hanging to her shoulder. "What did you do, Calhoun, trip over the dog?"

"Did you see him?" she demanded, and broke out of Sloan's hold to rush to the door.

"See who?"

"There was somebody upstairs." Her heart was pumping fast and hard. She hadn't noticed it before. Or the fact that her legs were shaky. "Someone was sneaking around on the third floor. I don't know what they did to Fred."

"Hold on." Gently now, he guided her back to the stairs and eased her down. "Let's have a look." He took the dog, then pulling up an eyelid, swore. When he looked back at Amanda, there was a flat grimness in his eyes she'd never seen before. "Somebody drugged him."

"Drugged him?" Amanda gathered Fred back to her breast. "Who would drug a poor little dog?"

"Someone who didn't want him to bark, I imagine. Tell me what happened."

"I heard someone on the third floor and went up to see. I found Fred, just lying there." She nuzzled the puppy. "When I started to pick him up, someone pushed me into the wall."

"Are you hurt?" His hands were instantly on her face.

"No." She let out a disgusted breath. "If it hadn't stunned me for a minute, I would have caught him."

Eyes narrowed, Sloan sat back on his heels. "Didn't it occur to you to call for help?"

"No." The baby's breath was tickling her shoulder, so she pulled it away.

"Idiot."

"Look, O'Riley, nobody's going to poke around in my house, and hurt my dog and get away with it. If he hadn't had a start on me, I'd have caught him."

"And then what?" he demanded. "God Almighty, Amanda, don't you realize he would have given you more than a push."

Actually she hadn't thought of it. But that didn't change the bottom line. "I can take care of myself. It's bad enough when people come to the door, or sneak around the grounds, but when they start breaking into the house, they're going to answer for it." She gave a nod of satisfaction as she rose. "I scared him good, anyway. The way he was running, he's halfway to the village by now. I don't think he'll be coming back. What about Fred?"

"I'll take care of him." He took the sleeping puppy from her. "He just needs to sleep it off. And you need to call the police."

"After the wedding." She shook her head before he could object. "I'm not spoiling this for C.C. and Trent just because some jerk decided to do some treasure hunting. What I will do is check the third floor and see if anything's missing. Then I'm going to go back out and make sure everything runs smoothly until it's time to throw rice at the bride and groom. After that, I'll call the police."

"Got it all figured out, nice and tidy, as usual." The hot edge of his temper seeped into his voice. "Things don't always work that way."

"I'll make it work."

"Sure you will. Can't have something like attempted robbery and a little assault mess up all your short-term plans. Just like you can't have someone like me messing up your long-term ones."

"I don't see what you're so upset about."

"You wouldn't," he said tightly. "You hear somebody in the house where they shouldn't be, get hit in the head, but you don't even think about calling for me. You don't think about asking somebody for help, not even when that somebody's in love with you."

The tightness in her chest returned, making her voice clipped. "I was just doing what I had to do."

"Yeah," he agreed with a slow nod. "You go ahead and do what you have to do now. I'll get out of your way."

Chapter 8

And he'd stay out of her way, Sloan promised himself. The woman had fuddled his brain long enough.

He stood out on the terrace off his bedroom, trying to enjoy the balmy May evening. He'd left The Towers as soon as it had been possible. Oh, he'd done his duty, he thought. Amanda wasn't the only one who could do what was expected of her. With the help of Suzanna and the children, he'd decorated the newlyweds' car. A smile plastered on his face, he'd tossed the rice. He'd even given Coco his handkerchief when her own proved inadequate for her happy tears. He'd waited with a worried Lilah until Fred had given his first groggy bark.

Then he'd gotten the hell out of there.

She didn't need him. The fact that he hadn't realized until now just how much he needed her to need him didn't make it any easier. Here he was, waiting to sweep her off her feet, and she was chasing after thieves or making dates with guys named William. Well, he was through making a fool of himself over her.

She had a job to do, and so did he. She had a life to live, and so did he. It was time he put things back in perspective. A man had to be crazy to think about saddling himself with an ornery, my-way-or-nothing female. A sane man wanted a nice, calm woman who'd give him some peace after a long day, not one who riled him up every time he took a breath.

So, he'd put Amanda Calhoun out of his mind and be a happier man for it.

"Sloan."

With one hand still braced on the railing, he turned. She was in the doorway, her fingers linked tight together. She'd changed the silk dress for a crisp cotton blouse and slacks. Very streamlined, very simple and certainly not sexy enough to make his heart start jumping as it was now.

"I knocked," she began, then with an uneasy movement of her shoulders, stepped onto the terrace. "I was afraid you wouldn't let me in, so I got a pass key."

"Isn't that against the rules?"

"Yes. I'm sorry, but I couldn't talk to you at home. I didn't even think I wanted to. Then after the police came and went, and everything was as close to normal as it gets, I couldn't settle down." She let out a long breath. Obviously he wasn't going to say anything to make it easier. He was just going to stand there, his white dress shirt unbuttoned and pulled out of the tuxedo pants, his feet bare and his eyes watchful. "I guess I'm not comfortable with unfinished business."

"All right." After lighting a cigar, he leaned back on the railing. "Finish it."

"It isn't as simple as that." A wayward breeze fluttered her hair. She shook it back impatiently. "I was upset and angry before—about there being someone in the house. My house.

I know you were concerned and I was very abrupt with you. And after I'd calmed down some I realized you were hurt that I hadn't asked you to help."

He blew out smoke. "I'll get over it."

"It's just that—" She broke off to pace the narrow width of the balcony. No, he wasn't going to make it easier. "I'm used to handling things myself. I've always been the one who's been able to find the logical solution, or the straightest route. It's part of my makeup. When something needs to be done, I do it. I have to, I guess. It's not as though I don't ever want help. It's just…it's just that I'm more used to being asked for it, than asking for it myself."

"One of the things I admire about you, Amanda, is the way you get things done." His eyes stayed on hers as he took a long, contemplative drag. "Why don't you tell me what you're going to do about me?"

"I don't know what to do." When her voice rose, she struggled to calm it and started moving again. "I don't like that. I always know what to do if I reason it out long enough. But no matter how much I think it all through, I can't find an answer."

"Maybe that's because two and two don't always make four."

"But they should," she insisted. "They always have for me. All I know is that you make me feel…different than I've ever felt before. It scares me." When she whirled back, her eyes were wide and dark with anger. "I know it's easy for you, but not for me."

"Easy for me?" he repeated. "You think this is easy for me?" In two furious motions, he tossed the cigar onto the terrace and ground it out. "I've been on slow burn since the minute I laid eyes on you. That isn't easy on a man, Amanda, believe me."

Because she found it hard to breathe, her voice came out in a whisper. "No one's ever wanted me the way you do. That frightens me." She pressed her lips together. "I've never wanted anyone the way I want you. That terrifies me."

He reached out to snag her hand by the wrist. "Don't expect to say that to me, or look at me the way you look right now, then ask me to let you go."

While panic and excitement warred inside her, she shook her head. "That's not what I'm asking."

"Then spell it out."

"Damn it, Sloan, I don't want you to be reasonable. I don't want to think. I want you to make me stop thinking, right now." On a moan, she threw her arms around him, pressed her lips to his and took exactly what she wanted.

There was fear. She was afraid she was taking a giant step off the edge of a very steep cliff.

There was exhilaration. She was taking that step with her eyes wide open.

And he was with her, all the way. His body was free-falling with hers, caught in the crosswinds, soaring on the current.

"Sloan—"

"Don't say a word." His arms locked tight around her as he pressed his mouth to her throat. The pulse hammering there matched exactly the rhythm of his own. That was what he wanted. That unity. He realized he'd never found it with another woman. "Not a word. Just come inside."

He led her from the balcony to the bedroom, leaving the door open to let in the sunset and the scent of water and flowers. He touched her hair first, watching his own fingers tangle and stroke. Then softly, a whispering touch, his lips on hers. No, he didn't want words from her, because he wasn't certain he could ever find the right ones to tell her what was in his heart. But he could show her.

Unsteady, she braced her hands on his chest. She didn't want to be weak now, but strong. Yet as those lips roamed over her face, she trembled.

Very slowly, barely touching her, he unbuttoned her blouse and slid it from her shoulders. Beneath was a white cotton chemise that made him smile. He should have known that beneath her practical clothes his Amanda would have more practicality. Watching her, he unhooked her slacks so that they slipped to the floor. When she reached out, he took her hands.

"No, just let me touch you. Let me see what it does to you."

Helpless, she closed her eyes as his fingers skimmed, lightly tracing the curve of her breasts. As if she were fashioned of the most delicate glass, he swept those fingertips over her. Elegantly erotic, the fragile caress had the blood rushing under skin, heating it, sensitizing it until she thought she might die from sheer pleasure.

Her head fell back, a shuddering moan escaped as he continued those lazy explorations with patient, gentle hands. He saw the dark delight flicker over her face, felt it shivering through her body. As excitement rioted through him, he circled his thumbs in a whispering touch over the nipples that strained against the cotton. Then his tongue replaced his hands and she gripped frantically at his shoulders for balance.

"Please…I can't…"

Now she was falling fast and hard, but he was there to catch her. When her knees gave way, he lifted her, cradling her in his arms, covering her mouth with his before laying her on the bed.

"Nobody," she murmured against his lips. "Nobody's ever made love to me like this."

"I'm just getting started."

He was true to his word. With a leisurely pace he took her places she had never been, had her lingering there before gently urging her on. With each touch he opened doors always firmly locked, then left them wide so that light and wind tunneled through. Each time she arched against him, shuddering, he soothed her until she floated down again.

Her taste was enough. Honey here, whiskey there, then as delicate as spun sugar. He filled himself with it, nibbling her skin. Down her arms, her throat, those long, lovely legs. Whenever he was tempted to hurry, to take his own release, he found himself greedy for one more taste.

He skimmed his hands up her ribs, pushing her shirt up, then over her head. At last, at long last, he sampled the smooth skin of her breast. Her hands were in his hair, pressing him closer as colors seemed to shatter behind her eyes.

Slow burn. Is that what he'd said? she wondered frantically as his clever mouth inched lower, still lower. She understood now, now when her body was on fire from the inside, heating degree by degree. The sparks were shooting through her, little pinpoints of unspeakable pleasure as ancient as the first stars that winked to life in the sky beyond the window.

He was tugging the last barrier aside, and she could do nothing but writhe under his hands, the breath sobbing in her lungs.

When he flicked his tongue over her, she arched against him, her hands grabbing at the bedspread in taut fists. Sensations hammered her, too fast, too sharp. She struggled to separate them, but they were one wild maze without beginning or end.

Did she know she was calling out his name over and over? he wondered. Did she know that her body was moving in that slow, sinuous rhythm, as if he were already inside her? He slid up her gradually, savoring each instant, absorbing each ache, each need, each longing. Her eyes fluttered open, dark and dazed.

She could only see his face, so close to hers—his eyes so intense. Gracefully her arms lifted to brush his shirt aside, to touch as thoroughly as she had been touched. She rose to him, to press her lips to his chest, to glide them up to his throat.

The light grew dimmer, softer. The breeze quieted. In an easy dance she moved over him, undressing him, needing to show him what he had done to her heart as well as her body. Her lips curved against his flesh as she felt him tremble as she had trembled. The glory flowed through her like water, clear and bright, so that when her arms came around him, when her mouth opened willingly beneath his, she let it pour into the kiss.

With a murmuring sigh, he slid into her. Her breath caught, then released gently. They moved together, the pace deliberately slow, deliciously easy. The sweetness brought tears to her eyes that he kissed away.

Gradually sweetness became heat, and heat a fresh burning. As passion misted her vision, she felt his fingers link with hers, holding tight as she rode to the top of the crest. His name tumbled from her lips as he swept to the peak with her.

He lay with his lips pressed against her throat, still haunted by the taste of her. Beneath him she was quiet, her breathing deep and steady. He wondered if she slept, and started to ease his weight aside. But her arms slid up and around him again.

"Don't." Her voice was a husky whisper that sent his blood singing again. "I don't want it to end yet."

To satisfy them both, he rolled, reversing positions. Her

hair brushed his cheek, a small thing that gave him tremendous happiness. "How's that?"

"Nice." She nuzzled her cheek against his. "It was all really, really nice."

"Is that the best you can do?"

"Umm. For right now. I don't think I've ever been this relaxed in my life."

"Good." Taking her hair in his hand, he pulled her head back to study her face. "It's getting too dark to see." Reaching over, he switched on the light.

Amanda brought up a hand to shield her eyes. "Why'd you do that?"

"Because I want to see you when we make love again."

"Again?" Chuckling, she dropped her head onto his shoulder. "You've got to be kidding."

"No, ma'am. I figure I might just get my fill of you by sunup."

Feeling deliciously lazy, she snuggled against him. "I can't stay the night."

"Wanna bet?"

"No, really." She arched like a cat when he stroked her back. "I wish I could, but I've got a whole list of things to do in the morning. Oh..." She shivered under his touch. "You've got such wonderful hands. Wonderful," she murmured as she lost herself in a long, dreamy kiss.

"Stay."

Her body shuddered as she felt him harden inside her. "Maybe for just a little while longer."

Drifting awake, she shifted. On a contented sigh, she reached out. Reluctantly she opened her eyes. Bright sunlight flooded the room, and she was alone in bed. Pushing her tumbled hair back, she sat up.

He'd gotten his way, she thought with a half smile. She had stayed the night, and he hadn't gotten enough of her—or she of him—until sunup.

It had been, she admitted freely, the most magnificent night of her life.

And where the hell was Sloan?

On cue, he walked in, pushing a room service cart. "Morning."

"Good morning." She smiled, though she felt awkward with him dressed and her still naked and in bed.

"I ordered us some breakfast." Sensing her dilemma, he plucked up a white terry-cloth robe from a chair. "Compliments of the BayWatch," he said as he handed it to her, then leaned over a bit farther to give her a leisurely kiss. "Why don't we eat on the terrace?"

"That'd be nice. Give me a minute."

When she joined him outside, there were plates set on the pale azure cloth, and a single rose in a clear vase. It touched her deeply that he would take as much care with the morning as he had with the night.

"You think of everything."

"Just of you." He grinned as he sat across from her. "We can look at this like a first date, since I never could convince you to have a meal with me before."

"No." Her gaze lowered as she poured coffee for both of them. "I guess you couldn't." Picking up her napkin, she began to pleat it with her fingers. They were having breakfast, she thought, after a long night of feasting. And they'd never even ridden in the same car, shared a pizza, talked on the phone.

It was idiotic, she told herself. It was scary.

"Sloan, I realize this might sound stupid at this stage, but I...I don't make a habit of spending the night with men in hotel rooms. I'm not usually intimate with someone I've known such a short time."

"You don't have to tell me that." He closed a hand over hers until she looked at him. "It's been a fast trip for both of us. Maybe it's because what happened between us is special. I'm in love with you, Amanda. No, don't pull away." He tightened his grip. "Normally I'm a patient man, but I have to work hard on it with you. I'm going to do my best to give you time."

"If I said I was in love with you—" she let out a cleansing breath "—what would happen next?"

In his eyes, something flickered and sent her already unsteady pulse jumping. "Sometimes you can't work out the answers first. You've got to be willing to gamble."

"I've never been much of a gambler." She bit her lip, determined to get over that last skip of fear. "I wouldn't have come here last night if I hadn't been in love with you."

He lifted her hand to press his lips to the palm. Over it, he smiled at her. "I know."

The laugh was as much from relief as amusement. "You knew, but you just had to hear me say it."

"That's right." His eyes were suddenly very sober. "I had to hear you say it. Women aren't the only ones who need words, Amanda."

No, she thought, they weren't. "I love you, but I'm still a little scared of it. I'd like to take it slow, one step at a time."

"Fair enough. We can start by having our first date before the eggs get cold."

At ease, she buttered a piece of toast and split it with him. "You know, as long as I've worked here, I've never sat on one of those terraces and looked out at the bay."

"Never snuck into an empty room and played guest?" He laughed. "No, you wouldn't. You wouldn't even think about it. So, how does it feel, seeing it from the other side of the desk?"

"Well, the bed's comfortable, the hotel robes are roomy and the view's wonderful." There was laughter in her eyes, contented, easy laughter. "However, at The Towers Retreat, we'll offer all that and more. Private spas, romantic fireplaces, complimentary champagne with each reservation—I have to run that by Trent—*cordon bleu* meals prepared by Coco, world-renowned chef, all in a turn-of-the-century setting, complete with ghosts and a legendary hidden treasure." She rested her chin on her hand. "Unless we manage to get our hands on the emeralds before we open."

"Do you really believe they still exist?"

"Yes. Oh, not with any of the mystic business Aunt Coco or Lilah subscribe to. It's simple logic. They did exist. If anyone in the family had sold them, it would have come out. Therefore, they still exist. A quarter of a million in jewels doesn't just disappear."

His brow lifted. "They're that valuable?"

"Oh, probably more so by now—that's not even counting the aesthetic or intrigue value."

It changed the complexion of things for him entirely. "So what we've got is five women and two kids, who've been living alone in a house loaded with antiques, plus a fortune in jewels. And no security system."

She frowned a little. "It's not exactly loaded with antiques since we've had to sell off a lot over the years. And there's never been a problem. It's not as though any of us are helpless."

"I know. Calhoun women can take care of themselves. I'm beginning to think that besides being tough, they're stupid."

"Now, wait a minute—"

"No, you wait." To emphasize the point, he poked his fork at her. "First thing in the morning, we're going to see about an alarm system."

She'd already decided the same thing herself after yesterday's incident. But that didn't mean he could tell her to. "You're not going to start taking over my life."

"So, to be stubborn, you'll ignore the obvious, because I brought it up, and take a chance that someone might break in and hurt one of the kids."

"Don't put words in my mouth," she tossed back. "I've been checking into alarms for the past two weeks."

"Why didn't you just say so?"

"Because you were too busy handing out orders." She might have said more, but the horn on one of the tourist boats distracted her. "What time is it?"

"About one."

"One?" Her eyes went huge. "In the afternoon? That's not possible, we just got up."

"It's real possible when you don't get to sleep until morning."

"I've got a million things to do." She was already pushing back from the table. "All that mess from the wedding has to be cleaned up. Trent's father was coming for brunch two hours ago, and William's coming by at three."

"Hold it." That brought him out of his chair. "You're not still going to see him?"

"Mr. St. James? He'll be gone by now. I can't believe I was so rude."

"William," he corrected, snagging her arm. "The attractive, intelligent man you had dinner with the other night."

"William? Well, of course I'm going to see him."

"No." He tugged her closer. "You're not."

The dangerous light in his eyes set off one in her own. "I just told you you weren't going to take over my life."

"I don't give a damn what you told me. There's no way in hell I'm going to let you waltz out of my bed and on to a date with another man."

With a little huff, she pulled her arm free. "You don't *let* me do anything. Get that straight. Next, it isn't a date. William Livingston is an antique dealer and I promised him I would show him through The Towers. He gets a busman's holiday, and I get a free assessment. Now move." She shoved past and headed for the shower. Muttering all the way, she slipped off the robe. She'd just finished adjusting the water temperature, stepping in and shutting the curtain when it was yanked open again.

"Damn it, Sloan!" She slicked the wet hair out of her eyes and glared.

"He's an antique dealer?"

"That's what I said."

"And he wants to look at furniture?"

"Exactly."

He hooked his thumbs in his belt loops. "I'm going with you."

"Fine." With a careless shrug, she picked up the soap and began to lather her shoulders. "Be a possessive bubblehead."

"Okay."

Telling herself she wasn't amused, she glanced over to see him pulling off his shirt. "What are you doing?"

Grinning, he tossed it aside. "I'll give you three guesses. A sharp lady like you should get it in one."

She bit back a chuckle as he unsnapped his jeans. "I don't have time for water games right now."

"Oh, I think we can sneak it in just under the wire."

"Maybe." She squeezed the wet soap between her hands and shot it at him, nodding approval when he caught it, chest high. "If you wash my back first."

Before stepping from his car, Livingston checked his microrecorder and the tiny camera in his pocket. He was very fond of technology and felt that the sophisticated equipment lent an air of elegance to the job. Since the moment he'd read about the Calhoun emeralds, he'd been obsessed by them, more than any other jewels he'd stolen in his long career. He was considered by Interpol, and indeed by himself, to be one of the most clever and elusive thieves on two continents.

The emeralds presented a challenge he couldn't resist. They weren't tucked in a vault or displayed in a museum. They weren't adoring some rich matron's neck. They were lying in wait somewhere in the odd old house, daring someone to find them. He intended to be that someone.

Though he wasn't opposed to employing violence in his work, he used it sparingly. He was sorry he'd had to use it on Amanda the day before, but he was much sorrier that she'd interrupted his search.

His own fault, he chided himself as he walked to the front door of The Towers. He'd been impatient and had decided that the wedding would be the perfect diversion, giving him the time and the privacy he required to case the interior of the house. Today, however, he would wander those rooms as a guest.

He might have been a thief from the South Side of Chicago, but when he put on a two-thousand-dollar suit, a trace of a British accent and polished manners, even the most discriminating invited him into their parlors.

He knocked and waited. The barking of the dog answered first, and Livingston's eyes hardened. He detested dogs, and the little bugger inside had nearly nipped him before he'd managed to give it a dose of phenobarbital.

When Coco answered the door, Livingston's eyes were clear and his charming smile already in place.

"Mr. Livingston, how nice to see you again." Coco started to offer a hand, then found it more judicious to grasp Fred's collar before the dog could leap at the man's calf. "Fred, stop that now. Mind your manners." Holding the snarling dog at bay, Coco offered a weak smile. "He really is a very gentle animal. He never acts like this, but he had an incident yesterday and isn't himself." After gathering Fred into her arms, she called for Lilah. "Let's go into the parlor, shall we?"

"I hope I'm not intruding on your Sunday, Mrs. McPike. I couldn't resist persuading Amanda to show me through your fascinating house."

"We're delighted to have you." Though she was becoming more disconcerted by the moment as Fred continued to snarl and snap. "Amanda's not here yet, though I can't think what's keeping her. She's always so prompt."

Lilah gave a half laugh as she came down the steps. "I can think exactly what's keeping her." There was no humor in her eyes as she studied their guest. "Hello again, Mr. Livingston."

"Miss Calhoun." He didn't care for the way she looked at him, as though she could see straight through the slick outer trappings to the ruthlessness inside.

"Fred's a bit high-strung today." With a quick pleading look, Coco passed the growling pup to Lilah. "Why don't you take him in the kitchen?" Her hands fluttered before she patted her hair. "Perhaps some herbal tea would soothe him."

"I'll take care of him." Lilah started down the hall, murmuring to the puppy, "I don't like him, either, Fred. Why do you suppose that is?"

"Well then." Relieved, Coco smiled again. "How about some sherry? You can enjoy it while I show you a particularly nice japanned cabinet. It's Charles II, I believe."

"I'd be delighted." He was also delighted to note that she was wearing an excellent set of pearls with matching earrings.

When Amanda arrived twenty minutes later, with Sloan stubbornly at her side, she found her aunt telling Livingston the family history while they admired an eighteenth-century credenza.

"William, I'm so sorry I'm late."

"Don't be." Livingston took one look at Sloan and concluded his entryway to The Towers wouldn't be Amanda after all. "Your aunt has been the most charming and informative of hostesses."

"Aunt Coco knows more about the furnishings than any of us," she told him. "This is Sloan O'Riley. Sloan is the architect who's designing the renovations."

"Mr. O'Riley." The handshake was brief. Sloan had already taken a dislike to the three-piece-suited, sherry-sipping antique dealer. "The work here must present quite a challenge."

"Oh, I'm getting by."

"I was just telling William how slow and tedious the job of sifting through all those old papers is. Not at all the exciting treasure the press makes it out to be." Coco beamed. "But I've decided to hold another séance. Tomorrow night, the first night of the new moon."

Amanda struggled not to groan. "Aunt Coco, I'm sure William isn't interested."

"On the contrary." He turned all his charm on Coco while a plan formed in his mind. "I'd love to attend myself, if I didn't have pressing business."

"The next time then. Perhaps you'd like to go upstairs—"

Before she could finish, Alex burst through the terrace doors, followed by a speeding Jenny and a laughing Suzanna. All three had dirt streaked on their hands and jeans. Eyes narrowed, Alex skidded to a halt in front of Livingston.

"Who's that?" he demanded.

"Alex, don't be a brat." Suzanna snagged his hand before he could spread any of his dirt over the buff-colored tailored pants. "I'm sorry," she began. "We've been in the garden. I made the mistake of mentioning ice cream."

"Don't apologize." Livingston forced his lips to curve. If he disliked anything more than dogs, it was small, grubby children. "They're...lovely."

Suzanna squeezed her son's hand before he could resort to violence at the term. "No, they're not," she said cheerfully. "But we're stuck with them. We'll just get out of your way." As she dragged them off to the kitchen, Alex shot a last look over his shoulder.

"He has mean eyes," he told his mother.

"Don't be silly." She tousled his hair. "He was just annoyed because you almost ran into him."

But Alex looked solemnly at Jenny, who nodded. "Like the snake on Rikki-Tikki-Tavi."

"You move, I strike," Alex said in a fair imitation of the evil cartoon voice.

"Okay, guys, you're giving me the creeps." She laughed off the quick shiver. "The last one in the kitchen has to wash the bowls." She gave them a head start while she rubbed the chill from her arms.

Chapter 9

"There, you see." Amanda gave Sloan a quick kiss on the cheek. "That wasn't so bad."

He wasn't quite ready to be placated. "He hung around for five hours. I don't see why Coco had to invite him for dinner."

"Because he's a charming, and single man." She laughed and slipped her arms around his neck. "Remember the tea leaves."

They stood at the seawall, inside an ornate pergola. Sloan decided it was as good a time as any to nibble on her neck. "What tea leaves?"

"The ones that…mmm. The ones that told Aunt Coco that there would be a man coming along who'd be important to us."

He switched to her ear. "I thought that was me."

"Maybe." She gave a surprised yip when he bit her. "Savage."

"Sometimes the Cherokee in me takes over."

She leaned back to study his face. In the bleeding lights of sunset, his skin was almost copper, his eyes so dark a green they were nearly black. Yes, she could see both sides of his heritage, the Celtic and the Cherokee, both warriors, in those knife-edged cheekbones, the sculpted mouth, the wild reddish hair.

"I really don't know anything about you." Yet it hadn't been like making love to a stranger. When he had touched her, she'd known everything. "Just that you're an architect from Oklahoma who went to Harvard."

"You know I like beer and long-legged women."

"There's that."

Because he could see it was important to her, he sat on the wall, his back to the sea. "Okay, Calhoun, what do you want to know?"

"I don't want to interrogate you." The old nerves resurfaced, making it impossible for her to settle. "It's just that you know everything about me, really. My family, my background, my ambitions."

Because he enjoyed watching her move, he took out a cigar, lighted it, then began to speak. "My great-great-grandfather left Ireland for the New World, and headed west to trap beaver. A genuine mountain man. He married a Cherokee woman, and hung around long enough to get three sons. One day he went off trapping and never came back. The sons started a trading post, did pretty well. One of them sent for a mail-order bride, a nice Irish girl. They had a passel of kids, including my grandfather. He was, and is, a wily old devil who bought up land while it was cheap enough, then hung on until he could sell it at a profit. Keeping up family tradition, he married Irish, a redheaded spitfire who supposedly drove him crazy. He must have loved her a lot, because he named the first oil well after her."

Amanda, who had been charmed thus far, blinked. "Oil well?"

"He called it Maggie," Sloan said with a grin as he blew out smoke. "She got such a kick out of it, he gave names to the rest of them, too."

"The rest of them," Amanda said faintly.

"My father took over the company in the sixties, but the old man hasn't stopped putting his two cents in. He's still ticked that I didn't go into the company, but I wanted to build, and I figured Sun Industries didn't need me."

"Sun Industries?" She nearly choked. It was one of the biggest conglomerates in the country. "You—I had no idea that you had money."

"My family does, anyway. Problem?"

"No. I just wouldn't want you to think that I..." She trailed off helplessly.

"That you were after the family fortune?" He let out a hoot of laughter. "Honey, I know you were after my body."

He had the uncanny ability to make her want to swear and laugh at the same time. "You really are a conceited jerk."

He tossed the cigar aside before making a grab for her. "But you love me."

"Maybe I do." With pretended reluctance, she slipped her arms around him. "A little." On a laugh, she lifted her lips to his. His mouth started off teasing, then heated with demands. His hands were light, then impatient, until she was wrapped tight around him, pouring herself mindlessly into the kiss.

"How do you do that to me?" she murmured as he nipped at her moist, parted lips.

"Do what?"

"Make me want you until it hurts."

On an unsteady moan, he pressed his lips to her throat. "Let's go inside. You can show me my room."

She tilted her head to give his busy mouth more freedom. "What room?"

"The room where we'll pretend I'm going to sleep when I'm sleeping with you."

"What are you talking about?"

"I'm talking about making love with you until we both need oxygen." Because he knew he was on the point of dragging her down on the hard, cold tiles, he set her away from him. "And I'm talking about the fact that I'm staying here until the alarm system's operational."

"But you don't need—"

"Oh, I need." He crushed his mouth to hers again to show her how much.

She waited for him, chiding herself for being as nervous as a new bride on her wedding night. Perhaps the waiting was more intense because she knew what they would bring to each other.

She slipped on a thin blue chemise, an impulsive extravagance that had been folded away for months. Unable to settle, she turned down the bed. There were candles she'd kept at the bedside and on the bureau for emergencies. But when she lighted them now, their glow was soft, romantic, and anything but practical. Suzanna had placed flowers in the room, as she always did. This time they were fragile lilies of the valley that added a haunting fragrance. Though there was no moonlight, she opened the terrace doors to let in the steady roar of the water on rocks.

Then he came to her, as she stood in the open doorway with the black night at her back.

The quick joke he'd meant to make melted from his mind. He could only stare, his hand growing damp on the knob, his heart bounding up to block his throat. To have her waiting for him, looking so desirable in the flicker of candlelight, to see that smile of welcome, was everything he'd ever wanted.

He wanted to be gentle with her, as he'd been so carefully gentle the night before. But when he crossed to her, the slow burn had already turned to fire. There was challenge instead of nerves in her eyes as she lifted her arms to take him in.

"I thought you'd never get here," she said, and, led by her own needs, crushed her mouth to his.

How could there be gentleness when there was such heat? How could there be patience when there was such urgency? Her body was already vibrating—Lord, he could feel each wild beat—as it fit itself to his. The flimsy material of her chemise teased the bare flesh of his chest, daring him to rip it aside and plunder. Her scent had wrapped itself around his system, taunting with dark secrets, seducing with fevered promises.

In that moment he was so full of her, he couldn't find himself.

Breathless, disoriented, he lifted his head. He knew his hands were big and could be rough if his heart didn't guide them. He knew his needs were huge and could be ruthless if he didn't retain control.

"Wait." He needed a moment to get back his breath and his sanity, but she was shaking her head.

"No." Her hands clutched in his hair, and she pulled him back to her.

She didn't know when the recklessness had burst through her, but it held sway now, as she fell with him onto the bed. Aggressive and desperate, her hands streaked over him. No weakness this time. No submission. She wanted the power, the power of knowing she could make him careless, make him as mindless and vulnerable as he made her.

In a tangle of arms and legs they rolled over the bed. Each time he tried to pull back, she was there, her mouth greedy, her low, sultry laughter pounding in his blood.

Her busy fingers rushed to unsnap his jeans, then tugged the denim over his hips. His muscles jumped and quivered when she danced those fingertips across his stomach. He swore, snatching her hands before she could drag him over that last jagged edge.

Breath heaving, he stared down at her, her wrists trapped in his hand. Her eyes were like cobalt, glistening dark in the shifting light. He could hear, over his own ragged breaths, the steady ticking of the bedside clock.

Then she smiled, a slow, lazy smile full of knowledge. And he heard nothing but the roar of his own needs.

Hot with hunger, his mouth fused with hers. Reckless with passion, his hands sought and took. She answered, demand for demand, pleasure for pleasure. Control snapped—he could almost hear the chain break as he sated himself with her. This was liberation, a world without reason. Desperate to feel her, he tore the chemise aside. Her quick gasp of surprise only fueled the fires.

Tossed in the whirlwind, she gave herself over to the speed, surrendered herself to the fury. No thought. No question. Only hot, damp flesh, ravenous, searching lips, quick, greedy hands.

His eyes open, fixed on hers, he drove himself into her, letting the shock of pleasure fill them both. Then she was rising up to meet him so that they drove each other into the dark.

"Yes, Mr. Stenerson." Amanda hummed a tune in her head as her supervisor droned on. And on. Ten more minutes, and she was off duty. Even the upcoming séance didn't dim her pleasure.

She would be with Sloan soon. Maybe there would be time for a walk before dinner.

"You don't seem to have your mind on your work, Miss Calhoun."

That brought her back with a jolt of guilt. "You were concerned about Mr. and Mrs. Wicken's complaint."

Glaring, he tapped his pencil on the desk. "I'm very concerned that one of our waiters spilled an entire tray of drinks in Mrs. Wicken's lap."

"Yes, sir. I arranged to have her slacks cleaned, and for a complimentary dinner for them any evening during their stay. They were satisfied."

"And you've fired the waiter?"

"No, sir."

His eyebrows rose up, wiggling like worms. "May I ask why not, when I specifically requested you do so?"

"Because Tim has been with us for three years, and could hardly be blamed for spilling the tray when the little Wicken boy stuck out his foot and tripped him. Several other waiters, and several of the guests saw it happen."

"Be that as it may, I gave you a specific order."

"Yes, sir." The cheerful little tune in her head became a throbbing headache. She'd meant to go over all of this with Stenerson before. "And after a closer review of the circumstances, I chose to handle it differently."

"Need I remind you who is in charge of this hotel, Miss Calhoun?"

"No, sir, but I would think after all the years I've worked at the BayWatch, you would trust my judgment." She took a deep breath, and a big risk. "If you don't, it might be best if I turned in my resignation."

He blinked three times, then cleared his throat. "Don't you feel that's a bit rash?"

"No, sir. If you don't feel I'm competent to make certain decisions, it undermines the system."

"It isn't your competence, but your lack of experience. However," he added, holding up a hand, "I'm sure you did what you felt was best in this case."

"Yes, sir."

By the time she left his office, her jaw was clenched. Amanda forced it to relax when William stopped her in the lobby.

"I just wanted to tell you again how much I enjoyed the tour of your home, and the wonderful meal."

"It was our pleasure."

"I have the feeling if I asked you to dinner again, you would have a different reason than hotel policy for saying no."

"William, I—"

"No, no." He patted her hand. "I understand. I'm disappointed, but I understand. I suppose Mr. O'Riley will attend the séance tonight?"

She laughed. "Whether he wants to or not."

"I really am sorry I'll miss it." He gave her hand a final squeeze. "It's at eight, did you say?"

"No, nine, sharp. Aunt Coco will have us all gathered around the dining table holding hands and sending out alpha waves or whatever."

"I hope you'll let me know if you receive any messages from...the other side."

"It's a deal. Good night."

"Good night." He glanced at his watch as she left. He had more than enough time to get ready.

"I thought I'd find you here." Amanda stepped into the large circular room the family called Bianca's tower. Lilah was curled on the window seat, as she often was, looking out to the cliffs.

"Yeah, just me and fierce Fred." Coming out of a private

dream, she ruffled the dozing dog's fur. "We're getting in tune for tonight's séance."

"Spare me." Amanda plopped onto the seat beside her.

"Well, what's wiped off that satisfied smile you had on your face this morning? Did you fight with Sloan?"

"No."

"Then it must be the dastardly Stenerson." At Amanda's brief oath, Lilah grinned. "Right the second time. Why do you put up with him, Mandy? The man's a weasel."

"Because I work for him."

"So quit."

"Easy for you to say." She shot Lilah an impatient look. "We can't all drift around from day to day like dreamy forest sprites." She cut herself off, letting out a disgusted breath. "Sorry."

Lilah only shrugged. "It sounds like you've got more needling you than Stenerson."

"He started it. He said I didn't have my mind on my work, and he was right."

"So your mind was wandering. Big deal."

"It is a big deal. Damn it, I like my job, and I'm good at it. But I haven't been concentrating, not on that or the necklace, or anything, since…"

"Since the big gun swaggered in from the West."

"It's not funny."

"Sure it is." Lilah wrapped her arms around her knees and rested her chin on them. "So you lose a little concentration, misplace one of your lists or miss an appointment by five minutes. So what?"

"I'll tell you so what. He's changing me and I don't know what to do about it. I have responsibilities, obligations. Damn it, I have goals. I have to think about tomorrow, and five years from tomorrow." The trouble was, when she did, she thought of Sloan. "What if he's just a glitch? A wonderful, exciting glitch that throws off everything I've planned out? A few weeks from now, he finishes up here and heads back to Oklahoma, and my life's a mess."

"What if he asks you to go with him?"

"That's worse." Flustered, Amanda rose to wander in distracted circles. "What am I supposed to do? Throw away everything I've worked for, everything I've hoped for just because he says saddle up?"

"Would you?"

Amanda shut her eyes. "I'm afraid I would."

"Then why don't you talk to him?"

"I can't." She sat again. "We haven't talked about the future. I guess neither of us wants to think about it. It was just that today, I started thinking—"

"You would get back to it."

"I started thinking," Amanda repeated, "that a month ago I didn't even know him. It's crazy to start planning my life around someone I've only known such a short time."

"And you've always been the sensible one," Lilah put in.

"Well, yes."

"Then relax." For encouragement she patted Amanda's shoulder. "When the time comes, you're bound to do the sensible thing."

"I hope you're right," Amanda murmured, then forced herself to add a decisive nod. "Of course, you're right. I'm going to work in the storeroom until dinner."

"See you're back on track already." Lilah chuckled to herself when Amanda strode out. "Come on, Fred." She nuzzled his nose. "Let's go see if we can derail her."

Sloan walked into the storeroom, armed with a bottle of champagne, a wicker basket and some of Lilah's sisterly advice. *Keep her off balance, big guy. The one thing you can't let her do is get logical on you.*

Though he wasn't exactly sure what had prompted Lilah's visit, he approved the spirit of it. Just as he approved the way Amanda looked, hunched over a desk in the storeroom, glasses on her nose, hair clipped back. There were neatly labeled file boxes stacked behind her, dozens of dusty cardboard boxes scattered alongside her and several fat piles of paper in front of her.

"Hey, Calhoun, ready for a break?"

"What?" Her head came up quickly, but it took a moment for her eyes to focus. "Oh, hi. I didn't hear you come in."

"Where were you?"

She lifted a ledger. "Back in 1929. It seems my illustrious great-grandpapa made a little pin money running liquor in from Canada during Prohibition."

"Good old Fergus."

"Greedy old Fergus," she corrected. "But a businessman through and through. If he kept such meticulous books of his illegal activities, he certainly would have a record of sale if he sold the emeralds."

"I thought Bianca hid them."

"That's the legend." She leaned back to rub her tired eyes. "I'd rather have the facts. I had this thought that maybe he put them in a safe-deposit box he didn't tell anyone about. But I can't find any record of that, either."

"Maybe you're looking in the wrong place." He set the bottle and basket down as he stood behind her. Gently he began to massage her neck muscles. "Maybe you should concentrate on Bianca. It was her necklace after all."

"We don't have a lot of information about Bianca." When her eyes started to drift closed, she popped them open again. "Great-Grandpapa destroyed all of her pictures, her letters, just about everything concerning her. We've only come across one of her date books so far."

"He must have been crazy mad."

"Crazy, anyway. Grieving, I'd think."

"No." Bending, he kissed the top of her head. "If he'd been grieving, he would have kept everything."

"Maybe it hurt to remember."

"If he'd loved her, he would have wanted to remember. He would have needed to. When you love someone, everything about them's precious." He felt her muscles knot under his fingers. "What's the problem, Amanda? You're all tied up."

"I've been sitting too long, that's all."

"Then my timing's perfect." He stepped back to pick up the champagne."

"What's that for?"

"Most people drink it." Sloan released the cork. After the pop came the seductive hiss. "I don't know about you, but I worked my butt off today. I thought we'd take a first-class coffee break."

She didn't need champagne to cloud her brain. He did that all by himself. And that, she reminded herself as she rose, was exactly what she needed to avoid. "It's a nice thought, but I should go help Aunt Coco with dinner."

"Lilah's helping her."

"Lilah?" Amanda's brows shot up. "You've got to be kidding."

"Nope." He opened the basket to take out two fluted glasses. "Suzanna's doing homework with the kids, and you and I are having dinner alone."

"Sloan, I'm really not dressed to go out."

"I like you in sweats." He poured the wine and, setting the bottle aside, lifted both glasses. "And we're not going anywhere."

"You just said—"

"I said we were having dinner alone, and we are. Right here."

"Here?" She gestured. "In the storeroom?"

"Yep. I got some of your aunt's pâté, some cold chicken and asparagus, and fresh strawberries." He tapped his glass against hers before drinking. "I've been thinking about you all day."

He didn't even have to try to make her knees weak. When he did sweet things, said sweet things, she dissolved into a puddle of love. "Sloan, we have to talk."

"Sure." But he bent down to rub his lips lazily over hers. "Why don't we get comfortable first?"

"What?" Already dizzy, she stared at him as he took out a blanket and spread it over the floor.

"Come on."

"I really think it would be better if we…" But he was already pulling her down to the blanket.

He took the glass from her hand, setting it on the floor before nuzzling her mouth. "This is better," he murmured. "Much better."

"The children are home," she managed as his hands slid under her shirt. "If someone came in—"

"I locked the door." Gently he skimmed the rough pad of his thumb over her nipples. "Pay attention, Calhoun, I'm going to show you how to relax."

She was so relaxed, she didn't think she could move. Heavy, her eyes fluttered partway open when Sloan lay a smidgen of pâté on her tongue.

"It's good," he told her, then spread a dab on her bare shoulder so he could lick it off. "Here." He lifted her, cradling her against his chest before he handed her the glass of champagne. "We were supposed to drink this first, but I got distracted."

It tasted like sin on her tongue. She sipped again, then opened her mouth obediently when he fed her more pâté, this time on a conventional cracker.

"More?"

She sighed her assent. They began to feed each other tidbits from the basket between kisses. Replete, she watched him pour the last of the champagne. "We're going to be late for the séance."

"Nope." He drew her back more comfortably against his chest. "Coco decided that the vibes weren't right. Something about interference from a dark presence."

"Sounds just like my levelheaded aunt."

"Now she wants to wait until the last night of the new moon." He nuzzled her neck. "We can stay in here all night."

She was beginning to believe that with him, anything was possible. "That would make it my first all-night picnic."

"After we're married, we'll make it a regular event."

Champagne slopped over her hand and onto his leg as she jolted straight.

"Easy, Calhoun, don't waste it."

She struggled around to face him. "What do you mean, married?"

"You know, like man and wife, that kind of thing."

With deliberate care, she set the glass down. Just like that, she thought, both panicked and angry. Just as she'd expected. With him it was *saddle up, Calhoun. We're getting hitched.* "What gave you the idea that we were getting married?"

He didn't like the fact that the line was back between her brows. "I love you, you love me. You're the logical one, Amanda. The next step's marriage from my point of view."

"It may be a step from your point of view, but it's a big leap from mine. You can't just assume I'm going to take it."

"Why not?"

"Because you can't. In the first place, I'm not planning on marriage for years yet. I've got my career to think about."

"What's one got to do with the other?"

"Everything. You've already messed up my concentration, had me shuffling around my priorities." Knowing it sounded foolish, she stopped to drag a hand through her hair. "Look at me," she demanded. "Just look at me. I'm sitting on the storeroom floor, naked, and arguing with a man I've only known for two weeks. This isn't me."

With deceptive laziness, he skimmed his gaze down, then up again. "Then who the hell is it?"

"I don't know." Frantic, she snatched up her sweats and began to pull them on. "I don't know who I am anymore, and it's your fault. Nothing's made sense since you ran into me on the sidewalk."

"You ran into me."

"That's beside the point." Shaken to the core, she yanked the sweatshirt over her head. "I'm daydreaming when I'm supposed to be working. I'm making love with you when I should be keeping appointments. I'm having naked picnics when I should be filing papers. It's got to stop."

"Maybe I should've just hit you over the head with the bottle of champagne instead of letting you drink it." Baffled, he scratched his head. "Why don't you sit down, Calhoun, and we'll talk this thing out?"

"No, I will not sit down. You'll start on me again, and I won't be able to think. You're not going to make plans for the rest of my life without consulting me, without even having the courtesy to ask. I'm taking back control of my life."

He rose then, naked and furious. "You're mad because I want you to marry me."

The breath hissed out between her clenched teeth. "You're just stupid." She grabbed the closest thing handy and ended up hurling her glasses at him. "Too stupid for words." With this she strode to the door, fought with and cursed the lock until she managed to open it. "You can take your incredibly romantic proposal and stuff it."

The hot and hazy afternoon was perfect for pleasure. Christian surprised me with a little basket of wine and cold ham. Together we sat in the wild grass beyond the rock and watched the boats glide by below. The light was so golden, like something poured out of a gilded pitcher. But it is always so when I'm with him. In this lovely fantasy of afternoons, there is nothing but sunlight and warm, fragrant air.

We talked of everything and nothing as he sketched me. He has already done two paintings of me since the summer began. Without risking modesty I can say he made me look beautiful. What woman is not when she is in love? And it was his eyes that studied me, his hands that drew my face, my hair. His feelings that guided his brush.

If I had not believed before how deep and true his love is for me, I would have seen it in the portraits he painted.

Will someone buy my portrait from him? It saddens me to think of it. Yet it makes me proud. That would be one way I could at last declare my feelings. Hanging on some pretty wall, the portrait of a woman whose eyes are filled with love for the man who painted her.

I say we talked of everything and nothing. We do not mention how quickly the days fly into weeks. There are so little of those weeks left before I must leave the island, and Christian. I think something in me will die this time.

Fergus and I attended a dinner dance tonight. He was very jolly, though there was much talk of war. He said that clever men know that there will always be war, and money to be made from it. I was stunned to hear him speak so, but he only brushed aside my concern.

"It's for you to think of how to spend the money, and for me to make it," he told me.

It upset me because it was not for money I married him, nor is it for money I stay with him. Both were for duty. Yet I have lived under his roof, eaten his food, taken his gifts without a thought.

It scrapes at my conscience to know that I appreciated the little picnic Christian brought to me so much more than I have ever appreciated all the sumptuous dinners Fergus's money has paid for.

Because it always pleases him, I wore the emeralds, and I have not yet put them away. They lie in the shadowed light, glinting at me, reminding me of both my grief and my joy.

If it were not for the children...but I can't think of it. There are the children. Whatever sins I commit, I will never desert them. They have needs that neither Christian nor I have a right to ignore. I know, in the loneliness ahead of me, they will be solace. Being blessed with them, it is not right to grieve for the child Christian and I must never conceive.

Yet, I do.

Tonight when I turn off the lamp I'll try to sleep quickly. For then it will be morning, and morning will become the golden afternoon, when I can see Christian again.

Chapter 10

The only thing that prevented Amanda from slamming the door was the fact that Suzanna would have already put the children to bed. But she did kick it.

Limping and muttering and occasionally sending a furious look over her shoulder, she started down the hallway. At that point, she wasn't certain if she was more angry with Sloan for taking her assent for granted, or with herself for wanting to give it to him. Marriage hadn't been in her plans, but damn it, she was good at taking the unexpected and making it work. But if he thought she would give him the satisfaction of just hopping on board because he said so, then he didn't know Amanda Kelly Calhoun.

When we get married, she fumed. Not if, not will you or would you. And the problem, the big problem was that under the instant panic and anger had been a thrill. She paused outside of her bedroom door as her own soft sigh caught up with her. Oh, Lord, she did want to marry him. Despite all the good, solid, sensible reasons against it, marrying him was exactly what she wanted. Living with him would mean living with the constant threat of upheaval. She smiled to herself. And what more satisfying life could there be for a woman so skilled at putting things back in place?

With her hand on the doorknob, she hesitated, debating whether she would go back, give in to the urge to throw herself laughing into his arms and say...yes!

No. Resolute, Amanda pushed open the door. She wasn't about to make it that easy for him. If he wanted her, really wanted her, then he was going to have to work a little harder. When he got it right—if he got it right—she corrected as she shut the door behind her, she would smile, slide her arms around him and say—

An arm whipped around her throat and cut off her breath. Instinctively she struggled, throwing both hands up to the barrier to yank and scratch as she fought to drag in the air to scream. Until the hard, cold barrel of a gun pressed against her temple.

"Don't." The voice was only a harsh whisper at her ear. "Be very still, and very quiet, and I won't have to hurt you."

Obediently she let her arms fall limply to her sides, but her mind was speeding. The children were just down the hall. Their safety came first. And Sloan...Sloan could come along at any moment, furiously demanding a showdown.

"That's better." The pressure on her windpipe eased slightly. "If you scream, people are going to get hurt—starting with you. I don't think you want that." She shook her head. "Good. Now—" He swore and tightened his grip again as Sloan bellowed in the corridor.

"Calhoun. I'm not finished with you."

"Be absolutely quiet," the man warned as he dragged her back. "Or I'll kill him."

Amanda shut her eyes and prayed.

Sloan shoved open the door of her room, but it was pitch-dark and silent inside. While he stood in the doorway, swearing, Amanda was pressed back into the corner, knowing the gun was now aimed in Sloan's direction. Her stomach seemed to be packed with ice as she stood, not even daring to breathe, willing him to turn and go. And when he did, when she heard his boots clanging on the stairs, she wondered if she would ever see him again.

"Now that we have a little privacy, we can talk." But the arm stayed around her throat and the gun at her temple. "About the emeralds."

"I don't know where they are."

"Yes. Initially I had trouble believing that, but now I'm sure you don't. So we'll play this a different way. We'll have to move quickly. First the storeroom. I'll take the papers you've yet to sort through. Then, to add a little flare to the trip, we'll fetch Coco's pearls, and a few of the smaller, more portable items."

"You'll never get out of the house."

"You just leave that up to me." There was a faint lilt of pleasure in the voice now, as if he would enjoy the challenge. "Now we're going to move quietly, and very quickly to the storeroom. If you try anything heroic, I'll regret shooting you."

She didn't dare, not with the children so close. But the storeroom, she thought, as she started out with him directly behind her. That was a different matter.

Sloan had left the lights on. The remnants of their picnic were spread over the floor. The air smelled, ever so lightly, of strawberries and champagne.

"Very sweet," Livingston murmured, then shut the door behind them. "It would have been more convenient for me if you had had the séance instead of a tryst." He loosened his hold so that she could step away, but kept his gun level.

Amanda stared at the man she knew as William Livingston. He was all in black with a soft leather pouch worn crosswise over his chest. On his hands were thin surgical gloves. The gun he carried was small, but she didn't doubt it was lethal, not when she looked into his eyes.

"No recriminations, Amanda?" His brow lifted when she said nothing. "I'd hoped you and I could enjoy each other while I was conducting business, but...let's not waste time." From his pouch he pulled out a denim duffel bag. "Just the papers from those boxes there. I'm sure you're too efficient to have filed away anything useful."

She bent to pick up the bag he'd tossed at her. "You've lost your accent."

"It's lost its purpose. Be quick, Amanda." His eyes narrowed as he gestured with the gun. "Very quick."

She began to stuff papers into the bag. He was stealing her history, she thought furiously. Her family. "These won't do you any good."

"I doubt you believe that, or you wouldn't be wasting your time with them." His posture seemed almost relaxed now as he stood between Amanda and the door. "You're much too practical. In my profession, it pays to do your homework. I know your family quite well." To hurry her along, he waved the gun. "Which is why I chose to concentrate on you, the most efficient and straightforward of the Calhoun women."

If his ego was the only thing she could strike at, she'd take her best shot. "I hope you weren't expecting me to fall for you." She flicked a coolly dismissive glance over him. "You're not my type—then or now."

It hit the mark. His vanity was as huge as his ambition. "It's a pity that the lack of time prevents me from testing that. Perhaps when I come back, we'll pick up where we left off."

"Even if you get away tonight, you'll never get back in this house again."

He only smiled. "We'll see. Running into you like this complicates my plans, but it doesn't alter the final goal. The necklace. I want it very badly. Some jewels have power, and I have a feeling about this necklace. A strong feeling."

The air in the room was suddenly cold, bone-chilling cold. The expression in Livingston's eyes changed. "Drafts," he muttered uneasily. "The place is full of drafts."

But Amanda felt it, too, and was Calhoun enough to recognize it.

"It's Bianca," she said, and despite the gun, despite the odds, felt completely safe. "If you've done your homework, then you'll know she's still here." The darting nerves in his eyes made her smile. "I don't think she wants you to have the papers, or the necklace."

"Ghosts?" he laughed, but the sound was strained. Though he could see with his own eyes that nothing had changed, he was no longer sure he was alone in the room with Amanda. "That's unworthy of you."

"Then why are you frightened?"

"I'm not frightened, I'm in a hurry. That's enough." He found himself desperate to get out of the room, out of the house. Despite the eerie chill, a line of sweat dribbled down his back. "You carry the bag. Since this has taken longer than expected, we'll have to forgo Coco's pearls, for now." Impatient, he waved the gun at her. "Out the terrace doors."

Amanda debated heaving the duffel bag at him and running. But then he would have the papers. Instead, she struggled with it, then fumbled at the door. "It's stuck."

She was braced when he came up behind her to fight with the old latch. The minute the door opened, she stuck a foot behind him, threw her weight against him, then ran.

Wanting to lead him away from her family, she headed toward the west wing. As she hit the first set of stone stairs, she shouted for Sloan. The heavy bag bumped each step as she dragged it with her. She could hear him behind her, closing in, and zigged around a corner as the first bullet pinged off granite.

She didn't stop to catch her breath, though her lungs were beginning to burn. The May night was warm, oppressively warm after the cold of the storeroom. The air was heavy with the threat of rain.

The sensation of safety she had felt in the storeroom had vanished. There was no protection now, except for her knowledge of the complex layout of the terraces and stairs. But she was straining, fighting her way through the dark and through the sudden certainty that she could not handle this alone.

Then she saw Sloan, heading toward her from the opposite direction. The relief lasted only an instant before she heard another shot.

Lights were flashing everywhere inside the house. Sloan shouted at her before he came forward like a charging bull. Unarmed, Amanda realized, blind with fury, and straight into a loaded gun.

Without hesitation, she whirled away from Sloan and heaved the bag of papers at Livingston. As he snatched it up, she could hear raised voices from inside, Jenny's crying, the dog's frantic barks. Wanting to protect as much as be protected, Amanda raced toward Sloan. When she reached him, arms outstretched, he shoved her aside.

"Get in the house."

"He's got a gun," she said, desperately clinging to his arm. "Just let him go."

"I said get inside." He shook her off, then before her astonished eyes, leaped over the wall.

With her heart in her throat, she raced to it, to see him scrambling up from the terrace below. Even as Lilah burst through a door, Amanda was giving chase.

"What the hell's going on?" Lilah shouted after her.

"Call the police." After the single order, Amanda saved her breath for running, following the sound of stampeding feet and Fred's furious barks.

There was no moonlight to guide her, but she plunged heedlessly into the dark, screaming for Sloan when she heard the explosion of gunfire. She flew down the steps, tearing around the house in a dead run. Over her own ragged gasps, she heard a shouted curse, then the sound of tires squealing on asphalt.

In her hurry, she stumbled once, scrambling back up from the driveway with gravel stinging her palms. Then for an instant, a terrifying instant, there was only the sound of the sea and the wind and her own thundering pulse.

Her legs trembled as she dashed down the slope, so blind with fear that she didn't see Sloan until she rammed into him.

"Oh, God." Her hands were instantly on his face. "I thought he'd killed you."

He was too infuriated at having lost his quarry to appreciate her concern. "Not for lack of trying. Are you all right?"

"Yes, yes, I'm fine. It was—"

"You're bleeding." Every other thought in his head vanished. "There's blood on your hands."

"I fell." She dropped her head onto his shoulder. "It was so dark, and I couldn't see." Fighting tears, she held on to him as Fred whined at their feet. In an abrupt change of mood, she pulled back, pushing at his chest with her sore hands. Her damp eyes sizzled. "Are you crazy, chasing after him that way? I told you he had a gun. He could have shot you."

"He damn near shot you," Sloan retorted. "And didn't I tell you to stay inside?"

"I don't take orders from you," she began.

"You're both alive," Lilah commented. Flashlight in hand, she strolled toward them. "I could hear you arguing from the end of the driveway." The light shot across papers scattered in the road. "What's all this?"

"Oh, God, he must have dropped some." Amanda was already down on her hands and knees, gathering them up.

"Must've been when Fred bit his leg." Far from pacified, Sloan bent to snatch up a paper before it blew away.

"Fred bit him?" Amanda and Lilah said in unison.

"Good and hard from the sound of it." It was a small but sweet satisfaction. "We might have had him, too, but he had a car stashed down the road."

"And he might have shot both of you," Amanda retorted.

"Excuse me." Lilah felt she was doing her part by shining the light so they could see to find papers. "Who is he?"

"Livingston," Sloan told her, then added a string of curses. "You'll have to get the details from your sister."

"Inside," Lilah suggested. "The rest of the family is in an uproar."

"You called the police?"

"Yes." Right before she'd rushed out of the house, barefoot, to chase her sister down the graveled driveway. When Fred stopped to perk his ears then give a long, ululant howl, she laughed. "And I'd say they're on the way. Fred already hears the sirens."

Because her arms were full, Amanda pushed the papers into Lilah's arms, then began to pick up more as they started back. "He didn't get everything," she muttered, then thought of that moment in the storeroom when the air had changed. "I knew he wouldn't."

At the door of the house Suzanna stood, a slim gladiator, armed with a fireplace poker. "Is everyone all right?"

"Fine." Amanda let out an exhausted breath. "The kids?"

"In the parlor with Aunt Coco. Oh, honey, your hands."

"I just scraped them."

"I'll get some antiseptic."

"And some brandy," Lilah added, before laying the papers on a table in the hallway.

Twenty minutes later, the story had been related to the police, and the family was left alone to absorb it. Sloan paced behind the sofa while the Calhoun women huddled together.

"We had that—that thief to dinner." Coco glared into her brandy. "I baked a chocolate soufflé. And all the time he was plotting to steal from us."

"The police will shoot him," Alex piped up. "Bang! Between the eyes."

"I think we've had enough excitement for one night." Suzanna kissed the top of his head. Less sure of himself than he wanted to be, Alex slipped a hand into hers and held tight.

"He got most of the papers." With a sigh, Amanda reached for the pile she'd tossed onto the coffee table. "I hope Fred took a good chunk out of him."

"Good boy, Fred." Lilah cuddled the dog in her lap. "I don't think they'll do Livingston—or whoever he is—any good. He's not meant to find the emeralds. We are."

"He won't get the chance," Sloan said grimly. "Not with the security system I'm putting in." He shot a look at Amanda, daring her to argue, but she was staring at one of the papers.

"It's a letter," she murmured. "A letter from Bianca to Christian."

"Oh, my dear." Coco leaned forward. "What does it say?"
Amanda read,

"My love,
I'm writing this as the rain continues to fall and keeps me from you. I wonder what you are doing, if you paint today in the gloomy light and think of me. When I'm alone like this in my tower, separated from the reality of my duties, I let the memories sweep over me. Of the first time I saw you, standing on the cliffs. Of the last time I touched you. I'm praying for the sun, Christian, so that we can make more memories. I cannot tell you how you have changed me, how much more my eyes see, now that they see with my heart. I can't imagine how empty my life would have been without this time we had together. I know now that love is very rare, very precious. It is something to be cherished and held on to tightly while too often it is smothered, or brushed carelessly away. Remember, even when our time together ends, I will hold your love. It will live in my heart long after that heart stops beating.

Bianca."

Coco let out a long, dreamy sigh. "Oh, how much they must have loved each other."

"Yucky," Alex said sleepily, and rested his head on his mother's breast.

Amanda smoothed the letter out, hating the fact that it had become crumpled. "I guess she never got the chance to send it to him. All these years it's been mixed up with receipts and account sheets."

"And tonight *we* found it, not Livingston," Lilah reminded her.

"Luck," Amanda murmured.

"Fate," her sister insisted.

When the phone rang, Amanda was the first up to answer. "It's the police," she said, then settled back to listen. "I see. Yes, thank you for letting us know." She hung up, blowing out a disgusted breath. "Looks like he got away. He didn't go back to the BayWatch for any of his things, or he slipped in and took what he wanted and left the rest."

"Do they think he'll come back?" Alarmed, Coco patted her chest.

"No, but they're going to keep an eye on the house until they're sure he's left the island."

"I imagine he's halfway to New York by now." Suzanna shifted the drowsy children on her lap. "And if he comes back, we'll be ready for him."

"More than ready," Amanda agreed. "They have an APB out, but…I guess that's all that can be done for tonight."

"No." Sloan crossed the room to her. "There's a little more that has to be done." He nodded to the rest of the room as he pulled her toward the doorway. "You'll excuse us."

"They might, but I don't," Amanda told him. "Let go of my arm."

"Okay." He did, then nipping her by the waist, hauled her over his shoulder. "It's always the hard way with you."

"I will not be slung around like a sack of potatoes." As he climbed the stairs, she wriggled, trying for one clear shot with her foot.

"We left some loose ends before you stormed off to go tangle with an armed robber. Now we're damn well going to tie them up. You like straight talk, Calhoun, and you're about to get some."

"You don't know what I like." She slammed a fist into his back. "You don't know anything."

"Then it's time I found out." He kicked open the door of her room, stalked over and dumped her onto the bed. When she scrambled up, fists raised, he shoved her down again. "You sit where I put you. So help me, we're going to have this out once and for all."

Amanda stunned them both by covering her face with her hands and bursting into tears. She couldn't stop them. Everything that had happened in the past few hours reared up to set off an emotional jag that knocked her flat. On an oath, Sloan stepped toward her, then away, then dragged a helpless hand through his hair.

"Don't do that, Mandy."

She only shook her head and continued to sob.

"Come on now, please." His voice gentled as he crouched in front of her. "I didn't mean to make you cry." Lost, he stroked her hair, patted her shoulder. "I'm sorry, honey. I know you've been through hell tonight. I should have waited to start on this." Cursing himself, he rubbed her arm. "Look, you can hit me if it'd make you feel better."

She sniffled, drew in a hitching breath, then clipped him hard enough to send him sprawling. Through a veil of tears, she studied him as he dabbed at his mouth with the back of his hand.

"I forgot how literal minded you were." He sat where he was as they watched each other. "You finished crying?"

"I think so." Sniffling again, she dug into her pocket for a tissue. "Your lip's bleeding."

"Yeah." He started to reach for the tissue, but she was wiping her face with it. Laughing, he sat back again. "God Almighty, you're a piece of work."

"I'm glad you think this whole thing is a big joke. Men breaking into the house, waving guns around. You're lucky I didn't find you facedown in the road with a hole in your head."

He saw the tears welling again and took her hands. "Is that what this is about?" He pressed a kiss to her freshly bandaged palms. "You're upset because I went after him?"

"I told you not to."

"Hey." His gaze fixed on hers, he raised a hand to cup her chin. "Do you think I could stand around after he'd taken a potshot at you? The only thing I regret is that I didn't catch up with him, so I could rearrange that pretty face of his."

"That's just stupid machismo," she said, but turned her cheek into his hand.

"That's the second time tonight you've called me stupid. I'd like to get back to the first time."

Instantly she pulled back and pokered up. "I don't want to talk about it."

"Too bad. That little chase was quite a diversion, but it's done now. We're not. How come you jumped all over me when I mentioned marriage?"

"Mentioned it? You ordered it."

"I just said that—"

"You just assumed," she interrupted, then pushed by him to stand up. "Just because I love you, just because I've made love with you, doesn't give you any right to take me for granted. I told you before that I make my own plans."

"I've had it with your plans, Calhoun." He took her arm to hold her still. "I've got plans, too, and needs. It so happens they all include you. I love you, damn it." He emphasized the point with a quick, frustrated shake. "You're the only woman I've ever needed, really needed. The only woman I've ever wanted to spend my life with, have children with, make a home with. God knows why when you're as ornery as a mule with two heads, but that's the way it is."

"Then why didn't you just ask?"

Baffled, he shook his head. "Ask what?"

She made a strangled sound and began to pace again. "It's not like I'm asking for Byron or Shelley. I don't expect you to get down on your knees with a hand over your heart. Maybe a little violin music wouldn't have hurt," she muttered. "Or some candlelight."

"Violin music?"

"Forget it." She stopped, hands on her hips, to face him down. "Do you think just because I'm sensible and organized that I don't need any trappings, any romance? You come here, change my entire life, make me love you so much I can't see straight, then you don't even have the good sense to do it right."

"Hold on." He held up a hand before she could stride by him again. "Are you saying you're mad because I didn't ask you fancy enough?"

The sound came again, louder this time. Her face was flushed with temper, her eyes glowing with it. "You didn't ask at all, but why should you? You already know the answer."

Trying to figure women, he thought while he rubbed his hands over his face, was like…trying to figure women. "You wait here," he told her, and strode out.

"Typical," Amanda called after him, then plopped down onto the bed. She was still stewing, her chin on her hand, when he came back in. "Now what?" she demanded.

"Just shut up a minute." He set the tape recorder he'd borrowed on her dresser, then pulled out a pack of matches. Systematically he began to light candles, moving from one part of the room to another while she scowled at him. When he was satisfied, he turned off the lights.

"What are you doing?"

"I'm getting things ready so I can ask you to marry me without having you throw something at me again."

Chin up, she jumped out of bed. "Now you're making fun of me."

"No, I'm not. Damn it, woman, are you going to argue with me all night or let me try to do this right?"

There was enough exasperation in his voice to make her stop and consider him. He didn't look terribly comfortable, she noted. And because he didn't, she wanted to smile. He was doing it for her, she realized. Because he loved her.

"I guess I'll let you try. What's that?" he asked, gesturing to the tape recorder.

"It's Lilah's." He punched the Play button. The soft, weeping sound of violins flowed into the room. Now she did smile, though her heart was beginning to thud.

"It's lovely."

"So are you, I should have made a point of telling you that more often." Stepping toward her, he held out a hand.

"Now's a good time to start." She placed her hand in his.

"I love you, Amanda." Very gently, he touched his lips to hers. "I love everything about you. The woman who makes lists and lines up her shoes in the closet. The woman who goes swimming in freezing water, just so she can be alone for a while. I love the incredibly sexy woman I found in bed, and the tough one, who knows her own mind. It's all the things you are I don't want to live without."

"I love you, too." She lifted a hand to his face. "I meant it when I said you'd changed my life. Tonight, when I read Bianca's letter, I understood how she felt. I'll never feel about anyone the way I feel about you. I'll never want to."

Smiling, he caught her wrist, turning it so that he could brush a kiss over her hand. "Then you're going to marry me?"

She laughed as she threw her arms around him. "I thought you'd never ask."

* * * * *

Suzanna's Surrender

THE CALHOUNS

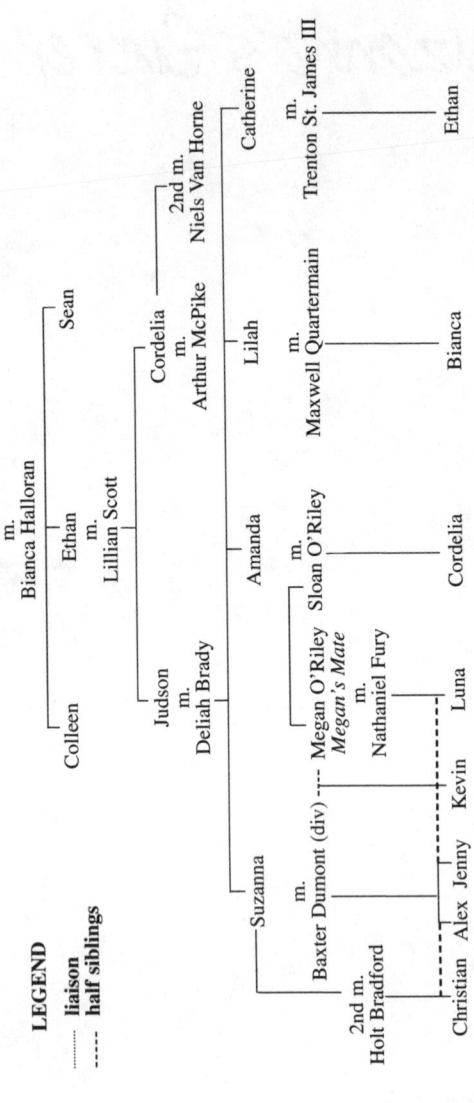

For my mother, with love

Prologue

Bar Harbor, 1965

The moment I saw her, my life was changed. More than fifty years have passed since that moment, and I'm an old man whose hair has turned white, whose body has grown frail. Yet my memories are full of color and strength.

Since my heart attack, I am to rest every day. So I have come back here to the island—her island—where it all began for me. It has changed, as I have. The great fire in '47 destroyed much. New buildings, new people have come. Cars crowd the streets without the charm of the jingling carriages. But I am lucky to be able to see it as it was, and as it is.

My son is a man now, a good one who chose to make his living from the sea. We have never understood each other, but have dealt together well enough. He has a quiet, lovely wife and a son of his own. The boy, young Holt, brings me a special kind of joy. Perhaps it is because I can see myself in him so clearly. The impatience, the fire, the passions that were once mine. Perhaps he, too, will feel too much, want too much. Yet I can't be sorry for it. If I could tell him one thing, it would be to grab hold of life and take.

My life has been full, and I'm grateful for the years I had with Margaret. I was no longer young when she became my wife. What we shared was not a blaze, but the quiet warmth of a banked fire. She brought me comfort, and I hope I gave her happiness. She's been gone for nearly ten years, and my memories of her are sweet.

Yet it is the memory of another woman that haunts me. This memory is so painfully clear, so complete. No amount of time could dull it. The years have not faded my image of her, nor have they altered by a single degree the desperate love I felt. Yes, feel still—will always feel though she is lost to me.

Perhaps now that I have brushed so close to death, I can open myself to it again, let myself remember what I have never been able to forget. Once it was too painful, and I lost the pain in a bottle. Finding no comfort there, I at last buried my misery in my work. Painting again, I traveled. But always, always, was pulled back here where I had once begun to live. Where I know I will one day die.

A man loves that way only once, and only if he is fortunate. For me, it was Bianca. It has always been Bianca.

It was June, the summer of 1912, before the Great War ripped the world apart. The summer of peace and beauty, of art and poetry, when the village of Bar Harbor opened itself to the wealthy and gave refuge to artists.

She came to the cliffs where I worked, her hand holding that of a child. I turned from my canvas, the brush still in my hand, the mood of the sea and the painting still on me. There she was, slender and lovely, the sunset hair swept up off her neck. The wind tugged at it, and at the skirts of the pale blue frock she wore. Her eyes were the color of the sea I was so frantically trying to recreate on canvas. They watched me, curious, wary. She had the pale and luminous skin of the Irish.

The moment I saw her, I knew I had to paint her. And I think I knew, as we stood in the wind, that I would have to love her.

She apologized for interrupting my work. The faint and musical lilt of Ireland was in the soft, polite voice. The child now in her arms was her son. She was Bianca Calhoun, another man's wife. Her summer home was on the ridge above. The Towers, the elaborate castle Fergus Calhoun had built. Even though I had only been on Mount Desert Island a short time, I had heard of Calhoun, and his home. Indeed I had admired the arrogant and fanciful lines of it, the turrets and peaks, the towers and parapets.

Such a place suited the woman who stood before me. She had a timeless beauty, a quiet steadiness, a graciousness that could never be taught, and banked passions simmering in her large green eyes. Yes, I was already in love, but then it was only with her beauty. As an artist, I wanted to interpret that beauty in my own way, with paint or pencils. Perhaps I frightened her by staring so intently. But the child, his name was Ethan, was fearless and friendly. She looked so young, so untouched, that it was difficult to believe the child was hers, and that she had two more besides.

She didn't stay long that day, but took her son and went home to her husband. I watched her walk through the wild roses, the sun in her hair.

I couldn't paint the sea anymore that day. Her face had already begun to haunt me.

Chapter 1

She wasn't looking forward to this. It had to be done, of course. Suzanna dragged a fifty-pound bag of mulch over to her pickup, then muscled it into the bed. That small physical task wasn't the problem. In fact, she was pleased to be able to make the delivery her second stop on her way home.

It was the first stop she wished she could avoid. But for Suzanna Calhoun Dumont, duty could never be avoided.

She'd promised her family that she would speak to Holt Bradford, and Suzanna kept her promises. Or tried to, she thought, and wiped a forearm over her sweaty brow.

But damn it, she was tired. She'd put in a full day in Southwest Harbor, landscaping a new house, and she had a full schedule the next day. That wasn't taking into account that her sister Amanda was getting married in little more than a week, or that The Towers was mass confusion in preparation for the wedding and with the remodeling of the west wing. It didn't even begin to deal with the fact that she had two energetic children at home who would want, and deserved, their mother's time and attention that evening. Or the paperwork that was piling up on her desk—or the fact that one of her part-time employees had quit just that morning.

Well, she'd wanted to start a business, Suzanna reminded herself. And she'd done it. She glanced back at her shop, locked for the night with the display of summer blooms in the window, at the greenhouse just behind the main building. It belonged to her—and the bank, she thought with a little smile—every pansy, petunia and peony. She'd proven she wasn't the incompetent failure her ex-husband had told her she was. Over and over again.

She had two beautiful children, a family who loved her and a landscaping-and-gardening business that was holding its own. She didn't even suppose Bax's claim that she was dull could apply now. Not when she was in the middle of an adventure that had started eighty years before.

There certainly wasn't anything mundane about searching for a priceless emerald necklace, or being dogged by international jewel thieves who would stop at nothing to get their hands on her great-grandmother Bianca's legacy.

Not that she'd been much more than a supporting player so far, Suzanna mused as she climbed into the truck. It had been her sister C.C. who had started it by falling in love with Trenton St. James III, of the St. James Hotels. It had been his idea to turn part of the financially plagued family home into a luxury retreat. In doing so, the old legend of the Calhoun emeralds had leaked to the ever-eager press and had set off a chain reaction that had run a course from the absurd to the dangerous.

It had been Amanda who had nearly been killed when the desperate and obsessed thief going by the name of William Livingston had stolen family papers he'd hoped would lead him to the lost emeralds. And it had been her sister Lilah who had had her life threatened during the latest attempt.

In the week that had passed since that night, the police hadn't turned up a trace of Livingston, or his latest known alias, Ellis Caufield.

It was odd, she thought as she joined the stream of traffic, how The Towers and the lost emeralds had affected the entire family. The Towers had brought C.C. and Trent together. Then Sloan O'Riley had come to design the retreat and had fallen in love with Amanda. The shy history professor, Max Quartermain, had lost his heart to Suzanna's free-spirited sister, Lilah, and both of them had nearly been killed. Again, because of the emeralds.

There were times Suzanna wished they could forget about the necklace that had belonged to her great-grandmother. But she knew, as they all knew, that the necklace Bianca had hidden away before her death was meant to be found.

So they continued, following up every lead, exploring every dusty path. Now it was her turn. During his research, Max had uncovered the name of the artist Bianca had loved.

It was a story that never failed to make Suzanna wistful, but it was just her bad luck that the connection with the artist led to his grandson.

Holt Bradford. She sighed a little as she drove through the traffic-jammed streets of the village. She couldn't claim to know him well—wasn't sure anyone could. But she remembered him as a teenager. Surly, bad tempered and aloof. Of course, girls had been attracted by his go-to-hell attitude. The attraction helped along, no doubt, by the dark, brooding looks and angry gray eyes.

Odd she should remember the color of his eyes, she mused. But then again, the one time she had seen them up close and personal he'd all but burned her alive with them.

He'd probably forgotten the altercation, she assured herself. She hoped so. Altercations made her shaky and sweaty, and she'd had enough of them in her marriage to last a lifetime. Certainly Holt wouldn't still hold a grudge—it had been more than ten years. After all, he hadn't been hurt very much when he'd taken a header off his motorcycle. And it had been his fault, she thought, setting her chin. She'd had the right of way.

In any case, she had promised Lilah she would talk to him. Any connection with Bianca's lost emeralds had to be followed up. As Christian Bradford's grandson, Holt might have heard stories.

Since he'd come back to Bar Harbor a few months before, he had taken up residence in the same cottage his grandfather had lived in during his romance with Bianca. Suzanna was Irish enough to believe in fate. There was a Bradford in the cottage and Calhouns in The Towers. Surely between them, they could find the answers to the mystery that had haunted both families for generations.

The cottage was on the water, sheltered by two lovely old willows. The simple wooden structure made her think of a doll's house, and she thought it a shame that no one had cared enough to plant flowers. The grass was freshly mowed, but her professional eye noted that there were patches that needed reseeding, and the whole business could use a good dose of fertilizer.

She started toward the door when the barking of a dog and the rumble of a man's voice had her skirting around to the side.

There was a rickety pier jutting out above the calm, dark water. Tied to it was a neat little cabin cruiser in gleaming white. He sat in the stern, patiently polishing the brass. He was shirtless, his tanned skin taut over bone and muscle, and gleaming with sweat. His black hair was curled past where his collar would be if he'd worn one. Apparently he didn't find it necessary to cover himself with anything more than a pair of ripped and faded cutoffs. She noticed his hands, limber, long fingered, and wondered if he had inherited them from his artist grandfather.

Water lapped quietly at the boat. Behind it, she saw a fish hawk soar then plummet. It gave a cry of triumph as it rose up again, a silver fish caught wriggling in its claws. The man in the boat continued to work, untouched by or oblivious to the drama of life and death around him.

Suzanna fixed what she hoped was a polite smile on her face and walked toward the pier. "Excuse me."

When his head shot up, she stopped dead. She had the quick but vivid impression that if he'd had a weapon, it would have been aimed at her. In an instant, he had gone from relaxed to full alert, with an edgy kind of violence in the set of his body that had her mouth going dry.

As she struggled to steady her heartbeat, she noted that he had changed. The surly boy was now a dangerous man. There was no other word that came to mind. His face had matured so that it was all planes and angles, sharply defined. The stubble of a two-day beard added to the rough-and-ready look.

But it was his eyes once again, that dried up her throat. A man with eyes that sharp, that potent, needed no weapon.

He squinted at her but didn't rise or speak. He had to give himself a moment to level. If he'd been wearing his weapon, it would have been out and in his hand. That was one of the reasons he was here, and a civilian again.

He might have forced himself to relax—he knew how—but he remembered her face. A man didn't forget that face. God knows, he hadn't. Timeless. In one of his youthful fantasies, he'd imagined her as a princess, lost and lovely in flowing silks. And himself as the knight who would have slain a hundred dragons to have her.

The memory made him scowl.

She'd hardly changed, he thought. Her skin was still pale Irish roses and cream, the shape of her face still classically oval. Her mouth had remained full and romantically soft, her eyes that deep, deep, dreamy blue, luxuriously lashed. They were watching him now with a kind of baffled alarm as he took his time looking her over.

She'd pulled her hair back in a smooth ponytail, but he remembered how it had flowed, long and loose and gleaming blond over her shoulders.

She was tall—all the Calhoun women were—but she was too thin. His scowl deepened at that. He'd heard she'd been married and divorced, and that both had been difficult experiences. She had two children, a boy and girl. It was difficult to believe that the slender wand of a woman in grubby jeans and a sweaty T-shirt had ever given birth.

It was harder to believe, harder to accept, that she could jangle his nerves just by standing ten feet away.

With his eyes still on hers, he went back to his polishing. "Do you want something?"

She let out the breath she hadn't been aware she was holding. "I'm sorry to just drop in this way. I'm Suzanna Dumont. Suzanna Calhoun."

"I know who you are."

"Oh, well..." She cleared her throat. "I realize you're busy, but I'd like to talk with you for a few minutes. If this isn't a good time—"

"What about?"

Since he was being so gracious, she thought, annoyed, she'd get right to the point. "About your grandfather. He was Christian Bradford, wasn't he? The artist?"

"That's right. So?"

"It's kind of a long story. Can I sit down?"

When he only shrugged, she walked to the pier. It groaned and swayed under her feet, and she lowered herself carefully.

"Actually, it started back in 1912 or '13, with my great-grandmother, Bianca."

"I've heard the fairy tale." He could smell her now, flowers and sweat, and it made his stomach tighten. "She was an unhappy wife with a rich and difficult husband. She compensated by taking a lover. Somewhere along the line, she supposedly hid her emerald necklace. Insurance if she got up the guts to leave. Instead of taking off into the sunset with her lover, she jumped out of the tower window, and the emeralds were never found."

"It wasn't precisely—"

"Now your family's decided to start a treasure hunt," he went on as if she hadn't spoken. "Got a lot of press out of it, and more trouble than I imagine you bargained for. I heard you had some excitement a couple of weeks ago."

"If you can call my sister being held at knifepoint excitement, yes." The fire had come into her eyes. She wasn't always good at defending herself, but when it came to her family, she was a scrapper. "The man who was working with Livingston, or whatever the bastard's calling himself now, nearly killed Lilah and her fiancé."

"When you've got priceless emeralds with a legend attached, the rats gnaw through the woodwork." He knew about Livingston. Holt had been a cop for ten years, and though he'd spent most of that time in Vice, he'd read reports on the slick and often violent jewel thief.

"The legend and the emeralds are my family's business."

"So why come to me? I turned in my shield. I'm retired."

"I didn't come to you for professional help. It's personal."

She took another breath, wanting to be clear and concise. "Lilah's fiancé used to be a history professor at Cornell. A couple of months ago, Livingston, going under the name of Ellis Caufield, hired him to go through the family's papers he'd stolen from us."

Holt continued to polish the brightwork. "Doesn't sound like Lilah developed any taste."

"Max didn't know the papers were stolen," Suzanna said between her teeth. "When he found out, Caufield nearly killed him. In any case, Max came to The Towers and continued his research for us. We've documented the emeralds' existence, and we've even interviewed a servant who worked at The Towers the year Bianca died."

Holt shifted and continued to work. "You've been busy."

"Yes. She corroborates the story that the necklace was hidden, and that Bianca was in love, and planning to leave her husband. The man she was in love with was an artist." She waited a beat. "His name was Christian Bradford."

Something flickered in his eyes then was gone. Very deliberately he set down his rag. He pulled a cigarette from a pack, flicked on a lighter then slowly blew out a haze of smoke.

"Do you really expect me to believe that little fantasy?"

She'd hoped for surprise, even amazement. She'd gotten boredom. "It's true. She used to meet him on the cliffs near The Towers."

He gave her a thin smile that was very close to a sneer. "Saw them, did you? Oh, I've heard about the ghost, too." He drew in more smoke, lazily released it. "The melancholy spirit of Bianca Calhoun, drifting through her summer home. You Calhouns are just full of—stories."

Her eyes darkened, but her voice remained very controlled. "Bianca Calhoun and Christian Bradford were in love. The summer she died, they met often on the cliffs just below The Towers."

That touched a chord, but he only shrugged. "So what?"

"So there's a connection. My family can't afford to overlook any connection, particularly one so vital as this one. It's very possible she told him where she put the emeralds."

"I don't see what a flirtation—an unsubstantiated flirtation—between two people some eighty years ago has to do with emeralds."

"If you could get past this prejudice you seem to have toward my family, we might be able to figure it out."

"Not interested in either part." He flipped open the top of a small cooler. "Want a beer?"

"No."

"Well, I'm fresh out of champagne." Watching her, he twisted off the top, tossed it toward a plastic bucket, then drank deeply. "You know, if you think about it, you'd see it's a little tough to swallow. The lady of the manor, well-bred, well-off, and the struggling artist. Doesn't play, babe. You'd be better off dropping the whole thing and concentrating on planting your flowers. Isn't that what you're doing these days?"

He could make her angry, she thought, but he wasn't going to shake her from her purpose. "My sisters' lives were threatened, my home has been broken into. Idiots are sneaking around in my garden and digging up my rosebushes." She stood, tall and slim and furious. "I have no intention of dropping the whole thing."

"Your business." He flicked the cigarette away before jumping effortlessly onto the pier. It shook and swayed beneath them. He was taller than she remembered, and she had to angle her chin to keep her eyes level. "Just don't expect to suck me into it."

"All right then. I'll just stop wasting my time and yours."

He waited until she'd stepped off the pier. "Suzanna." He liked the way it sounded when he said it. Soft and feminine and old-fashioned. "You ever learn to drive?"

Eyes stormy, she took a step back toward him. "Is that what this is all about?" she demanded. "You're still steaming because you fell off that stupid motorcycle and bruised your inflated male ego?"

"That wasn't the only thing that got bruised—or scraped, or lacerated." He remembered the way she'd looked. God, she couldn't have been more than sixteen. Rushing out of her car, her hair windblown, her face pale, her eyes dark and drenched with concern and fear.

And he'd been sprawled on the side of the road, his twenty-year-old pride as raw as the skin the asphalt had abraded.

"I don't believe it," she was saying. "You're still mad, after what, twelve years, for something that was clearly your own fault."

"My fault?" He tipped the bottle toward her. "You're the one who ran into me."

"I never ran into you or anyone. You fell."

"If I hadn't ditched the bike, you would have run into me. You weren't looking where you were going."

"I had the right of way. And you were going entirely too fast."

"Bull." He was starting to enjoy himself. "You were checking that pretty face of yours in the rearview mirror."

"I certainly was not. I never took my eyes off the road."

"If you'd had your eyes on the road, you wouldn't have run into me."

"I didn't—" She broke off, swore under her breath. "I'm not going to stand here and argue with you about something that happened twelve years ago."

"You came here to try to drag me into something that happened eighty years ago."

"That was an obvious mistake." She would have left it at that, but a very big, very wet dog came bounding across the lawn. With two happy barks, the animal leaped, planting both muddy feet on Suzanna's shirt and sending her staggering back.

"Sadie, down!" As Holt issued the terse command, he caught Suzanna before she hit the ground. "Stupid bitch."

"I beg your pardon?"

"Not you, the dog." Sadie was already sitting, thumping her dripping tail. "Are you all right?" He still had his arms around her, bracing her against his chest.

"Yes, fine." He had muscles like rock. It was impossible not to notice. Just as it was impossible not to notice that his breath fluttered along her temple, that he smelled very male. It had been a very long time since she had been held by a man.

Slowly he turned her around. For a moment, a moment too long, she was face-to-face with him, caught in the circle of his arms. His gaze flicked down to her mouth, lingered. A gull wheeled overhead, banked, then soared out over the water. He felt her heart thud against his. Once, twice, three times.

"Sorry," he said as he released her. "Sadie still sees herself as a cute little puppy. She got your shirt dirty."

"Dirt's my business." Needing time to recover, she crouched down to rub the dog's head. "Hi, there, Sadie."

Holt pushed his hands into his pockets as Suzanna acquainted herself with his dog. The bottle lay where he'd tossed it, spilling its contents onto the lawn. He wished to God she didn't look so beautiful, that her laugh as the dog lapped at her face didn't play so perfectly on his nerves.

In that one moment he'd held her, she'd fit into his arms

as he'd once imagined she would. His hands fisted inside his pockets because he wanted to touch her. No, that wasn't even close. He wanted to pull her inside the cottage, toss her onto the bed and do incredible things to her.

"Maybe a man who owns such a nice dog isn't all bad." She tossed a glance over her shoulder and the cautious smile died on her lips. The way he was looking at her, his eyes so dark and fierce, his bony face so set had the breath backing up in her lungs. There was violence trembling around him. She'd had a taste of violence from a man, and the memory of it made her limbs weak.

Slowly he relaxed his shoulders, his arms, his hands. "Maybe he isn't," he said easily. "But it's more a matter of her owning me at this point."

Suzanna found it more comfortable to look at the dog than the master. "We have a puppy. Well, he's growing by leaps and bounds so he'll be as big as Sadie soon. In fact, he looks a great deal like her. Did she have a litter a few months ago?"

"No."

"Hmm. He's got the same coloring, the same shaped face. My brother-in-law found him half-starved. Someone had dumped him, I suppose, and he'd managed to get up to the cliffs."

"Even I draw the line at abandoning helpless puppies."

"I didn't mean to imply—" She broke off because a new thought had jumped into her mind. It was no crazier than looking for missing emeralds. "Did your grandfather have a dog?"

"He always had a dog, used to take it with him wherever he went. Sadie's one of the descendants."

Carefully she got to her feet again. "Did he have a dog named Fred?"

Holt's brows drew together. "Why?"

"Did he?"

Holt was already sure he didn't like where this was leading. "The first dog he had was called Fred. That was before the First World War. He did a painting of him. And when Fred exercised the right *de seigneur* around the neighborhood, my grandfather took a couple of the puppies."

Suzanne rubbed suddenly damp hands on her jeans. It took all of her control to keep her voice low and steady. "The day before Bianca died, she brought a puppy home to her children. A little black puppy she called Fred." She saw his eyes change and knew she had his attention, and his interest. "She'd found him out on the cliffs—the cliffs where she went to meet Christian." She moistened her lips as Holt continued to stare at her and say nothing. "My great-grandfather wouldn't allow the dog to stay. They argued about it, quite seriously. We were able to locate a maid who'd worked there, and she'd heard the whole thing. No one was sure what happened to that dog. Until now."

"Even if that's true," Holt said slowly, "it doesn't change the bottom line. There's nothing I can do for you."

"You can think about it, you can try to remember if he ever said anything, if he left anything behind that could help."

"I've got enough to think about." He paced a few feet away. He didn't want to be involved with anything that would bring him into contact with her again and again.

Suzanna didn't argue. She could only stare at the long, jagged scar that ran from his shoulder to nearly his waist. He turned, met her horrified eyes and stiffened.

"Sorry, if I'd known you were coming to call, I'd have put on a shirt."

"What—" She had to swallow the block of emotion in her throat. "What happened to you?"

"I was a cop one night too long." His eyes stayed steady on hers. "I can't help you, Suzanna."

She shook away the pity he obviously would detest. "You won't."

"Whatever. If I'd wanted to dig around in other people's problems, I'd still be on the force."

"I'm only asking you to do a little thinking, to let us know if you remember anything that might help."

He was running out of patience. Holt figured he'd already given her more than her share for one day. "I was a kid when he died. Do you really think he'd have told me if he'd had an affair with a married woman?"

"You make it sound sordid."

"Some people don't figure adultery's romantic." Then he shrugged. It was nothing to him either way. "Then again, if one of the partners turns out to be a washout, I guess it's tough to come down on the other for looking someplace else."

She looked away at that, closing in on a private pain. "I'm not interested in your views on morality, Holt. Just your memory. And I've taken up enough of your time."

He didn't know what he'd said to put that sad, injured look in her eyes. But he couldn't let her leave with that haunting him. "Look, I think you're reaching at straws here, but if anything comes to mind, I'll let you know. For Sadie's ancestor's sake."

"I'd appreciate it."

"But don't expect anything."

With a half laugh she turned to walk to her truck. "Believe me, I won't." It surprised her when he crossed the lawn with her.

"I heard you started a business."

"That's right." She glanced around the yard. "You could use me."

The faint sneer came again. "I ain't the rosebush type."

"The cottage is." Unoffended, she fished her keys out of her pocket. "It wouldn't take much to make it charming."

"I'm not in the market for posies, babe. I'll leave the puttering around the rose garden to you."

She thought of the aching muscles she took home with her every night and climbed into the truck to slam the door. "Yes, puttering around the garden is something we women do best. By the way, Holt, your grass needs fertilizer. I'm sure you have plenty to spread around."

She gunned the engine, set the shift in reverse and pulled out.

Chapter 2

The children came rushing out of the house, followed by a big-footed black dog. The boy and the girl skimmed down the worn stone steps with the easy balance and grace of youth. The dog tripped over his own feet and somersaulted. Poor Fred, Suzanna thought as she climbed out of the truck. It didn't look as though he would ever outgrow his puppy clumsiness.

"Mom!" Each child attached to one of Suzanna's jean-clad legs. At six, Alex was already tall for his age and dark as a gypsy. His sturdy tanned legs were scabbed at the knees and his bony elbows were scraped. Not from clumsiness, Suzanna thought, but from derring-do. Jenny, a year younger and blond as a fairy princess, carried the same badges of honor. Suzanna forgot her irritation and fatigue the moment she bent to kiss them.

"What have you two been up to?"

"We're building a fort," Alex told her. "It's going to be impregnant."

"Impregnable," Suzanna corrected, tweaking his nose.

"Yeah, and Sloan said he could help us with it on Saturday."

"Can you?" Jenny asked.

"After work." She bent to pet Fred, who was trying to push his way through the children for his rightful share of affection. "Hello, boy. I think I met one of your relatives today."

"Does Fred have relatives?" Jenny wanted to know.

"It certainly looked that way." She walked over to sit with the children on the steps. It was a luxury to sit, to smell the sea and flowers, to have a child under each arm. "I think I met his cousin Sadie."

"Where? Can she come to visit? Is she nice?"

"In the village," Suzanna said, answering Alex's rapid-fire questions in turn. "I don't know, and yes, she's very nice. Big, like Fred's going to be when he grows into his feet. What else did you do today?"

"Loren and Lisa came over," Jenny told her. "We killed hundreds of marauders."

"Well, we can all sleep easy tonight."

"And Max told us a story about storming the beach at Normally."

Chuckling, Suzanna kissed the top of Jenny's head. "I think that was Normandy."

"Lisa and Jenny played dolls, too." Alex gave his sister a brotherly smirk.

"She wanted to. She got the brand-new Barbie and her car for her birthday."

"It was a Ferrari," Alex said importantly, but didn't want to admit that he and Loren had played with it when the girls were out of the room. He inched closer to toy with his mother's ponytail. "Loren and Lisa are going to Disney World next week."

Suzanna bit back a sigh. She knew her children dreamed

of going to that enchanted kingdom in central Florida. "We'll go someday."

"Soon?" Alex prompted.

She wanted to promise, but couldn't. "Someday," she repeated. The weariness was back when she rose to take each child by the hand. "You guys run and tell Aunt Coco I'm home. I need to shower and change. Okay?"

"Can we go to work with you tomorrow?"

She gave Jenny's hand a quick squeeze. "Carolanne's watching the shop tomorrow. I have site work." She felt their disappointment as keenly as her own. "Next week. Go ahead now," she said as she opened the massive front door. "And I'll look at your fort after dinner."

Satisfied with that, they barreled down the hall with the dog at their heels.

They didn't ask for much, Suzanna thought as she climbed the curving stairs to the second floor. And there was so much more she wanted to give them. She knew they were happy and safe and secure. They had a huge family who loved them. With one of her sisters married, and two others engaged, her children had men in their lives. Maybe uncles didn't replace a father, but it was the best she could do.

They hadn't heard from Baxter Dumont for months. Alex hadn't even rated a card on his birthday. The child support check was late again—as it was every month. Bax was too sharp a lawyer to neglect the payment completely, but he made certain it arrived weeks after its due date. To test her, she knew. To see if she would beg for it. Thank God she hadn't needed to yet.

The divorce had been final for a year and a half, but he continued to take out his feelings for her on the children—the only truly worthwhile thing they had made together.

Perhaps that was why she had yet to get over the nagging

disillusionment, the sense of betrayal and loss and inadequacy. She no longer loved him. That love had died before Jenny had been born. But the hurt...Suzanna shook her head. She was working on it.

She stepped into her room. Like most of the rooms in The Towers, Suzanne's bedroom was huge. The house had been built in the early 1900s by her great-grandfather. It had been a showpiece, a testament to his vanity, his taste for the opulent and his need for status. It was five stories of somber granite with fanciful peaks and parapets, two spiraling towers and layering terraces. The interior was lofty ceilings, fancy woodwork, mazelike hallways. Part castle, part manor house, it had served first as summer home, then as permanent residence.

Through the years and financial reversals, the house had fallen on hard times. Suzanna's room, like the others, showed cracks in the plaster. The floor was scarred, the roof leaked and the plumbing had a mind of its own. As one, the Calhouns loved their family home. Now that the west wing was under renovation, they hoped it would be able to pay its own way.

She went to the closet for a robe, thinking that she'd been one of the lucky ones. She'd been able to bring her children here, into a real home, when their own had crumbled. She hadn't had to interview strangers to care for them while she made a living. Her father's sister, who had raised Suzanna and her sisters after their parents had died, was now caring for Suzanna's children. Though Suzanna was aware that Alex and Jenny were a handful, she knew there was no one better suited for the task than Aunt Coco.

And one day soon they would find Bianca's emeralds, and everything would settle back to what passed for normal in the Calhoun household.

"Suze." Lilah gave the door a quick knock then poked her head in. "Did you see him?"

"Yes, I saw him."

"Terrific." Lilah, her red hair curling to her waist, strolled in. She stretched out diagonally on the bed, plumping a pillow against the tiered headboard. Easily she settled into her favorite position. Horizontal. "So tell me."

"He hasn't changed much."

"Oh-oh."

"He was abrupt and rude." Suzanna pulled the T-shirt over her head. "I think he considered shooting me for trespassing. When I tried to explain what was going on, he sneered." Remembering that look, she tugged down the zipper of her jeans. "Basically, he was obnoxious, arrogant and insulting."

"Mmm. Sounds like a prince."

"He thinks we made the whole thing up to get publicity for The Towers when we open the retreat next year."

"What a crock." That stirred Lilah enough to have her sitting up. "Max was nearly killed. Does he think we're crazy?"

"Exactly." With a nod, Suzanna dragged on her robe. "I couldn't begin to guess why, but he seems to have a grudge against the Calhouns in general."

Lilah gave a sleepy smile. "Still stewing because you knocked him off his motorcycle."

"I did not—" On an oath, Suzanna gave up. "Never mind, the point is I don't think we're going to get any help from him." After pulling the band out of her hair, she ran her hands through it. "Though after the business with the dog, he did say he'd think about it."

"What dog?"

"Fred's cousin," she said over her shoulder as she walked into the bath to turn on the shower.

Lilah came to the doorway just as Suzanna was pulling the curtain closed. "Fred has a cousin?"

Over the drum of the water, Suzanna told her about Sadie, and her ancestors.

"But that's fabulous. It's just one more link in the chain. I'll have to tell Max."

With her eyes closed, Suzanna stuck her head under the shower. "Tell him he's on his own. Christian's grandson isn't interested."

He didn't want to be. Holt sat on the back porch, the dog at his feet, and watched the water turn to indigo in twilight.

There was music here, the symphony of insects in the grass, the rustle of wind, the countermelody of water against wood. Across the bay, Bar Island began to fade and merge into dusk. Nearby someone was playing a radio, a lonely alto sax solo that suited Holt's mood.

This was what he wanted. Quiet, solitude, no responsibilities. He'd earned it, hadn't he? he thought as he tipped the beer to his lips. He'd given ten years of his life to other people's problems, their tragedies, their miseries.

He was burned out, bone-dry and tired as hell.

He wasn't even sure he'd been a good cop. Oh, he had citations and medals that claimed he had been. But he also had a twelve-inch scar on his back that reminded him he'd nearly been a dead one.

Now he just wanted to enjoy his retirement, repair a few motors, scrape some barnacles, maybe do a little boating. He'd always been good with his hands and knew he could make a decent living repairing boats. Running his own business, at his own pace, in his own way. No reports to type, no leads to follow up, no dark alleys to search.

No knife-wielding junkies springing out of the shadows to rip you open and leave you bleeding on the littered concrete.

Holt closed his eyes and took another pull of beer. He'd

made up his mind during the long, painful hospital stay. There would be no more commitment in his life, no more trying to save the world from itself. From that point on, he would start looking out for himself. Just himself.

He'd taken the money he'd inherited and had come home, to do as little as possible with the rest of his life. Sun and sea in the summer, roaring fires and howling winds in the winter. It wasn't so damn much to ask.

He'd been settling in, feeling pretty good about himself. Then she'd come along.

Hadn't it been bad enough that he'd looked at her and felt—Lord, the way he'd felt when he'd been twenty years old. Churned up and hungry. He was still hung up on her.

The lovely, and unattainable, Suzanna Calhoun of the Bar Harbor Calhouns. The princess in the tower. She'd lived high up in her castle on the cliffs. And he had lived in a cottage on the edge of the village. His father had been a lobsterman, and Holt had often delivered a catch to the Calhouns' back door—never going beyond the kitchen. But he'd sometimes heard voices or laughter or music. And he had wondered and wanted.

Now she had come to him. But he wasn't a love-struck boy any longer. He was a realist. Suzanna was out of his league, just as she had always been. Even if it had been different, he wasn't interested in a woman who had home and hearth written all over her.

As far as the emeralds went, there was nothing he could do to help her. Nothing he wanted to do.

He'd known about the emeralds, of course. That particular story had made national press. But the idea that his grandfather had been involved, had loved and been loved by a Calhoun woman. That was fascinating.

Even with the coincidence about the dogs, he wasn't sure

he believed it. Holt hadn't known his grandmother, but his grandfather had been the hero of his childhood. He'd been the dashing and mysterious figure who had gone off to foreign places, come back with fabulous stories. He'd been the man who had been able to perform magic with a canvas and brush.

He could remember climbing up the stairs to the studio as a child to watch the tall man with the snow-white hair at work. Yet it had seemed more like combat than work. An elegant and passionate duel between his grandfather and the canvas.

They would take long walks, the young boy and the old man, along the shore, across the rocks. Up on the cliffs. With a sigh, Holt sat back. Very often they had walked to the cliffs just below The Towers. Even as a child he'd understood that as his grandfather had looked out to sea, he had gone someplace else.

Once, they had sat on the rocks there and his grandfather had told him a story about the castle on the cliffs, and the princess who'd lived there.

Had he been talking about The Towers, and Bianca?

Restless, Holt rose to go inside. Sadie glanced up, then settled her head on her front paws again as the screen door slammed.

The cottage suited him more than the home he'd grown up in. That had been a neat and soulless place with worn linoleum and dark paneled walls. Holt had sold it after his mother's death three years before. Recently he'd used the profits for some repairs and modernization of the cottage, but preferred keeping the old place much as it had been in his grandfather's day.

It was a boxy house, with plaster walls and wood floors. The original stone fireplace had been pointed up, and Holt looked forward to the first cool night when he could try it out.

The bedroom was tiny, almost an afterthought that jutted out from the main structure. He liked lying in bed at night and listening to rain drumming on the tin roof. The stairs to his grandfather's studio had been reinforced, as well as the railing that skirted along the open balcony. He climbed up now, to look at the wide, airy space, dim with twilight.

Now and then he thought about putting skylights in the angled roof, but he never considered refinishing the floor. The dark old wood was splattered with paint that had dripped from brush or palette. There were streaks of carmine and turquoise, drops of emerald green and canary yellow. His grandfather had preferred the vivid, the passionate, even the violent in his work.

Against one wall, canvases were stacked, Holt's legacy from a man who had only begun to find critical and financial success in his last years. They would, he knew, be worth a hefty sum. Yet as he never considered sanding the paint from the floors, he had never considered selling this part of his inheritance.

Crouching down, he began to look through the paintings. He knew them all, had studied them countless times, wondering how he could have come from a man with such vision and talent. Holt turned over the portrait, knowing that was why he had come up here.

The woman was as beautiful as a dream—the fine-featured oval face, the alabaster skin. Rich red-gold hair was swept up off a graceful neck. Full, soft lips were curved, just a little. But it was the eyes that drew Holt, as they always had. They were green, like a misty sea. It wasn't their color that pulled at him, but the expression in them, the look, the emotion that had been captured by his grandfather's brush and skill.

Such quiet sadness. Such inner grief. It was almost too

painful to look at, because to look too long was to feel. He had seen that expression today, in Suzanna's eyes.

Could this be Bianca? he wondered. The resemblance was there, in the shape of the face, the curve of the mouth. The coloring was certainly wrong and the similarities slight. Except the eyes, he thought. When he looked at them, he thought of Suzanna.

Because he was thinking of her too much, he told himself. He rose, but he didn't turn the portrait back to the wall. He stood staring at it for a long time, wondering if his grandfather had loved the woman he'd painted.

It was going to be another hot one, Suzanna thought. Though it was barely seven, the air was already sticky. They needed rain, but the moisture hung in the air and stubbornly refused to fall.

Inside her shop, she checked on the refrigerated blooms and left a note for Carolanne to push the carnations by selling them at half price. She checked the soil in the hanging pots of impatiens and geraniums, then moved on to the display of gloxinia and begonias.

Satisfied, she took her sprayer out to drench the flats of annuals and perennials. The rosebushes and peonies were moving well, she noted. As were the yews and junipers.

By seven-thirty, she was checking on the greenhouse plants, grateful that her inventory was dwindling. What didn't sell, she would winter over. She would also take cuttings for next year's plants. But winter, and that quiet work, was months away.

By eight her pickup was loaded, and she was on her way to Seal Harbor. She would put in a full day's work there on the grounds of a newly constructed home. The buyers were from Boston, and wanted their summer home to have an established yard, complete with shrubs, trees and flower beds.

It would be hot, sweaty work, Suzanne mused. But it would also be quiet. The Andersons were in Boston this week, so she would have the yard to herself. She liked nothing better than working with the soil and living things, tending something she had planted and watching it grow and thrive.

Like her children, she thought with a smile. Her babies. Every time she put them to bed at night or watched them run in the sunlight, she knew that nothing that had happened to her before, nothing that would happen to her in the future would dim that glow of knowing they were hers.

The failed marriage had left her shaken and uncertain, and there were times she still had terrible doubts about herself as a woman. But not as a mother. Her children had the very best she could give them. The bond nourished her, as well as them.

Over the past two years, she'd begun to believe that she could be a success in business. Her flair for gardening had been her only useful skill and had been a kind of salvation during the last months of her dying marriage. In desperation she had sold her jewelry, taken out a loan and had plunged into Island Gardens.

It had made her feel good to use her maiden name. She hadn't wanted any frivolous or clever name for the business, but something straightforward. The first year had been rough—particularly when she'd been pouring every cent she could spare into legal fees to fight a custody suit.

The thought of that, the memory of it, still made her blood run cold. She couldn't have lost them.

Bax hadn't wanted the children, but he'd wanted to make things difficult for her. When it had been over, she'd lost fifteen pounds, countless hours of sleep and had been up to her neck in debt. But she had her children. The ugly battle had been won, and the price meant nothing.

Gradually she was pulling out. She'd gained back a few of the pounds, had caught up a bit on her sleep and was slowly, meticulously hacking away at the debt. In the two years since she'd opened the business, she'd earned a reputation as dependable, reasonable and imaginative. Two of the resorts had tried her out, and it looked as though they'd be negotiating long-term contracts.

That would mean buying another truck, hiring on full-time labor. And maybe, just maybe, that trip to Disney World.

She pulled up in the driveway of the pretty Cape Cod house. Now, she reminded herself, it meant getting to work.

The grounds took up about a half acre and were gently sloped. She had had three in-depth meetings with the owners to determine the plan. Mrs. Anderson wanted plenty of spring flowering trees and shrubs, and the long-term privacy factor of evergreens. She wanted to enjoy a perennial bed that was carefree and full of summer color. Mr. Anderson didn't want to spend his summers maintaining the yard, particularly the side portion, which fell in a more dramatic grade. There, Suzanna would use ground covers and rockeries to prevent erosion.

By noon, she had measured off each area with stakes and strings. The hardy azaleas were planted. Two long-blooming fairy roses flanked the flagstone walk and were already sweetening the air. Because Mrs. Anderson had expressed a fondness for lilacs, Suzanna placed a trio of compact shrubs near the master bedroom window, where the next spring's breezes would carry the scent indoors.

The yard was coming alive for her. It helped her ignore the aching muscles in her arms as she drenched the new plants with water. Birds were chirping, and somewhere in the near distance, a lawn mower was putting away.

One day, she would drive by and see that the fast-growing hedge roses she had planted along the fence had spread and bloomed until they covered the chain link. She would see the azaleas bloom in the spring and the maple leaves go red in the fall, and know that she'd been part of that.

It was important, more important than she could admit to anyone, that she leave a mark. She needed that to remind herself that she wasn't the weak and useless woman who had been so callously tossed aside.

Dripping with sweat, she picked up her water bottle and shovel and headed around to the front of the house again. She'd put in the first of the flowering almonds and was digging the hole for the second when a car pulled into the driveway behind her truck. Resting on her shovel, Suzanna watched Holt climb out.

She let out a little huff of breath, annoyed that her solitude had been invaded, and went back to digging.

"Out for a drive?" she asked when his shadow fell over her.

"No, the girl at the shop told me where to find you. What the hell are you doing?"

"Playing canasta." She shoveled some more dirt. "What do you want?"

"Put that shovel down before you hurt yourself. You've got no business digging ditches."

"Digging ditches is my business—more or less. Now, what do you want?"

He watched her dig for another ten seconds before he snatched the shovel away from her. "Give me that damn thing and sit down."

Patience had always been her strong point, but she was

hard-pressed to find it now. Working at it, she adjusted the brim of the fielder's cap she wore. "I'm on a schedule, and I have six more trees, two rosebushes and twenty square feet of ground cover to plant. If you've got something to say, fine. Talk while I work."

He jerked the shovel out of her reach. "How deep do you want it?" She only lifted a brow. "How deep do you want the hole?"

She skimmed her gaze down, then up again. "I'd say a little more than six feet would be enough to bury you in."

He grinned, surprising her. "And you used to be so sweet." Plunging the shovel in, he began to dig. "Just tell me when to stop."

Normally she repaid kindness with kindness. But she was going to make an exception. "You can stop right now; I don't need any help. And I don't want the company."

"I didn't know you had a stubborn streak." He glanced up as he tossed dirt aside. "I guess I had a hard time getting past that pretty face." That pretty face, he noted, was flushed and damp and had shadows of fatigue under the eyes. It annoyed the hell out of him. "I thought you sold flowers."

"I do. I also plant them."

"Even I know that thing there is a tree."

"I plant those, too." Giving up, she took out a bandanna and wiped at her neck. "The hole needs to be wider, not deeper."

He shifted to accommodate her. Maybe he needed to do a little reevaluating. "How come you don't have anybody doing the heavy work for you?"

"Because I can do it myself."

Yes, there was stubbornness in the tone, and just a touch of nastiness. He liked her better for it. "Looks like a two-man job to me."

"It is a two-man job—the other man quit yesterday to be a rock star. His band got a gig down in Brighton Beach."

"Big time."

"Hmm. That's fine," she said, and turned to heft the three-foot tree by its balled roots. As Holt frowned at her, she lifted it, then set it carefully in the hole.

"Now I guess I fill it back in."

"You've got the shovel," she pointed out. As he worked, she dragged a bag of peat moss closer and began to mix it with the soil.

Her nails were short and rounded, he noted as she dug her already grimed fingers into the soil. There was no wedding ring on her finger. In fact, she wore no jewelry at all, though she had hands that were meant to wear beautiful things.

She worked patiently, her head down, her cap shielding her eyes. He could see the nape of her neck and wondered what it would be like to press his lips there. Her skin would be hot now, and damp. Then she rose, switching on the garden hose to drench the dirt.

"You do this every day?"

"I try to take a day or two in the shop. I can bring the kids in with me." With her feet, she tamped down the damp earth. When the tree was secure, she spread a thick lawyer of mulch, her moves competent and practiced. "Next spring, this will be covered with blooms." She wiped the back of her wrist over her brow. The little tank top she wore had a line of sweat down the front and back that only emphasized her fragile build. "I really am on a schedule, Holt. I've got some aspens and white pine to plant out in back, so if you need to talk to me, you're going to have to come along."

He glanced around the yard. "Did you do all this today?"

"Yes. What do you think?"

"I think you're courting sunstroke."

A compliment, she supposed, would have been too much to ask. "I appreciate the medical evaluation." She put a hand on the shovel, but he held on. "I need this."

"I'll carry it."

"Fine." She loaded the bags of peat and mulch into a wheelbarrow. He swore at her, tossed the shovel on top then nudged her away to push the wheelbarrow himself.

"Where out back?"

"By the stakes near the rear fence."

She frowned after him when he started off, then followed him. He began digging without consulting her so she emptied the wheelbarrow and headed back to her truck. When he glanced up, she was pushing out two more trees. They planted the first one together, in silence.

He hadn't realized that putting a tree in the ground could be soothing, even rewarding work. But when it stood, young and straight in the dazzling sunlight, he felt soothed. And rewarded.

"I was thinking about what you said yesterday," he began when they set the second tree in its new home.

"And?"

He wanted to swear. There was such patience in the single word, as if she'd known all along he would bring it up. "And I still don't think there's anything I can do, or want to do, but you may be right about the connection."

"I know I'm right about the connection." She brushed mulch from her hands to her jeans. "If you came out here just to tell me that, you've wasted a trip."

She rolled the empty wheelbarrow to the truck. She was about to muscle the next two trees out of the bed when he jumped up beside her.

"I'll get the damn things out." Muttering, he filled the wheelbarrow and rolled it back to the rear of the yard. "He never mentioned her to me. Maybe he knew her, maybe they had an affair, but I don't see how that helps you."

"He loved her," Suzanna said quietly as she picked up the shovel to dig. "That means he knew how she felt, how she thought. He might have had an idea where she would have hidden the emeralds."

"He's dead."

"I know." She was silent a moment as she worked. "Bianca kept a journal—at least we're nearly certain she did, and that she hid it away with the necklace. Christian might have kept one, too."

Annoyed, he grabbed the shovel again. "I never saw it."

She suppressed the urge to snap at him. However much it might grate, he could be a link. "I suppose most people keep a private journal in a private place. Or he might have kept some letters from her. We found one Bianca wrote him and was never able to send."

"You're chasing windmills, Suzanna."

"This is important to my family." She set the white pine carefully in the hole. "It's not the monetary value of the emeralds. It's what they meant to her."

He watched her work, the competent and gentle hands, the surprisingly strong shoulders. The delicate curve of her neck. "How could you know what they meant to her?"

She kept her eyes down. "I can't explain that to you in any way you'd understand or accept."

"Try me."

"We all seem to have some kind of bond with her—especially Lilah." She didn't look up when she heard him digging the next hole. "We'd never seen the emeralds, not even a photograph. After Bianca died, Fergus, my great-grandfather, destroyed all pictures of her. But Lilah...she drew a sketch of them one night. It was after we'd had a séance."

She did look up then and caught his look of amused disbelief. "I know how it sounds," she said, her voice stiff and defensive. "But my aunt believes in that sort of thing. And after that night, I think she may be right to. My youngest sister, C.C. had an...experience during the séance. She saw them—the emeralds. That's when Lilah drew the sketch. Weeks later, Lilah's fiancé found a picture of the emeralds in a library book. They were exactly as Lilah had drawn them, exactly as C.C. had seen them."

He said nothing for a moment as he set the next tree in place. "I'm not much on mysticism. Maybe one of your sisters saw the picture before, and had forgotten about it."

"If any of us had seen a picture, we wouldn't have forgotten. Still, the point is that all of us feel that finding the emeralds is important."

"They might have been sold eighty years ago."

"No. There was no record. Fergus was a maniac about keeping his finances." Unconsciously she arched her back, rolled her shoulders to relieve the ache. "Believe me, we've been through every scrap of paper we could find."

He let it drop, mulling it over as they planted the last of the trees.

"You know the bit about the needle in the haystack?" he asked as he helped her spread mulch. "People don't really find it."

"They would if they kept looking." Curious, she sat back on her heels to study him. "Don't you believe in hope?"

He was close enough to touch her, to rub the smudge of dirt from her cheek or run a hand down the ponytail. He did neither. "No, only in what is."

"Then I'm sorry for you." They rose together, their bodies nearly brushing. She felt something rush along her skin, something race through her blood, and automatically stepped back.

"If you don't believe in what could be, there isn't any use in planting trees, or having children or even watching the sun set."

He'd felt it, too. And resented and feared it every bit as much as she. "If you don't keep your eye on what's real, right now, you end up dreaming your life away. I don't believe in the necklace, Suzanna, or in ghosts, or in eternal love. But if and when I'm certain that my grandfather was involved with Bianca Calhoun, I'll do what I can to help you."

She gave a half laugh. "You don't believe in hope or love, or anything else apparently. Why would you agree to help us?"

"Because if he did love her, he would have wanted me to." Bending, he picked up the shovel and handed it back to her. "I've got things to do."

Chapter 3

Suzanna pulled up to the shop, pleased that she had to squeeze between a station wagon and a hatchback in the graveled parking area. There were a few people wandering around the flats of annuals, and a young couple deliberating over the climbing roses. A woman, hugely pregnant, strolled about, carrying a tray of mixed pots. The toddler by her side held a single geranium like a flag.

Inside, Carolanne was ringing up a sale and flirting with the young man who held a ceramic urn of pink double begonias. "Your mother will love them," she said, and swept her long lashes over doe-colored eyes. "There's nothing like flowers for a birthday. Or anytime. We're having a special on carnations." She smiled and tossed her long, curling brown hair. "If you have a girlfriend."

"Well, no..." He cleared his throat. "Not really. Right now."

"Oh." Her smile warmed several degrees. "That's too

bad." She gave him his change and a long look. "Come back anytime. I'm usually here."

"Sure. Thanks." He shot a glance over his shoulder, trying to keep her in sight, and nearly ran over Suzanna. "Oh. Sorry."

"That's all right. I hope your mother enjoys them." Chuckling, she joined the pert brunette at the cash register. "You're amazing."

"Wasn't he cute? I love it when they blush. Well." She turned her smile on Suzanna. "You're back early."

"It didn't take as long as I thought." She didn't feel it was necessary to add she'd had unexpected and unwanted help. Carolanne was a hard worker, a skilled salesperson, and an inveterate gossip. "How are things here?"

"Moving along. All this sunshine must be inspiring people to beef up their gardens. Oh, Mrs. Russ was back. She liked the primroses so much, she made her husband build her another window box so she could buy more. Since she was in the mood, I sold her two hibiscus—and two of those terra-cotta pots to put them in."

"I love you. Mrs. Russ loves you, and Mr. Russ is going to learn to hate you." At Carolanne's laugh, Suzanna looked out through the glass. "I'll go and see if I can help those people decide which roses they want."

"The new Mr. and Mrs. Halley. They both wait tables over at Captain Jack's, and just bought a cottage. He's studying to be an engineer, and she's going to start teaching at the elementary school in September."

Shaking her head, Suzanna laughed. "Like I said, you're amazing."

"No, just nosy." Carolanne grinned. "Besides, people buy more if you talk to them. And boy, do I love to talk."

"If you didn't, I'd have to close up shop."

"You'd just work twice as hard, if that's possible." She waved a hand before Suzanna could protest. "Before you go, I asked around to see if anyone needed any part-time work." Carolanne lifted her hands. "No luck yet."

It wasn't any use moaning, Suzanna thought. "This late in the season, everyone's already working."

"If Tommy the creep Parotti hadn't jumped ship—"

"Honey, he had a chance to make a break and do something he's always wanted to do. We can't blame him for that."

"You can't," Carolanne muttered. "Suzanna, you can't keep doing all the site work yourself. It's too hard."

"We're getting by," she said absently, thinking of the help she'd had that day. "Listen, Carolanne, after we deal with these customers, I have another delivery to make. Can you handle things until closing?"

"Sure." Carolanne let out a sigh. "I'm the one with a stool and a fan, you're the one with the pick and the shovel."

"Just keep pushing the carnations."

An hour later, Suzanna pulled up at Holt's cottage. It wasn't just impulse, she told herself. And it wasn't because she wanted to pressure him. Lecturing herself, she climbed out of the truck. It certainly wasn't because she wanted his company. But she was a Calhoun, and Calhouns always paid their debts.

She walked up the steps to the porch, again thinking it was a charming place. A few touches—morning glories climbing up the railing, a bed of columbine and larkspur, with some snapdragons and lavender.

Day lilies along that slope, she thought as she knocked. A border of impatiens. Miniature roses under the windows. And there, where the ground was rocky and uneven, a little herb bed, set off with spring bulbs.

It could be a fairy-tale place—but the man who lived there didn't believe in fairy tales.

She knocked again, noting that his car was there. As she had before, she walked around the side, but he wasn't in the boat this time. With a shrug, she decided she would do what she'd come to do.

She'd already picked the spot, between the water and the house, where the shrub could be seen and enjoyed through what she'd determined was the kitchen window. It wasn't much, but it would add some color to the empty backyard. She wheeled around what she needed, then began to dig.

Inside his work shed, Holt had the boat engine broken down. Rebuilding it would require concentration and time. Which was just what he needed. He didn't want to think about the Calhouns, or tragic love affairs, or responsibilities.

He didn't even glance up when Sadie rose from her nap on the cool cement and trotted outside. He and the dog had an understanding. She did as she chose, and he fed her.

When she barked, he kept on working. As a watchdog, Sadie was a bust. She barked at squirrels, at the wind in the grass, and in her sleep. A year before there'd been an attempted burglary in his house in Portland. Holt had relieved the would-be thief of his stereo equipment while Sadie had napped peacefully on the living room rug.

But he did look up, he did stop working when he heard the low, feminine laughter. It skimmed along his skin, light and warm. When he pushed away from the workbench, his stomach was already in knots. When he stood in the doorway and looked at her, the knots yanked tight.

Why wouldn't she leave him alone? he wondered, and shoved his hands into his pockets. He'd told her he'd think about it, hadn't he? She had no business coming here again.

They didn't even like each other. Whatever she did to him physically was his problem, and so far he'd managed quite nicely to keep his hands off her.

Now here she was, standing in his yard, talking to his dog. And digging a hole.

His brows drew together as he stepped out of the shed. "What the hell are you doing?"

Her head shot up. He saw her eyes, big and blue and alarmed. Her face, flushed from the heat and her work, went very pale. He'd seen that kind of look before—the quick, instinctive fear of a cornered victim. Then it was gone, fading so swiftly he nearly convinced himself he'd imagined it. Color seeped slowly into her cheeks again as she managed to smile.

"I didn't think you were here."

He stayed where he was and continued to scowl. "So, you decided to dig a hole in my yard."

"I guess you could say that." Steady now, annoyed with herself for the instinctive jolt, she plunged the shovel in again, braced her foot on it and deepened the hole. "I brought you a bush."

Damned if he was going to take the shovel from her this time and dig the hole himself. But he did cross to her. "Why?"

"To thank you for helping me out today. You saved me a good hour."

"So you use it to dig another hole."

"Uh-huh. There's a breeze off the water today." She lifted her face to it for a moment. "It's nice."

Because looking at her made his palms sweat, he scowled down at the tidy shrub pregnant with sassy yellow blooms. "I don't know how to take care of a bush. You put it there, you're condemning it to death row."

With a laugh, she scooped out the last of the dirt. "You

don't have to do much. This one's very hardy, even when it's dry, and it'll bloom for you into the fall. Can I use your hose?"

"What?"

"Your hose?"

"Yeah." He raked a hand through his hair. He hadn't a clue how he was supposed to react. It was certainly the first time anyone had given him flowers—unless you counted the batch the guys at the precinct had brought in when he'd been in the hospital. "Sure."

At ease with her task, she continued to talk as she went to the outside wall to turn on the water. "It'll stay neat. It's a very well behaved little bush and won't get over three feet." She petted Sadie, who was circling the bush and sniffing. "If you'd like something else instead..."

He wasn't going to let himself be touched by some idiotic plant or her misplaced gratitude. "It doesn't matter to me. I don't know one from the other."

"Well, this is a *hypericum kalmianum.*"

His lips quirked into what might have been a smile. "That tells me a lot."

Chuckling, she set it in place. "A sunshine shrub in layman's terms." Still smiling, she tilted her head back to look at him. If she didn't know better, she'd have thought he was embarrassed. Fat chance. "I thought you could use some sunshine. Why don't you help me plant it? It'll mean more to you then."

He'd said he wasn't going to get sucked in, and damn it, he'd meant it. "Are you sure this isn't your idea of a bribe? To get me to help you out?"

Sighing a little, she sat back on her heels. "I wonder what makes someone so cynical and unfriendly. I'm sure you have your reasons, but they don't apply here. You did me a favor today, and I'm paying you back. Very simple. Now if you don't want the bush, just say so. I'll give it to someone else."

He lifted a brow at the tone. "Is that how you keep your kids in line?"

"When necessary. Well, what's it to be?"

Maybe he was being too hard on her. She'd made a gesture and he was slapping it back in her face. If she could be casually friendly, so could he. "I've already got a hole in my yard," he pointed out then knelt beside her. The dog lay down in the sunlight to watch. "We might as well put something in it."

And that, she supposed, was his idea of a thank-you. "Fine."

"So how old are your kids?" Not that he cared, he told himself. He was just making conversation.

"Five and six. Alex is the oldest, then Jenny." Her eyes softened as they always did when she thought of them. "They're growing up so fast, I can hardly keep up."

"What made you come back here after the divorce?"

Her hands tensed in the soil, then began to work again. It was a small and quickly concealed gesture, but he had very sharp eyes. "Because it's home."

There was a tender spot, he thought and eased around it. "I heard you're going to turn The Towers into a hotel."

"Just the west wing. That's C.C.'s husband's business."

"It's hard to picture C.C. married. The last time I saw her she was about twelve."

"She's grown up now, and beautiful."

"Looks run in the family."

She glanced up, surprised, then back down again. "I think you've just said something nice."

"Just stating a fact. The Calhoun sisters were always worth a second look." To please himself, he reached out to toy with the tip of her ponytail. "Whenever guys got together, the four of you were definitely topics of conversation."

She laughed a little, thinking how easy life had been back then. "I'm sure we'd have been flattered."

"I used to look at you," Holt said slowly. "A lot."

Wary, she lifted her head. "Really? I never noticed."

"You wouldn't have." His hand dropped away again. "Princesses don't notice peasants."

Now she frowned, not only at the words but at the clipped tone. "What a ridiculous thing to say."

"It was easy to think of you that way, the princess in the castle."

"A castle that's been crumbling for years," she said dryly. "And as I recall, you were too busy swaggering around and juggling girls to notice me."

He had to grin. "Oh, between the swaggering and juggling, I noticed you all right."

Something in his eyes set off a little warning bell. It might have been some time since she'd heard that particular sound, but she recognized it and heeded it. She looked down again to firm the dirt around the bush.

"That was a long time ago. I imagine we've both changed quite a bit."

"Can't argue with that." He pushed at the dirt.

"No, don't shove at it, press it down—firm, but gentle." Scooting closer, she put her hands over his to show him. "All it needs is a good start, and then—"

She broke off when he turned his hands over to grip hers.

They were close, knees brushing, bodies bent toward each other. He noted that her hands were hard, callused, a direct and fascinating contrast to the soft eyes and tea rose complexion. There was a strength in her fingers that would have surprised him if he hadn't seen for himself how hard she worked. For reasons he couldn't fathom, he found it incredibly erotic.

"You've got strong hands, Suzanna."

"A gardener's hands," she said, trying to keep her voice light. "And I need them to finish planting this bush."

He only tightened his grip when she tried to draw away. "We'll get to it. You know, I've thought about kissing you for fifteen years." He watched the faint smile fade away from her face and the alarm shoot into her eyes. He didn't mind it. It might be best for both of them if she was afraid of him. "That's a long time to think about anything."

He released one hand, but before she could let out a sigh of relief, he had cupped the back of her neck. His fingers were firm, his grip determined. "I'm just going to get it out of my system."

She didn't have time to refuse. He was quick. Before she could deny or protest, his mouth was on hers, covering and conquering. There was nothing soft about him. His mouth, his hands, his body when he pulled her against him, were hard and demanding. The swift frisson of fear had her lifting a hand to push against his shoulder. She might as well have tried to move a boulder.

Then the fear turned to an ache. She fisted her hand against him, forced to fight herself now rather than him.

She was taut as a wire. He could feel her nerves sizzle and snap as he clamped her against him. He knew it was wrong, unfair, even despicable, but damn it, he needed to wipe out this fever that continued to burn in him. He needed to convince himself that she was just another woman, that his fantasies of her were only remnants of a boy's foolish dreams.

Then she shuddered. A soft, yielding sound followed.

And her lips parted beneath his in irresistible and avid invitation. Swearing, he plunged, dragging her head back by the hair so that he could take more of what she so mindlessly offered.

Her mouth was a banquet, and he too racked with hunger to stem the greed. He could smell her hair, fresh as rainwater, her skin, seductively musky with heat and labor, and the rich and primitive fragrance of earth newly turned. Each separate scent slammed into his system, pumping through his blood, roaring through his head to churn a need he'd hoped to dispel.

She couldn't breathe, or think. All of the weighty and worrisome cares she carried in her vanished. In their place, rioting sensations sprinted. The tensed ripple of muscle under her fingers, the hot and desperate taste of his mouth, the thunder of her heartbeat that raced with dizzying speed. She was wrapped around him now, her fingers digging in, her body straining, her mouth as urgent and impatient as his.

It had been so long since she had been touched. So long since she had tasted a man's desire on her lips. So long since she had wanted any man. But she wanted now—to feel his hands on her, rough and demanding, to have his body cover hers on the soft, sunny grass. To be wild and willful and wanton until this clawing ache was soothed.

The sheer power of that want ripped through her, tearing through her lips in a sobbing moan.

His fingers were curled into her shirt, had nearly ripped it aside before he caught himself, cursed himself. And released her. Her shallow ragged breaths were both condemnation and seduction as he forced himself to pull away. Her eyes had gone to cobalt and were wide with shock.

Small wonder, he thought in livid self-disgust. The woman had nearly been shoved to the ground and ravished in broad daylight.

Her lashes lowered before he could see the shame.

"I hope you feel better now."

"No." His hands were far from steady, so he curled them into fists. "I don't."

She didn't look at him, couldn't. Nor could she afford to think, just at this moment, of what she had done. To comfort herself she began to spread mulch around the newly planted bush. "If it stays dry, you'll have to water this regularly until it's established."

For a second time, he gripped her hands. This time she jolted. "Aren't you going to belt me?"

Using well-honed control, she relaxed and looked up. There was something in her eyes, something dark and passionate, but her voice was very calm. "There doesn't seem to be much point in that. I'm sure you're of the opinion that a woman like me would be…needy."

"I wasn't thinking about your needs when I kissed you. It was a purely selfish act, Suzanna. I'm good at being selfish."

Because his grip was light, she slipped her hands from under his. "I'm sure you are." She brushed her palms on her thighs before she rose. The only thought in her head was of getting away, but she made herself load the wheelbarrow calmly. Until he gripped her arm and whirled her around.

"What the hell is this?" His eyes were stormy, his voice as rough as his hands. He wanted her to rage at him—needed it to soothe his conscience. "I all but took you on the ground, without giving a hell of a lot of consideration to whether you'd have liked it or not, and now you're going to load up your cart and go away?"

She was very much afraid she would have liked it. That was why it was imperative that she stay very calm and very controlled. "If you want to pick a fight or a casual lover, Holt, you've come to the wrong person. My children are expecting me home, and I'm very tired of being grabbed."

Yes, her voice was calm, he thought, even firm, but her arm was trembling lightly under his hold. There was something here, he realized, some secrets she held behind those sad and beautiful eyes. The same stubbornness that had had him pursuing his gold shield made it essential that he discover them.

"Grabbed in general, or just by me?"

"You're the one doing the grabbing." Her patience was wearing thin. The Calhoun temper was always difficult to control. "I don't like it."

"That's too bad, because I have a feeling I'm going to be doing a lot more of it before we're through."

"Maybe I haven't made myself clear. We are through." She shook loose and grabbed the handles of the wheelbarrow.

He simply put his weight on it to stop her. He wasn't sure if she realized she'd just issued an irresistible challenge. His grin came slowly. "Now you're getting mad."

"Yes. Does that make you feel better?"

"Quite a bit. I'd rather have you claw at me than crawl off like a wounded bird."

"I'm not crawling anywhere," she said between her teeth. "I'm going home."

"You forgot your shovel," he told her, still grinning.

She snatched it up and tossed it into the wheelbarrow with a clatter. "Thanks."

"You're welcome."

He waited until she'd gone about ten feet. "Suzanna."

She slowed but didn't stop, and tossed a look over her shoulder. "What?"

"I'm sorry."

Her temper eased a bit as she shrugged. "Forget it."

"No." He dipped his hands into his pockets and rocked back on his heels. "I'm sorry I didn't kiss you like that fifteen years ago."

Swearing under her breath, she quickened her pace. When she was out of sight, he glanced back at the bush. Yeah, he thought, he was sorry as hell, but planned to make up for lost time.

She needed some time to herself. That wasn't a commodity Suzanna found very often in a house as filled with people as The Towers. But just now, with the moon on the rise and the children in bed, she took a few precious moments alone.

It was a clear night, and the heat of the day had been replaced by a soft breeze that was scented with the sea and roses. From her terrace she could see the dark shadow of the cliffs that always drew her. The distant murmur of water was a lullaby, as sweet as the call of a night bird from the garden.

Tonight it wouldn't ease her into sleep. No matter how tired her body was, her mind was too restless. It didn't seem to matter how often she told herself she had nothing to worry about. Her children were safely tucked into bed, dreaming about the day's adventures. Her sisters were happy. Each one of them had found her place in the world, just as each one of them had found a mate who loved her for who and what she was. Aunt Coco was happy and healthy and looking forward to the day when she would become head chef of The Towers Retreat.

Her family, always Suzanna's chief concern, was content and settled. The Towers, the only real home she'd ever known, was no longer in danger of being sold, but would remain the Calhoun home. It was pointless to worry about the emeralds. The family was doing all that could be done to find the necklace.

If they hadn't been exploring every avenue, she would never have gone to Holt Bradford. Her fingers curled on the stone wall. That, she thought, had been a useless exercise. He was Christian Bradford's grandson, but he didn't feel the connection. It was obvious that the past held no interest for him. He thought only about the moment, about himself, about his own comfort and pleasures.

Catching herself, Suzanna sighed and forced herself to relax her hands. If only he hadn't made her so angry. She despised losing her temper, and it had come dangerously close to breaking loose that day. It was her own fault, and her own problem that something else had broken loose.

Needs. She didn't want to need anyone but her family— the family she could love and depend on and worry about. She'd already learned a painful lesson about needing a man, one man. She didn't intend to repeat it.

He'd kissed her on impulse, she reminded herself. It had been a kind of dare to himself. There had certainly been no affection in it, no softness, no romance. The fact that it had stirred her was strictly chemical. She'd cut herself off from men for more than two years. And the last year or so of her marriage—well, there had been no affection, softness or romance there, either. She'd learned to do without those things when it came to men. She could continue to do without them.

If only she hadn't responded to him so...blatantly. He might as well have knocked her over the head with a club and dragged her into a cave by the hair for all the finesse he'd shown. Yet she had thrown herself into the moment, clinging to him, answering those hard and demanding lips with a fervor she'd never been able to show her own husband.

By doing so, she'd humiliated herself and amused Holt. Oh, the way he had grinned at her at the end had had her steaming for hours afterward. That was her problem, too, she thought now. Just as it was her problem that she could still taste him.

Perhaps she shouldn't be so hard on herself. As embarrassing as the moment had been, it had proved something. She was still alive. She wasn't the cold shell of a woman that Bax had tossed so carelessly aside. She could feel, and want.

Closing her eyes, she pressed a hand to her stomach. Want too much, it seemed. It was like a hunger, and the kiss, like a crust of bread after a long fast, had stirred the juices. She could be glad of that—to feel something again besides remorse and disillusionment. And feeling it, she could control it. Pride would prevent her from avoiding Holt. Just as pride would save her from any new humiliation.

She was a Calhoun, she reminded herself. Calhoun women went down fighting. If she had to deal with Holt again in order to widen the trail to the emeralds, then she would deal with him. She would never, never let herself be dismissed and destroyed by a man again. He hadn't seen the last of her.

"Suzanna, there you are."

Her thoughts scattered as she turned to see her aunt striding through the terrace doors. "Aunt Coco."

"I'm sorry, dear, but I knocked and knocked. Your light was on so I just peeked in."

"That's all right." Suzanna slipped an arm around Coco's sturdy waist. This was a woman she'd loved for most of her life. A woman who had been mother and father to her for more than fifteen years. "I was lost in the night, I guess. It's so beautiful."

Coco murmured an agreement and said nothing for a moment. Of all of her girls, she worried most about Suzanna. She had watched her ride away, a young bride radiant with hope. She had been there when Suzanna had come back, barely four years later, a pale, devastated woman with two small children. In the years since, she'd been proud to see Suzanna gain her feet, devoting herself to the difficult task of single parenthood, working hard, much too hard, to establish her own business.

And she had waited, painfully, for the sad and haunted look that clouded her niece's eyes, to finally fade forever.

"Couldn't you sleep?" Suzanna asked her.

"I haven't even thought about sleep yet." Coco let out a huff of breath. "That woman is driving me out of my mind."

Suzanna managed not to smile. She knew *that woman* was her great-aunt Colleen, the eldest of Bianca's children, and the sister of Coco's father. The rude, demanding and perpetually cranky woman had descended on them a week before. Coco was certain the move had been made with the sole purpose of making her life a misery.

"Did you hear her at dinner?" Tall and stately in her draping caftan, Coco began to pace. Her complaints were issued in an indignant whisper. Colleen might have been well past eighty, her bedroom may have been two dozen feet away, but she had ears like a cat. "The sauce was too rich, the asparagus too soft. The idea of her telling *me* how to prepare coq au vin. I wanted to take that cane and wrap it around her—"

"Dinner was superb, as always," Suzanna soothed. "She has to complain about something, Aunt Coco, otherwise her day wouldn't be complete. And as I recall, there wasn't a crumb left on her plate."

"Quite right." Coco drew in a deep breath, releasing it slowly. "I know I shouldn't let the woman get on my nerves. The fact is, she's always frightened me half to death. And she knows it. If it wasn't for yoga and meditation, I'm sure

I'd have already lost my sanity. As long as she was living on one of those cruise ships, all I had to do was send her an occasional duty letter. But actually living under the same roof." Coco couldn't help it—she shuddered.

"She'll get tired of us soon, and sail off down the Nile or the Amazon or whatever."

"It can't be too soon for me. I'm afraid she's made up her mind to stay until we find the emeralds. Which is what this is all about anyway." Coco calmed herself enough to stand at the wall again. "I was using my crystal to meditate. So soothing, and after an evening with Aunt Colleen—" She broke off because she was clenching her teeth. "In any case, I was just drifting along, when thoughts and images of Bianca filled my head."

"That's not surprising," Suzanne put in. "She's on all of our minds."

"But this was very strong, dear. Very clear. There was such melancholy. I tell you, it brought tears to my eyes." Coco pulled a handkerchief out of her caftan. "Then suddenly, I was thinking of you, and that was just as strong and clear. The connection between you and Bianca was unmistakable. I realized there had to be a reason, and thinking it through, I believe it's because of Holt Bradford." Coco's eyes were shining now with discovery and enthusiasm. "You see, you've spoken to him, you've bridged the gap between Christian and Bianca."

"I don't think you can call my conversations with Holt a bridge to anything."

"No, he's the key, Suzanna. I doubt he understands what information he might have, but without him, we can't take the next step. I'm sure of it."

With a restless move of her shoulders, Suzanna leaned against the wall. "Whatever he understands, he isn't interested."

"Then you have to convince him otherwise." She put a hand on Suzanna's and squeezed. "We need him. Until we find the emeralds, none of us will feel completely safe. The police haven't been able to find that miserable thief, and we don't know what he may try next time. Holt is our only link with the man Bianca loved."

"I know."

"Then you'll see him again. You'll talk to him."

Suzanna looked toward the cliffs, toward the shadows. "Yes, I'll see him again."

I knew she would come back. However unwise, however wrong it might have been, I looked for her every afternoon. On the days she did not come to the cliffs, I would find myself staring up at the peaks of The Towers, aching for her in a way I had no right to ache for another man's wife. On the days she walked toward me, her hair like melted flame, that small, shy smile on her lips, I knew a joy like no other.

In the beginning, our conversations were polite and distant. The weather, unimportant village gossip, art and literature. As time passed, she became more at ease with me. She would speak of her children, and I came to know them through her. The little girl, Colleen, who liked pretty dresses and yearned for a pony. Young Ethan who only wanted to run and find adventure. And little Sean, who was just learning to crawl.

It took no special insight to see that her children were her life. Rarely did she speak of the parties, the musicals, the social gatherings I knew she attended almost nightly. Not at all did she speak of the man she had married.

I admit I wondered about him. Of course, it was common knowledge that Fergus Calhoun was an ambitious and wealthy man, one who had turned a few dollars into an empire during the course of his life. He commanded both respect and fear in the business world. For that I cared nothing.

It was the private man who obsessed me. The man who had the right to call her wife. The man who lay beside her at night, who touched her. The man who knew the texture of her skin, the taste of her mouth. The man who knew how it felt to have her move beneath him in the dark.

I was already in love with her. Perhaps I had been from the moment I had seen her walking with the child through the wild roses.

It would have been best for my sanity if I had chosen another place to paint. I could not. Already knowing I would have no more of her, could have no more than a few hours of conversation, I went back. Again and again.

She agreed to let me paint her. I began to see, as an artist must see, the inner woman. Beyond her beauty, beyond her composure and breeding was a desperately unhappy woman. I wanted to take her in my arms, to demand that she tell me what had put that sad and haunted look in her eyes. But I only painted her. I had no right to do more.

I have never been a patient or a noble man. Yet with her, I found I could be both. Without ever touching me, she changed me. Nothing would be the same for me after that summer—that all too brief summer when she would come, to sit on the rocks and look out to sea.

Even now, a lifetime later, I can walk to those cliffs and see her. I can smell the sea that never changes, and catch the drift of her perfume. I have only to pick a wild rose to remember the fiery lights of her hair. Closing my eyes, I hear the murmur of the water on the rocks below and her voice comes back as clear and as sweet as yesterday.

I am reminded of the last afternoon that first summer,

when she stood beside me, close enough to touch, as distant as the moon.

"We leave in the morning," she said, but didn't look at me. "The children are sorry to go."

"And you?"

A faint smile touched her lips but not her eyes. "Sometimes I wonder if I've lived before. If my home was an island like this. The first time I came here, it was as if I had been waiting to see it again. I'll miss the sea."

Perhaps it was only my own needs that made me think, when she glanced at me, that she would miss me, as well. Then she looked away again and sighed.

"New York is so different, so full of noise and urgency. It's hard to believe such a place exists when I stand here. Will you stay on the island through the winter?"

I thought of the cold and desolate months ahead and cursed fate for taunting me with what I could never have. "My plans change with my mood." I said it lightly, fighting to keep the bitterness out of my voice.

"I envy you your freedom." She turned away then to walk back to where her nearly completed portrait rested on my easel. "And your talent. You've made me more than what I am."

"Less." I had to curl my hands into fists to keep from touching her. "Some things can never be captured with paint and canvas."

"What will you call it?"

"Bianca. Your name is enough."

She must have sensed my feelings, though I tried desperately to hold them in myself. Something came into her eyes as she looked at me, and the look held longer than it should. Then she stepped back, cautiously, like a woman who had wandered too close to the edge of a cliff.

"One day you'll be famous, and people will beg for your work."

I couldn't take my eyes off her, knowing I might never see her again. "I don't paint for fame."

"No, and that's why you'll have it. When you do, I'll remember this summer. Goodbye, Christian."

She walked away from me—for what I thought was the last time—away from the rocks, through the wild grass and the flowers that fight through both for the sun.

Chapter 4

Coco Calhoun McPike didn't believe in leaving things up to chance—particularly when her horoscope that day had advised her to take a more active part in a family matter and to visit an old acquaintance. She felt she could do both by paying an informal call on Holt Bradford.

She remembered him as a dark, hot-eyed boy who had delivered lobster and loitered around the village, waiting for trouble to happen. She also remembered that he had once stopped to change a flat for her while she'd been struggling on the side of the road trying to figure out which end of the jack to put under the bumper. He'd refused—stiffly, she recalled—her offer of payment and had hopped back on his motorcycle and ridden off before she'd properly thanked him.

Proud, defiant, rebellious, she mused as she maneuvered her car into his driveway. Yet, in a grudging sort of way, chivalrous. Perhaps if she was clever—and Coco thought that she was—she could play on all of those traits to get what she wanted.

So this had been Christian Bradford's cottage, she mused. She'd seen it before, of course, but not since she'd known of the connection between the families. She paused for a moment. With her eyes closed she tried to *feel* something. Surely there was some remnant of energy here, something that time and wind hadn't washed away.

Coco liked to consider herself a mystic. Whether it was a true evaluation, or her imagination was ripe, she was certain she did feel some snap of passion in the air. Pleased with it, and herself, she trooped to the house.

She'd dressed very carefully. She wanted to look attractive, of course. Her vanity wouldn't permit otherwise. But she'd also wanted to look distinguished and just the tiniest bit matronly. She felt the old and classic Chanel suit in powder blue worked very well.

She knocked, putting what she hoped was a wise and comforting smile on her face. The wild barking and the steady stream of curses from within had her placing a hand on her breast.

Five minutes out of the shower, his hair dripping and his temper curdled, Holt yanked open the door. Sadie bounded out. Coco squeaked. Good reflexes had Holt snatching the amorous dog by the collar before she could send Coco over the porch railing.

"Oh my." Coco looked from dog to man, juggling the plate of double-fudge brownies. "Oh, goodness. What a very *large* dog. She certainly does look like our Fred, and I'd so hoped he'd stop growing soon. Why you could practically *ride* her if you liked, couldn't you?" She beamed a smile at Holt. "I'm so sorry, have I interrupted you?"

He continued to struggle with the dog, who'd gotten a good whiff of the brownies and wanted her share. Now. "Excuse me?"

"I've interrupted," Coco repeated. "I know it's early, but on days like this I just can't stay in bed. All this sun and twittering birds. Not to mention the sawing and hammering. Do you suppose she'd like one of these?" Without waiting for an answer, Coco took one of the brownies off the plate. "Now you sit and behave."

With what was certainly a grin, Sadie stopped straining, sat and eyed Coco adoringly.

"Good dog." Sadie took the treat politely then padded back into the house to enjoy it. "Well, now." Pleased with the situation, Coco smiled at Holt. "You probably don't remember me. Goodness, it's been years."

"Mrs. McPike." He remembered her, all right, though the last time he'd seen her, her hair had been a dusky blond. It had been ten years, he thought, but she looked younger. She'd either had a first-class face-lift or had discovered the fountain of youth.

"Why, yes. It's so flattering to be remembered by an attractive man. But you were hardly more than a boy the last time. Welcome home." She offered the plate of brownies.

And left him no choice but to accept it and ask her in.

"Thanks." He studied the plate as she breezed inside. Between plants and brownies, the Calhouns were making a habit of bearing gifts. "Is there something I can do for you?"

"To tell you the truth, I've just been dying to see the place. To think this is where Christian Bradford lived and worked." She sighed. "And dreamed of Bianca."

"Well, he lived and worked here anyway."

"Suzanna tells me you're not quite convinced they loved each other. I can appreciate your reluctance to fall right in with the story, but you see, it's a part of my family history. And yours. Oh, what a glorious painting!"

She crossed the room to a misty seascape hung above the

stone fireplace. Even through the haze of fog, the colors were ripe and vivid, as though the vitality and passion were fighting to free themselves from the thin graying curtain. Turbulent whitecaps, the black and toothy edge of rock, the gloom-crowned shadows of islands marooned in a cold, dark sea.

"It's powerful," she murmured. "And, oh, lonely. It's his, isn't it?"

"Yes."

She let out a shaky sigh. "If you'd like to see that view, you've only to walk on the cliffs beneath The Towers. Suzanna walks there, sometimes with the children, sometimes alone. Too often alone." Shaking off the mood, Coco turned back. "My niece seems to feel that you're not particularly interested in confirming Christian and Bianca's relationship, and helping to find the emeralds. I find that difficult to believe."

Holt set the plate aside. "It shouldn't be, Mrs. McPike. But what I told your niece was that if and when I was convinced there had been a connection of any importance, I'd do what I could to help. Which, as I see it, is next to nothing."

"You were a police officer, weren't you?"

Holt hooked his thumbs in his pockets, not trusting the change of subject. "Yeah."

"I have to admit I was surprised when I heard you'd chosen that profession, but I'm sure you were well suited to the job."

The scar on his back seemed to twinge. "I used to be."

"And you'd have solved cases, I suppose."

His lips curved a little. "A few."

"So you'd have looked for clues and followed them up until you found the right answer." She smiled at him. "I always admire the police on television who solve the mystery and tidy everything up before the end of the show."

"Life's not tidy."

On certain men, she thought, a sneer was not at all unattractive. "No, indeed not, but we could certainly use someone on our side who has your experience." She walked back toward him, and she was no longer smiling. "I'll be frank. If I had known what trouble it would cause my family, I might have let the legend of the emeralds die with me. When my brother and his wife were killed, and left their girls in my care, I was also left the responsibility of passing along the story of the Calhoun emeralds—when the time was right. By doing what I consider my duty, I've put my family in danger. I'll do anything in my power, and use anyone I can, to keep them from being hurt. Until those emeralds are found, I can't be sure my family is safe."

"You need the police," he began.

"They're doing what they can. It isn't enough." Reaching out, she put a hand on his. "They aren't personally involved, and can't possibly understand. You can."

Her faith and her obstinate logic made him uneasy. "You're overestimating me."

"I don't think so." Coco held his hand another moment, then gave it a brief squeeze before releasing it. "But I don't mean to nag. I only came so I could add my input to Suzanna's. She has such a difficult time pushing for what she wants."

"She does well enough."

"Well, I'm glad to hear it. But with her work and Mandy's wedding, and everything else that's been going on, I know she hasn't had time to speak with you again for the last couple of days. I tell you, our lives have been turned upside down for the last few months. First C.C.'s wedding, and the renovations, now Amanda and Sloan—and Lilah already setting a date to marry Max." She paused and hoped to look wistful. "If I could only find some nice man for Suzanna, I'd have all my girls settled."

Holt didn't miss the speculative look. "I'm sure she'll take care of that herself when she's ready."

"Not when she doesn't give herself a moment to look. And after what that excuse for a man did to her." She cut herself off there. If she started on Baxter Dumont, it would be difficult to stop. And it would hardly be proper conversation. "Well, in any case, she keeps herself too busy with her business and her children, so I like to keep my eye out for her. You're not married, are you?"

At least no one could accuse her of being subtle, Holt thought, amused. "Yeah. I've got a wife and six kids in Portland."

Coco blinked, then laughed. "It was a rude question," she admitted. "And before I ask another, I'll leave you alone." She started for the door, pleased that he had enough manners to accompany her and open it for her. "Oh, by the way, Amanda's wedding is Saturday, at six. We're holding the reception at the ballroom in The Towers. I'd like for you to come."

The unexpected curve had him hesitating. "I really don't think it's appropriate."

"It's more than appropriate," she corrected. "Our families go back quite a long way, Holt. We'd very much like to have you there." She started toward her car then turned, smiling again. "And Suzanna doesn't have an escort. It seems a pity."

The thief called himself by many names. When he had first come to Bar Harbor in search of the emeralds, he had used the name Livingston and had posed as a successful British businessman. He had only been partially successful and had returned under the guise of Ellis Caufield, a wealthy eccentric. Due to bad luck and his partner's fumbling, he'd had to abandon that particular cover.

His partner was dead, which was only a small inconvenience. The thief now went under the name of Robert Marshall and was developing a certain fondness for this alter ego.

Marshall was lean and tanned and had a hint of a Boston accent. He wore his dark hair nearly shoulder length and sported a drooping mustache. His eyes were brown, thanks to contact lenses. His teeth were slightly bucked. The oral device had cost him a pretty penny, but it had also changed the shape of his jaw.

He was very comfortable with Marshall, and delighted to have signed on as a laborer on The Towers renovation. His references had been forged and had added to his overhead. But the emeralds would be worth it. He intended to have them, whatever the price.

Over the past months they had gone from being a job to an obsession. He didn't just want them. He needed them. He found the risk of working so close to the Calhouns only added spice to the game. He had, in fact, passed within three feet of Amanda when she had come into the west wing to talk to Sloan O'Riley. Neither of them, who had known him only as Livingston, had given him a second glance.

He did his job well, hauling equipment, cleaning up debris. And he worked without complaint. He was friendly with his co-workers, even joining them occasionally for a beer after work.

Then he would go back to his rented house across the bay and plan.

The security at The Towers posed no problem—not when it would be so easy for him to disengage it from the inside.

By working for the Calhouns, he could stay close, he could be certain he would hear about any new developments in their search for the necklace. And with care and skill, he could do some searching on his own.

The papers he had stolen from them had offered no real clue as yet. Unless it came from the letter he'd discovered. One that had been written to Bianca and signed only "Christian." A love letter, Marshall mused as he stacked lumber. It was something he had to look into.

"Hey, Bob. Got a minute?"

Marshall looked up and gave his foreman an affable smile. "Sure, nothing but minutes."

"Well, they need some tables moved into the ballroom for that wedding tomorrow. You and Rick give the ladies a hand."

"Right."

Marshall strolled along, fighting back a trembling excitement at being free to walk through the house. He took his instructions from a flustered Coco, then hefted his end of the heavy hunt table to move it up to the next floor.

"Do you think he'll come?" C.C. asked Suzanna as they finished washing down the glass on the mirrored walls.

"I doubt it."

C.C. brushed back her short cap of black hair as she stood aside to search for streaks. "I don't see why he wouldn't. And maybe if we all gang up on him, he'll break down and join ranks."

"I don't think he's a joiner." Suzanna glanced around and saw the two men struggling in with the table. "Oh, it goes against that wall. Thanks."

"No problem," Rick managed through gritted teeth. Marshall merely smiled and said nothing.

"Maybe if he sees the picture of Bianca and hears the tape

from the interview Max and Lilah had with the maid who used to work here back then, he'll pitch in. He's Christian's only surviving family."

"Hey!" Rick muffled a curse when Marshall bobbled the table.

"I don't think he's big on family feeling," Suzanna put in. "One thing that hasn't changed about Holt Bradford is that he's still a loner."

Holt Bradford. Marshall committed the name to memory before he called across the room. "Is there anything else we can do for you ladies?"

Suzanna glanced over her shoulder with an absent smile. "No, not right now. Thanks a lot."

Marshall grinned. "Don't mention it."

"Some lookers, huh?" Rick muttered as they walked back out.

"Oh, yeah." But Marshall was thinking of the emeralds.

"I tell you, bud, I'd like to—" Rick broke off when two other women and a young boy came to the top of the stairs. He gave them both a big, toothy smile. Lilah gave him a lazy one in return and kept walking.

"Man, oh, man," Rick said with a hand to his heart. "This place is just full of babes."

"Pardon the leers," Lilah said mildly. "Most of them don't bite."

The slim strawberry blonde gave a weak smile. At the moment a couple of leering carpenters were the least of her worries. "I really don't want to get in the way," she began in a soft Southwestern drawl. "I know what Sloan said, but I really think it would be best if Kevin and I checked into a hotel for the night."

"This late in the season, you couldn't check into a tent. And we want you here. All of us. Sloan's family is our family now." Lilah smiled down at the dark-haired boy who was gawking at everything in sight. "It's a wild place, isn't it? Your uncle's making sure it doesn't come crashing down on our heads." She walked into the ballroom.

Suzanna was standing on a ladder, polishing glass, while C.C. sat on the floor, hitting the low spots. Lilah bent to the boy. "I was supposed to be in on this," she whispered. "But I played hooky."

The idea made him laugh, and the laughter, so much like Alex's, had Suzanna glancing over.

She was expecting them. Their arrival had been anticipated for weeks. But seeing them here, knowing who they were, had her nerves jolting.

The woman wasn't just Sloan's sister, nor was the boy just his nephew. A short time before, Suzanna had learned that Megan O'Riley had been her husband's lover, and the boy his child. The woman who was staring at her now, the boy's hand gripped in hers, had been only seventeen when Baxter had charmed her into bed and seduced her with vows of love and promises of marriage. And all the while, he had been planning to marry Suzanna.

Which one of us, Suzanna wondered, had been the other woman?

It didn't matter now, she thought, and she climbed down. Not when she could see the nerves so clearly in Megan O'Riley's eyes, the tension in the set of her body, and the courage in the angle of her chin.

Lilah made introductions so smoothly that an outsider might have thought there was nothing but pleasantries in the ballroom. As Suzanna offered a hand, all Megan could think was that she had overdressed. She felt stiff and foolish in the trim bronze-colored suit, while Suzanna seemed so relaxed and lovely in faded jeans.

This was the woman she had hated for years, for taking away the man she'd loved and stealing the father of her child. Even after Sloan had explained Suzanna's innocence, even knowing the hate had been wasted, Megan couldn't relax.

"I'm so glad to meet you." Suzanna put both hands over Megan's stiff one.

"Thank you." Feeling awkward, Megan drew her hand away. "We're looking forward to the wedding."

"So are we all." After a bracing breath, Suzanna let herself look down at Kevin, the half brother to her children. Her heart melted a little. He was taller than her son, and a full year older. But they had both inherited their father's dark good looks. Unconsciously Suzanna reached out to brush back the lock of hair that fell, the twin of Alex's, over Kevin's brow.

Megan's arm came around his shoulders in an instinctive move of defense. Suzanna let her hand drop to her side.

"It's nice to meet you, Kevin. Alex and Jenny could hardly sleep last night knowing you'd be here today."

Kevin gave her a fleeting smile, then glanced up at his mother. She'd told him he was going to meet his half brother and sister, and he wasn't too sure he was happy about it. He didn't think his mother was, either.

"Why don't we go down and find them?" C.C. put a hand on Suzanna's shoulder, gently rubbing. Megan noted that Lilah had already flanked her sister's other side. She didn't blame them for sticking together against an outsider, and her chin came up to prove it.

"It might be best if we—"

She never got to finish. Alex and Jenny came clattering down the hall to burst into the room, breathless and flushed. "Is he here?" Alex demanded. "Aunt Coco said he was, and we want to see—" He cut himself off, skidding to a halt on the freshly polished floor.

The two boys eyed each other, interested and cautious, like two terriers. Alex wasn't sure he was pleased that his new brother was bigger than he was, but he'd already decided it would be neat to have something besides a sister.

"I'm Alex and this is Jenny," Alex said, taking over introductions. "She's only five."

"Five and a half," Jenny put in, and marched up to Kevin. "And I can beat you up if I have to."

"Jenny, I don't think that'll be necessary." Suzanna spoke mildly, but the lifted brows said it all.

"Well, I could," Jenny muttered, still sizing him up. "But Mom says we have to be nice 'cause we're family."

"Do you know any Indians?" Alex demanded.

"Yeah." Kevin was no longer gripping his mother's hand for dear life. "Lots of them."

"Want to see our fort?" Alex asked.

"Yeah." He sent a pleading glance at his mother. "Can I?"

"Well, I—"

"Lilah and I'll take them out." C.C. gave Suzanna's shoulder a final squeeze.

"They'll be fine," Suzanna assured Megan as her sisters hustled the children along. "Sloan designed the fort, so it's sturdy." She picked up her rag again to run it through her hands. "Does Kevin know?"

"Yes." Megan turned her purse over and over in restless hands. "I didn't want him to meet your children without understanding." She took a deep breath and prepared to launch into the speech she'd prepared. "Mrs. Dumont—"

"Suzanna. This is hard for you."

"I don't imagine it's easy, or comfortable for either of us. I wouldn't have come," she continued, "if it hadn't been so important to Sloan. I love my brother, and I won't do anything to spoil his wedding, but you must see that this is an impossible situation."

"I can see it's a painful one for you. I'm sorry." Her hands lifted then fell. "I wish I had known sooner, about you, about Kevin. It's unlikely that I could have made any difference as far as Bax is concerned, but I wish I had known." She glanced down at the rag she was gripping too tightly, then put it aside. "Megan, I realize that while you were giving birth to Kevin, alone, I was in Europe, honeymooning with Kevin's father. You're entitled to hate me for that."

Megan could only stare and shake her head. "You're nothing like I expected. You were supposed to be cool and remote and resentful."

"It would be hard to resent a seventeen-year-old girl who was betrayed and left alone to raise a child. I wasn't much older than that when I married Bax. I understand how charming he could be, how persuasive. And how cruel."

"I thought we'd live happily ever after," Megan said with a sigh. "Well, I grew up quickly, and I learned fast." She let out another long breath as she studied Suzanna. "I hated you, for having everything I thought I wanted. Even when I'd stopped loving him, it helped get me through to hate you. And I was terrified of meeting you."

"That's something else we have in common."

"I can't believe I'm here, talking to you like this." To relieve her nerves she wandered around the ballroom. "I imagined it so many times all those years ago. I'd face you down, demand my rights." She gave a soft laugh. "Even today, I had a whole speech planned out. It was very sophisticated, very mature—maybe just a little vicious. I didn't want to believe that you hadn't known about Kevin, that you'd been a victim, too. Because it was so much easier to think of myself as the only one who'd been betrayed. Then your children came in." She closed her eyes. "How do you deal with the hurt, Suzanna?"

"I'll let you know when I figure it out."

Smiling a little, Megan glanced out of the window. "It hasn't affected them. Look."

Suzanna walked over. Down in the yard she could see her children, and Megan's son, climbing into the plywood fort.

Holt gave it a lot of thought. Up until the moment when he dragged the suit out of his closet, he'd been certain he wasn't going. What the devil was he supposed to do at a society wedding? He didn't like socializing or making small talk or picking at those tiny little canapés. You never knew what the hell was in them anyway.

He didn't like strangling himself with a tie or having to iron a shirt.

So why was he doing it?

He loosened the hated knot of the tie and frowned at himself in the dusty mirror over the bureau. Because he was an idiot and couldn't resist an invitation to the castle on the cliffs. Because he was twice an idiot and wanted to see Suzanna again.

It had been over a week since they had planted the yellow bush. A week since he'd kissed her. And a week since he'd admitted that one kiss, however turbulent, wasn't going to be enough.

He wanted to get a handle on her and thought the best way was to observe her in the midst of the family she seemed to love so much. He wasn't quite sure if she was the cool and remote princess of his youth, the hot-blooded woman he'd held in his arms or the vulnerable one whose eyes were haunting his dreams.

Holt was a man who liked to know exactly what he was up against, whether it was a suspect, a dinky motor or a woman. Once he had Suzanna pegged, he'd move at his own pace.

He didn't want to admit that she'd gotten to him with her fervent belief in the connection between his grandfather and her ancestor. More, he hated to admit that the visit by Coco McPike had made him feel guilty and responsible.

He wasn't going to the wedding to help anyone, he reminded himself. He wasn't making any commitments. He was going to please himself. This time he didn't have to stop at the kitchen door.

It wasn't a long drive, but he took his time, drawing it out. His first glimpse of The Towers bounced him back a dozen years. It was, as it had always been, a fanciful place, a maze of contrasts. It was built of somber stone, yet it was flanked with romantic towers. From one angle, it seemed formidable, from another graceful. At the moment, there was scaffolding on the west side, but instead of looking unsightly, it simply looked productive.

The sloped lawn was emerald green and guarded by gnarled and dignified trees, dashed with fragile and fragrant flowers. There was already a crowd of cars, and Holt felt foolish handing over the keys to his rusted Chevy to the uniformed valet.

The wedding was to take place on the terrace. Since it was about to begin, Holt kept well to the back of the crowd of people. There was organ music, very stately. He had to force himself not to drag at his tie and light a cigarette. There were a few murmured comments and sighs as the bridesmaids started down a long white runner spread over the lawn.

He barely recognized C.C. as the stunning goddess in the long rose-colored dress. Yeah, the Calhoun girls had always been lookers, he thought, and skimmed his gaze over the woman who walked behind her. Her dress was the color of sea foam, but he hardly noticed. It was the face—the face in the portrait in his grandfather's loft. Holt let out the breath between his teeth. Lilah Calhoun was a dead ringer for her great-grandmother. And Holt wasn't going to be able to deny the connection any longer.

He stuffed his hands into his pockets, wishing he hadn't come after all.

Then he saw Suzanna.

This was the princess of his youthful imagination. Her pale gold hair fell in soft curls to her shoulders under a fingertip veil of misty blue. The dress of the same color flowed around her, skirts billowing in the breeze as she walked. She carried flowers in her hands; more were scattered in her hair. When she passed him, her eyes as soft and dreamy as the dress, he felt a longing so deep, so intense, he could barely keep from speaking her name.

He remembered nothing about the brief and lovely ceremony except how her face had looked when the first tear slipped down her cheek.

As it had been so many years ago, the ballroom was filled with light and music and flowers. As for the food, Coco had outdone herself. The guests were treated to lobster croquettes, steamship round, salmon mousse and champagne by the bucket. Dozens of chairs had been set up in corners and along the mirrored walls, and the terrace doors had been thrown open to allow the guests to spill outside.

Holt held himself apart, sipping the cold, frothy wine and using the time to observe. As his first visit to The Towers, it was quite a show, he decided. Mirrors tossed back the reflection of women in pastel dresses as they stood or sat or were lured out to dance. Music and the scent of gardenias filled the air.

The bride was stunning, tall and regal in white lace, her face luminous as she danced with the big, bronzed man who was now her husband. They looked good together, Holt thought idly. The way people were meant to, he supposed, when they were in love. He saw Coco dancing with a tall, fair man who looked as if he'd been born in a tuxedo.

Then he looked back, as he already had several times, at Suzanna. She was leaning over now, saying something to a dark-haired little boy. Her son? Holt wondered. It was obvious the kid was on the verge of some kind of rebellion. He was shuffling his feet and tugging at the bow tie. He had Holt's sympathy. There couldn't be anything much worse for a kid on a summer evening then being stuck in a mini tuxedo and having to hang around with adults. Suzanna whispered something in his ear, then tugged on it. The boy's mutinous expression turned into a grin.

"Still brooding in corners, I see."

Holt turned and was once again struck by Lilah Calhoun's resemblance to the woman his grandfather had painted. "Just watching the show."

"It is worth the price of a ticket. Max." Lilah laid a hand on the arm of the tall, lanky man at her side. "This is Holt Bradford, whom I was madly in love with for about twenty-four hours some fifteen years ago."

Holt's brow lifted. "You never told me."

"Of course not. At the end of the day I decided I didn't want to be in love with the surly, dangerous sort after all. This is Max Quartermain, the man I'm going to love for the rest of my life."

"Congratulations." Holt took Max's offered hand. Firm grip, Holt mused, steady eyes and a slightly embarrassed smile. "You're the teacher, right?"

"I was. And you're Christian Bradford's grandson."

"That's right," Holt agreed, and his voice had cooled.

"Don't worry, we're not going to hound you as long as you're a guest." Studying him, Lilah ran a fingertip around the rim of her glass. "We'll do that later. I'll have Max show you the scar he got while we were having our little publicity stunt."

"Lilah." Max's voice was soft with an underlying command.

Lilah merely shrugged and sipped champagne. "You remember C.C." She gestured as her sister joined them.

"I remember a gangly kid with engine grease on her face." He relaxed enough to smile. "You look good."

"Thanks. My husband, Trent. Holt Bradford."

It was Coco's dance partner, Holt noted as the two men summed each other up during the polite introductions.

"And the bride and groom," Lilah announced, toasting the couple before she drank again.

"Hello, Holt." Though she was still glowing, Amanda's eyes were steady and watchful. "I'm glad you could come." As she introduced Sloan, Holt realized he'd been surrounded quite neatly. They didn't press. No, the emeralds were never mentioned. But they'd joined ranks, he thought, in a solid wall of determination he had to admire, even as he resented it.

"What is this, a family meeting?" Suzanna hurried up. "You're supposed to be mingling, not huddling in a corner. Oh. Holt." Her smile wavered a bit. "I didn't know you were here."

"Your aunt invited me."

"Yes, I know, but—" She broke off and put her hostess's smile back in place. "I'm glad you could make it."

Like hell, he thought and lifted his glass. "It's been… interesting so far."

At some unspoken signal, her family drifted away, leaving them alone in the corner beside a tub of gardenias. "I hope they didn't make you uncomfortable."

"I can handle it."

"That may be, but I wouldn't want you badgered at my sister's wedding."

"But it doesn't bother you if it's someplace else."

Before she could retort, small impatient hands were tugging at her skirt. "Mom, when can we have the cake?"

"When Amanda and Sloan are ready to cut it." She skimmed a finger down Alex's nose.

"But we're hungry."

"Then go over to the buffet table and stuff your little face."

He giggled at that but didn't relent. "The cake—"

"Is for later. Alex, this is Mr. Bradford."

Not particularly interested in meeting another adult who would pat his head and tell him what a big boy he was, Alex pouted up at Holt. When he was offered a very manly handshake, he perked up a bit.

"Are you the policeman?"

"I used to be."

"Did you ever get shot in the head?"

Holt muffled a chuckle. "No, sorry." For some reason he felt as though he'd lost face. "I did catch one in the leg once."

"Yeah?" Alex brightened. "Did it bleed and bleed?"

He had to grin. "Buckets."

"Wow. Did you shoot lots of bad guys?"

"Dozens of them."

"Okay! Wait a minute." He raced off.

"I'm sorry," Suzanna began. "He's going through a murder-and-mayhem stage."

"I'm sorry I didn't get shot in the head."

She laughed. "Oh, that's all right, you made up for it by telling him you shot lots of bad guys." She wondered, but didn't ask, if he'd been telling the truth.

"Suzanna, would—"

"Hey." Alex skidded to a halt, with two other children in tow. "I told them how you got shot in the leg."

"Did it hurt?" Jenny wanted to know.

"Some."

"It bled and bled," Alex said with relish. "This is Jenny, she's my sister. And this is my brother, Kevin."

Suzanna wanted to kiss him. She wanted to pull Alex up in her arms and smother him with kisses for accepting so easily what adults had made so complicated. Instead, she brushed a hand over his hair.

The three of them bombarded Holt with questions until Suzanna called a halt. "I think that's enough gore for now."

"But, Mom—"

"But, Alex," she mimicked. "Why don't you go get some punch?"

Since it seemed like a pretty good idea, they trooped off.

"Quite a brood," Holt murmured, then looked back at Suzanna. "I thought you had two kids."

"I do."

"Seems to me I just saw three."

"Kevin is my ex-husband's son," she said coolly. "Now, if you'll excuse me."

He put a hand on her arm. Another secret, he thought, and decided he would dig up that answer, as well. Not now. Now he was going to do something he'd thought about doing since he'd seen her walk down the white satin runner in the floaty blue dress.

"Would you like to dance?"

Chapter 5

She couldn't quite relax in his arms. She told herself it was foolish, that the dance was just a casual social gesture. But his body was so close, so firm, the hand at her back so possessive. It reminded her too clearly of the moment he had pulled her against him to send her soaring into a kiss.

"It's quite a house," he said, and gave himself the pleasure of feeling her hair against his cheek. "I always wondered what it was like inside."

"I'll have to give you a tour sometime."

He could feel her heart thud against his. Experimenting, he skimmed his hand up her spine. The rhythm quickened. "I'm surprised you haven't been back to nag me."

There was annoyance in her eyes as she drew her head back. "I have no intention of nagging you."

"Good." He brushed his thumb over her knuckles and felt her tremble. "But you will come back."

"Only because I promised Aunt Coco."

"No." He increased the pressure on her spine and brought her an inch closer. "Not only because of that. You wonder what it would be like, the same way I've wondered half my life."

A little line of panic followed his fingers up her spine. "This isn't the place."

"I choose my own ground." His lips hovered bare inches from hers. He watched her eyes darken and cloud. "I want you, Suzanna."

Her heart had leaped up to throb in her throat so that her voice was husky and uneven. "Am I supposed to be flattered?"

"No. You'd be smart to be scared. I won't make things easy on you."

"What I am," she said with more control, "is uninterested."

His lips curved. "I could kiss you now and prove you wrong."

"I won't have a scene at my sister's wedding."

"Fine, then come to my place tomorrow morning."

"No."

"All right then." He lowered his head. She turned hers away so that his lips brushed her temple, then nibbled on her ear.

"Stop it. My children—"

"Should hardly be shocked to see a man kiss their mother." But he did stop, because his knees were going weak. "Tomorrow morning, Suzanna. There's something I need to show you. Something of my grandfather's."

She looked up again, struggling to steady her pulse. "If this is some sort of game, I don't want to play."

"No game. I want you, and this time I'll have you. But there is something of my grandfather's you have the right to see. Unless you're afraid to be alone with me."

Her spine stiffened. "I'll be there."

* * *

The next morning, Suzanna stood on the terrace with Megan. They watched their children race across the lawn with Fred.

"I wish you could stay longer."

With a half laugh, Megan shook her head. "I'm surprised to say I wish I could, too. I have to be back at work tomorrow."

"You and Kevin are welcome here anytime. I want you to know that."

"I do." Megan shifted her gaze to meet Suzanna's. There was a sadness there she understood, though she rarely allowed herself to feel it. "If you and the kids decide to visit Oklahoma, you've got a home with us. I don't want to lose touch. Kevin needs to know this part of his family."

"Then we won't." She stooped to pick up a rose petal that had drifted from a bouquet to float to the terrace. "It was a beautiful wedding. Sloan and Mandy are going to be happy—and we'll have nieces and nephews in common."

"God, the world's a strange place." Megan took Suzanna's hand. "I'd like to think we can be friends, not only for our children's sakes or for Sloan and Amanda."

Suzanna smiled. "I think we already are."

"Suzanna!" Coco signaled from the kitchen door. "A phone call for you." She was chewing her lip when Suzanna reached her. "It's Baxter."

"Oh." Suzanna felt the simple pleasure of the morning drain. "I'll take it in the other room."

She braced herself as she walked down the hallway. He couldn't hurt her any longer, she reminded herself. Not physically, not emotionally. She slipped into the library, took a long, steadying breath, then picked up the phone.

"Hello, Bax."

"I suppose you considered it sly to keep me waiting on the phone."

And there it was again, she thought, that clipped, critical tone that had once made her shiver. Now she only sighed. "I'm sorry. I was outside."

"Digging in the garden, I suppose. Are you still pretending to make a living pruning rosebushes?"

"I'm sure you didn't call to see how my business is going."

"Your business, as you call it, is nothing to me but a slight embarrassment. Having my ex-wife selling flowers on the street corner—"

"Clouds your image, I know." She passed a hand over her hair. "We're not going to go through that again, are we?"

"Quite the little shrew these days." She heard him murmur something to someone else, then laugh. "No, I didn't call to remind you you're making a fool of yourself. I want the children."

Her blood turned to ice. "What?"

The shaky whisper pleased him enormously. "I believe it states quite clearly in the custody agreement that I'm entitled to two weeks during the summer. I'll pick them up on Friday."

"You...but you haven't—"

"Don't stammer, Suzanna. It's one of your more annoying traits. If you didn't comprehend, I'll repeat. I'm exercising my parental rights. I'll pick the children up on Friday, at noon."

"You haven't seen them in nearly a year. You can't just pick them up and—"

"I most certainly can. If you don't choose to honor the agreement, I'll simply take you back to court. It isn't legal or wise for you to try to keep the children from me."

"I've never tried to keep them from you. You haven't bothered with them."

"I have no intention of rearranging my schedule to suit

you. Yvette and I are going to Martha's Vineyard for two weeks, and have decided to take the children. It's time they saw something of the world besides the little corner you hide in."

Her hands were shaking. She gripped the receiver more tightly. "You didn't even send Alex a card on his birthday."

"I don't believe there's anything in the agreement about birthday cards," he said shortly. "But it is very specific on visitation rights. Feel free to check with your lawyer, Suzanna."

"And if they don't want to go?"

"The choice isn't theirs—or yours." But his, he thought, which was exactly as he preferred it. "I wouldn't try to poison them against me."

"I don't have to," she murmured.

"See that they're packed and ready. Oh, and Suzanna, I've been reading quite a bit about your family lately. Isn't it odd that there wasn't any mention of an emerald necklace in our settlement agreement?"

"I didn't know it existed."

"I wonder if the courts would believe that."

She felt tears of frustration and rage fill her eyes. "For God's sake, didn't you take enough?"

"It's never enough, Suzanna, when you consider how very much you disappointed me. Friday," he said. "Noon." And hung up.

She was trembling. Even when she lowered carefully into a chair, she couldn't stop. She felt as though she'd been jerked back five years, into that terrible helplessness. She couldn't stop him. She'd read the custody agreement word for word before signing it, and he was within his rights. Oh, technically she could have demanded more notice, but that would only postpone the inevitable. If Bax had made up his mind, she couldn't change it. The more she fought, the more she argued, the harder he would twist the knife.

And the more difficult he would make it on the children.

Her babies. Rocking, she covered her face with her hands. It was only for a short time—she could survive it. But how would they feel when she shipped them off, giving them no choice?

She would have to make it sound like an adventure. With the right tone, the right words, she could convince them this was something they wanted to do. Pressing her lips together, she rose. But not now. She would never be able to convince them of anything but her own turmoil if she spoke with them now.

"Damn place is like Grand Central Station." The familiar thump of a cane nearly had Suzanna sinking back into the chair again. "People coming and going, phone ringing. You'd think nobody ever got married before." Suzanna's great-aunt Colleen, her magnificent white hair swept back and diamonds glittering at her ears, stopped in the doorway. "I'll have you know those little monsters of yours tracked dirt up the stairs."

"I'm sorry."

Colleen only huffed. She enjoyed complaining about the children, because she had grown so fond of them. "Hooligans. The one blessed day of the week there's not hammering and sawing every minute, and there's packs of children shrieking through the house. Why the hell aren't they in school?"

"Because it's July, Aunt Colleen."

"Don't see what difference that makes." Her frown deepened as she studied Suzanna. "What's the matter with you, girl?"

"Nothing. I'm just a little tired."

"Tired my foot." She recognized the look. She'd seen it

before—the weary desperation and helplessness—in her own mother's eyes. "Who was that on the phone?"

Suzanna's chin came up. "That, Aunt Colleen, is none of your business."

"Well, you've climbed on your high horse." And it pleased her. She preferred that her grandniece bite back rather than take a slap. Besides, she'd just badger Coco until she learned what was going on.

"I have an appointment," Suzanna said as steadily as possible. "Would you mind telling Aunt Coco that I've gone out?"

"So now I'm a messenger boy. I'll tell her, I'll tell her," Colleen muttered, waving her cane. "It's high time she fixed me some tea."

"Thank you. I won't be long."

"Go out and clear your head," Colleen said as Suzanna started by. "There's nothing a Calhoun can't handle."

Suzanna sighed and kissed Colleen's thin cheek. "I hope you're right."

She didn't allow herself to think. She left the house and climbed into her pickup, telling herself she would handle whatever needed to be handled—but she would calm herself first.

She had become very skilled at pulling in her emotions. A woman couldn't sit in a courtroom with her children's futures hanging in the balance and not learn control.

It was possible to feel panic or rage or misery and function normally. When she was certain she could, she would speak with the children.

There was an appointment to be kept. Whatever Holt had to show her might distract her enough to help her keep control of her emotions until they leveled.

She thought she was calm when she pulled up at his

house. As she got out of the truck, she combed a hand through her windblown hair. When she realized she was gripping her keys too hard she deliberately relaxed her fingers. She slid the keys into her pocket and knocked.

The dog sent up a din. Holt had one hand on Sadie's collar as he opened the door. "You made it. I thought I might have to come after you."

"I told you I'd be here." She stepped inside. "What do you have to show me?"

When he was sure Sadie would do no more than sniff and whine for attention, he released her. "Your aunt showed a lot more interest in the cottage."

"I'm a little pressed for time." After giving the dog an absent pat, she stuck her hands into the pockets of her baggy cotton slacks. "It's very nice." She glanced around, took in nothing. "You must be comfortable here."

"I get by," he said slowly, his eyes keen on her face. There wasn't a trace of color in her cheeks. Her eyes were too dark. He'd wanted to make her aware of him, maybe uncomfortably aware, but he hadn't wanted to make her sick with fear at the thought of seeing him again.

"You can relax, Suzanna." His voice was curt and dismissive. "I'm not going to jump you."

Her nerves stretched taut on the thin wire of control. "Can we just get on with this?"

"Yeah, we can get on with it, as soon as you stop standing there as if you're about to be chained and beaten. I haven't done anything—yet—to make you look at me that way."

"I'm not looking at you in any way."

"The hell you're not. Damn it, your hands are shaking." Furious, he grabbed them. "Stop it," he demanded. "I'm not going to hurt you."

"It has nothing to do with you." She yanked her hands

away, hating the fact that she couldn't stop them from trembling. "Why should you think that anything I feel, any way I look depends on you? I have my own life, my own feelings. I'm not some weak, terrified woman who falls apart because a man raises his voice. Do you really think I'm afraid of you? Do you really think you could hurt me after—"

She broke off, appalled. She'd been shouting, and the furious tears were still burning her eyes. Her stomach was clenched so tight she could hardly breathe. Sadie had retreated to a corner and sat quivering. Holt stood a foot away, staring at her, eyes narrowed in speculation.

"I have to go," she managed, and bolted for the door. His hand slapped the wood and held it shut. "Let me go." When her voice broke, she bit down on her lip. She struggled with the door then whirled on him, eyes blazing. "I said let me go."

"Go ahead," he said with surprising calm, "take a punch at me. But you're not going anywhere while you're churned up like this."

"If I'm churned up, it's my own business. I told you, this has nothing to do with you."

"Okay, so you're not going to hit me. Let's try another release valve." He put his hands firmly on either side of her face and covered her mouth with his.

It wasn't a kiss meant to soothe or comfort. It did neither. This was raw and turbulent emotion and matched her own feelings completely.

Her arms were caught between them, her hands still fisted. Her body trembled; her skin heated. At the first flicker of response, he dived into the rough, desperate kiss until he was certain the only thing she was thinking about was him.

Then he took a moment longer, to please himself. She was a volcano waiting to erupt, a storm ready to blow. Her pent-up passion packed a punch more stunning than her fist could have. He intended to be around for the explosion, but he could wait.

When he released her, she leaned back against the door, her eyes closed, breath hitching. Watching her, he realized he'd never seen anyone fight so hard for control.

"Sit down." She shook her head. "All right, stand." With a dismissive shrug, he moved away to light a cigarette. "Either way you're going to tell me what set you off."

"I don't want to talk to you."

He sat on the arm of a chair and blew out a stream of smoke. "Lots of people haven't wanted to talk to me. But I usually find out what I want to know."

She opened her eyes. They were dry now, which relieved him considerably. "Is this an interrogation?"

With another shrug, he brought the cigarette to his lips again. It wouldn't do her any good if he caved in and offered soft words. He wasn't even sure he had them. "It can be."

She thought about pulling the door open and leaving. But he would only stop her. She'd learned the hard way that there were some battles a woman couldn't win.

"It isn't worth it," she said wearily. "I shouldn't have come while I was upset, but I thought I had gotten myself under control."

"Upset about what?"

"It isn't important."

"Then it shouldn't be a problem to tell me."

"Bax called. My ex-husband." To comfort herself she began to roam the room.

Holt studied the tip of his cigarette, reminding himself that jealousy was out of place. "Looks like he can still stir you up."

"One phone call. One, and I'm back under his thumb." There was a bitterness in her voice he hadn't expected from her. He said nothing. "There's nothing I can do. Nothing. He's going to take the children for two weeks. I can't stop him."

Holt let out an impatient breath. "For God's sake, is that what all this hysteria's about? So the kids go off with Daddy for a couple of weeks." Disgusted, he crushed out his cigarette. And to think he'd been worried about her. "Save the vindictive-wife routine, babe. He's got a right."

"Oh yes, he's got the right." Her voice shook with an emotion so deep that Holt's head snapped up again. "Because it says so on a piece of paper. And he was there when they were conceived, so that makes him their father. Of course, that doesn't mean he has to love them, or worry about them or struggle to raise them without malice. It doesn't mean he has to remember Christmas or birthdays. It's just as Bax told me on the phone. There's nothing in the custody agreement that obligates him to send birthday cards. But it does obligate me to turn the children over to him when he has the whim."

There were tears threatening again, but she refused them. Tears in front of a man never brought anything but humiliation. "Do you think this is about me? He can't hurt me anymore. But my children don't deserve to be used so that he can try to pay me back for being so much less than he wanted."

Holt felt something hot and lethal spread in his gut. "He did a good job on you, didn't he?"

"That isn't the point. Alex and Jenny are the point. Somehow I have to convince them that the father who hasn't bothered to contact them in months, who could barely tolerate them when they lived under the same roof, is going to take them on a wonderful two-week vacation." Suddenly tired, she pushed her hands through her hair. "I didn't come here to talk about this."

"Yes, you did." Calmer, Holt lit another cigarette. If he didn't do something with his hands, he was going to touch her again, and he wasn't sure either of them could handle it. "I'm not family, so I'm safe. You can dump on me and figure I won't lose any sleep over it."

She smiled a little. "Maybe you're right. Sorry."

"I didn't ask for an apology. How do the kids feel about him?"

"He's a stranger."

"Then they probably don't have any preset expectations. Seems to me they might think of the whole thing as an adventure—and that you're letting him push your buttons. If he is using them to get to you, he hit a bull's-eye."

"I'd already come to those same conclusions myself. I needed to vent some excess frustration." She tried a smile again. "Usually I just pull some weeds."

"I think kissing me worked better."

"It was different anyway."

He tapped out his cigarette and rose. The hell with what they could handle. "Is that the best description you can come up with?"

"Off the top of my head. Holt," she began when he slid his arms around her.

"Yeah?" He nipped at her chin, then her mouth.

"I don't want to be held." But she did, too much.

"That's too bad." His arms tightened, bringing her closer.

"You asked me to come here so you could…" She made a little sound of distress when he closed his teeth over her earlobe. "You could show me something of your grandfather's."

"That's right." Her skin smelled like the air high on the cliffs—laced with the sea and wildflowers and hot summer sunlight. "I also asked you here so I could get my hands on you again. We'll just take one thing at a time."

"I don't want to get involved." But even as she said it, her mouth was moving to meet his.

"Me, either." He changed the angle and sucked on her bottom lip.

"This is just—oh—chemistry." Her fingers tangled in his hair.

"You bet." His rough-palmed hands slipped under her shirt to explore.

"It can't go anywhere."

"It already has."

He was right about that, as well. For one brief moment she let herself fall into the kiss, into the heat. She needed something, someone. If she couldn't have comfort or compassion, she would take desire. But the more she took, the more her body strained for something just out of reach. Something she couldn't afford to want or need again.

"This is too fast," she said breathlessly, and struggled away. "I'm sorry, I realize it must seem as though I'm sending you mixed signals."

He was watching her eyes, just her eyes, as his body pulsed. "I think I can sort them out."

"I don't want to start something I won't be able to finish." She moistened her lips still warm from his. "And I have too many responsibilities, too much to worry about right now to even think about having…"

"An affair?" he finished. "You're going to have to think about it." With his eyes still on hers, he gathered her hair in his hand. "Go ahead, take a few days. I can afford to be patient as long as I get what I want. And I want you."

Nerves skittered along her spine. "Just because I find you attractive, physically, doesn't mean I'm going to jump into bed with you."

"I don't much care whether you jump, crawl or have to

be dragged. We can decide on the method later." Before she could think of a name to call him, he grinned, kissed her then stepped back. "Now that that's settled, I'll take you up and show you the portrait."

"If you think it's settled because you—what portrait?"

"You take a look, then tell me."

He led the way up into the loft. Torn between curiosity and fury, Suzanna followed him. The only thing she was certain of at the moment was that since she'd met Holt Bradford again, her emotions had been on a roller coaster. All she wanted out of life was a nice smooth, uneventful ride.

"He worked up here."

The simple statement captured her attention and her interest. "Did you know him well?"

"I don't think anyone did." Holt moved over to open a tilt-out window. "He came and went pretty much as he pleased. He'd come back here for a few days, or a few months. I'd sit up here sometimes and watch him work. If he got tired of me hanging around, he'd send me out with the dog, or into the village for ice cream."

"There's still paint on the floor." Unable to resist, Suzanna bent down to touch. She glanced up, met Holt's eyes and understood.

He'd loved his grandfather. These splotches of paint, more than the cabin itself, were memories. She reached a hand out for his, rising when their fingers linked. Then she saw the portrait.

The canvas was tilted against the wall, its frame old and ornate. The woman looked back at her, with eyes full of secrets and sadness and love.

"Bianca," Suzanna said, and let her own tears come. "I knew he must have painted her. He'd have had to."

"I wasn't certain until I saw Lilah yesterday."

"He never sold it," Suzanna murmured. "He kept it, because it was all he had left of her."

"Maybe." He wasn't entirely comfortable that the exact thought had occurred to him. "I've got to figure there was something between them. I don't see how that helps you get any closer to the emeralds."

"But you'll help."

"I said I would."

"Thank you." She turned to face him. Yes, he would help, she thought. He wouldn't break his word no matter how much it annoyed him to keep it.

"The first thing I have to ask you, is if you'll bring the portrait to The Towers so my family can see it. It would mean a great deal to them."

At Suzanna's insistence, they took Sadie as well. She rode in the back of the pickup, grinning into the wind. When they arrived at The Towers, they saw Lilah and Max sitting out on the lawn. Fred, spotting the truck, tore across the yard, then came to a stumbling halt when Sadie leaped nimbly out of the back.

Body aquiver, he approached her. The dogs gave each other a thorough sniffing over. With a flick of her tail, Sadie pranced across the yard. She sent Fred one come-hither look over her shoulder that had him scrambling after her.

"Looks like love at first sight for old Fred," Lilah commented as she walked with Max to the truck. "We wondered where you'd gone." She ran a hand down Suzanna's arm, letting her know without words that she knew about the call from Bax.

"Are the kids around?"

"No, they went into the village with Megan and her parents to help Kevin pick out some souvenirs before they leave."

With a nod, Suzanna took her hand. "There's something you have to see." Stepping back, she gestured. Through the open door of the truck, Lila saw the painting. Her fingers tightened on her sister's.

"Oh, Suze."

"I know."

"Max, can you see?"

"Yes." Gently he kissed the top of her head and looked at the portrait of a woman who was the double for the one he loved. "She was beautiful. This is a Bradford." He glanced at Holt with a shrug. "I've been studying your grandfather's work for the past couple of weeks."

"You've had this all along," Lilah began.

Holt let the accusation in the tone roll off him. "I didn't know it was Bianca until I saw you yesterday."

She subsided, studying his face. "You're not as nasty as you'd like people to think. Your aura's much too clear."

"Leave Holt's aura alone, Lilah," Suzanna said with a laugh. "I want Aunt Coco to see this. Oh, I wish Sloan and Mandy hadn't left on their honeymoon."

"They'll only be gone two weeks," Lilah reminded her.

Two weeks. Suzanna struggled to keep the smile in place as Holt carried the portrait inside.

The moment she saw it, Coco wept. But that was only to be expected. Holt had propped the painting on the love seat in the parlor, and Coco sat in the wing chair, drenching her handkerchief.

"After all this time. To have part of her back in this house."

Lilah touched her aunt's shoulder. "Part of her has always been in the house."

"Oh, I know, but to be able to look at her." She sniffled. "And see you."

"He must have loved her so much." Damp eyed, C.C. rested

her head on Trent's shoulder. "She looks just as I imagined her, just as I knew she looked that night when I felt her."

Holt kept his hands in his pocket. "Look, sentiment and séances aside, it's the emeralds you need. If you want my help, then I need to know everything."

"Séance." Coco dried her eyes. "We should hold another one. We'll hang the portrait in the dining room. With that to focus on we're bound to be successful. I've got to check the astrological charts." She got up and hurried out of the room.

"And she's off and running," Suzanna murmured.

Trent nodded. "Not to discredit Coco, but it might be best if I filled in Holt in a more conventional way."

"I'll make some coffee." Suzanna sent one last glance at the portrait before heading for the kitchen.

There wasn't so very much Trent could tell him, she thought as she ground beans. Holt already knew about the legend, the research they'd done, the danger her sisters had faced. It was possible that he might make more of it, with his training, than they had. But would he care, even a fraction of the amount her family did?

She understood that emotional motivation could change lives. And that without it, nothing worthwhile could be accomplished.

He had passion. But could his passions run deeper than a physical need? Not for her, she assured herself, measuring the coffee carefully. She'd meant what she'd said about not wanting to become involved. She couldn't afford to love again.

She was afraid he was right about an affair. If she couldn't be strong enough to resist him, she hoped she could be strong enough to hold her heart and her body separate. It couldn't be wrong to need to be touched and wanted. Perhaps by giving herself to him, in a physical way, she could prove to herself that she wasn't a failure as a woman.

God, she wanted to feel like a woman again, to experience that rush of pleasure and release. She was nearly thirty, she thought, and the only man with whom she'd been intimate had found her wanting. How much longer could she go on wondering if he was right?

She jolted when hands came down on her shoulders.

Slowly, aware of how easily she paled, Holt turned her to face him. "Where were you?"

"Oh. Up to my ears weeding pachysandra."

"That's a pretty good lie if you'd put more flare into it." But he let it go. "I'm going to run down and talk with Lieutenant Koogar. Rain check the coffee."

"All right, I'll drive you down."

"I'm hitching a ride with Max and Trent."

Her brow lifted. "Men only, I take it."

"Sometimes it works better that way." He rubbed a thumb over the line between her brows in a gentle gesture that surprised them both. Catching himself, he dropped his hand again. "You worry too much. I'll be in touch."

"Thank you. I won't forget what you're doing for us."

"Forget it." He hauled her against him and kissed her until she went limp. "I'd rather you remember that."

He strode out, and she sank weakly into a chair. She wouldn't have any choice but to remember it.

Chapter 6

He wasn't playing Good Samaritan, Holt assured himself. After getting a clearer handle on the situation, he was doing what he felt was best. Somebody had to keep an eye on her until Livingston was under wraps. The best way to keep an eye on her was to stick close.

Swinging into the graveled lot, he pulled up next to her pickup. He saw that she was outside the shop with customers, so amused himself by roaming around.

He'd driven by Island Gardens before but had never stopped in. There hadn't been any reason to. There were a lot of thriving blossoms crowded on wooden tables or sitting in ornamental pots. Though he couldn't tell one from the other, he could appreciate their appeal. Or maybe it was the fact that the air smelled like Suzanna.

It was obvious she knew what she was doing here, he reflected. There was a tidiness to the place, enhanced by a breezy informality that invited browsers to browse even as it tempted them to buy.

Colorful pictures were set up here and there, describing certain flowers, their planting instructions and maintenance. Along the side of the main building were stacks of fifty- and hundred-pound bags of planting medium and mulch.

He was looking over a tray of snapdragons when he heard a rustle in the bush behind him. He tensed automatically, and his fingers jerked once toward the weapon he no longer wore. Letting out a quiet breath, he cursed himself. He had to get over this reaction. He wasn't a cop anymore, and no one was likely to spring at his back with an eight-inch buck knife.

He turned his head slightly and spotted the young boy crouched behind a display of peonies. Alex grinned and popped up. "I got you!" He danced gleefully around the peonies. "I was a pygmy and I zapped you with my poison blow dart."

"Lucky for me I'm immune to pygmy poison. If it'd been Ubangi poison, I would've been a goner. Where's your sister?"

"In the greenhouse. Mom gave us seeds and stuff, but I got bored. It's okay for me to come out here," he said quickly, knowing how fast adults could make things tough for you. "As long as I don't go near the street or knock over anything."

He wasn't about to give the kid a hard time. "Have you killed many customers today?"

"It's pretty slow. 'Cause it's Monday, Mom says. That's why we can come to work with her and Carolanne can have the day off."

"You like coming here?"

Holt wasn't sure how it had happened, but he and the boy were walking among the flats of flowers, and Alex's hand was in his.

"Sure, it's neat. We get to plant things. Like, see those?" He pointed at an edging of multicolored flowers that sprang up beside the gravel. "Those are zinnias, and I planted them myself, so I get to water them and stuff. Sometimes we get to carry things to the car for people, and they give you quarters."

"Sounds like a good deal."

"And Mom closes up at lunchtime and we walk down the street and get pizza and play the video games. We get to come almost every Monday. Except—" He broke off and kicked at the gravel.

"Except what?"

"Next week we'll have to be on vacation, and Mom won't come."

Holt looked down at the boy's bent head and wondered what the hell to do. "I, ah, guess she's pretty busy here."

"Carolanne or somebody could work, and she could come. But she won't."

"Don't you figure she'd go with you if she could?"

"I guess." Alex kicked at the gravel again and, when Holt didn't scold, kicked a third time. "We have to go to somebody named Martha's yard, with my father and his new wife. Mom says it'll be fun, and we'll go to the beach and have ice cream."

"Sounds pretty good."

"I don't want to go. I don't see how come I have to. I want to go to Disney World with Mom."

When the little voice broke, Holt let out a deep breath and crouched down. "It's tough having to do things you don't want to. I guess you'll have to look after Jenny while you're gone."

Alex shrugged and sniffled. "I guess. She's scared to go. But she's only five."

"She'll be okay with you. Tell you what, I'll look after your mom while you're gone."

"Okay." Feeling better, Alex wiped his nose with the back of his hand. "Can I see on your leg where they shot you?"

"Sure." Holt pointed to a scar about six inches above his kneecap on his left leg.

"Wow." Since Holt didn't seem to mind, Alex ran a fingertip over it. "I guess since you were a policeman and all, you'll take good care of Mom."

"Sure I will."

Suzanna wasn't sure what she felt when she saw Holt and her son, dark heads bent close. But she knew something warm stirred when Holt lifted a hand and brushed it through Alex's hair.

"Well, what's all this?"

Both males looked over then back at each other to exchange a quick and private look before Holt rose. "Man talk," he said, and gave Alex's hand a squeeze.

"Yeah." Alex pushed out his chest. "Man talk."

"I see. Well, I hate to interrupt, but if you want pizza, you'd better go wash your hands."

"Can he come?" Alex asked.

"His name," Suzanna said, "is Mr. Bradford."

"His name is Holt." Holt sent Alex a wink and got a grin in return.

"Can he?"

"We'll see."

"She says that a lot," Alex confided, then raced off to find his sister.

"I suppose I do." Suzanna sighed then turned back to Holt. "What can I do for you?"

She was wearing her hair loose, with a little blue cap over it that made her look about sixteen. Holt suddenly felt as foolish and awkward as a boy asking for his first date.

"Do you still need part-time help?"

"Yes, without any luck." She began to pinch off begonias. "All the high school and college kids are set for the summer."

"I can give you about four hours a day."

"What?"

"Maybe five," he continued as she stared at him. "I've got a couple of repair jobs, but I call my own hours."

"You want to work for me?"

"As long as I only have to haul and plant the things. I ain't selling flowers."

"You can't be serious."

"I mean it. I won't sell them."

"No, I mean about working for me at all. You've already started up your own business, and I can't afford to pay more than minimum wage."

His eyes went very dark, very fast. "I don't want your money."

Suzanna blew the hair out of her eyes. "Now, I am confused."

"Look, I figured we could trade off. I'll do some of the heavy work for you, and you can fix up my yard some."

Her smile bloomed slowly. "You'd like me to fix up your yard?"

Women always made things complicated, he thought and stuffed his hands into his pockets. "I don't want you to go crazy or anything. A couple more bushes maybe. Now do you want to make a deal or don't you?"

Her smile turned to a laugh. "One of the Andersons' neighbors admired our team effort. I'm scheduled to start tomorrow." She held out a hand. "Be here at six."

He winced. "A.M.?"

"Exactly. Now, how about lunch?"

He put his hand in hers. "Fine. You're buying."

* * *

Good God, the woman worked like an elephant. She worked like two elephants, Holt corrected as the sweat poured down his back. He had a pick or shovel in his hand so often, he might as well be on a chain gang.

It should've been cooler up here on the cliffs. But the lawn they were landscaping—attacking, he thought as he brought the pick down again—was nothing but rock.

In the three days he'd worked with her, he'd given up trying to stop her from doing any of the heavy work. She only ignored him and did as she pleased. When he went home in the midafternoon, every muscle twinging, he wondered how in holy hell she kept it up.

He couldn't put in more than four or five hours and juggle his own jobs. But he knew she worked eight to ten every day. It wasn't difficult to see that she was throwing herself into her work to keep from thinking about the fact that the kids were leaving the next day.

He brought the pick down again, hit rock. The shock sang up his arms. At the low, steady swearing, Suzanna glanced up from her own work. "Why don't you take a break. I can finish that."

"Did you bring the dynamite?"

The smile touched her lips for only a moment. "No, really. Go get a drink out of the cooler. We're nearly ready to plant."

"Fine." He hated to admit that the whole business was wearing him out. There were blisters on top of his blisters, his muscles felt as though he'd gone ten rounds with the champ—and lost. Wiping his face and neck dry, he walked over to the cooler they'd set in the shade of a beech tree. As he pulled out a ginger ale, he heard the pick ring against the rocky soil. It was no use telling her she was crazy, he thought as he guzzled down the cold liquid. But he couldn't help it.

"You're a lunatic, Suzanna. This is the kind of work they give to people with numbers across their chest."

"What we have here," she said in a thick Southern drawl, "is a failure to communicate."

Her quote of the line from *Cool Hand Luke* made him grin, but only for an instant. "Stark, raving mad," he continued, watching her swing the pick. "What the hell do you think's going to grow in that rock?"

"You'd be surprised." She took a moment to wipe at the sweat that was dripping in her eyes. "See those lilies on the bank there?" She gave a little grunt as she dislodged a rock. "I planted them two years ago in September."

He glanced at the profusion of tall, colorful flowers with grudging admiration. He had to admit that they were an improvement over the rough, rocky soil, but was it worth it?

"The Snyders gave me my first real job." She hefted a rock and tossed it into the wheelbarrow. Stretching her back, she listened to the fat bees buzzing in the gaillardia. "A sympathy job, seeing as they were friends of the family and poor Suzanna needed a break." Her breath whooshed out as she struck soil, and she blinked away the little red dots in front of her eyes. "Surprised them that I knew what I was doing, and I've been working here on and off ever since."

"Great. Would you put that damn thing down a minute?"

"Almost done."

"You won't be done until you keel over. Who's going to see a few posies wilting all the way up here?"

"The Snyders will see them, their guests will see them." She shook her head to clear a haze brought on by the heat. "The photographer from *New England Gardens* will see them." Lord, the bees were loud, she thought as the buzzing filled her head. "And nothing's going to wilt. I'm putting in pinks and campanula and some coreopsis, some lavender for scent and monarda for the hummingbirds." She pressed a hand to her head, ran it over her eyes. "In September we'll plant some bulbs. Dwarf irises and windflowers. Some tuberoses and..." She staggered under a hot wave of dizziness. Holt made the dash from shade to sun as the pick slid out of her hands. When he grabbed her she seemed to melt into his arms.

Cursing her helped relieve the fright as he carried her over and laid her down under the tree. Her body was like hot wax he could all but pour onto the cool grass. "That's it." He plunged his hand into the cooler then rubbed icy water over her face. "You're finished, do you understand? If I see a pick in your hands again, I'll murder you."

"I'm all right." Her voice was weak, but the irritation was clear enough. "Just a little too much sun." The water on her face felt heavenly, even if his hands were a bit rough. She took the ginger ale from him and drank carefully.

"Too much sun," he was ranting, "too much work. And not enough food or sleep from the look of you. You're a mess, Suzanna, and I'm tired of it."

"Thank you very much." She pushed his hands away and leaned back against the tree. She needed a minute, she'd admit. But she didn't need a lecture. "I should have taken a break," she said in disgust. "I know better, but I've got things on my mind."

"I don't care what you've got on your mind." God, she was white as a sheet. He wanted to hold her until the color came back into her cheeks, to stroke her hair until she was strong and rested again. But the concern came out in fury. "I'm taking you home and you're going to bed."

Steadier, she set the bottle aside. "I think you're forgetting who works for whom."

"When you pass out on me, I take over."

"I didn't pass out," she said irritably. "I got dizzy. And nobody takes over for me, not now, not ever again. Stop splashing water in my face, you're going to drown me."

She was recovering fast enough, he thought, but it didn't cool his temper. "You're stubborn, hardheaded and just plain stupid."

"Fine. If you've finished yelling at me, I'm going to take my lunch break." She knew she had to eat. She didn't mind being stubborn or hardheaded, but she did mind being stupid. Which, she thought as she snatched a sandwich out of the cooler, was exactly what she had been to skip breakfast.

"Maybe I haven't finished yelling."

She shrugged as she unwrapped the sandwich. "Then you can yell while I eat. Or you can stop wasting time and have some lunch."

He considered dragging her to the truck. He liked the idea, but the benefits would only be short-term. Short of tying her up and locking her in a room, he couldn't stop her from working herself into the ground.

At least she was eating, he reflected. And the color had seeped back into her cheeks. Maybe there was another tack to getting his way. Casually he took out a sandwich.

"I've been thinking about the emeralds."

The change in topic and attitude surprised her. "Oh?"

"I read the transcript Max put together from the interview with Mrs. Tobias, the maid. And I listened to the tape."

"What do you think?"

"I think she's got a good memory, and that she was impressed by Bianca. From her viewpoint, the setup was that Bianca was unhappy in her marriage, devoted to her children and in love with my grandfather. She and Fergus were already on shaky ground when they had the blowout over the dog. We'll figure that was the straw that broke it. She decided to leave him, but she didn't go that night. Why?"

"Even if she'd finally made the decision," Suzanna said slowly, "there would have been arrangements to make. She'd have had to consider the children." This she understood all too well. "Where could she take them? How could she be certain she could provide for them? Even if the marriage was a disaster, she would have to plan carefully how to tell them she was taking them away from their father."

"So when Fergus left for Boston after they fought, she started to work it out. We have to figure she went to my grandfather, because he ended up with the dog."

"She loved him," Suzanna murmured. "She would have gone to him first. And he loved her, so he would have wanted to go away with her and the children."

"If we go with that, we take it to the next step. She went back to The Towers to pack, to get the kids together. But instead of meeting my grandfather and riding off into the sunset, she takes a jump out of the tower window. Why?"

"She was in turmoil." With her eyes half-closed, Suzanna stared into the sunlight. "She was about to take a step that would end her marriage, separate her children from their father. Break her vows. It's so difficult, so frightening. Like dying. Maybe she thought she was a failure, and when her husband came home, and she had to face him and herself, she couldn't."

Holt ran a hand over her hair. "Is that what it was like for you?"

Her shoulders stiffened. "We're talking about Bianca. And I don't see what her reasons for killing herself have to do with the emeralds."

Holt took his hand away. "First we decide why she hid them, then we go for where."

Slowly she relaxed again. "Fergus gave them to her when their first son was born. Not their first child. A girl didn't rate." She took another sip of her ginger ale and washed away some of her own bitterness. "She would have resented that, I think. To be rewarded—like a prize mare—for producing an heir. But, they were hers because the child was hers."

Because her eyes were heavy, she let them drift closed. "Bax gave me diamonds when Alex was born. I didn't feel guilty about selling them to start the business. Because they were mine. She might have felt the same way. The emeralds would have bought a new life for her, for the children."

"Why did she hide them?"

"To make certain he didn't find them if he stopped her from leaving. So that she knew she'd have something of her own."

"Did you hide your diamonds, Suzanna?"

"I put them in Jenny's diaper bag. The last place Baxter would look." With a half laugh, she plucked at the grass. "That sounds so melodramatic."

But he wasn't smiling or sneering, she noted. He was frowning out at the dianthiums where the bees hovered and hummed. "It sounds damn smart to me. She spent a lot of time in the tower, right?"

"We've looked there."

"We'll look again, and take her bedroom apart."

"Lilah will love that." Suzanna closed her eyes again. The food and the shade were making her sleepy. "It's her bedroom now. And we've looked there, too."

"I haven't."

"No." She decided it wouldn't hurt to stretch out while they finished talking it through. The grass was blissfully cool and soft. "If we found her journal, we'd know the answers. Mandy went through every book in the library, just in case it got mixed in like the purloined letter."

He began to stroke her hair again. "We'll take another look."

"Mandy wouldn't have missed anything. She's too organized."

"I'd rather check over old ground than depend on a séance."

She made a sound that was half laugh and half sigh. "Aunt Coco'll talk you into it." Her voice grew heavy with fatigue. "We need to plant the pinks first."

"Okay." He'd moved his hands down and was gently massaging her shoulders.

"It'll trail right over the rocks and down the bank. It doesn't give up," she murmured, and was asleep.

"You're telling me."

He left her there in the shade and walked back into the sunlight.

The grass was tickling her cheek when she woke. She'd rolled over onto her stomach and had slept like a stone. Groggy, she opened her eyes. She saw Holt sitting back against the tree, his legs crossed at the ankles. He was watching her as he brought a cigarette to his lips.

"I must have dozed off."

"You could say that."

"Sorry." She pushed herself up on her elbow. "We were talking about the emeralds."

He flicked the cigarette away. "We've talked enough for now." In one swift move, he hooked his hands under her arms and pulled her against him. Before she was fully awake, she was in his lap and his mouth was on hers.

He'd watched her sleep. And as he had watched her sleep, the need to touch her had boiled inside him until his blood was like lava. She'd looked so perfect, the sleeping princess, creamy skin dappled by hazy shade, her cheek resting on her hand, her hand on the grass.

He'd wanted those soft, warm lips under his, to feel that long, fragile body molded to him, to hear that quick little catch in her breathing. So he took, feverishly.

Disarmed, disoriented, she struggled back. Her blood had gone from slow and cool to rapid and hot. Her body, relaxed by sleep, was now taut as a bow. She dragged in a single ragged breath. All she could see was his face, his eyes dark and dangerous, his mouth hard and hungry. Then all was a blur as his lips brushed down on hers again.

She let him take what he seemed to need to take so desperately. Under the shade of the beech she pressed against him, answering each demand. When the dizziness came again, she reveled in it. This was not a weakness she had to fight. It was one she had wanted to feel as long as she could remember.

On an oath, he buried his face at her throat where her pulse jackhammered. Nothing and no one had ever made him feel like this. Frantic and shaky. Each time his mouth came back to hers it was with a new edge of desperation, each keener than the last. Dozens of sensations knifed into him, all sharp and deadly. He wanted to shove her aside, walk away before they cut him to ribbons. He wanted to roll with her on the cool, soft grass and drive out all the aches and jagged needs.

But her arms were around him, her hands moving restlessly through his hair while her body trembled. Then her cheek was against his, nuzzling there in a gesture that was almost unbearably sweet.

"What are we going to do?" she murmured. Wanting comfort, she turned her lips to his skin and sighed.

"I think we both know the answer to that."

Suzanna closed her eyes. It was so simple for him. She rested against him a moment, listening to the bees buzz in the flowers. "I need time."

He put his hands on her shoulders, pushing her back until

they were face-to-face. "I may not be able to give it to you. We're not children anymore, and I'm tired of wondering what it would be like."

She let out a shaky breath. The turmoil wasn't only hers, she realized. She could feel it, shimmering out of him. "If you ask for more than I can give, we'll both be disappointed. I want you." She bit back a gasp when his fingers tightened. "But I can't make another mistake."

His eyes darkened and narrowed. "Do you want promises?"

"No," she said quickly. "No, I don't. But I have to keep the ones I made to myself. If I come to you, I have to be sure it's not just something I want, but something I can live with." Reaching out, she laid a hand on his cheek. "The one thing I can promise you is that if we're lovers, I won't regret it."

He couldn't argue, not when she looked at him that way. "When," he corrected.

"When," she said with a nod, then rose. Her legs weren't as shaky as she'd thought they would be. She felt stronger. *When,* she thought again. Yes, she'd already accepted that it was only a matter of time. "But for now, we'll have to take things as they come. We've got a job to finish."

"It's finished." He pulled himself to his feet as she turned.

The plants were in place, the ground smoothed and mulched. Where there had only been rocks and thin, thirsty soil were bright hopeful young flowers and tender green leaves.

"How?" she began, already hurrying over to study his work.

"You slept three hours."

"Three—" Appalled, she looked back at him. "You should have woken me up."

"I didn't," he said simply. "Now I've got to get back, I'm running late."

"But you shouldn't have—"

"It's done." Impatience shimmered around him. "Do you want to rip the damn things out and do it yourself?"

"No." As she studied him she realized he wasn't just angry, he was embarrassed. Not only had he done something sweet and considerate, but he'd spent three hours planting what he still sneeringly called posies.

So he stood there, she thought, looking very male and ruffled in the streaming sun, the charming rockery at his feet and his rough, clever hands stuffed in his pockets. Thank me and I'll snarl, he seemed to say.

It was then, facing him on the rocky slope, that she realized what she had refused to admit in his arms. What she had insisted was only passion and need. She loved him. Not just for the hot-blooded kisses or the demanding hands. But for the man beneath. The man who would run a careless hand over her son's hair or answer her little girl's incessant questions. The man who would leave paint splattered on the floor in memory of his grandfather.

The one who would plant flowers for her while she slept.

As she continued to stare, Holt shifted uncomfortably. "Look, if you're going to faint again, I'm going to leave you where you fall. I haven't got time to play nursemaid."

A smile moved slowly, beautifully over her face, confusing him. She loved him for that, too—that snapping impatience that covered the compassion. She would need time to think, of course. Time to adjust. But for now, for this moment, she could simply hold tight to this rush of feeling and be content.

"You did a good job."

He glanced back at the flowers, certain he'd rather cut out his tongue than admit how much he'd enjoyed the work. "You stick them in and cover them up." He moved his shoulders in dismissal. "I put the tools and stuff in the truck. I've got to go."

"I put the Bryce job off until Monday. Tomorrow—I have to be home tomorrow."

"All right. See you later."

As he walked off to his car, Suzanna knelt down to touch the fragile new blooms.

In the cottage near the water, the man who called himself Marshall completed a thorough search. He found a few things of minor interest. The ex-cop liked to read and didn't cook. There were shelves of well-worn books in the bedroom, and only a few scattered supplies in the kitchen. He kept his medals in a box tossed in the bottom of a drawer, and a loaded .32 at the ready in the nightstand.

After rifling through a desk, Marshall discovered that Christian's grandson had made a few shrewd investments. He found it amusing that a former Vice cop had had the sense to create a tidy nest egg. He also found it interesting that training had caused Holt to write up a detailed report on everything he knew about the Calhoun emeralds.

His temper threatened as he read of the interview with the former servant—the servant that Maxwell Quartermain had located. That grated. Quartermain should have been working for him. Or he should have been dead. Marshall was tempted to wreck the place, to toss furniture, break lamps. To give in to an orgy of destruction.

But he forced himself to stay calm. He didn't want to tip his hand. Not yet. Perhaps he hadn't found anything particularly enlightening, but he knew as much as the Calhouns did.

Very carefully, he put the papers back in place, shut the drawers. The dog was beginning to bark out in the yard. He detested dogs. Sneering at the sound, he rubbed at the scar on his leg where the little Calhoun mutt had bitten him. They would have to pay for that. They would all have to pay.

And so they would, he thought. When he had the emeralds. He left the cottage precisely as he had found it.

I will not write of the winter. That is not a memory I wish to relive. But I did not leave the island. Could not leave it. She was never out of my mind in those months. In the spring, she remained with me. In my dreams.

And then, it was summer.

It isn't possible for me to write how I felt when I saw her running to me. I could paint it, but I could never find the words. I haunted those cliffs, waiting for her, hoping for her. It had become easy to convince myself that it would be enough just to see her, just to speak with her again. If she would only walk down the slope, through the wildflowers and sit on the rocks with me.

Then all at once, she was calling my name, running, her eyes so filled with joy. She was in my arms, her mouth on mine. And I knew she had suffered as I had suffered. She loved as I loved.

We both knew it was madness. Perhaps I could have been stronger, could have convinced her to go and leave me. But something had changed in her over the winter. No longer would she be content with only emptiness, as I learned her marriage was for her. Her children, so dear to her, could not forge a bond between her and the husband who wanted only obedience and duty. Yet I could not allow her to give herself to me, to take the step that could cause her guilt or shame or regret.

So we met, day after day on the cliffs, in all innocence. To talk and laugh, to pretend the summer was endless. Sometimes she brought the children, and it was almost as if we were a family. It was reckless, but somehow we didn't believe anything could touch us while we stood, cupped between sky and sea, with the peaks of the house far up at our backs.

We were happy with what we had. There have been no happier days in my life before or since. Love like that has no beginning or end. It has no right or wrong. In those bright summer days, she was not another man's wife. She was mine.

A lifetime later, I sit here in this aging body and look out at the water. Her face, her voice, come so clearly to me.

She smiled. "I used to dream of being in love."

I had taken the pins from her hair so that my hands could lose themselves in it. A small, precious pleasure. "Do you still?"

"Now I don't have to." She bent toward me, to touch her lips to mine. "I'll never have to dream again. Only wish."

I took her hand to kiss it, and we watched an eagle soar. "There's a ball tonight. I'll wish you were there, to waltz with me."

I got to my feet, drew her to hers and began to dance with her through the wild roses. "Tell me what you'll wear, so I can see you."

Laughing, she lifted her face to mine. "I shall wear ivory silk with a low bodice that bares my shoulders and a draped beaded skirt that catches the light. And my emeralds."

"A woman shouldn't look sad when she speaks of emeralds."

"No." She smiled again. "These are very special. I've had them since Ethan was born, and I wear them to remind me."

"Of what?"

"That no matter what happens, I've left something behind. The children are my real jewels." As a cloud came over the sun she pressed her head to my shoulder. "Hold me closer, Christian."

Neither of us spoke of the summer that was so quickly coming to an end, but I know we both thought of it at that moment when my arms held her tight and our hearts beat together in the dance. The fury of what I was soon to lose again rushed through me.

"I would give you emeralds, and diamonds, sapphires." I crushed my mouth to hers. "All that and more, Bianca, if I could."

"No." She brought her hands to my face, and I saw the tears sparkling in her eyes. "Only love me," she said.

Only love me.

Chapter 7

Holt was home for less than three minutes when he knew someone had broken in. He might have turned in his shield, but he still had cop's eyes. There was nothing obviously out of place—but an ashtray was closer to the edge of the table, a chair was pulled at a slightly different angle to the fireplace, a corner of the rug was turned up.

Braced and at alert, he moved from the living room into the bedroom. There were signs here, as well. He noted them—the fractional rearrangement of the pillows, the different alignment of the books on the shelves—as he crossed to get his gun from the drawer. After checking the clip, he took his weapon with him as he searched the house.

Thirty minutes later, he replaced the gun. His face was set, his eyes flat and hard. His grandfather's canvases had been moved, not much, but enough to tell Holt that someone had touched them, studied them. And that was a violation he couldn't tolerate.

Whoever had tossed the place had been a pro. Nothing had been taken, little had been disturbed, but Holt was certain every inch of the cottage had been combed.

He was also certain who had done the combing. That meant that Livingston, by whatever guise he was using, was still close. Close enough, Holt thought, that he had discovered the Bradford connection to the Calhouns. And the emeralds.

Now, he decided as he dropped a hand on the head of the dog who whined at his feet, it was personal.

He went through the kitchen door to sit on the porch with his dog and a beer and watch the water. He would let his temper cool and his mind drift, sorting through all the pieces of the puzzle, arranging and rearranging until a picture began to form.

Bianca was the key. It was her mind, her emotions, her motivations he had to tap into. He lit a cigarette, resting his crossed ankles on the porch rail as the light began to soften and pearl toward twilight.

A beautiful woman, unhappily married. If the current crop of Calhoun women were anything to go by, Bianca would also have been strong willed, passionate and loyal. And vulnerable, he added. That came through strongly in the eyes of the portrait, just as it came through strongly in Suzanna's eyes.

She'd also been on the upper rungs of society's ladder, one of the privileged. A young Irishwoman of good family who had married extremely well.

Again, like Suzanna.

He drew on the cigarette, absently stroking Sadie's ears when she nuzzled her head into his lap. His gaze was drawn toward the little yellow bush, the slice of sunshine Suzanna had given him. According to the interview with the former maid, Bianca had also had a fondness for flowers.

She had had children, and by all accounts had been a good

and devoted mother, while Fergus had been a strict and disinterested father. Then Christian Bradford had come into the picture.

If Bianca had indeed taken him as a lover, she had also taken an enormous social risk. Like Caesar's wife, a woman in her position was expected to be unblemished. Even a hint of an affair—particularly with a man beneath her station— and her reputation would have been in tatters.

Yet she had become involved.

Had it all grown to be too much for her? Holt wondered. Had she been eaten up by guilt and panic, hidden the emeralds away as some kind of last-ditch show of defiance, only to despair at the thought of the disgrace and scandal of divorce. Unable to face her life, she had chosen death.

He didn't like it. Shaking his head, Holt blew out a slow stream of smoke. He just didn't like the rhythm of it. Maybe he was losing his objectivity, but he couldn't see Suzanna giving up and hurling herself onto the cliffs. And there were too many similarities between Bianca and her great-granddaughter.

Maybe he should try to get inside Suzanna's head. If he understood her, maybe he could understand her star-crossed ancestor. Maybe, he admitted with a pull on the beer, he could understand himself. His feelings for her seemed to undergo radical changes every day, until he no longer knew exactly what he felt.

Oh, there was desire, that was clear enough. But it wasn't simple. He'd always counted on it being simple.

What made Suzanna Calhoun Dumont tick? Her kids, Holt thought immediately. No contest there, though the rest of her family ran a dead heat. Her business. She would work herself ragged making it run. But Holt suspected that her thirst to succeed in business doubled right back around to her children and family.

Restless, he rose to pace the length of the porch. A whippoorwill came to roost in the old wind-bent maple and lifted its voice in its three-note call. Roused, the insects began to whisper in the grass. The first firefly, a lone sentinel, flickered near the water that lapped the bank.

This, too, was something he wanted. The simple quiet of solitude. But as he stood, looking out into the night, he thought of Suzanna. Not just the way she had felt in his arms, the way she made his blood swim. But what it would be like to have her beside him now, waiting for moonrise.

He needed to get inside her head, to make her trust him enough to tell him what she felt, how she thought. If he could make the link with her, he would be one step closer to making it with Bianca.

But he was afraid he was already in too deep. His own thoughts and feelings were clouding his judgment. He wanted to be her lover more than he had ever wanted anything. To sink into her, to watch her eyes darken with passion until that sad, injured look was completely banished. To have her give herself to him the way she had never given herself to anyone—not even the man she had married.

Holt pressed his hands to the rail, leaned out into the growing dark. Alone, with night to cloak him, he admitted that he was following the same pattern as his grandfather.

He was falling in love with a Calhoun woman.

It was late before he went back inside. Later still before he slept.

Suzanna hadn't slept at all. She had lain awake all night trying not to think about the two small suitcases she had packed. When she managed to get her mind off that, it had veered toward Holt. Thoughts of him only made her more restless.

She'd been up at dawn, rearranging the clothes she'd

already packed, adding a few more things, checking yet again to be sure she had included a few of their favorite toys so that they wouldn't feel homesick.

She'd been cheerful at breakfast, grateful that her family had been there to add support and encouragement. Both children had been whiny, but she'd nearly joked them out of it by noon.

By one, her nerves had been frayed and the children were cranky again. By two she was afraid Bax had forgotten the entire thing, then was torn between fury and hope.

At three the car had come, a shiny black Lincoln. Fifteen horrible minutes later, her children were gone.

She couldn't stay home. Coco had been so kind, so understanding, and Suzanna had been afraid they would both dissolve into puddles of tears. For her aunt's sake as much as her own, she decided to go to work.

She would keep herself busy, Suzanna vowed. So busy that when the children got back, she hardly would have noticed they'd been gone.

She stopped by the shop, but Carolanne's sympathy and curiosity nearly drove her over the edge.

"I don't mean to badger you," Carolanne apologized when Suzanna's responses became clipped. "I'm just worried about you."

"I'm fine." Suzanna was selecting plants with almost obsessive care. "And I'm sorry for being short with you. I'm feeling a little rough today."

"And I'm being too nosy." Always good-natured, Carolanne shrugged. "I like the salmon-colored ones," she said as Suzanna debated over the group of New Guinea impatiens. "Listen, if you want to blow off some steam, just call me. We can have a girls' night out."

"I appreciate that."

"Anytime," Carolanne insisted. "It'll be fine. That's a really nice grouping," she added as Suzanna began to load her choices into the truck. "Are you putting in another bed?"

"Paying off a debt." Suzanna climbed into the truck, gave a wave then drove off. On the way to Holt's, she busied her mind by designing and redesigning the arrangement for the flower bed. She'd already scouted out the spot, bordering the front porch so he could enjoy it whenever he came or went from the cottage. Whether he wanted to or not.

The job would take her the rest of the day, then she would unwind by walking along the cliffs. Tomorrow she would put in a full day at the shop, then spend the cool of the evening working the gardens at The Towers.

One by one, the days would pass.

She didn't bother to announce herself after she'd parked the truck, but set right to work staking out the bed. The result was not what she'd hoped for. As she dug and hoed and worked the soil there was no soothing response. Her mind didn't empty of worries and fill with the pleasure of planting. Instead a headache began to work nastily behind her eyes. Ignoring it, she wheeled over a load of planting medium and dumped it. She was raking it smooth when Holt stepped out.

He'd watched her from the window for nearly ten minutes, hating the fact that the strong shoulders were slumped and her eyes dull with sadness.

"I thought you were taking the day off."

"I changed my mind." Without glancing up, she rolled the wheelbarrow back to the truck and loaded it with flats of plants.

"What the hell are all of those?"

"Your paycheck." She started with snapdragons, delphiniums and bright shasta daisies. "This was the deal."

Frowning, he came down a couple of steps. "I said maybe you could put in a couple of bushes."

"I'm putting in flowers." She packed down the soil. "Anyone with an ounce of imagination can see that this place is crying for flowers."

So she wanted to fight, he noted, rocking back on his heels. Well, he could oblige her. "You could have asked before you dug up the yard."

"Why? You'd just sneer and make some nasty macho remark."

He came down another step. "It's my yard, babe."

"And I'm planting flowers in it. *Babe*." She tossed her head up. Yeah, she was mad enough to spit nails, he noted. And she was also miserable. "If you don't want to bother to give them any water or care, then I will. Why don't you go back inside and leave me to it?"

Without waiting for a response, she went back to work. Holt took a seat while she added lavender and larkspur, dahlias and violas. He smoked lazily, noting that her hands were as sure and graceful as usual.

"Planting posies doesn't seem to be improving your mood today."

"My mood is just fine. In fact, it's dandy." She snapped a sprig off some freesia and swore. "Why shouldn't it be, just because I had to watch Jenny get in that damn car with tears running down her cheeks? Just because I had to stand there and smile when Alex looked back at me, his little mouth quivering and his eyes begging me not to make him go."

When her eyes filled, she shook the tears away. "And I had to stand there and take it when Bax accused me of being an overprotective, smothering mother who was turning his children, *his* children into timid weaklings."

She hacked her spade into the dirt. "They're not timid or

weak," she said viciously. "They're just children. Why shouldn't they be afraid to go with him, when they hardly know him? And with his wife who stood there in her silk suit and Italian heels looking distressed and helpless. She won't have a clue what to do if Jenny has a bad dream or Alex gets a stomachache. And I just let them go. I just stood there and let them get in that awful car with two strangers. So I'm feeling just fine. I'm feeling terrific."

She sprang up to shove the wheelbarrow back to the truck. When she came back to do the mulching, he was gone. She forced herself to do the work carefully, reminding herself that at least here, over this one thing, she had control.

Holt came back, dragging the hose from around the other side of the house and holding two beers. "I'll water them. Have a beer."

Swiping a hand over her brow, she frowned at the bottles. "I don't drink beer."

"That's all I've got." He shoved one into her hand, then pushed the lever for the sprayer. "I think I can handle this part by now," he said dryly. "Why don't you have a seat?"

Suzanna walked to the steps and sat. Because she was thirsty she took one long sip, then rested her chin on her hand and watched him. He'd learned not to drown the plants, or pound them with a heavy spray. She let out a little sigh, then sipped again.

No words of sympathy, she thought. No comforting pats or claims to understand just how she felt. Instead, he'd given her exactly what she'd needed, a silent wall to hurl her misery and anger against. Did he know he'd helped her? She couldn't be sure. But she knew she had come here, to him, not only to plant flowers, not only to get out of the house, but because she loved him.

She hadn't given herself time to think about that, not since the feeling had opened and bloomed inside of her. Nor had she given herself a chance to wonder what it would mean to either of them.

It wasn't something she wanted. She wanted never to love again, never to risk hurt and humiliation at a man's hands again. But it had happened.

She hadn't looked for it. She had looked only for peace of mind, for security for her children, for simple contentment for herself. Yet she had found it.

And what would his reaction be if she told him. Would it please his ego? Would it shock or appall or amuse? It didn't matter, Suzanna told herself as she slipped an arm around the dog who had come to join her. For now, perhaps for always, the love was hers. She no longer expected emotions to be shared.

Holt shut off the spray. The colorful bed added charm to the simple wooden cottage. It even pleased him that he recognized some of the blooms by name. He wasn't going to ask her about the ones that were unfamiliar. But he'd look them up.

"It looks pretty good."

"They're mostly perennials," she said in the same casual tone. "I thought you might find it rewarding to see them come back year after year."

He might, but he also thought he would remember, much too vividly, how hurt and unhappy she'd looked when she'd planted them. He didn't dare dwell on how much it upset him to picture Alex and Jenny climbing tearfully into a car and driving away.

"They smell okay."

"That's the lavender." She took a deep breath of it herself before rising. "I'll go around and turn off the hose." She'd nearly turned the corner when he called her name.

"Suzanna. They'll be all right."

Not trusting her voice, she nodded and continued around back. She was crouched down, the dog's face in hers when he joined her.

"You know, if you put some day lilies and some sedum on that bank, you'd solve most of the erosion problem."

He cupped a hand under her elbow to pull her to her feet. "Is working the only thing you use to take your mind off things?"

"It does the job."

"I've got a better idea."

Her heart gave a quick jolt. "I really don't—"

"Let's go for a ride."

She blinked. "A ride?"

"In the boat. We've got a couple of hours before dark."

"A ride in the boat," she said, unaware that she amused him with her long, relieved sigh. "I'd like that."

"Good." He took her hand and pulled her to the pier. "You cast off." When the dog jumped in beside him, Suzanna realized this was an old routine. For a man who didn't want to appear to have any sentiment, it was a telling thing that he took a dog along for company when he set out to sea.

The engine roared to life. Holt waited only until Suzanna had climbed on board before he headed into the bay.

The wind slapped against her face. Laughing, she clapped a hand to her cap to keep it from flying off. After she'd pulled it on more securely, she joined him at the wheel.

"I haven't been out on the water in months," she shouted over the engine.

"What's the use of living on an island if you never go out on the water?"

"I like to watch it."

She turned her head and caught the bright glint of window glass from the secluded houses on Bar Island. Overhead gulls wheeled and screamed. Sadie barked at them, then settled on the boat cushions with her head on the side so that the wind could send her ears flying.

"Has she ever jumped out?" Suzanna asked him.

He glanced back at the dog. "No. She just looks stupid."

"You'll have to bring her by the house again. Fred hasn't been the same since he met her."

"Some women do that to a man." The salt breeze was carrying her scent to him, wrapping it around his senses so that he drew her in with every breath. She was standing close, braced against the boat's motion. The expression in her eyes was still far off and troubled, and he knew she wasn't thinking of him. But he thought of her.

He moved expertly through the bay traffic, keeping the speed slow and steady as he maneuvered around other boats, passed a hotel terrace where guests sat under striped umbrellas drinking cocktails or eating an early dinner. Far to starboard, the island's three-masted schooner streamed into port with its crowd of waving tourists.

Then the bay gave way to the sea and the water became less serene. The cliffs roared up into the sky. Arrogantly, defiantly, The Towers sat on its ridge overlooking village and bay and sea. Its somber gray stone mirrored the tone of the rain clouds out to the west. Its old, wavy glass glinted with fanciful rainbows. Like a mirage, there were streaks and blurs of color that were Suzanna's garden.

"Sometimes when I went lobstering with my father, I'd look up at it." And think of you. "Castle Calhoun," Holt murmured. "That's what he called it."

Suzanna smiled, shading her eyes with the flat of her hand as she studied the imposing house on the cliffs. "It's just home. It's always been home. When I look up at it I think of Aunt Coco trying out some new recipe in the kitchen and Lilah napping in the parlor. The children playing in the yard or racing down the stairs. Amanda sitting at her desk and working her meticulous way through the mounds of bills it takes to hold a home together. C.C. diving under the hood of the old station wagon to see if she could make a miracle happen and get one more year out of the engine. Sometimes I see my parents laughing at the kitchen table, so young, so alive, so full of plans." She turned around to keep the house in sight. "So many things have changed, and will change. But the house is still there. It's comforting. You understand that or you wouldn't have chosen to live in Christian's cottage, with all his memories."

He understood exactly, and it made him uneasy. "Maybe I just like having a place on the water."

Suzanna watched Bianca's tower disappear before she shifted to face him. "Sentiment doesn't make you weak, Holt."

He frowned out over the water. "I could never get close to my father. We came at everything from different directions. I never had to explain or justify anything I felt or wanted to my grandfather. He just accepted. I guess I figured there was a reason he left me the place when he died, even though I was only a kid."

It moved her in a very soft, very lovely way that he had shared even that much with her. "So you came back to it. We always come back to what we love." She wanted to ask him more, what his life had been like during the span of years he'd been away. Why he had turned his back on police work to repair boat motors and props. Had he been in love, or had his heart broken? But he hit the throttle and sent the boat streaking out over the wide expanse of water.

He hadn't come out to think deep thoughts, to worry or to wonder. He had come to give her, and himself, an hour of relaxation, a respite from reality. Wind and speed worked that particular miracle for him. It always had. When he heard her laugh, when she tossed her face up into the sun, he knew he'd chosen well.

"Here, take the wheel."

It was a challenge. She could hear the dare in his voice, see it in his eyes when he grinned at her. Suzanna didn't hesitate, but took his place at the helm.

She gloried in the control, in the power vibrating under her fingertips. The boat sliced through the water like a blade, racing to nowhere. There was only sea and sky and unlimited freedom. The Atlantic roughened, adding a dash of danger. The air took on a bite that shivered along the skin and made each breath a drink of icy wine.

Her hands were firm and competent on the wheel, her body braced and ready. The wistful look in her eyes had been replaced by a bright fearlessness that quickened his blood. Her face was flushed with excitement, dampened by the spray. She didn't look like a princess now, but like a queen who knew her own power and was ready to wield it.

He let her race where she chose, knowing that she would end where he had wanted her for most of his life. He wouldn't wait another day. Not even another hour.

She was breathless and laughing when she gave him the wheel again. "I'd forgotten what it was like. I haven't handled a boat in five years."

"You did all right." He kept the speed high as he turned the boat in a wide half circle.

Still laughing, she rubbed her hands over her arms. "Lord, it's freezing."

He glanced toward her and felt the punch low in his gut. She was glowing—her eyes as blue as the sky and only more vital, the thin cotton pants and blouse plastered against her slender body, her hair streaming out from under the cap.

When his palms grew damp and unsteady on the wheel, he looked away. Not falling in love, he realized. He'd stopped falling and had hit the ground with a fatal smack. "There's a jacket in the cabin."

"No, it feels wonderful." She closed her eyes and let the sensations hammer her. The wild wind, the golden evening sun, the smell of salt and sea and the man beside her, the roar of the motor and the churning wake. They might have been alone, completely, with nothing but excitement and speed, with either of them free to take the wheel and spear off into that fabulous aloneness.

She didn't want to go back. Suzanna drank deeply of the tangy air and thought how liberating it would be to race and race in no direction at all, then to drift wherever the current took her.

But the air was already warming. They were no longer alone. She heard the long, droning horn of a tourist boat as Holt cut the speed and glided toward the harbor.

This too was lovely, she thought. Coming home. Knowing your place, certain of your welcome. She let out a little sigh at the simple familiarity. The blue water of Frenchman Bay deepening now with evening, the buildings crowded with people, the clang of buoys. It was all the more comforting after the frantic race to nowhere.

They said nothing as he navigated across the bay and circled around to drift to his pier. But she was relaxed when she jumped out to secure the lines, when she ran her hands over the dog who leaned against her legs, begging for attention.

"You're quite the sailor, aren't you, girl?" She crouched down to give the dog a good rub. "I think she wants to go again."

Holt stepped nimbly to the dock and stood a foot apart. "There's a storm coming in."

Suzanna glanced up and saw that the clouds were blowing slowly but determinedly inland. "You're right. We can certainly use the rain." Foolish, she thought, to feel awkward now and start talking of the weather. She rose, uncertain of her moves now that he was standing here, tension in every line of his body, his eyes dark and intent on hers. "Thanks for the ride. I really enjoyed it."

"Good." The pier swayed when he started forward. Suzanna took two steps back and felt better when her feet hit solid ground.

"If you get a chance, maybe you can bring Sadie to visit Fred this weekend. He'll be lonely without the kids around."

"All right."

She was halfway across the yard, and he was still a foot away. If it hadn't seemed so paranoid, she would have said he was stalking her. "The bush is doing well." She ran her fingers over it as she passed. "But you really need to feed this lawn. I could recommend a simple and inexpensive program."

His lips curved slightly, but his eyes stayed on hers. "You do that."

"Well, I...it's getting late. Aunt Coco—"

"Knows you're a big girl." He took her arm to hold her still. "You're not going anywhere tonight, Suzanna."

Perhaps if she'd been wiser or more experienced, she would have gauged his mood before he touched her. There was no mistaking it now, not when his fingers had closed over her with taut possession, not when his needs, and his intention of satisfying them, were so clear in those deep gray eyes.

She wished she could have been so certain of her own mood and her own needs.

"Holt, I told you I needed time."

"Time's up," he said simply, with an underlying edge that had her pulse jerking.

"This isn't something I intend to take casually."

Heat flashed into his eyes. From miles away came the violent rumble of thunder. "There's nothing casual about it. We both know that."

She did know it, and the knowledge was terrifying. "I think—"

He swore and swept her into his arms. "You think too much."

The moment the shock wore off she began to struggle. By then he had already carried her onto the back porch. "Holt. I won't be pressured." The screen door slammed behind them. Didn't he know she was afraid? That she was so afraid if she took this step he would find her dull, shrug her off and leave her shattered? "I'm not going to be rushed into this."

"If you had your way, it would take another fifteen years." He kicked open the door to the bedroom then dropped her onto the bed. It wasn't what he had planned, but he was too knotted up with terror and longings to struggle with soft words.

She was off the bed in a shot to stand beside it, slim and straight as an arrow. The lowering light, already gathering gloom, crept through the window at her back. "If you think you can cart me in here and throw me on the bed—"

"That's exactly what I've done." His eyes stayed hard on hers as he pulled his shirt over his head. "I'm tired of waiting, Suzanna, and I'm damn tired of wanting you. We're going to do this my way."

It had been like this for her before, she thought as her heart sank to her stomach like a stone. Only then it had been Bax, ordering her into bed, peeling off his clothes before he climbed on top of her to take his marital rights, quick and hard and without affection. And after, there would come his derision and disgust for her.

"Your way's hardly new," she said tightly. "And it doesn't interest me. I'm not obligated to go to bed with you, Holt. To let you demand and take and tell me I'm not good enough to satisfy. I'm not going to be used again, by anyone."

He caught her arms before she could storm from the room, dragged her struggling and swearing against him to crush his heated mouth to hers. The force of it sent her reeling. She would have stumbled away if his arms hadn't banded her so tightly.

Over the fear and the anger her own needs swelled. She wanted to scream at him for pulling them from her, for leaving her raw and naked and defenseless. But she could only hold on.

He yanked her away, arm's length, his breath already ragged and shallow. Her eyes were dark as midnight and held as many secrets. He would uncover them, that he promised himself. One by one he would learn them all. And tonight, he would begin.

"No one is going to be used here, and I'm only going to take what you give." His tensed fingers flexed on her arms. "Look at me, Suzanna. Look at me and tell me you don't want me, and I'll let you go."

Her lips parted on a shaky breath. She loved him, and she was no longer a girl who could hold love to herself like a comforting pillow in the night. If she was not as strong as she hoped and able to hold her heart and body separate, then she had no choice but to unite them. If that heart was broken, she would survive.

Hadn't she promised them both there would be no regrets?

She lifted a hand to his gently though she expected no gentleness in return. The choice was one she made freely.

"I can't tell you I don't want you. There's no need to wait any longer."

Chapter 8

If his nerves hadn't been so tangled, if the need hadn't been so acute, he might have been able to show her tenderness. If his blood hadn't been so hot, desire so greedy, he would have tried to give her some romance. But he was certain if he didn't possess now, possess quickly, he would shatter into hundreds of jagged shards of desperation.

So his mouth was fevered with impatience, his hands rough with urgency. At the first potent taste he understood she was already his. But it wasn't enough. Maybe it could never be enough.

She didn't tremble or hesitate. The vulnerability was cloaked inside a generosity that urged him to take his fill. As her hands roamed restlessly over his back he felt only her hunger, and none of her doubt.

He pushed the cap from her hair, then yanked the band from it so that his hands could take fistfuls of honey-colored silk. And the hands that gripped were unsteady, even as his mouth ruthlessly devoured hers.

She opened for him, releasing a soft and sultry moan of pleasure as his tongue plunged to duel with hers. He wanted so badly, and that want vibrating from him aroused her own. She had risen on her toes, unaware that she was fighting to meet him flare for flare. Her body was quaking with passions long suppressed.

And there was fear in that, fear in not knowing what would become of her if she lost that last toehold on control. She had to show him that she could give pleasure, make him enjoy and continue to want. If she fumbled now, lessened her grip on proving herself a woman, might he not find her less than his fantasy?

Yet she had never been wanted like this. Not like this with the violence of desire pulsing in the air so that every breath was like breathing temptation. She strained against him, hoping what she had to give would be enough while her system jolted along the battering tide of sensations.

His mouth raced over her face, down her throat where his teeth and the rough stubble of beard scraped. And his hands—Lord, his hands were fast and lethal.

She had to keep her head, but her knees were watery and her mind was spinning from the onslaught. Desperately she dug her nails into his back as she struggled away from the edge and tried to remember what a man would like.

She was quivering like a plucked bow, so tensed and wired he thought she might snap in two in his hands. She was holding back. The knowledge that she could do so when he was half-crazed brought on a kind of virulent fury. He tore the blouse aside as he pushed her onto the bed.

"Damn you, I want it all." Breath heaving, he encircled her wrists and dragged her arms over her head. "I'll have it all." When his mouth swooped down to capture hers, her hands strained under his grip, her pulse jittering in quick, rabbit jumps under his fingers.

His body was like a furnace, hot damp flesh fusing with hers in a way that made her shudder from the sheer wonder of it. Like iron, his fingers clamped hers still while his free hand raked over her in a merciless assault. She could feel the anger, taste the frustrated and furious desire. Desperate, she tried to pull in a breath to beg him to wait, to give her a moment, but all she could manage were jagged moans.

The wind kicked the curtains aside, letting dusk pour through. The first drops of rain hit the roof, sounding to her sensitized ears like gunshots that echoed the war he was waging on her. Again thunder rumbled, closer now, warning of a reckless power.

When his mouth found her breast, he let out a hot groan of pleasure. Here she was as soft as a summer breeze and as potent as whiskey. As she writhed beneath him, he dampened and tugged on the taut nipple, losing himself in the taste and texture while her heartbeat hammered against his mouth.

And she wanted as he wanted. He could feel the urgent excitement raging through her, hear it in her quick, sobbing breaths. Her hips arched and plunged against his until he was senseless. He ranged lower, his teeth nipping at her rib cage, his tongue laying a line of wet heat over her belly.

Her hands were free now and her fingers gripped his hair, then tore at the bedspread. She couldn't breathe. She needed to tell him. Her body was too full of aches and heat. She needed…

She needed.

Someone cried out. Suzanna heard the quick desperate sound, felt it tear from her own throat as her body arched up. Whole worlds exploded inside of her with a roar more huge than the thunder that stalked just overhead. Stunned, she lay shuddering under him as he lifted his head to stare at her.

Her eyes were dark, her face flushed with fresh fever. Beneath his, her body shook with aftershocks even as her hands slipped limply from his back to the ravaged bed. He hadn't guessed what it would do to him to see that kind of dazed pleasure on her face.

But he knew he wanted more.

He was driving her up again before she could recover. Now she could only embrace the speed and the thrill of danger. As the rain began to pound, she rolled with him, too giddy to be shocked by her own greed. Her hands were as rough and ready as his now, her mouth as merciless. When he dragged the slacks down her legs, her quick gasp was one of triumph. Her fingers were equally impatient as they yanked the denim over his hips, as they streaked and pressed over slick, heated flesh.

She wanted to touch as urgently as she needed to be touched. To possess even as she was possessed. She craved the madness, the turbulent hunger she hadn't known she could feel, and this tempestuous desire that reared up like a wild wolf to consume.

There was no thought of control now, not from either of them. When he sent her racing up again, then again, she rode each slashing crest only frantic for more. More was what he wanted to give her, and what he wanted to take. As the blood fired through his veins he drove himself into her, claiming possession in a frenzy of speed and heat. She matched him, beat for wild beat, the long, nurturing fingers digging into his hips.

They were alone again, but this time the sea was violently churning and the air was flaming hot. Here, at last was the power and the freedom. The speed was reckless, the journey a glorious risk. She felt him shudder, bury his face in her hair as he reached the end. Suzanna locked tight around him, and followed.

He'd wondered what it would be like for fifteen years. From boy to man he had dreamed about her, imagined her, wanted her. None of his fantasies had come close. She had been like a volcano, smoldering and shuddering, then erupting hot. Now she lay like warm wax beneath him, her body meltingly soft with passions spent. Her hair smelled of sun and sea. He thought he could stay just so for eternity, molded against her with the rain drumming on the roof and the wind blowing the curtains.

But he wanted to see her.

When he shifted, she made a small sound of protest and reached out. He said nothing, only kissed her until she relaxed again. Her eyes were drifting shut when he turned the lamp beside the bed on low.

Lord, she was beautiful, with her hair fanned out on the pillows, her skin glowing, her mouth soft and full. She tensed, but he ignored her discomfort as he took a long, silent study of the rest of her.

"Like I said," he murmured when his eyes came back to hers. "The Calhoun women are all lookers."

She didn't know what she was supposed to say or how she was expected to act. She knew that he had taken her to a new place, an extraordinary place, but she had no idea if he had experienced the same mind-spinning ride. Then he frowned and her stomach twisted. With his eyes narrowed, he traced a finger down her throat, over the swell of her breasts.

"I should have shaved," he said abruptly, hating the fact that he'd scraped and reddened her skin. "You could have told me I was hurting you."

"I guess I didn't notice."

"Sorry." He touched his lips gently to her throat. Her look of dazed surprise made him feel like an idiot. When he rolled away, she reached out tentatively for his hand.

"You didn't hurt me," she said softly. "It was wonderful." And she waited, hopeful that he would tell her the same.

"I've got to let the dog in." His voice was rough, but he gave her fingers a quick squeeze before he left the room.

Suzanna heard it now, the whining howls, the scratching at the screen. She told herself it wasn't a rejection. It only meant that he could go from passion to practicality more quickly than she. They had shared something, something vital. She could cling to that. She sat up, more than a little amazed to see the state of the bed. The spread was a heap on the floor, the sheets a tangled knot at the foot. Her clothes—what was left of them—were scattered with his.

She rose and, uncomfortable naked, tugged on his shirt before she lifted her own. One button out of five remained, hanging by a thread. Laughing, she hugged it to herself. To have been wanted like that. With a little sigh, she bent down to search for her buttons. Maybe now he could be cool and collected, maybe his life hadn't been changed as hers had, but she had been wanted, desperately. She would never forget it.

"What are you doing?"

She looked up to see him standing in the doorway. Obviously walking around buck naked didn't concern him in the least, she thought and felt her steady pulse jerk and dance again. He looked angry. She wished she understood what she had done, or hadn't done, to put that scowl on his face.

"My blouse," she said. "I found the buttons." She gripped them in one hand, the thin cotton in the other. "Do you have a needle and thread?"

"No." Didn't she know what she did to him, standing there in nothing but his shirt, her hair tousled, her eyes heavy? Did she want him to get down on his knees and beg?

"Oh." She swallowed and tried to smile. "Well, I can fix it at home. If I could just borrow your shirt. I'd better get back."

He closed the door behind him. "No," he said again, and crossed the room to take her.

The rain stopped at dawn, leaving the air washed clean. Suzanna awoke to the lazy music of water dripping from the gutters. Before her mind had adjusted to where she was, her mouth was captured in a hot, hungry kiss. Her body catapulted from sleep to desire in one breathless leap.

He'd awakened wanting her. That burning need wouldn't ease no matter how much he took, how willingly she gave. There were no words, none he knew, that could express what she had come to mean to him. From a boy's fantasy to a man's salvation.

He could only show her.

He covered her. He filled her. Watching her face in the watery morning sunlight, he knew he would never be content unless she was with him.

"You're mine." He threw the words out like a curse as her body shuddered beneath his. "Say it." His hands fisted on the sheets and he buried his face against her throat. "Damn it, Suzanna, say it."

She could say nothing but his name as he dragged her over the edge.

When her hands slid limply from his back, he rolled over, locking her close so that she lay over him. He could be content with her head resting on his heart. He told himself that he'd already pushed her hard and fast enough. But he'd wanted badly to hear the words.

His hands were fisted in her hair. As if, she thought dizzily, he would yank her back if she tried to move. Her body felt achy and bruised and glorious. She smiled, listening to the rapid thud of his heart and the liquid beauty of morning birdsong.

Her eyes flew open, her head up. He did pull her hair, but more from reflex than intent. "It's morning," Suzanna said.

"That usually happens when the sun comes up."

"No, I—ouch."

"Sorry," he muttered, and reluctantly released her hair.

"I must have fallen asleep."

"Yeah." He ran his hands up and down her back. He liked the long, smooth feel of it. "You dozed off before I could interest you in another round."

Her color fluctuated, but when she tried to scramble up, he held her firmly in place.

"Going somewhere?"

"I have to get home. Aunt Coco must be frantic."

"She knows where you are." Because it was easier to keep her in place, he reversed positions again and began to nibble at her throat. Nothing could have pleased him more than feeling the instant quickening of her pulse under his lips. "And in all likelihood, she's got a pretty good idea what you've been up to."

Without much hope of dislodging him, she pushed at his shoulder. "I didn't tell her where I was going."

"I called her last night when I let Sadie in. Scratch my back, will you? Base of the spine."

She obliged automatically, even while her thoughts spun. "You—you told my aunt that I..."

"I told her you were with me. I figure she could put the rest together. That's good. Thanks."

Suzanna let out a long breath. Oh yes, Aunt Coco wouldn't have any trouble adding two and two. And there was absolutely no reason to feel uncomfortable or embarrassed. But she was both. Not only relating to her aunt but to the man whose naked body was spread over hers.

It had been one thing to face him at night. But the morning...

He lifted his head to study her. "What's the problem?"

"Nothing." When he lifted a brow she shifted in what passed for a shrug. "It's just that I'm not sure what to do now. I've never done this before."

He grinned at her. "How'd you get two kids?"

"I don't mean that I've never...I mean I've never..."

His grin only widened. "Well, get used to it, babe." Considering, he trailed a finger over her jawline. "Want me to help you out with morning-after etiquette?"

"I want you to stop leering at me."

"No, you see that's part of the form." He replaced his trailing finger with a light nip of his teeth. "I'm supposed to leer at you in the morning so you don't start feeling that you look like a hag."

"A—" The word caught in her throat. "A hag?"

"And you're supposed to tell me I was incredible."

Her brow lifted. "I am?"

"That, and any other superlatives you can come up with. Then—" he rolled her over again "—you're supposed to go fix me breakfast, to show me your talents are versatile."

"I can't tell you how grateful I am that you're filling me in on the procedure."

"No problem. And after you fix me breakfast, you should seduce me back into bed."

She laughed and pressed her cheek to his in a move that disarmed and delighted him. "I'll have to practice up on that, but I could probably handle a couple of scrambled eggs."

"Let me know if you find any."

"Have you got a robe?"

"What for?"

She looked up again. He was still leering. "Never mind." Sliding away, she instinctively turned her back as she groped on the floor for his shirt. "And what do you do while I'm fixing breakfast?"

He caught the ends of her hair, let them shift through his fingers. "I watch you."

And he enjoyed it, seeing her move around his kitchen, his shirt skimming her thighs with the scent of coffee ripening the air and her voice low and amused as she spoke to the dog.

She felt more at ease here, with familiar chores. The bush they had planted was a cloud of sunlight outside the window, and the breeze still smelled of rain.

"You know," she said as she grated cheese into the eggs, "you could use more than a toaster, one pot and a skillet."

"Why?" He kicked back in the chair and took a comfortable drag on his cigarette.

"Well, some people actually use this room to prepare entire meals."

"Only if they haven't heard of take-out." He saw that the coffee had dripped through and rose to pour them both a cup. "What do you take in this?"

"Just black. I need the kick."

"If you ask me, what you need is more sleep."

"I have to be at work in an hour or so." With the bowl of eggs in her hands, she stopped to stare out of the window. He recognized the look in her eyes and rubbed a hand over her shoulder.

"Don't."

"I'm sorry." She turned to the stove to pour the beaten eggs into the skillet. "I can't help but wonder what they're doing, if they're having a good time. They've never been away before."

"Hasn't he taken them for a weekend?"

"No, just a couple of afternoons that weren't terribly successful." She made an effort to shake the mood as she stirred the eggs. "Well, there's only thirteen days left to go."

"You're not helping them or yourself by getting worked up." His impotence grated as he fought to massage the tension from her shoulders.

"I'm fine. I will be fine," she corrected. "I've got more than enough to keep me busy for the next couple of weeks. And with the kids gone, I can put in more time trying to find the emeralds."

"You leave that to me."

She glanced over her shoulder. "This is a team effort, Holt. It always has been."

"I'm involved now, and I'll handle it."

She dished the eggs up as carefully as she chose her words. "I appreciate your help. All of us do. But they're called the Calhoun emeralds for a reason. Two of my sisters have been threatened because of them."

"Exactly my point. You're out of your league with Livingston, Suzanna. He's smart and he's brutal. He won't ask you nicely to get out of his way."

Turning, she handed him his plate. "I'm accustomed to smart, brutal men, and I've already spent enough of my life being afraid."

"What's that supposed to mean?"

"Just what I said." She lifted her plate, and the mug of coffee. "I won't let some thief intimidate me or make me afraid to do what's best for myself and my family."

But Holt was shaking his head. That wasn't the answer he'd wanted. "Are you afraid of Dumont? Physically?"

Her gaze wavered then leveled. "We're talking about the emeralds." She tried to move by him, but Holt blocked her path. His eyes had gone dark, but when he spoke his voice was softer, more controlled than she had ever heard it.

"Did he hit you?"

Her color deepened, then raced away from her cheeks. "What?"

"I want to know if Dumont ever hit you."

Nerves were tightening her throat. No matter how quiet his voice, there was a terrible gleam of violence in his eyes. "The eggs are getting cold, Holt, and I'm hungry."

He fought back the urge to hurl the plate against the wall. He sat, waited for her to take the seat across from him. She looked very frail and very composed in the stream of sunlight. "I want an answer, Suzanna." He picked up his coffee and sipped as she toyed with her food. He knew how to wait and how to push.

"No." Her voice was flat as she took the first bite. "He never hit me."

"Just knocked you around?" He kept his voice casual and ate without tasting. Her gaze flicked up to his, then away.

"There are a lot of ways to intimidate and demoralize, Holt. After that, humiliation is a snap." Picking up a slice of toast, she buttered it carefully. "You're nearly out of bread."

"What did he do to you?"

"Let it go."

"What," he repeated slowly, "did he do to you?"

"He made me face facts."

"Such as?"

"That I was pitifully inadequate as a wife of a corporate lawyer with social and political ambitions."

"Why?"

She slammed down the knife. "Is this how you interrogate suspects?"

Anger, he thought. That was better. "It's a simple question."

"And you want a simple answer? Fine. He married me because of my name. He thought there was a bit more money as well as prestige attached to it, but the Calhoun name was more than adequate. Unfortunately it became quickly apparent that I wasn't the social boon he'd imagined. My dinner party conversation was pedestrian at best. I could be dressed up to look the part of the prominent wife of a politically ambitious attorney, but I could never quite pull it off. It was, as he told me often, a huge disappointment that I couldn't get it through my head what was expected of me. That I was boring, in the drawing room, the dining room and the bedroom."

She sprang up to scrape the rest of her meal into Sadie's bowl. "Does that answer your question?"

"No." Holt pushed his plate away and pulled out a cigarette. "I'd like to know how he convinced you that you were at fault."

Keeping her back to him, she straightened. "Because I loved him. Or I loved the man I thought I'd married, and I wanted, very badly, to be the woman he'd be proud of. But the harder I tried, the more I failed. Then I had Alex, and it seemed...I had done something so incredible. I'd brought that beautiful baby into the world. And it was so easy, so natural for me to be a mother. I never had any doubts, any missteps. I was so happy, so focused on the child and the family we'd begun, that I didn't realize that Bax was discreetly finding more exciting companionship. Not until I found out I was going to have Jenny."

"So he cheated on you." His voice was deceptively mild. "What did you do about it?"

She didn't turn around, but began to run water in the sink to wash the dishes. "You can't understand what it's like to be betrayed that way. To already feel as though you're inadequate. To be carrying a man's child and find out that you've already been replaced."

"No, I can't. But it seems to me I'd be ticked off."

"Was I angry?" She nearly laughed. "Yes, I was angry, but I was also...wounded. I don't like to remember how easy it was for him to shatter me. Alex was only a few months old, and Jenny hadn't been planned. But I was so happy to be pregnant. He didn't want her. Nothing he'd done to me before had hurt or shocked me the way his reaction did when I told him I was pregnant again. He wasn't angry so much as...irked." She decided on a half laugh and plunged her hands into the soapy water.

"He had a son," she continued, "so the Dumont name would continue. He didn't intend to clutter up his life with children, and he certainly didn't want to have to drag me around the social wheel a second time while I was fat and tired and unattractive. The most practical solution was to terminate the pregnancy. We fought horribly about that. It was the first time I'd had the nerve to stand up to him—which only made it worse. Bax was used to getting his own way, he always had. Since he couldn't force me to do what he wanted, he paid me back, expertly."

Calmer now, she set the dish aside to drain and began to wash out the skillet. "He was still discreet publicly with his affairs, but he made sure I knew about them, and how sadly I compared to the women he slept with. He took my name off the checking and charge accounts so that I had to ask him whenever I needed money. That was one of his more subtle humiliations. The night Jenny was born, he was with another woman. He made certain I knew about that when he came to the hospital so the press could snap his picture while he played the proud father."

Holt hadn't moved. He didn't trust himself to move. "Why did you stay with him?"

"At first, because I kept hoping I would wake up beside the man I'd fallen in love with. Then, when I started to consider that my marriage was a failure, I had one child and was pregnant with another." She picked up a cloth and began to dry the dishes. "And I stayed because for a long time, a very long time I was convinced he was right about me. I wasn't clever and witty and sharp. I wasn't sexy or seductive. So the least I could be was loyal. When I realized I couldn't even be that, I had to consider the effect on the children. They weren't to be hurt. I couldn't have stood it if dissolving my marriage to Bax had hurt them. One day, I suddenly understood that it was all for nothing, that I was not only wasting my life but probably doing more harm to Alex and Jenny by pretending there was a marriage. Bax paid little attention to his son, and none at all to his daughter. He spent a great deal more time with his lover than he did with his family."

She sighed, set the dishes down. "So I hid my diamonds in Jenny's diaper bag and asked for a divorce." When she turned, the weariness was back on her face. "Does that answer your question?"

Very slowly, his eyes on hers, he rose. "Did it ever occur to you, did it ever once cross your mind that he was inadequate, that he was a failure? That he was a spoiled, selfish bastard?"

Her lips curved a little. "Well, the last part certainly occurred to me. It also occurs to me that my little story is one-sided. I imagine Bax's view of our relationship would differ from mine, and not without some merit."

"He's still pushing your buttons," Holt said with barely suppressed fury. "So you're not clever? I guess anyone could manage to raise two kids and run a business. Dull, too?" He took a step toward her, only more furious when he saw her instinctive move to brace. "Yeah, I don't know when I've been so bored by anyone, but then most men are bored with women with brains and guts, especially when they're softhearted and hardheaded. Nothing puts me to sleep faster than a woman who'll sweat all day to make sure her kids are provided for. God knows you're not sexy. I just didn't have anything better to do last night than to spend it going crazy over you."

He'd trapped her against the sink with his body and with an anger so ripe she could almost taste it. "You asked and I answered. I don't know what you want me to say now."

"I want you to say you don't give a damn about him." He grabbed her by the shoulders, his face close to hers. "I want you to tell me what I told you to tell me when I was inside you, when I was so full of you I couldn't breathe. You're mine, Suzanna. Nothing that happened before counts because you're mine now. That's what I want to hear."

His hands slipped down to clamp over her wrists. Even as she opened her mouth to speak he saw the quick wince of pain. Swearing, he looked down and saw the bruises he'd already put on her. He jerked back as if she'd slapped him.

"Holt—"

He raised a hand to silence her, turning away until he could clear the red haze of fury from his mind. He'd put marks on her skin. It had been done in passion and without intention, but that didn't erase them. By putting them there, he was no better than the man who had bruised her soul.

He jammed his hands into his pockets before he turned. "I've got things to do."

"But—"

"We got off the track, Suzanna. My fault. I know you have to get to work, and so do I."

So that was that, she thought. She'd bared her soul, now he would walk away. "All right. I'll see you on Monday."

With a nod, he headed for the back door, then swore, stopping with his hand on the screen. "Last night meant something to me. Do you understand that?"

She let out a quiet breath. "No."

His hand curled into a fist on the screen. "You're important to me. I care about you, and having you here, this way, is…I need you. Is that clear enough?"

She studied him—a fist on the door, impatience in his eyes, his body rigid with passions she couldn't quite understand. It was enough, she realized. For now it was more than enough.

"Yes, I think it's clear."

"I don't want it to end there." He turned his head, and his eyes were dark and fierce again. "It's not going to end there."

She continued to study his face, keeping her voice calm. "Are you asking me to come back?"

"You know damn well—" He cut himself off and closed his eyes. "Yes, I'm asking you to come back. And I'm asking you to think about spending time with me that isn't at work or in bed. If that doesn't spell it out for you, then—"

"Would you like to come to dinner?"

He gave her a blank stare. "What?"

"Would you like to come to dinner, tonight? Maybe we could take a drive after."

"Yeah." He dragged a hand through his hair, not sure if he was relieved or uneasy that it had been so simple. "That would be good."

Yes, it would be good, she thought and smiled. "I'll see you about seven then. Bring Sadie if you like."

Chapter 9

It wasn't candlelight and moonbeams, Suzanna thought, but it was a romance. She hadn't believed she would find it again, or want it. Flexing her back as she drove up the curving road to The Towers, she smiled.

Of course, a relationship with Holt Bradford was lined with rough edges, but it had its softer moments. She'd had a lovely time discovering them over the past few days. And nights.

There was the way he'd shown up at the shop once or twice, just before lunchtime. He hadn't said anything about the children, or her missing the routine—just that he'd come into the village for some parts and felt like eating.

Or how he'd come up behind her at odd moments to rub the tension out of her shoulders. The evening he'd surprised her after a particularly grueling day by dragging her and a wicker basket filled with cold chicken into the boat.

He was still demanding, often abrupt, but he never made

her feel less than what she wanted to be. When he loved her, he loved her with an urgency and ferocity that left no doubt as to his desire.

No, she hadn't been looking for romance, she thought as she parked the truck behind Holt's car. But she was terribly glad she'd found it.

The moment she opened the door, Lilah pounced. "I've been waiting for you."

"So I see." Suzanna lifted a brow. Lilah was still in her park service uniform. Knowing her schedule, Suzanna was sure her sister had been home nearly an hour. As a matter of routine, Lilah should have been in her most comfortable clothes and spread out dozing on the handiest flat surface. "What's up?"

"Can you do anything with that surly hulk you've gotten tangled up with?"

"If you mean Holt, not a great deal." Suzanna pulled off her cap to run her hands through her hair. "Why?"

"Right now, he's upstairs, taking my room apart inch by inch. I couldn't even change my clothes." She aimed a narrowed glance up the steps. "I told him we'd already looked there, and that if I'd been sleeping in the same room as the emeralds all these years, I'd know it."

"And he ignored you."

"He not only ignored me, he kicked me out of my own bedroom. And Max." She let out a hiss of breath and sat on the stairs. "Max grinned and said it was a damn good idea."

"Want to gang up on them?"

A wicked gleam came into Lilah's eyes. "Yeah." She rose then swung an arm over Suzanna's shoulders as they started up. "You're really serious about him, aren't you?"

"I'm taking it one step at a time."

"Sometimes when you love someone it's better to take it by leaps and bounds." Then she yawned and swore. "I missed my nap. It'd be satisfying if I could say I disliked that pushy jerk, but I can't. There's something too solid and steady under the bad manners."

"You've been looking at his aura again."

Lilah laughed and stopped at the top of the stairs. "He's a good guy, as much as I'd like to belt him right now. It's good to see you happy again, Suze."

"I haven't been unhappy."

"No, just not happy. There's a difference."

"I suppose there is. Speaking of happy, how are the wedding plans coming?"

"Actually, Aunt Coco and the relative from hell are in the kitchen arguing over them right now." She turned laughing eyes to her sister. "And having a delightful time. Our great-aunt Colleen is pretending she simply wants to make certain the event will live up to the Calhoun reputation, but the fact is, she's getting a big kick out of making guest lists and shooting down Aunt Coco's menus."

"As long as she's entertained."

"Wait until she gets hold of you," Lilah warned. "She has some very creative ideas for floral arrangements."

"Terrific." Suzanna stopped in Lilah's doorway. Holt was definitely hard at work. Never particularly ordered, Lilah's room looked as though someone had scooped up every piece of furniture and dropped it down again like pick-up sticks. At the moment, he had his head in the fireplace, and Max was crawling on the floor.

"Having fun, boys?" Lilah said lazily.

Max looked up and grinned. She was mad, all right, he thought. He'd learned to handle and enjoy her temper. "I found that other sandal you've been looking for. It was under the cushion of the chair."

"There's good news." She lifted a brow, noting that Holt

was now sitting on Lilah's hearth, looking at Suzanna. And Suzanna was looking at him. "You need a break, Max."

"No, I'm fine."

"You definitely need a break." She walked in to take his hand and pull him to his feet. "You can come back and help Holt invade my privacy later."

"I told you she wouldn't like it," Suzanna said when Lilah dragged Max from the room.

"That's too bad."

With her hands on her hips she surveyed the damage. "Did you find anything?"

"Not unless you count the two odd earrings and one of those lacy things we found behind the dresser." He tilted his head. "You got any of those lacy things?"

"Not really." She looked down at her sweaty T-shirt. "Up until a few days ago, I didn't think I'd need any."

"You've got a real nice way of wearing denim, babe." He rose, and since she wasn't coming any closer, moved to her. "And…" He ran his hands over her shoulders, down her back to her hips. "I get a real charge out of taking it off you." He kissed her hard, in the deep and urgent way she'd come to expect. Then he nipped her bottom lip and grinned. "But anytime you want to borrow one of those lacy things from Lilah…"

She laughed and gave him a quick, affectionate hug, the kind she gave so freely that never failed to warm him from the inside out. "Maybe I'll surprise you. How long have you been here?"

"I came straight from the site. Did you get the rest of those whatdoyoucallits in?"

"Russian olives, yes." And her back was still aching. "You were a lot of help on the retaining wall."

"You were out of your mind to think you could build that thing on your own."

"I had a part-time laborer when I contracted."

He shook his head and went back to searching the fireplace. "You may be tough, Suzanna, but you're not equipped to haul around lumber and swing a sledgehammer."

"I'd have done it—"

"Yeah." He glanced around. "I know." He tested another brick. "It did look pretty good."

"It looked terrific. And since you didn't swear at me more than half a dozen times when you were hefting landscape timbers, why don't I reward you?"

"Oh, yeah?" He lost his interest in the bricks.

"I'll go get you a beer."

"I'd rather have—"

"I know." She laughed as she walked out. "But you'll have to settle for a beer. For now."

It felt good, she thought, to be able to joke like that. Not to be embarrassed or edgy. There was no need to feel anything but content, knowing he cared for her. In time, they might have something deeper.

Full of energy and hope, she rounded the last step and turned into the hall. All at once, there was chaos. She heard the dogs first, Fred and Sadie, barking fiendishly, then the clatter of feet on the porch and two high bellowing shouts.

"Mom!" Both Jenny and Alex yelled the single syllable as they burst into the house.

The rich and fast joy came first as she bent to scoop them up in her arms. Laughing, she smothered them both with kisses as the dogs dashed in mad circles.

"Oh, I missed you. I missed you both so much. Let me look at you." When she drew them back arm's length, her smile faltered. They were both on the edge of tears. "Baby?"

"We wanted to come home." Jenny's voice trembled as

she buried her face against her mother's shoulder. "We hate vacation."

"Shh." She stroked Jenny's hair as Alex rubbed a fist under his eyes.

"We were unmanageable and bad," he said in a trembly voice. "And we don't care, either."

"Just the attitude I've come to expect," Bax said as he walked through the open front door. Jenny's arms tightened around Suzanna's neck, but Alex turned and threw out his Calhoun chin.

"We didn't like the dumb party, and we don't like you, either."

"Alex!" Her tone sharp, she dropped a hand on his shoulder. "That's enough. Apologize."

His lips quivered, but the stubborn gleam remained in his eyes. "We're sorry we don't like you."

"Take your sister upstairs," Bax said tightly. "I want to speak with your mother in private."

"You and Jenny go in the kitchen." Suzanna brushed a hand over Alex's cheek. "Aunt Coco's there."

Bax took a careless swipe at Fred with his foot. "And take these damn mutts with you."

"Chéri?" This from the svelte brunette who continued to hover in the doorway.

"Yvette." Keeping her arms around the children, Suzanna rose. "I'm sorry, I didn't see you."

The Frenchwoman waved distracted hands. "I beg your pardon, it's so confusing, I see. I just wondered—Bax, the children's bags?"

"Have the driver bring them in," he snapped. "Can't you see I'm busy?"

Suzanna sent the frazzled woman a look of sympathy. "He can just leave them here in the hall. If you'd like to come into the parlor…go see Aunt Coco," she told the children. "She'll be so happy you're back."

They went, holding each other's hand, with the dogs prancing at their heels.

"If you could spare a moment of your time," Bax said, then cast a glance up and down her work clothes, "out of your obviously fascinating day."

"The parlor," she repeated and turned. She struggled for calm, knowing it was essential. Whatever had caused him to change his plans and bring the children home a full week early was undoubtedly going to fall on her head. That she could handle. But the fact that the children had been upset was a different matter.

"Yvette—" Suzanna gestured to a chair "—can I get you something?"

"Oh, if you would be so kind. A brandy?"

"Of course. Bax?"

"Whiskey, a double."

She went to the liquor cabinet and poured, grateful her hands were steady. As she served Yvette, she thought she caught a glance of apology and embarrassment.

"Well, Bax, would you like to tell me what happened?"

"What happened began years ago when you had the mistaken idea you could be a mother."

"Bax," Yvette began, and was rounded on.

"Get out on the terrace. I prefer to do this privately."

So that hadn't changed, Suzanna thought. She gripped her hands together as Yvette crossed the room and exited through the glass doors.

"At least this little experiment should have rid her of the notion of having a child."

"Experiment?" Suzanna repeated. "Your visit with the children was an experiment?"

He sipped at the whiskey and watched her. He was still a striking man with a charmingly boyish face and fair hair. But temper, as it always had, added an edge to his looks that was anything but appealing.

"My reasons for taking the children are my concern. Their unforgivable behavior is yours. They haven't any conception of how to act in public and in private. They have the manners and dispositions of heathens and as little control. You've done a poor job, Suzanna, unless it was your intention to raise two miserable brats."

"Don't think you can stand here and speak about them that way in my house." Eyes dangerously bright, she walked toward him. "I don't give a damn if they fit your standards or not. I want to know why you've brought them back this way."

"Then listen," he suggested, and shoved her into a chair. "Your precious children don't have a clue what's expected of a Dumont. They were loud and unmanageable in restaurants, whiny and fidgety on the drive. When corrected they became defiant or sulky. At the resort, among several of my acquaintances, their behaviour was an embarrassment."

Too incensed for fear, Suzanna pulled herself out of the chair. "In other words, they were children. I'm sorry your plans were upset, Baxter, but it's difficult to expect a five- and six-year-old to present themselves as socially correct on all occasions. Even more difficult when they're thrust into a situation that wasn't any of their doing. They don't know you."

He swirled whiskey, swallowed. "They're perfectly aware that I'm their father, but you've seen to it that they have no respect for that relationship."

"No, you've seen to it."

Deliberately he set the whiskey aside. "Do you think I don't know what you tell them? Sweet, harmless little Suzanna." She stepped back automatically, pleasing him.

"I don't tell them anything about you," she said, furious with herself for retreating.

"Oh, no? Then you didn't mention the fact that they had a bastard brother out in Oklahoma?"

So that was it, she realized, struggling to settle. "Megan O'Riley's brother married my sister. There was no way to keep the situation a secret, even if I had wanted to."

"And you just couldn't wait to sling my name around." He gave her another shove that sent her stumbling back.

"The boy's their half brother. They accept that, and they're too young to understand what a despicable thing you did."

"My affairs are mine. Don't you forget it." Gripping her shoulders, he pushed her up against the wall. "I have no intention of letting you get away with your pitiful plots for revenge."

"Take your hands off me." She twisted, but he forced her back again.

"When I'm damn good and ready. Let me warn you, Suzanna. I won't have you spreading my private business around. If even a hint of this gets out, I'll know where it started, and you know who'll pay for it."

She kept herself rigid, kept her eyes steady. "You can't hurt me anymore."

"Don't count on it. You make sure your children keep this business of half brothers to themselves. If it's mentioned again—" he tightened his grip and jerked her up on her toes "—ever, you'll be very sorry."

"Take your threats and get out of my house."

"Yours?" He closed a hand around her throat. "Remember, it's only yours because I didn't want this crumbling anachronism. Push me, and I'll have you back in court in a heartbeat. And I'll have it all this time. Those children might benefit from a nice, Swiss boarding school, which is exactly where they'll be if you don't watch your step."

He saw her eyes change, but it wasn't the fear he'd expected. It was fury. She lifted a hand, but before she could strike out, he was jerked away and tumbling to the floor. She watched Holt drag him up again by the collar, then send him crashing into a Louis Quinze table.

She'd never seen murder in a man's eyes before, but she recognized it in Holt's as he pounded a fist into Baxter's face.

"Holt, don't—"

She started forward only to have her arm gripped with surprising strength. "Let him alone," Colleen said, her mouth grim, her eyes bright.

He wanted to kill him, and might have, if the man had fought back. But Bax slumped in his hold, nose and mouth seeping blood. "You listen to me, you bastard." Holt slammed him against the wall. "Put your hands on her again, and you're dead."

Shaken, hurting, Bax fumbled for a handkerchief. "I can have you arrested for assault." Holding the cloth to his nose, he looked around and saw his wife standing inside the terrace doors. "I have a witness. You assaulted me and threatened my life." It was his first taste of humiliation, and he detested it. His glance veered toward Suzanna. "You'll regret this."

"No, she won't," Colleen put in before Holt could give in to the satisfaction of smashing his fist into the sneering mouth. "But you will, you miserable, quivering, spineless swine." She leaned heavily on her cane as she walked toward him. "You'll regret it for what's left of your worthless life if you ever lay hands on any member of my family again. Whatever you think you can do to us, I can do only more viciously to you. If you're unclear about my abilities, my name is Colleen Theresa Calhoun, and I can buy and sell you twice over."

She studied him, a pitiful man in a rumpled suit, bleeding into a silk handkerchief. "I wonder what the governor of your state—who happens to be my godchild—will have to say if I mention this scene to him." She gave a slow, satisfied nod when she saw she was understood. "Now get your miserable hide out of my house. Young man—" she inclined her head to Holt "—you'll be so kind as to show our guest to the door."

"My pleasure." Holt dragged him into the hall. The last thing Suzanna saw when she ran from the house was Yvette's fluttering hands.

"Where did she go?" Holt demanded when he found Colleen alone in the parlor.

"To lick her wounds, I suppose. Get me a brandy. Damn it, she'll keep a minute," she muttered when he hesitated. Colleen eased herself into a chair and waited for her heart rate to settle. "I knew she'd had a difficult time, but I wasn't fully aware of the extent of it. I've had this Dumont looked into since the divorce." She took the brandy and drank deeply. "Pitiful excuse for a man. I still wasn't aware he had abused her. I should have been, the first time I saw that look in her eyes. My mother had the same look." She closed her own and leaned back. "Well, if he doesn't want to see his political ambitions go up in smoke, he'll leave her be." Slowly she opened her eyes and gave Holt a steely look. "You did well for yourself—I admire a man who uses his fists. I only regret I didn't use my cane on him."

"I think you did better. I just broke his nose, you scared the—"

"I certainly did." She smiled and drank again. "Damn good feeling, too." She noted that Holt was staring at the open terrace doors, his hands still fisted. Suzanna could do worse, she thought and swirled the remaining brandy. "My mother used to go to the cliffs. You might find Suzanna there. Tell her the children are having cookies and spoiling their dinner."

* * *

She had gone to the cliffs. She didn't know why when she'd needed to run, that she had run there. Only for a moment, she promised herself. She would only need a moment alone.

She sat on a rock, covered her face and wept out the bitterness and shame.

He found her like that, alone and sobbing, the wind carrying off the sounds of her grief, the sea pounding restlessly below. He didn't know where to begin. His mother had always been a sturdy woman, and whatever tears she had shed, had been shed in private.

Worse, he could still see Suzanna pushed against the wall, Dumont's hand on her throat. She'd looked so fragile, and so brave.

He stepped closer, laid a hesitant hand on her hair. "Suzanna."

She was up like a shot, choking back tears, wiping them from her damp face. "I have to get back in. The children—"

"Are in the kitchen stuffing themselves with cookies. Sit down."

"No, I—"

"Please." He sat, easing her down beside him. "I haven't been here in a long time. My grandfather used to bring me. He used to sit right here and look out to sea. Once he told me a story about a princess in the castle up on the ridge. He must have been talking about Bianca, but later, when I remembered it, I always thought of you."

"Holt, I'm so sorry."

"If you apologize, you're only going to make me mad."

She swallowed another hot ball of tears. "I can't stand that you saw, that anyone saw."

"What I saw was you standing up to a bully." He turned

her face to his. When he saw the fading red marks on her throat, he had to force back an oath. "He's never going to hurt you again."

"It was his reputation. The children must have talked about Kevin."

"Are you going to tell me?"

She did, as clearly as she was able. "When Sloan told me," she finished, "I knew it was important that the children understand they had a brother. What Bax doesn't realize is that I never thought about him, never cared. It was the children who mattered, all of them. The family."

"No, he wouldn't understand that. Or you." He brought her hand to his lips to kiss it gently. The stunned look on her face had him scowling out to sea. "I haven't been Mr. Sensitivity myself."

"You've been wonderful."

"If I had you wouldn't look like I hit you with a rock when I kiss your hand."

"It just isn't your style."

"No." He shrugged and dug out a cigarette. "I guess it's not." Then he changed his mind and slipped an arm around her shoulders instead. "Nice view."

"It's wonderful. I've always come here, to this spot. Sometimes…"

"Go ahead."

"You'll just laugh at me, but sometimes it's as if I can almost see her. Bianca. I can feel her, and I know she's here, waiting." She rested her head on his shoulder and shut her eyes. "Like right now. It's so warm and real. Up in the tower, her tower, it's bittersweet, more of a longing. But here, it's anticipation. Hope. I know you think I'm crazy."

"No." When she started to shift, he pulled her closer so

that her head nestled back on his shoulder. "No, I can't. Not when I feel it, too."

From the west tower, the man who called himself Marshall watched them through field glasses. He didn't worry about being disturbed. The family no longer came above the second floor in the west wing, and the crew had knocked off thirty minutes before. He'd hoped to take advantage of the time that Sloan O'Riley was away with his new bride on his honeymoon to move more freely around the house. The Calhouns were so accustomed to seeing men in tool belts that they rarely gave him a second glance.

And he was interested, very interested in Holt Bradford, finding it fascinating that he was being drawn into this generation of Calhouns. It pleased him that he could continue his work right under the nose of an ex-cop. Such irony added to his vanity.

He would continue to keep tabs, he thought, while the cop completed his search. And he would be there to take what was his the moment the treasure was found. Whoever was in the way would simply be eliminated.

Suzanna spent all evening with her children, soothing ruffled feathers and trying to turn their unhappy experience into a silly misadventure. By the time she got them tucked into bed, Jenny was no longer clinging and Alex had rebounded like a rubber ball.

"We had to ride in the car for hours and hours." He bounced on his sister's bed while Suzanna smoothed Jenny's sheets. "And they had dumb music on the radio the *whole* time. People were singing like this." He opened his mouth wide and let out what he thought passed for an operatic aria. "And you couldn't understand a word."

"Not like that, like this." Jenny let out a screech that could have shattered crystal. "And we had to be quiet and appreciate."

Suzanna held her temper and tweaked her daughter's nose. "Well, you appreciated that it was awful, didn't you?"

That made Jenny giggle and reach up for another kiss. "Yvette said we could play a word game, but he said it gave him a headache, so she went to sleep."

"And that's what you should do, right now."

"I liked the hotel," Alex continued, hoping to postpone the inevitable. "We got to jump on the beds when nobody was looking."

"You mean like you do in your room?"

He grinned. "They had little bars of soap in the bathroom, and they put candy on your pillow at night."

Suzanna cocked her head. "You can forget that idea, toadface."

After Jenny was settled with her night-light and army of stuffed animals, Suzanna carried Alex to his room. He didn't let her pick him up and cuddle often anymore, but tonight, he seemed to need it as much as she did.

"You've been eating bricks again," she murmured, and nuzzled his neck.

"I had five bricks for lunch." He flew out of her arms and onto the bed. She wrestled with him until he was breathless. He flopped back, laughing, then leaped out of bed again.

"Alex—"

"I forgot."

"You've already stretched it tonight, kid. In the bed or I'll have you cooked over a slow fire."

He pulled something out of the jeans he'd been wearing when he'd come home. "I saved it for you."

Suzanna took the flattened, broken chocolate wrapped in

gold paper. It was more than a little melted, certainly inedible and more precious than diamonds.

"Oh, Alex."

"Jenny had one, too, but she lost it."

"That's all right." She brought him close for a fierce hug. "Thanks. I love you, you little worm."

"I love you, too." It didn't embarrass him to say it as it sometimes did, and he cuddled against her a moment longer. When his mother tucked him into bed, he didn't complain when she stroked his hair. "Night," he said, ready to sleep.

"Good night." She left him alone, weeping a little over the smashed mint. In her room, she opened the little case that had once held her diamonds, and tucked her son's gift inside.

She undressed then slipped into a thin white nightgown. There was paperwork waiting on her desk in the corner, but she knew her mind and nerves were still too rattled. To soothe herself, she opened the terrace doors and, taking her brush, walked outside to feel the night.

There was an owl hooting, crickets singing, the quiet whoosh of the sea. Tonight the moon was gilded and its light clear as glass. Smiling to herself, she lifted her face to it and skimmed the brush lazily through her hair.

Holt had never seen anything more beautiful than Suzanna brushing her hair in the moonlight. He knew he made a poor Romeo and was deathly afraid he'd make a fool of himself trying, but he had to give her something, to somehow show her what it meant to have her in his life.

He came out of the garden and started up the stone steps. He moved quietly, and she was dreaming. She didn't know he was there until he said her name.

"Suzanna."

She opened her eyes and saw him standing only a foot away, his hair ruffled by the breeze, his eyes dark in the shimmering light. "I was thinking about you. What are you doing here?"

"I went home, but…I came back." He wanted her to go on brushing her hair, but was certain the request would sound ridiculous. "Are you all right?"

"I'm fine, really."

"The kids?"

"They're fine, too. Sleeping. I didn't even thank you before. Maybe it's petty, but now that I've had a chance to settle, I can admit I really enjoyed seeing Bax's nose bleed."

"Anytime," Holt said, and meant it.

"I don't think it'll be necessary again, but I appreciate it." She reached out to touch his hand, and pricked her finger on a thorn. "Ow."

"That's a hell of a start," he mumbled, and thrust the rose at her. "I brought you this."

"You did?" Absurdly touched, she brushed the petals to her cheek.

"I stole it out of your garden." He stuck his hands into his pockets and wished for a cigarette. "I don't guess it counts."

"It certainly does." She had had two gifts that night, she thought, from the two men she loved. "Thank you."

He shrugged and wondered what to do next. "You look nice."

She smiled and glanced down at the simple white gown. "Well, it's not lacy."

"I watched you brushing your hair." His hand came out of his pocket of its own volition to touch. "I just stood there, down at the edge of the garden and watched you. I could hardly breathe. You're so beautiful, Suzanna."

Now it was she who couldn't breathe. He'd never looked at her just this way. His voice had never sounded so quiet. There was a reverence in it, as in the hand that stroked over her hair.

"Don't look at me like that." His fingers tightened in her hair and he had to force them to relax again. "I know I've been rough with you."

"No, you haven't."

"Damn it, I have." He fought against a welling impatience as she only stared at him. "I've pushed you around and grabbed on. I ripped your blouse."

A smile touched her lips. "When I sewed the buttons back on I remembered that night, and what it felt like to be needed that way." More than a little baffled, she shook her head. "I'm not fragile, Holt."

Couldn't she see how wrong she was? Didn't she know how she looked right now, her hair smooth and shining in the moonlight, the thin white gown flowing down?

"I want to be with you tonight." He slid his hand down to touch her cheek. "Let me love you tonight."

She couldn't have denied him anything. When he lifted her to carry her in, she pressed her lips to his throat. But his mouth didn't turn hot and ready to hers. He laid her down carefully, took the brush and rose from her to set it on the nightstand. Then he turned the lights low.

When his mouth came to hers at last, it was soft as a whisper. His hands didn't race to excite, but moved with exquisite patience to seduce.

He felt her confusion, heard it in the unsteady murmur of his name, but he only rubbed his lips over hers, tracing the shape with his tongue. His strong hands moved with an artist's grace over the tensed slope of her shoulders.

"Trust me." He took his mouth on a slow, quiet journey over her face. "Let go and trust me, Suzanna. There's more than one way." Over her jaw, down the line of her throat, back to her trembling lips his mouth whispered. "I should have showed you before."

"I can't..." Then his kiss had her sinking, deep, deeper still into some thick velvet haze. She couldn't right herself. Didn't want to. Surely this endless, echoing tunnel was paradise.

He touched, hardly touching at all, and left her weak. His mouth, gliding like a cool breeze over her flesh, was rapture. She could hear him murmur to her, incredible promises, soft, lovely words. There was passion in them, in the fingertips that seemed designed only to bring her pleasure, yet this was a passion to give she had never expected.

He stroked her through the thin cotton, delighting in the liquid movements of her body beneath his hands. He could watch her face in the lamplight, feed on that alone, knowing she was steeped in him, in what he offered her. There was no need to strap down greed, desire was no less, but it had taken a different hue.

When she sighed, he brought his lips back to hers to swallow the flavor of his name.

He undressed her slowly, bringing the gown down inch by inch, wallowing in the delight of warming newly bared skin. Fascinated with each tremor he brought her, he lingered. Then took her gently over the first crest.

Unbearably sweet. Each movement, each sigh. Exquisitely tender. Every touch, every murmur. He had imprisoned her in a world of silk, gently bringing dozens of pulses to a throbbing ache that was like music. Never had she been more aware of her body than now as he explored it so thoroughly, so patiently.

At last she felt his flesh against hers, the warm, hard body she had come to crave. Opening heavy eyes, she looked. Lifting weighted limbs, she touched.

He hadn't known a need could be so strong yet so quiet. She enfolded him. He slipped into her. For both, it was like coming home.

* * *

I could not have foreseen that the day would be my last with her. Would I have looked more closely, held more tightly? The love could have been no greater, but could it have been treasured more completely?

There is no answer.

We found the little dog, cowering and half-starved in the rocks by our cliffs. Bianca found such pleasure in him. It was foolish, I suppose, but I think we both felt this was something we could share, since we had found him together.

We called him Fred, and I must admit I was sad to see him go when it was time for her to return to The Towers. Of course it was right that she take the orphaned pup to her children so that they could make him a family. I went home alone, to think of her, to try to work.

When she came to me, I was stunned that she should have taken such a risk. Only once before had she been to the cottage, and we had not dared chance that again. She was frantic and overwrought. Under her cloak, she carried the puppy. Because she was pale as a ghost, I made her sit and poured her brandy.

She told me, as I sat, hardly daring to speak, of the events that had taken place since we'd parted.

The children had fallen in love with the dog. There had been laughter and light hearts until Fergus had returned. He refused to have the dog, a stray mutt, in his home. Perhaps I could have forgiven him for that, thought of him only as a rigid fool. Bianca told me that he had ordered the dog destroyed, holding firm even on the tears and pleas of his children.

On the girl, young Colleen, he had been the hardest. Fearing a harsher, perhaps a physical reprisal, Bianca had sent the children and the dog up to their nanny.

The argument that had followed was bitter. She did not tell me all, but her tremors and the flash of fear in her eyes said enough. In his fury, he had threatened and abused her. It was then I saw in the light of my lamp, the marks on her throat where his hands had squeezed.

I would have gone then. I would have killed him. But her terror stopped me. Never before and never again in my life have I felt a rage such as that. To love as I loved, to know that she had been hurt and frightened. There are times I wish to God I had gone, and had killed. Perhaps things would have been different. But I'll never be sure.

I didn't leave her, but stayed while she wept and told me that he had gone to Boston, and that when he returned he intended to bring a new governess of his choosing. He had accused her of being a poor mother, and would take the care and control of the children from her.

If he had threatened to cut out her heart, he could not have done more damage. She would not see her children raised by a paid servant, overseen by a cold, ambitious father. She feared most for her daughter, knowing if nothing was done, Colleen would one day be bartered off into marriage—even as her mother had been.

It was this great fear that forced her decision to leave him.

She knew the risks, the scandal, the position she would be giving up. Nothing could sway her. She would take her children away where she knew they would be safe. Her wish was for me to go with them, but she did not beg or call upon my love.

She did not need to.

I would make the arrangements the next day, and she would prepare the children. Then she asked me to make her mine.

For so long I had wanted her. Yet I had promised myself I would not take her. That night I broke one promise, and I made another. I would love her eternally.

I still remember how she looked, her hair unbound, her eyes so dark. Before I touched her I knew how she would feel. Before I laid her in my bed, I knew how she would look there. Now it is only a dream, the sweetest memory of my life. The sound of the water and the crickets, the smell of wildflowers.

In that timeless hour, I had everything a man could want. She was beauty and love and promise. Seductive and innocent, shy and wanton. Even now, I can taste her mouth, smell her skin. And ache for her.

Then she was gone. What I had thought was a beginning was an end.

I took what money I had, sold paints and canvases for more and bought four tickets on the evening train. She did not come. There was a storm brewing. Hot lightning, vicious thunder, heavy wind. I told myself it was the weather that turned my blood so cold. But God help me, I think I knew. There was such a sharp, terrifying pain, such unreasonable fear. It consumed me.

For the first time, and the last, I went to The Towers. The rain began to slash as I beat on the door. The woman who answered was hysterical. I would have pushed past her, run through the house calling for Bianca, but at that moment, the police arrived.

She had jumped from the tower, thrown herself through the window onto the rocks. This is unclear now, as it was even then. I remember running, shouting for her over the howling wind. The lights of the house were blinding, slashing through the gloom. Men were already scrambling on the ridge and below with lanterns. I stood, looking down at her. My love. Taken from me. Not by her own hand. I could never accept that. But gone. Lost.

I would have leaped off that ridge myself. But she stopped me. I will swear it was her voice that stopped me. Instead, I sat on the ground, the rain pouring over me.

I could not join her then. Somehow I would have to live out my life without her. I have done so, and perhaps some good has come from the time I have spent here. The boy, my grandson. How Bianca would have loved him. There are times I take him to our cliffs and I'm sure she's there with us.

There are still Calhouns in The Towers. Bianca would have wanted that. Her children's children, and theirs. Perhaps one day another lonely young woman will walk those cliffs. I hope her fate is a kinder one.

I know, in my heart, that it is not ended yet. She waits for me. When my time comes at last, I will talk with Bianca again. I will love her as I once promised. Eternally.

Chapter 10

Holt waited for Trent in the pergola along the seawall. Lighting a cigarette, he looked over the wide lawn to The Towers. One of the gargoyles along the center peak had lost its head while the other sat grinning down, more charming than ferocious. There were clematis—he recognized it now—and roses climbing up to the first terrace. The old stone glowered in the hazy sunlight. There was really no other word for it, but the flowers gave it a kind of magical, Sleeping Beauty aura. Towers and turrets speared up, arrogant of form, dignified with age.

Scaffolding bracketed the west end, and the high whine of a power saw cut the air. A lift truck was parked under the balcony, its mechanism groaning as it hefted its load of equipment to a trio of bare-backed men. A radio jolted out hard rock.

Maybe it was right and just that the house held so tenaciously to the past even while it accepted the present, Holt mused. If it was possible for stone and mortar to absorb emotion and memory, The Towers had done so. Already he felt as though it harbored some of his.

The windows of the room where he had spent most of the night with Suzanna winked back at him. He remembered every second of those hours, every sigh, every movement. He also remembered that he had confused her. No, tenderness wasn't his style, he thought, but it had been easy with her.

She hadn't asked him for softness. She hadn't asked him for anything. Was that why he felt compelled to give? Without trying, she had tapped into something inside him he hadn't known was there—and was still more than a little uncomfortable with. Finding it, feeling it left him as vulnerable as she. He'd yet to work out the right way to tell her.

She deserved the music, the candlelight, the flowers. She deserved the soft poetic words. He was going to try to give them to her, no matter how big a fool it made him feel.

In the meantime, he had a job to do. He was going to find those damn emeralds for her. And he was going to put Livingston behind bars.

Holt tossed the cigarette away as he saw Trent come out of the house. In the pergola, they would have relative privacy. The clatter of construction echoed in countertime to the beat and drum of waves. Whatever they said wouldn't carry above ten feet. Anyone looking out of the house would see two men sharing a late-afternoon beer, away from the women.

Trent stepped inside and offered a bottle.

"Thanks." Holt leaned negligently against a post and lifted the beer. "Did you get the list?"

"Yeah." Trent took a seat on one of the stone benches so that he could watch the house as he drank. "We've only signed on four new men in the last month."

"References?"

"Of course." The faint annoyance in his tone was instinctive. "Sloan and I are well aware of security."

Holt merely shrugged. "A man like Livingston wouldn't have any problem getting references. They'd cost him." Holt drank deeply. "But he'd get them."

"You'd know more about that sort of thing than I." Trent's eyes narrowed as he watched two of the men replacing shingles on the roof of the west wing. "But I have a hard time buying that he could be here, working right under our noses."

"Oh, he's here." Holt took out another cigarette, lighted it, then took a thoughtful drag. "Whoever tossed my place knew about the connection almost as soon as you did. Since none of you go around talking about the situation at cocktail parties, he'd have heard something here, in the house. He didn't sign on at the start of the job, because he was busy elsewhere. But the last few weeks..." He paused as the children ran out, dogs in tow, to race to their fort. "He wouldn't just sit and wait, not as long as there's a possibility you could knock out a wall and have the emeralds fall into your hand. And where better to keep an eye on things than inside?"

"It fits," Trent admitted. "But I don't like the idea of my wife, or any of the others, being that close." He thought of C.C., the baby she carried, and his eyes darkened. "If there's a chance you're right, I want to move on it."

"Give me the list, and I'll check it out. I've still got connections." Holt's gaze remained on the children. "He's not going to hurt any of them. That's a fact."

Trent nodded. He was a businessman and had never done anything more violent than a little boxing in college. But he would do whatever it took to protect his wife and unborn child. "I filled Max in, and Sloan and Amanda decided to break off their honeymoon. They should be here in a couple of hours."

That was good, Holt thought. It was best having the family all in one place. "What did Sloan tell her?"

"That there was some problem with the job." More comfortable now that wheels were in motion, Trent grinned a little. "If she finds out he's stringing her along, there'll be hell to pay."

"The less the women know, the better."

This time Trent laughed. "If any of them heard you say that, you'd lose three layers of skin. They're a tough bunch."

Holt thought of Suzanna. "They think they are."

"No, they are. It took me quite a while to accept it. Individually they're strong—velvet-coated steel. Not to mention stubborn, impulsive and feverishly loyal. Together..." Trent smiled again. "Well, I'll admit I'd rather face a pair of sumo wrestlers than the Calhoun women on a roll."

"When it's over, they can be as mad as they want."

"As long as they're safe," Trent finished, and noted that Holt was watching the children. "Great kids," he commented.

"Yeah. They're okay."

"They've got a hell of a mother." Trent drank contemplatively. "Too bad they don't have a real father."

Even the thought of Baxter Dumont made Holt's blood boil. "How much do you know about him?"

"More than I like. I know he put Suzanna through hell. He nearly broke her with the custody suit."

"Custody suit?" Stunned, Holt looked back. "He went after the kids?"

"He went after her," Trent corrected. "What better way? She doesn't talk about it. I got the story from C.C. Apparently he was annoyed that she filed for the divorce. Not good for his image, particularly since he's got his eye on a senate seat. He dragged her through a long, ugly court battle, trying to prove she was unstable and unfit."

"Bastard." Choking on rage, Holt turned away to flick the cigarette onto the rocks.

"He didn't want them. The idea was to ship them off to a boarding school. Or that was the threat. He backed off when Suzanna made the settlement."

His hands were on the stone rail now, fingers digging in. "What settlement?"

"She gave him damn near everything. He dropped the case so the arrangements could be made privately. He got the house, all the property, along with a chunk of her inheritance. She could have fought it, but she and the kids were already an emotional mess. She didn't want to take any chances with them, or put them through any more stress."

"No, she wouldn't." Holt drank in a futile attempt to wash the bitterness from his throat. "He's not going to hurt her or the kids anymore. I'll see to it."

"I thought you would." Trent rose, satisfied. He pulled a list out of his pocket and exchanged it for Holt's empty bottle. "Let me know what you find out."

"Yeah."

"The séance tonight." Trent saw Holt grimace and laughed again. "It may surprise you."

"The only thing that surprises me is that Coco talked me into it."

"If you plan on sticking around, you'll have to get used to being talked into all manner of things."

He was going to stick around, all right, Holt thought as Trent walked away. He just needed to find the right way to tell Suzanna. After glancing at the names on the list, Holt tucked it away. He'd make a couple of calls and see what he could dig up.

As he started across the lawn, the dogs galloped up to him, Fred devotedly pressing to Sadie's side. When they stopped jumping long enough to be petted, Fred lapped frantically at her face. Sadie tolerated it, then turned away and ignored him.

"They've got a name for women like you," Holt told her.

"Remember the Alamo!" Alex shouted. He stood spread legged on the roof of his fort, a plastic sword in his hand. Because he counted on his challenge being answered, his eyes gleamed as they met Holt's. "You'll never take us alive."

"Oh yeah?" Unable to resist, Holt moved closer. "What makes you think I want you, monkey brain?"

"'Cause we're the patriots and you're the evil invaders."

Jenny popped her head through an opening that served as a window. Before Holt could evade it, he was hit dead center of the chest with a splat of water from her pistol. Alex let out a triumphant hoot as Holt scowled down at his shirt.

"I suppose you know," Holt said slowly, "this means war."

As Jenny shrieked, he grabbed her and pulled her through the window. To her delight, he held her upside down so that her two blond ponytails brushed the grass.

"He's taken a hostage!" Alex bellowed. "Death to the last man." He scrambled inside then burst out of the doorway, brandishing his sword. Holt barely had time to right Jenny before the little missile plowed into him. "Off with his head," Alex chanted, echoed by his sister. Holt let his body go lax and took them both to the ground with him.

There were screams and giggles as he wrestled with them. It wasn't as easy as he'd supposed. They were both agile and slick, wriggling out of his hold to attack. He found himself at a disadvantage as Alex sat on his chest and Jenny found a spot on his ribs to tickle.

"I'm going to have to get rough," he warned them. When

he took a spray of water in the face, he swore, making them both howl with laughter. A quick roll and he dislodged the pistol, then snatched it up to drench them both. With shrieks and giggles, they fell on him.

It was a wet and messy battle, and when he finally managed to pin them, they were all out of breath.

"I massacred you both," Holt managed. "Say uncle." Jenny poked a finger in his ribs, making him twitch. In defense he lowered his cheek to her neck and rubbed a day's worth of stubble over her skin.

"Uncle, uncle, uncle!" She screamed, gurgling with laughter. Satisfied, he used the same weapon on Alex until victorious, he rolled over and lay stomach down on the grass.

"You killed us," Alex admitted, not displeased. "But you're morally wounded."

"Yeah, but I think you mean mortally."

"Are you going to take a nap?" Jenny climbed onto his back to bounce. "Lilah sleeps in the grass sometimes."

"Lilah sleeps anywhere," Holt muttered.

"You can take a nap in my bed if you want," she invited, then pressed a curious finger on the edge of the scar she saw beneath his hitched-up T-shirt. "You have a hurt on your back."

"Uh-huh."

Alex was already scrambling to look. "Can I see?"

Holt tensed automatically, then forced himself to relax. "Sure."

As Alex pushed up the shirt, both children's eyes widened. It wasn't like the neat little scar they had both admired on his leg. This was long and jagged and mean, slashing from the waist so high up on his back they couldn't push the shirt up enough to see the end of it.

"Gee," was all Alex could think to say. He swallowed, then

gamely touched a finger to the scar. "Did you get in a big fight?"

"Not exactly." He remembered the pain, the incredible flash of white heat. "One of the bad guys got me," he said, and hoped it would satisfy. When he felt Jenny's little mouth lower to his back, he went very still.

"Does it feel better now?" she asked.

"Yeah." He had to let out a long breath to steady his voice. "Thanks." Turning over, he sat up to brush a hand through her hair.

Suzanna stood a few feet away, watching them with her heart in her throat. She'd seen the battle from the kitchen doorway. It had touched her to see how easily Holt had joined in the game with her children. She'd been smiling when she'd started out to join them—then she had watched Jenny and Alex examining the scar on Holt's back, and Jenny's kiss to make it better. She had seen the look of ragged emotion on Holt's face when he'd turned to sweep his hand over her little girl's hair.

Now the three of them were on the grass, Jenny cuddled on his lap, Alex's arm slung affectionately around his shoulder. She took a moment to make certain her eyes were dry before she continued toward them.

"Is the war over?" she asked, and three pair of eyes lifted.

"He won," Alex told her.

"It doesn't look as though it was an easy victory." She scooped Jenny up when the girl lifted her arms. "You're all wet."

"He blasted us—but I got him first."

"That's my girl."

"And he's ticklish," Jenny confided. "*Real* ticklish."

"Is that so?" Suzanna sent Holt a slow smile. "I'll keep that in mind. Now you two scat. I noticed nobody put away the game you were playing."

"But, Mom—" Alex had his excuses ready, but she stopped them with a look.

"If you don't clean it up, I will," she said mildly. "But then I'll have your share of strawberry shortcake tonight."

That was a tough one. Alex agonized over it for a minute, then caved in. "I'll do it. Then I get Jenny's share."

"Do not." Jenny sprinted toward the house with her brother giving chase.

"Very smooth, Mom," Holt commented as he rose.

"I know their weaknesses." She put her arms around him, surprising and pleasing him. It was very rare for her to make the first move. "You're all wet, too."

"Sniper fire, but I picked them off like flies." Bringing her closer, he rested his cheek on her hair. "They're terrific kids, Suzanna. I'm, ah…" He didn't know how to tell her he'd fallen in love with them, any more than he knew how to tell her he'd fallen in love with their mother. "I'm getting you wet." Feeling awkward, he drew away.

Smiling, she touched a hand to his cheek. "Want to take a walk?"

He thought of the list in his pocket. It could wait an hour, he decided, and took her hand.

He'd known she would head to the cliffs. It seemed right that they would walk there as the shadows lengthened and the air cooled toward evening. She talked a little of the job she'd finished that day, he of the hull he'd repaired. But their minds weren't on work.

"Holt." She looked out to sea, her hand in his. "Will you tell me why you resigned from the force?" She felt his fingers stiffen, but didn't turn.

"It's done," he said flatly. "There's nothing to tell."

"The scar on your back—"

"I said it's done." He withdrew and pulled out a cigarette.

"I see." She absorbed the rejection. "Your past and your personal feelings about it are none of my business."

He took an impatient drag. "I didn't say that."

"You certainly did. You have the right to know all there is to know about me. I'm supposed to trust you with everything, unquestioningly. But I'm not to pry into what's yours."

He turned angry eyes on her. "What is this, some kind of test?"

"Call it what you like," she tossed back. "I'd hoped you trusted me by now, that you cared enough to let me in."

"I do care, damn it. Don't you know it still rips me up to remember it? Ten years of my life, Suzanna. Ten years." He whirled away to flick the cigarette over the edge.

"I'm sorry." Instinctively she put her hands on his shoulders to soothe. "If anyone knows how painful it is to dredge up old wounds, it's me. Why don't we go back? I'll see if I can find you a clean shirt."

"No." His jaw was clenched, his body tight as a spring. "You want to know, you've got a right. I tossed it in because I couldn't handle it. I spent ten years telling myself I could make a difference, that none of the crap I had to wade through would affect me. I could rub shoulders with dealers and pimps and victims all day and not lose any sleep at night. If I had to kill somebody, it was line of duty. Not something you want to think about too much, but something you live with. I saw a few cops burn out along the way, but it wasn't going to happen to me."

She said nothing, just continued to rub at the knotted muscles of his shoulders while she waited for him to go on. He kept looking out to sea, smelling her, and the dusky scent of the wild roses that were at peak.

"Vice takes you into the pits, Suzanna. You get so you understand the people you're trying to wipe out. You think like them. You have to when you go under, or you don't come out again. There are things I'm never going to tell you, because I do care. Ugly things, and I just..." He closed his eyes, and jammed his hands into his pockets. "I just didn't want to see it anymore. I was already thinking about coming back here—just sort of kicking it around."

Suddenly weary, he lifted his hands to rub the heels over his eyes. "I was tired, Suzanna, and I wanted to live like a normal person again. The kind who doesn't strap on a gun every day or make deals with slime in back rooms. We were on a routine investigation, looking for a small-time dealer who we thought we could pressure information out of. Doesn't matter why," he said impatiently. "Anyway, we got a tip where to find him, and when we cornered him in this little dive, he snapped. Turned out the jerk had about twenty thousand in coke strapped under his clothes, and more than a couple lines in his system. He panicked. He dragged some half-stoned woman with him and bolted."

His palms were beginning to sweat, so he wiped them against his jeans. "My partner and I separated to cut him off. He pulled the woman out in the alley. With us on either end, he didn't have any hope of getting away. I had my weapon out. It was dark. The garbage had turned."

He could still smell it, rank and fetid, as the sweat began to run down his back. "I could hear my partner coming up the other side, and hear the woman crying. He'd sliced her up a little and she was balled up on the concrete. I couldn't be sure how bad she was hurt. I remember thinking the creep was going to be up for more than distribution. Then he jumped me. He had the knife in before I could get off a shot."

He could still feel it ripping through his flesh, still smell his own blood. "I knew I was dead, and I kept thinking that I wouldn't be able to come home. That I was going to die in that damn alley with the stink of that garbage. I killed him as I went down. That's what they told me. I don't remember. The thing I remember next was waking up in the hospital feeling like I'd been sliced in half and sewn back together. I told myself that if I made it, I was coming back here. Because I knew if I had to walk down another alley, I wouldn't come back out."

Suzanna had her arms tight around him now, her cheek pressed against his back. "Do you think because you came home instead of facing another alley, you failed?"

"I don't know."

"I did, for a long time. No one had put a knife in my back, but I came to understand that if I stayed with Bax, if I'd kept that promise, part of me would die. I chose survival, do you think I should be ashamed of that?"

"No." He turned, taking her shoulder. "No."

She lifted her hands to cup his face. In her eyes was understanding, and the sympathy he couldn't have accepted even a week before. "Neither do I. I hate what happened to you, but I'm glad it brought you here." Offering comfort, she touched her lips to his. Slowly, with a sweetness that was unbearably moving, she felt him let go.

His body relaxed against hers even as he pulled her closer. His mouth softened even as it heated. Here, at last, was the next level. There was not only passion, not only tenderness, but trust. As the wind whispered through the wild grass and the bright, brave flowers, she thought she heard something else, something so quiet and lovely that it brought tears to her eyes. When he lifted his head, when she saw his face, she knew he'd heard it, too. She smiled.

"We're not alone here," she murmured. "They must have stood in this same spot, holding each other like this. Wanting each other like this." Filled with the moment, she pressed his hand to her lips. "Holt, do you believe that fate and time can run in a circle?"

"I'm beginning to."

"They still come here, to wait. I wonder if they ever find each other. I think they will, if we can make things right." She kissed him again, then slipped an arm around his waist. "Let's go home. I have a feeling it's going to be an interesting evening."

"Suzanna," he began as they started back. "After the séance..." He trailed off, looking pained, and made her laugh.

"Don't worry, at The Towers we only have friendly ghosts."

"Right. Just don't expect me to put much stock in chanting and trances, but anyway, I was wondering if after—look, I know you don't like to leave the kids, but I thought you could come back to my place for a little while. There's some stuff I want to talk to you about."

"What stuff?"

"Just—stuff," he said lamely. If he was going to ask her to marry him, he wanted to do it right. "I'd appreciate it if you could get away for an hour or two."

"All right, if it's important. Is it about the emeralds?"

"No. It's...I'd rather wait, okay? Listen, I've got a couple of things to do before we start calling up spirits."

"Aren't you going to stay for dinner?"

"I can't. I'll be back." As they came up the slope and passed the stone wall, he pulled her against him for a brief, hard kiss. "See you later."

She frowned after him and might have pursued, but her name was called from the second-level terrace. Shading her eyes, she saw her sister.

"Amanda!" With a laugh, she raced across the lawn and up the stone steps. "What are you doing back?" She gathered the new bride into her arms and squeezed. "You look wonderful—but you were supposed to be gone nearly another week. Is anything wrong?"

"No, nothing." She kissed both of Suzanna's cheeks. "Come on, I'll fill you in."

"Where are we going?"

"Bianca's tower. Family meeting."

They climbed up, then went inside to ascend the narrow circular stairs that led to the tower. C.C. and Lilah were already waiting.

"Aunt Coco?" Suzanna asked.

"We'll let her know what we discuss," Amanda answered. "But it would look too suspicious if we pulled her up here now."

With a nod, Suzanna took a seat on the floor at Lilah's feet. "So I take it this is women only?"

"No more than they deserve," C.C. said, and crossed her arms. "They've been skulking off to have their boy's club meetings for days now. It's time we set things straight."

"Max has definitely got something up his sleeve," Lilah put in. "He's acting much too innocent. And, he's been hanging around the construction crew for the last couple of days."

"I don't suppose he wants to learn how to set tile," Suzanna murmured.

"If he did, he'd have twenty books on it by now." Lilah rolled her shoulders and leaned back. "And this afternoon when I got home from work, I saw Trent and Holt powwowing in the pergola. Somebody who didn't know better might have thought they were just hanging out and having a beer, but something was going on."

"So they know something they're not telling us." Thoughtful, Suzanna drummed her fingers on her knees. She'd had a feeling something was going on, but Holt had done such a good job of distracting her, she hadn't acted on it.

"Sloan had a long, mumbling conversation with Trent on the phone two days ago. He claimed there was some problem with materials that he had to see to personally." Tossing her hair, Amanda gave a sniff. "And he thought I was stupid enough to buy it. He wanted to get back because they're on to something—and they want to keep the little women out of the way."

"Fat chance," C.C. muttered. "I'm for marching downstairs right now and demanding they tell us whatever they know. If Trent thinks I'm going to sit around twiddling my thumbs while he handles Calhoun business, he's got another think coming."

"Bamboo shoots and brass knuckles," Lilah mused, not terribly displeased with the image. "That'll just make them more stubborn. Male egos on the line, ladies. Get out your hard hats and flak jackets."

Suzanna laughed and patted her leg. "You've got a point. Let's see what we know… Sloan gets called back so they must think they're getting close. I can't see them being secretive if they thought they'd hit on the location of the emeralds."

"Neither can I." Because she thought best on her feet, Amanda paced. "Remember how stiff-necked they got when we decided to look for the yacht Max had jumped off? Sloan threatened to…what was it? Hog-tie," she said viciously. "Yes, that was it. He threatened to hog-tie me if I so much as thought about trying to find Livingston on my own."

"Trent won't even discuss Livingston with me," C.C. added, then wrinkled her nose. "It isn't good for me to be upset in my delicate condition."

From her sprawled perch on the window seat, Lilah gave a hoot. "I'd like to see any man go through childbirth then have the nerve to call a woman delicate."

"Holt says that Livingston is out of our league. *Ours,*" Suzanna explained, making a circular motion with her finger. "Not his."

"Jerk." C.C. plopped down on the window seat beside Lilah. "So are we agreed? They've got a line on Livingston and they're keeping it to themselves."

The vote was unanimous.

"Now, we need to find out what they know." Amanda stopped pacing and tapped her foot. "Suggestions?"

"Well…" Suzanna looked down at her nails and smiled. "I say divide and conquer. The four of us should be able to dig information out of them—each in our own way. Then we rendezvous here, tomorrow, same time, and put the pieces together."

"I like it." Lilah sat up to put a hand on Suzanna's shoulder. "The poor guys haven't got a chance."

Suzanna reached up to lay her hand on Lilah's as Amanda and C.C. added theirs. "And when it's over," she said, "maybe they'll realize the Calhoun women take care of their own."

Chapter 11

Holt had never felt more ridiculous in his life. He was about to take part in a séance. If that wasn't bad enough, before the night was over, he was going to ask the woman who was currently laughing at him, to be his wife.

"It isn't a firing squad." Chuckling, Suzanna patted his cheek. "Relax."

"Damn foolishness is what it is." From the foot of the table, Colleen scowled at everyone in general. "The idea of talking to spirits. Hogwash. And you—" She stabbed a finger toward Coco. "Not that you ever kept an ounce of sense in that flighty head of yours, but I'd have thought even you would know better than to raise these girls on such bilge."

"It isn't bilge." As always, the steely gaze made Coco tremble, but she felt fairly safe with the length of the table between them. "You'll see after we begin."

"What I see is a table full of dolts." Though her face remained in stern lines, Colleen's heart melted as she looked up at the portrait of her mother, which had been hung over the fireplace. "I'll give you ten thousand for it."

Holt shrugged. She'd been dogging him for days about buying the painting. "It isn't for sale."

"If you think you're going to hose me, young man, you're mistaken. I know a hustle."

He grinned at her. He would have bet his last nickel she'd hustled plenty herself. "I'm not selling it."

"It's worth more, anyway," Lilah put in, unable to resist. "Isn't that right, Professor?"

"Well, actually, yes." Max cleared his throat. "Christian Bradford's early work is increasing in value. At Sotheby's two years ago, one of his seascapes went for thirty-five thousand."

"What are you," Colleen snapped, "his agent?"

Max swallowed a grin. "No, ma'am."

"Then hush. Fifteen thousand, and not a penny more."

Holt ran his tongue around his teeth. "Not interested."

"Maybe if we got on with the matter at hand." Coco held her breath, waiting for her aunt's wrath to fall. When Colleen only muttered and scowled, she relaxed. "Amanda, dear, light the candles. Now we must all try to empty our minds of all worries, all doubts. Concentrate on Bianca." When the candles were glowing, and the chandelier extinguished, she gave a last glance around the table. "Join hands."

Holt grumbled under his breath but took Suzanna's hand in his right, Lilah's in his left.

"Focus on the picture," Coco whispered, closing her eyes to bring it into her mind since it was behind her on the wall. Tingles of anticipation raced up and down her spine. "She's close to us, very close to us. She wants to help."

Holt let his mind drift because it helped him forget what he was doing. He tried to imagine what it would be like when he and Suzanna were alone in the cottage. He'd bought candles. Not the sturdy type he kept in the kitchen drawer for power outages, but slender white tapers that smelled of jasmine.

There was champagne chilling beside the six-pack in his refrigerator, and two new clear flutes beside his coffee mugs. Even now the jeweler's box was burning a hole in his hip pocket.

Tonight, he thought, he'd take the step. The words would come exactly as he planned. The music would be playing. She would open the box, look inside....

Her hands were draped with emeralds. He frowned, giving himself a little shake. That wasn't right. He hadn't bought her emeralds. But the image focused so clearly. Suzanna on her knees holding emeralds. Three glittering tiers flanked by icy diamonds and centered by a glowing teardrop stone of dreamy green.

The Calhoun necklace. He felt the chill on his neck and ignored it. He'd seen the picture Max had found in the old library book. He knew what the emeralds looked like. It was the atmosphere, the humming silence and the flickering candles that made him think of them. That made him see them.

He didn't believe in visions. But when he closed his eyes to clear it from his mind, it seemed imprinted there. Suzanna kneeling on the floor with emeralds dripping from her fingers.

He felt a hand on his shoulder and looked around. There was no one there, only shadows and light thrown by the candles. But the feeling remained, with an urgency that had his hackles rising.

It was crazy, he told himself. And it was time to put an end to the whole insane business.

"Listen," he began. And the portrait of Bianca crashed to the floor.

Coco gave a piping squeak and jolted out of the chair. "Oh, my. Oh, my goodness," she murmured, patting her speeding heart.

Amanda was already racing forward. "Oh, I hope it isn't damaged."

"I don't think it will be." Lilah released Holt's hand. "Do you?"

The clear and steady gaze made him uncomfortable. Ignoring her, he turned to Suzanna. Her hand was like ice in his. "What is it? What's wrong?"

"Nothing." But she gave a quick shudder. "I think you'd better check the portrait."

He rose to go over where the others were crouched. As he did, Suzanna looked down the length of the table at her great-aunt. Colleen's white skin had paled like glass. Her eyes were dark and damp. Without a word, Suzanna rose and poured her a brandy. "It's going to be all right," she murmured, laying a hand on the thin shoulder.

"The frame cracked." Sloan ran a finger along it before he rose. "Funny that it would fall that way. Those nails are sturdy."

Holt started to shrug it off, but when he bent closer to where the frame had separated from the backing, he went very still. "There's something between the canvas and the back." Hefting the portrait, he laid it facedown on the table. "I need a knife."

Sloan pulled out his pocketknife and offered it. Holt made a long thin slit just beneath the cracked frame and slid out several sheets of paper.

"What is it?" The question was muffled as Coco had her hands pressed to her mouth.

"It's my grandfather's writing." The emotion sprang up strong and fast. It churned in Holt's eyes as he lifted them to Suzanna's. "It looks like a kind of diary. It's dated 1965."

"Sit down, dear." Coco put a comforting hand on his shoulder. "Trent, would you pour the brandy? I'll brew some tea for C.C."

He did need to sit, and he hoped the drink would steady him. For now, he could only stare at the papers and see his grandfather. Sitting on the back porch of the cottage, watching the water. Standing in his loft, slashing paint on canvas. Walking on the cliffs, telling a young boy stories.

When Suzanna came back to lay a hand on his, he turned his palm up and gripped her fingers. "It's been there all this time, and I didn't know."

"You weren't meant to know," she said quietly. "Until tonight." When he looked at her again, she curled her fingers tight around his. "Some things we just have to take on faith."

"Something happened tonight. Something upset you."

"I'll tell you. Not yet."

Composed, Coco brought in the tea, then took her seat. "Holt, whatever your grandfather wrote belongs to you. No one here will ask you to share it. If after you read it, you feel you prefer to keep it to yourself, we'll understand."

He glanced down at the papers again, then lifted the first sheet. "We'll read it together." He took a long breath, kept Suzanna's hand tight in his. "'The moment I saw her, my life changed.'"

No one spoke as Holt read through his grandfather's memories. But around the table, hands linked again. There was no sound but his voice and the wind breathing through the trees outside the windows. When he was finished, the room remained silent.

Lilah spoke first, her voice thick with tears while others slid down her cheeks. "He never stopped loving her. Always, even though he made a life for himself, he loved her."

"How he must have felt, to come here that night and

find out she was gone." Amanda leaned her head on Sloan's shoulder.

"But he was right." Suzanna watched one of her tears drop on the back of Holt's hand. "She didn't take her own life. She couldn't have. Not only did she love him too much, but she would have tolerated anything to protect her children."

"No, she didn't jump." Colleen whispered the words. She lifted her snifter with a trembling hand, then set it down again. "I've never spoken of that night, not to anyone. Through the years I've sometimes thought what I saw was a dream. A terrible, terrible nightmare."

Determined, she cleared her blurred vision and strengthened her voice. "He understood her, her Christian. He couldn't have written about her that way and not have known her heart. She was beautiful, but she was also kind and generous. I have never been loved as I was loved by my mother. And I have never hated as I hated my father."

She straightened her shoulders. Already the burden had lessened. "I was too young to understand her unhappiness or her desperation. In those days a man ruled his home, his family, as he chose. No one dared to question my father. But I remember the day she brought the puppy home, the little puppy my father would not have in his home. She did send us upstairs, but I hid at the top and listened. I had never heard her raise her voice to him before. Oh, she was valiant. And he was cruel. I didn't understand the names he called her. Then."

She paused to drink again, for her throat was dry and the memory bitter. "She defended me against him, knowing as even I knew he barely tolerated me, a female. When he left the house after the argument, I was glad. I prayed that night he would never come back. The next day, my mother told me we were going to take a trip. She hadn't told my brothers yet, but I was the eldest. She wanted me to understand that she would take care of us, that nothing bad would happen.

"Then, he came back. I knew she was upset, even frightened. I was to stay in my room until she came for me. But she didn't come. It grew late, and there was a storm. I wanted my mother." Colleen pressed her lips together. "She wasn't in her room, so I went up to the tower where she often spent her time. I heard them as I crept up the stairs. The door was open and I heard them. The terrible argument. He was raging, crazed with fury. She told him that she would no longer live with him, that she wanted nothing from him but her children and her freedom."

Because Colleen was shaking, Coco rose and walked down to take her hand.

"He struck her. I heard the slap and raced to the door. But I was afraid, too afraid to go in. She had a hand to her cheek, and her eyes were blazing. Not with fear, with fury. I will always remember that there was no fear in her at the end. He threatened her with scandal. He screamed at her that if she left his house, she would never lay eyes on any of his children again. She would never ruin his reputation. She would never throw an obstacle in the path of his ambitions."

Though her lips trembled, Colleen lifted her chin. "She did not beg. She did not weep. She hurled words back at him like thunderbolts." Fisting a hand, she pressed it to her mouth to smother her own tears. "She was magnificent. Her children would never be taken from her, and scandal be damned. Did he think she cared what people thought of her? Did he think she feared his power to have society shun her? She would take her children and she would make a life where both she and they could be loved. And I think it was that which drove him mad. The idea that she would choose another man over him. Over him. Fergus Calhoun. That she would toss his money and power and position back at him, rather than bow to his wishes. He grabbed her, lifting her from her feet, shaking her, screaming into her face while his own purpled with rage. I think I screamed then, and hearing me, she began to fight. When she struck him, he threw her aside. I heard the crash of the glass. He ran to it, roaring for her, but she was gone. How long he stood there while the wind and rain poured in, I don't know. When he turned his face was white, his eyes glazed. He walked past me without even seeing me. I went inside, over to the broken window and looked down until Nanny came and carried me away."

Coco pressed a kiss to the white hair, then gently stroked. "Come with me, dear. I'll take you upstairs. Lilah will bring you a nice cup of tea."

"Yes, I'll be right there." Lilah wiped her cheeks dry. "Max?"

"I'll come with you." He slipped an arm around her waist as Coco led Bianca's daughter from the room.

"Poor little girl," Suzanna murmured, and let her head rest on Holt's shoulder as he drove away from The Towers. "To have seen something so horrible, to have had to live with it all of her life. I think of Jenny—"

"Don't." He put a firm hand over hers. "You got out. Bianca didn't." He waited a moment. "You knew, didn't you? Before Colleen told us the story."

"I knew she hadn't committed suicide. I can't explain how, but tonight, I knew. It was as if she was standing right behind me."

He thought of the sensation of having a hand on his shoulder. "Maybe she was. After a night like this, it's hard for me to convince myself the picture falling off the wall was a coincidence."

Suzanna closed her eyes. "It was beautiful, what your grandfather wrote about her. If we never find the emeralds, we have that—we'll know she had that. To love that way," she said on a sigh. "It hardly seems possible. I don't want to think of the tragedy or sadness, but of the time they had together. Dancing in the wild roses."

He'd never danced with her in the sunlight, Holt thought. Or read her poetry or promised her eternal love.

When they reached the cottage, Sadie leaped out the back window of the car to race around the yard and sniff at the flower bed she'd planted for him. When Holt leaned across her, Suzanna looked down in surprise.

"What are you doing?"

"I'm opening the door for you." He shoved it open. "If I'd gotten out to do it, you wouldn't have waited."

Amused, Suzanna stepped out. "Thank you."

"You're welcome." When he reached the house, he unlocked the front door, then held that open. Keeping her face sober, Suzanna inclined her head as she slipped past him.

"Thank you."

Holt just let the screen slam shut. Brow lifted, Suzanna scanned the room.

"You've done something different."

"I cleaned it up," he muttered.

"Oh. It looks nice. You know, Holt, I've been meaning to ask you if you think Livingston is still on the island."

"Why? Did something happen?"

His response was much too abrupt, Suzanna noted and moved casually around the room. "No, I've just been wondering where he may be staying, what his next move might be." She ran a fingertip down one of the candles he'd bought. "Any ideas?"

"How should I know?"

"You're the expert on crime."

"And I told you to leave Livingston to me."

"And I told you I couldn't do that. Maybe I'll start poking around on my own."

"Try it and I'll handcuff you and lock you in a closet."

"The urban counterpart to hog-tying," she murmured. "I wouldn't have to try it if you'd tell me what you know. Or what you think."

"What brought this up now?"

She moved her shoulder. "Since we have a little time to ourselves, I thought we could talk about it."

"Look, why don't you just sit down?" He pulled out his lighter.

"What are you doing?"

"I'm lighting candles." His nerves were stretching like taffy. "What does it look like I'm doing?"

She did sit, and steepled her hands. "Since you're so cranky, I have to assume that you do know something."

"You don't have to assume anything except that you're ticking me off." He stalked to the stereo.

"How close are you?" she asked as a bluesy sax filled the air.

"I'm nowhere." Since that was a lie, he decided to temper it with part of the truth. "I think he's in the area because he broke in here and took a look around a couple of weeks ago."

"What?" She catapulted out of the chair. "A couple of weeks ago, and you didn't tell me?"

"What were you going to do about it?" he countered. "Pull out a magnifying glass and deer-hunter's hat?"

"I had a right to know."

"Now you know. Just sit down, will you? I'll be back in a minute."

He stalked out and she began to pace. Holt knew more than he was saying, but at least she'd annoyed a piece from him. Livingston was close, close enough that he'd known Holt might have something of interest. The fact that Holt was wound like a top at the moment made her think something more was working on him. It shouldn't be difficult, she thought, now that she already had him irritated, to push a little more out of him.

The candles were scented, she noted, and smiled to herself. She couldn't imagine that he'd bought jasmine candles on purpose. Especially a half a dozen of them. She traced a finger over the calla lilies he'd stuck—not very artistically—in a vase. Maybe working with flowers was getting to him, she thought. He wasn't pretending so hard not to like them.

When he came back in, she smiled then looked puzzled. "Is that champagne?"

"Yeah." And he was thoroughly disgusted. He'd imagined she'd be charmed. Instead she questioned everything. "Do you want some or not?"

"Sure." The curt invitation was so typical she didn't take offense. After he'd poured, she tapped her glass absently against his. "Now, if you're sure it was Livingston who broke in, I think—"

"One more word," he said with dangerous calm. "One more word about Livingston and I'll pour the rest of the bottle over your hard head."

She sipped, knowing she'd have to be careful if she didn't want to waste a bottle of champagne and end up with sticky hair. "I'm only trying to get a clear picture."

He let out what was close to a roar of frustration and spun away. Champagne sloshed over his glass as he paced. "She wants a clear picture, and she's blind as a bat. I shoveled two months' worth of dust out of this place. I bought candles and flowers. I had to listen to some jerk try to teach me about wine. That's the picture, damn it."

She'd wanted to irritate information from him, not infuriate him. "Holt—"

"Just sit down and shut up. I should have known this would get screwed up. God knows why I tried to do it this way."

A light dawned, and she smiled. He'd set the stage, but she'd been too focused on her own scheme to take note. "Holt, it's very sweet of you to do all of this. I'm sorry if I didn't seem to appreciate it. If you wanted me to come here tonight so we could make love—"

"I don't want to make love with you." He swore, viciously. "Of course I want to make love with you, but that's not it. I'm trying to ask you to marry me, damn it, so will you sit *down!*"

Since her legs had dissolved from knees to toe, she slid into a chair.

"This is perfect." He gulped down champagne and started pacing again. "Just perfect. I'm trying to tell you that I'm crazy about you, that I don't think I can live without you, and all you can do is ask me what I'm doing and nag me about some obsessed jewel thief."

Cautiously she brought the glass to her lips. "Sorry."

"You should be sorry," he said bitterly. "I was ready to make a fool of myself tonight for you, and you won't even let me do that. I've been in love with you nearly half my life. Even when I moved away, I couldn't get you out of my mind. You spoiled every other woman for me. I'd start to get close to someone, and then...they weren't you. They just weren't you, and I'd never even gotten past your back door."

In love. The two words reeled in her head. *In love.* "I thought you didn't even like me."

"I couldn't stand you." He raked his free hand through his hair. "Every time I looked at you I wanted you so much I couldn't breathe. My mouth would go dry and my stomach would knot, and you'd just smile and keep walking." His dark and turbulent eyes locked on hers. "I wanted to strangle you. Then you ran into me and knocked me off my bike and I was lying there bleeding and—and mortified. You were leaning over me, smelling like heaven and running your hands over me to see if anything was broken. One more minute of that and I'd have dragged you onto the asphalt with me." He rubbed his hand over his face. "Lord, you were only sixteen."

"You swore at me."

His face was a picture of anger and disgust. "Damn right, I swore at you. You were better off with that than with what I wanted to do to you." He was calming, little by little. He sipped again but kept pacing. "I talked myself into believing it was just an adolescent fantasy. Even a crush, and that was tough to swallow. Then you came walking across my yard. I looked at you and my throat went dry, my stomach knotted up. We were both past being adolescents."

He set his glass down, noting that she was gripping hers with both hands. Her eyes were huge and fixed on his. Cursing both of them, he fumbled for a cigarette then tossed it aside.

"I'm not good at this, Suzanna. I thought I could pull it off. Set the mood, you know? And after you'd had enough champagne, I'd convince you I could make you happy."

She couldn't relax her grip. She tried but couldn't. "I don't need champagne and candlelight, Holt."

He smiled a little. "Babe, you were born for it. I could lie to you and tell you I'll remember to give it to you every night. But I won't."

She looked down at her glass and wondered if she was

ready to take this sort of chance again. Loving him was one thing. Being loved by him was incredible. But marriage...
"Why don't you just tell me the truth then?"

He walked over to sit on the arm of the couch and face her. "I love you. I've never felt about anyone the way I feel about you. Whatever happens, I'll never feel like this about anyone else again. There's no taking back what's happened to either of us in the last few years, but maybe we can make things better for both of us. For the kids."

Her eyes changed, darkened. "It may never be easy. Bax would always be their legal father."

"He wouldn't be the one who loved them." When her eyes filled, he shook his head. No, she hadn't needed candlelight and champagne to make her vulnerable and open to his needs. Only a mention of her children. "I won't use them to get to you. I know I could, but first it has to be between you and me. Maybe I'm stuck on them, and I want to—I think I could be pretty good at being their father, but I don't want you to marry me for them."

She took a deep breath. Odd, her fingers had relaxed on the stem of the glass without her being aware. "I never wanted to love anyone again. And I certainly never wanted to get married." Her lips curved. "Until you." Setting the glass aside, she reached for his hand. "I can't claim to have loved you as long, but you couldn't love me more than I love you."

He didn't settle for her hand, but pulled her into his arms. When he at last managed to tear his mouth from hers, he buried his face in her hair. "Don't tell me you need to think about it, Suzanna."

"I don't need to think about it." She couldn't remember the last time her heart and mind had been so at peace. "I'll marry you."

Before the words were out of her mouth, she was tumbling with him onto the couch. She was laughing as they tugged at each other's clothes, laughing still when the frantic movements sent them rolling onto the floor.

"I knew it." She nipped his bare shoulder. "You did bring me here to make love."

"Can I help it if you can't keep your hands off me?" He trailed a necklace of quick kisses around her throat.

She smiled, tilting her head to give him easy access. "Holt, did you really think about pulling me down on the street after you'd fallen off your bike?"

"After you'd run into me," he corrected, nuzzling her ear. "Yeah. Let me show you what I had in mind."

Later they lay like rag dolls on the floor, a tangle of limbs. When she could manage it, she lifted her head from his chest. "It was much better that we didn't try that twelve years ago."

Lazily he opened his eyes. She was smiling down at him, her hair brushing his shoulders, the candlelight glowing in her eyes. "Much better. I wouldn't have had any skin left on my back."

She chuckled then shifted to trace the shape of his face. "You always scared me a little. Looking so dark and dangerous. And, of course, the girls used to talk about you."

"Oh, yeah? What did they say?"

"I'll tell you when you're sixty. You could probably use it then." He pinched her, but she only laughed then rested her cheek on his. "When you're sixty, we'll be an old married couple with grandchildren."

He liked the thought of it. "And you still won't be able to keep your hands off me."

"And I'll remind you of the night you asked me to marry

you, when you gave me flowers and candlelight, then shouted at me and raged up and down the room, making me love you even more."

"If that's all it takes, you'll be delirious about me by the time I'm sixty."

"I already am." She lowered her mouth to his.

"Suzanna." He drew her closer, started to roll her under him, then swore. "It's your own fault," he said as he nudged her aside.

"What?"

"You were supposed to be sitting over there, dazed by my romantic abilities." He fought to untangle his jeans and pull the jeweler's box from the pocket. "Then I was going to get down on one knee."

Eyes wide, she stared at the box, then at him. "You were not."

"Yes, I was. I was going to feel like an idiot, but I was going to do it. You've got no one to blame but yourself that we're lying naked on the floor. Here."

"You bought me a ring," she whispered.

"There could be a frog in there for all you know." Impatient with her, he flipped up the top himself. "I didn't want to give you diamonds." He shrugged when she said nothing, only stared into the box. "I figured you'd already had those. I thought about emeralds, but those are something you will have. And this is more like your eyes."

When the tears blurred her vision, the light refracted. There were diamonds, tiny, lovely stones in a heart shape about the deep and brilliant sapphire. They weren't cold, as the ones she had sold, but warmed by the rich blue fire they encircled.

Holt watched the first tear fall with a great deal of discomfort. "If you don't like it, we can take it back. You can pick out what you want."

"It's beautiful." She dashed a tear away with the back of

her hand. "I'm sorry. I hate to cry. It's just so beautiful, and you bought it for me because you love me. And when I put it on—" she lifted drenched eyes to his "—I'm yours."

He dropped his brow to hers. Those were the words he'd wanted. The ones he'd needed. Taking the ring from the box, he slipped it onto her finger. "You're mine." He kissed her fingers, then her lips. "I'm yours." Bringing her close again, he remembered his grandfather's words. "Eternally."

Chapter 12

Suzanna took the children to the shop with her in the morning. She couldn't tell the rest of her family the news until she'd gauged Alex's and Jenny's feelings. The day was bright and hot. Knowing it would be a busy one, she arrived a full hour before opening. Because they wanted to check the herbs they had planted, she took them into the greenhouse to look at the tender shoots.

She let them argue for a while over whose plants would be the biggest or the best, supervising as they gave the shoots their morning drink.

"Do you guys like Holt?" she asked casually, nerves drumming.

"He's neat." Alex was tempted to turn the sprayer on his sister, but he'd gotten in trouble the last time he'd indulged himself.

"He plays with us sometimes." Jenny danced from foot to foot, waiting her turn. "I like when he throws me up in the air."

"I like him, too." Suzanna relaxed a little.

"Does he throw you up in the air?" Jenny wanted to know.

"No." With a laugh, Suzanna ruffled her hair.

"He could. He's got big muscles." Reluctantly Alex passed the sprayer to his sister. "He let me feel them." Screwing up his face, Alex flexed his own. Obliging, Suzanna pinched the tiny biceps.

"Wow. You're pretty tough."

"That's what he said."

"I was wondering..." Suzanna wiped nervous hands on her jeans. "How would you feel if he lived with us, all the time?"

"That'd be good," Jenny decided. "He plays with us even when we don't ask."

One down, Suzanna thought and turned to her son. "Alex?"

He shuffled his feet, frowning a little. "Are you going to get married like C.C. and Amanda?"

Sharp little devil, she thought, and crouched down. "I was thinking about it. What do you think?"

"Do I have to wear a dumb tuxedo again?"

She smiled and stroked his cheek. "Probably."

"Is he going to be our uncle, like Trent and Sloan and Max?" Jenny asked.

Suzanna got up to turn off the spray before answering her daughter. "No. He'd be your stepfather."

Brother and sister exchanged looks. "Would he still like us?"

"Of course he would, Jenny."

"Would we have to go away and live someplace else?"

She sighed and combed a hand through Alex's hair. "No. He would come to live with us at The Towers, or maybe we'd go and live with him at his cottage. We'd be a family."

Alex thought it over. "Would he be Kevin's stepfather, too?"

"No." She had to kiss him. "Megan's Kevin's mom, and maybe one day she'll fall in love and get married. Then Kevin will have a father."

"Did you fall in love with Holt?" Jenny asked.

"Yes, I did." She felt Alex shift uncomfortably and smiled. "I'd like to marry him so we could all live together. But Holt and I both wanted to see how you felt about it."

"I like him," Jenny announced. "He lets me ride on his shoulders."

Alex shrugged, a bit more cautious. "Maybe it's okay."

Concerned, Suzanna rose. "We can talk about it some more. Let's go set up."

They stepped out of the greenhouse just as Holt pulled up in the graveled lot. He knew he'd told her he'd wait until lunchtime, but he hadn't been able to. He'd awakened realizing he'd rather face another alley than those two kids who could so easily reject him. He stuffed his hands into his pockets and tried to look casual.

"Hi."

"Hi." Suzanna wanted to reach out to him, but her children held her hands.

"I thought I'd drop by and...how's it going?"

Jenny gave him a shy smile and huddled closer to her mother. "Mom says you're going to get married and be our stepfather and live with us."

Holt had to knock back an urge to shuffle his feet. "That's the plan."

Alex tightened his fingers around Suzanna's as he stared up at Holt. "Are you going to yell at us?"

After a quick glance at Suzanna, Holt stooped down until he was eye to eye with the boy. "Maybe. If you need it."

Alex trusted that answer more than he would have an unqualified no. "Do you hit?" He remembered the swats he'd received during his vacation. They'd insulted more than hurt, but he still resented it.

Holt put a hand under the boy's chin and held it firm. "No," he said, and the look in his eyes made Alex believe. "But I might hang you up by your thumbs, or boil you in oil. If I get really mad, I'll stake you to an anthill."

Alex's lips twitched, but he wasn't finished with the interrogation. "Are you going to make Mom cry like he did?"

"Alex," Suzanna began, but Holt cut her off.

"I might sometimes, if I'm stupid. But not on purpose. I love her a lot, so I want to make her happy. Sometimes I might screw up."

Alex frowned and considered. "Are you going to do all that kissing stuff? Since Trent and Sloan and Max came, there's always kissing."

"Yeah." Holt's face relaxed into a smile. "I'm going to do all that kissing stuff."

"But you won't like it," Alex said, hopeful. "You'll just do it 'cause Mom likes it."

"Sorry, I like it, too."

"Jeez," Alex muttered, deflated.

"Do it now." Jenny danced and giggled. "Do it now so I can see."

Willing to oblige, Holt straightened and pulled Suzanna close. When he took his lips from Suzanna's, Alex was red faced and Jenny was clapping. "I hate to tell you," Holt said soberly. "but one day you'll like it, too."

"Uh-uh. I'd rather eat dirt."

With a laugh, Holt hoisted him up, relieved and delighted when Alex slung a friendly arm around his neck. "Tell me that in ten years."

"I like it," Jenny insisted, and tugged on his leg. "I like it now. Kiss me." He hauled her in his other arm and kissed her tiny, waiting lips. She smiled, big blue eyes beaming. "You kissed Mom different."

"That's 'cause she's the mom and you're the kid."

She liked the way he smelled, the way his arm supported her. When she rubbed a hand over his cheek, she was a little disappointed that it was smooth today. "Can I call you Daddy?" she asked, and Holt felt his heart lurch in his chest.

"I—ah—sure. If you want."

"Daddy's for babies," Alex said in disgust. "But you can be Dad."

"Okay." He looked over at Suzanna. "Okay."

Holt wished he could have spent the day with them, but there were things that had to be done. He had a family now—it still dazed him—and he meant to protect them. He'd already put in calls to his contacts in Portland and was awaiting the rundowns on the four names from Trent's list. While he waited, he put in calls to the Department of Motor Vehicles, the credit bureau and the Internal Revenue, stretching it a bit by giving his old badge number and rank.

Between information and instinct, he whittled the four names down to two. While he waited for another call back, he read over his grandfather's diary.

He understood the feelings beneath the words, the longing, the devotion. He understood the rage his grandfather had felt when he'd learned the woman he loved had suffered abuse by the hands of the man she'd married. Was it coincidence or fate that his relationship with Suzanna had so many similarities to that of their ancestors? At least this time, the tale would have a happy ending.

Suzanna's diamonds, he thought, drumming his fingers on

the pages. Bianca's emeralds. Suzanna had hidden her jewels, the one material thing she felt belonged to her from the marriage, as security for her children. He had to believe Bianca had done the same.

So, where was the equivalent of Jenny's diaper bag? he wondered.

When the phone rang, he snatched it up on the first ring. Before he hung up again, Holt had little doubt he had his man. Going into the bedroom, he checked his weapon, balancing the familiar weight in his hand. He strapped it to his calf.

Fifteen minutes later, he was walking through the chaos of construction in the west wing. He found Sloan in what was a nearly completed two-level suite. There was a smell of new lumber and male sweat. Sloan, in a tool belt and jeans, was supervising the construction of a new staircase.

"I didn't know architects swung hammers," Holt commented.

Sloan grinned. "I got a personal interest in this job."

Nodding, Holt scanned the crew. "Which one's Marshall?"

Alerted, Sloan unbuckled the tool belt. "He's up on the next level."

"I'd like to have a little talk with him."

Sloan's eyes flashed, but he merely nodded again. "I'll go with you." He waited until they were out of range of the crew. "You think he's the one?"

"Robert Marshall didn't apply for a Maine driver's license until six weeks ago. He's never paid taxes under the name and social security number he's using. Employers don't usually check with the DMV or IRS when they hire a laborer."

Sloan swore and flexed his fingers. He could still see

Amanda racing along the terrace pursued by a man holding a gun. "I get first crack at him."

"I appreciate the sentiment, but you'll have to strap it in."

The hell he would, Sloan thought, and signaled the foreman. "Marshall," he said briefly.

"Bob?" The foreman pulled out a bandanna to wipe his neck. "You just missed him. I had him drive Rick into Emergency. Rick took a pretty good slice out of his thumb, figured he needed stitches."

"How long ago?" Holt demanded.

"'Bout twenty minutes, I guess. Told them to take the rest of the day, since we're knocking off at four." He stuffed the bandanna back into his pocket. "Problem?"

"No." Sloan bit down on temper. "Let me know if Rick's okay."

"Sure thing." He shouted at one of the carpenters, then lumbered off.

"I need an address," Holt said.

"Trent's got the paperwork." They started out. "Are you going to turn it over to Lieutenant Koogar?"

"No," Holt said simply.

"Good."

They found Trent in the office he'd thrown together on the first floor, a stack of files at his fingertips, a phone at his ear. He took one look at the two men. "I'll get back to you," he said into the phone and hung up. "Who is it?"

"He's using the name Robert Marshall." Holt pulled out a cigarette. "Foreman let him go early. I want an address."

Saying nothing, Trent crossed to a file cabinet to pull out a folder. "Max is upstairs. He has a stake in this, too."

Holt skimmed the information in Marshall's file. "Then get him. We'll do this together."

The apartment Marshall had listed was on the edge of the

village. The woman who opened the door after Holt's third booming knock was bent and withered and out of sorts.

"What? What?" she demanded. "I'm not buying any encyclopedias or vacuum cleaners."

"We're looking for Robert Marshall," Holt told her.

"Who? Who?" She peered through the thick lenses of her glasses.

"Robert Marshall," he repeated.

"I don't know any Marshalls," she grumbled. "There's a McNeilly next door and a Mitchell down below, but no Marshalls. I don't want to buy any insurance, either."

"We're not selling anything," Trent said in his most patient voice. "We're looking for a man named Robert Marshall who lives at this address."

"I told you there's no Marshalls here. I live here. Lived here for fifteen years, since that worthless clot I married passed on and left me with nothing but bills. I know you," she said abruptly, pointing a gnarled finger at Sloan. "Saw your picture in the paper." Reaching to the table beside the door, she hefted an iron bookend. "You robbed a bank."

"No, ma'am." Later, Sloan thought, much later, he might find the whole business amusing. "I married Amanda Calhoun."

The woman held on to the bookend while she considered. "One of the Calhoun girls. That's right. The youngest one—no, not the youngest one, the next one." Satisfied, she set the bookend down again. "Well, what do you want?"

"Robert Marshall," Holt said again. "He gave this building and this apartment as his address."

"Then he's a liar or a fool, because I've lived here for fifteen years ever since that no-account husband of mine caught pneumonia and died. Here one day, gone the next." She snapped her bent fingers. "And good riddance."

Thinking it was a dead end, Holt glanced at Sloan. "Give her a description."

"He's about thirty, six feet tall, trim, black hair, shoulder length, big droopy moustache."

"Don't know him. The boy downstairs, the Pierson boy's got hair past his shoulders. A disgrace if you ask me. Bleaches it, too, just like a girl. He's no more'n sixteen. You'd think his mother would make him cut that hair, but no. Plays the music so loud I have to bang on the floor."

"Excuse me," Max put in and described the man he had known as Ellis Caufield.

"Sounds like my nephew. Lives in Rochester with his second wife. Sells used cars."

"Thanks." Holt wasn't surprised the thief had given a phony address, but he was annoyed. As they came out of the building, he dug a quarter from his pocket.

"I guess we wait until morning," Max was saying. "He doesn't know we're on to him, so he'll show up for work."

"I'm finished waiting." Holt headed for a phone booth. After dropping in the coin, he punched in numbers. "This is Detective Sergeant Bradford, Portland P.D., badge number 7375. I need a cross-check." He reeled off the phone number from Marshall's file. Then he held on with a cop's patience while the operator set her computer to work. "Thanks." He hung up and turned to the three men. "Bar Island," he said. "We'll take my boat."

While their men prepared to sail across the bay, the Calhoun women met in Bianca's tower. "So," Amanda began, pad and pencil at the ready. "What do we know?"

"Trent's been cross-checking the personnel files," C.C. supplied. "He claimed there was some hitch in withholding taxes, but that's bull."

"Interesting," Lilah mused. "Max stopped me from going over to the west wing this morning. I'd wanted to see how things were going, and he made all kinds of lame excuses why I shouldn't distract the men while they were working."

"And Sloan shoved a couple of files into a drawer, and locked it when I came into the room last night." Amanda tapped her pencil on the pad. "Why wouldn't they want us to know if they're checking up on the crews?"

"I think I have an idea," Suzanna said slowly. She'd been chewing it over most of the day. "Last night I found out that Holt's cottage had been broken into and searched."

Her three sisters pounced on that, hammering her with questions.

"Just wait." She lifted a hand. "He was irritated with me, which is why it came out. He was even more irritated that it had. But he did tell me, because he wanted to scare me into backing off, that he was certain it was Livingston."

"Which means," Amanda concluded, "that our old friend knows Holt's connected. Who else knows besides us?" In her organized way, she began to list names.

"Oh, stop fussing," Lilah said with a negligent wave of her hand. "No one knows except the family. None of us have mentioned it outside of this house."

"Maybe he found out the same way Max did," C.C. suggested. "From the library."

"Max checked out the books." Lilah shook her head. "Maybe he found the information in the papers he stole from us."

"It's possible." Amanda noted it down. "But he's had the papers for weeks. When did he break into the cottage?"

"A couple weeks ago, but I don't think he made the connection that way. I think he got it from us."

There was an instant argument. Suzanna stood, throwing

up both hands to cut it off. "Listen, we're agreed that none of us have discussed this outside of the house. And we're agreed that the men are trying to keep us from finding out they're checking out the crews. Which means—"

"Which means," Amanda interrupted and shut her eyes. "The bastard's working for us. Like a fly on the wall, so he can pick up little pieces of information, poke around the house. We're so used to seeing guys hauling lumber, we wouldn't give him a second look."

"I think Holt already came to that conclusion." Suzanna lifted her hands again. "The question is, what do we do about it?"

"We give the construction boys a thrill tomorrow, and visit the west wing." Lilah straightened from the window seat. "I don't care what he's made himself look like this time, I'll know him if I get close enough." With that settled, she sat back. "Now, Suzanna, why don't you tell us when bad boy Bradford asked you to marry him?"

Suzanna grinned. "How did you know?"

"For an ex-cop, he's got great taste in jewelry." She took Suzanna's hand to show off the ring to her other sisters.

"Last night," she said as she was hugged and kissed and wept over. "We told the kids this morning."

"Aunt Coco's going to go through the roof." C.C. gave Suzanna another squeeze. "All four of us in a matter of months. She'll be in matchmaker heaven."

"All we need now is to get that creep behind bars and find the emeralds." Amanda dashed a tear away. "Oh, no! Do you realize what this means?"

"It means you have to organize another wedding," Suzanna answered.

"Not just that. It means we're going to be stuck with Aunt Colleen at least until the last handful of rice gets tossed."

* * *

Holt returned to The Towers in a foul mood. They'd found the house. Empty. They had no doubt that Livingston was living there. Bending the law more than a little, he had broken in and given the place as meticulous a search as Livingston had given his cottage. They'd found the stolen Calhoun papers, the lists the thief had made and a copy of the original blueprints of The Towers.

They'd also found a typed copy of each woman's weekly schedule, along with handwritten comments that left no doubt as to the fact that Livingston had followed and observed each one of them. There was a well-ordered inventory of the rooms he had searched and the items he'd felt valuable enough to steal.

They had waited an hour for his return, then uneasy about leaving the women alone, had phoned in the information to Koogar. While the police staked out the rented house on Bar Island, Holt and his companions returned to The Towers.

It was only a matter of waiting now. That was something he had learned to do well in his years on the force. But now it wasn't a job, and every moment grated.

"Oh, my dear, dear boy." Coco flew at him the moment he stepped into the house. He caught her by her sturdy hips as she covered his face with kisses.

"Hey," was all he could manage as she wept against his shoulder. Her hair, he noted, was no longer gleaming black but fire-engine red. "What'd you do to your hair?"

"Oh, it was time for a change." She drew back to blow her nose into her hankie, then fell into his arms again. Helpless, he patted her back and looked at the grinning men around him for assistance.

"It looks okay," he assured her, wondering if that was what she was weeping about. "Really."

"You like it?" She pulled back again, fluffing at it. "I thought I needed a bit of dash, and red's so cheerful." She buried her face in the soggy hankie. "I'm so happy," she sobbed. "So very happy. I had hoped, you see. And the tea leaves indicated that it would all work out, but I couldn't help but worry. She's had such a dreadful time, and her sweet little babies, too. Now everything's going to be all right. I'd thought it might be Trent, but he and C.C. were so perfect. Then Sloan and Amanda. Then almost before I could blink, our dear Max and Lilah. Is it any wonder I'm overwhelmed?"

"I guess not."

"To think, all those years ago when you'd bring lobsters to the back door. And that time you changed a tire for me and were too proud to even let me thank you. And now, now, you're going to marry my baby."

"Congratulations." Trent grinned and slapped Holt on the back while Max dug out a fresh handkerchief for Coco.

"Welcome to the family." Sloan offered a hand. "I guess you know what you're getting into."

Holt studied the weeping Coco. "I'm getting the picture."

"Stop all that caterwauling." Colleen clumped down the stairs. "I could hear you wailing all the way up in my room. For heaven's sake, take that mess into the kitchen." She gestured with her cane. "Pour some tea into her until she pulls herself together. Out, all of you," she added. "I want to talk to this boy here."

Like rats deserting a sinking ship, Holt thought as they left him alone. Gesturing for him to follow, Colleen strode into the parlor.

"So, you think you're going to marry my grand-niece."

"No. I am going to marry her."

She sniffed. Damned if she didn't like the boy. "I'll tell

you this, if you don't do better by her than that scum she had before, you'll answer to me." She settled into a chair. "What are your prospects?"

"My what?"

"Your prospects," she said impatiently. "Don't think you're going to latch on to my money when you latch on to her."

His eyes narrowed, pleasing her. "You can take your money and—"

"Very good," she said with an approving nod. "How do you intend to keep her?"

"She doesn't need to be kept." He whirled around the room. "And she doesn't need you or anyone else poking into her business. She's managed just fine on her own, better than fine. She came out of hell and managed to put her life together, take care of the kids and start a business. The only thing that's going to change is that she's going to stop working herself into the ground, and the kids'll have someone who wants to be their father. Maybe I won't be able to give her diamonds and take her to fancy dinner parties, but I'll make her happy."

Colleen tapped her fingers on the head of her cane. "You'll do. If your grandfather was anything like you, it's no wonder my mother loved him. So..." She started to rise, then saw the portrait over the mantel. Where her father's stern face had been was her mother's lovely one. "What's that doing there?"

Holt dipped his hands into his pockets. "It seemed to me that was where it belonged. That's where my grandfather would have wanted it."

Colleen eased herself back into the chair. "Thank you." Her voice was strained, but her eyes remained fierce. "Now go away. I want to be alone."

He left her, amazed that he was growing fond of her. Though he didn't look forward to another scene, he started toward the kitchen to ask Coco where he could find Suzanna.

But he found her himself, following the music that drifted down the hall. She was sitting at a piano, playing some rich, haunting melody he didn't recognize. Though the music was sad, there was a smile on her lips and one in her eyes. When she looked up, her fingers stilled, but the smile remained.

"I didn't know you played."

"We all had lessons. I was the only one they stuck with." She reached out a hand for his. "I was hoping we'd have a minute alone, so I could tell you how wonderful you were with the kids this morning."

With his fingers meshed with hers, he studied the ring he'd given her. "I was nervous." He laughed a little. "I didn't know how they'd take it. When Jenny asked if she could call me Daddy...it's funny how fast you can fall in love. Suzanna." He kept toying with her hands, studying the ring. "I think I understand now what a parent would feel, what he'd go through to make sure his kids were safe. I'd like to have more. I know you'd need to think about it, and I don't want you to feel that I would care less about Alex and Jenny."

"I don't have to think about it." She pressed a kiss to his cheek. "I've always wanted a big family."

He drew her close so her head rested on his shoulder. "Suzanna, do you know where the nursery was when Bianca lived here?"

"On the third floor of the east wing. It's been used as a storeroom as long as I can remember." She straightened. "You think she hid the necklace there?"

"I think she hid them somewhere Fergus wouldn't look, and I can't see him spending a lot of time in the nursery."

"No, but you'd think someone would have come across them. I don't know why I say that," she corrected. "The place is filled with boxes and old furniture. The Tower's version of a garage sale."

"Show me."

It was worse than he'd imagined. Even overlooking the cobwebs and dust, it was a mess. Boxes, crates, rolled-up rugs, broken tables, shadeless lamps stood, sat or reclined over every inch of space. Speechless, he turned to Suzanna who offered a sheepish grin.

"A lot of stuff collects in eighty-odd years," she told him. "Most of what's valuable's been culled out, and a lot of that was sold when we were—well, when things were difficult. This floor's been closed off for a long time, since we couldn't afford to heat it. We had to concentrate on keeping up the living space. Once we got everything under some kind of control, we were going to kind of attack the other sections a room at a time."

"You need a bulldozer."

"No, just time and elbow grease. We had plenty of the latter, but not nearly enough of the former. Over the last couple of months, we've gone through a lot of the old rooms, inch by inch, but it's a slow process."

"Then we might as well get started."

They worked for two grueling and dirty hours. They found a tattered parasol, an amazing collection of nineteenth-century erotica, a trunk full of musty clothes from the twenties and a box of warped phonograph records. There was also a crate filled with toys, a miniature locomotive, a sad, faded rag doll, assorted yo-yos and tops. Among them was a set of lovely old fairy-tale prints that Suzanna set aside.

"For our nursery," she told him. "Look." She held up a

yellow christening gown. "It might have been my grandfather's."

"You'd have thought this stuff would have been packed up with more care."

"I don't think Fergus ran a very tidy household after Bianca died. If any of this stuff belonged to his children, I'd wager the nanny bundled it away. He wouldn't have cared enough."

"No." He pulled a cobweb out of her hair. "Listen, why don't you take a break?"

"I'm fine."

It was useless to remind her that she'd been working all day, so he used another tactic. "I could use a drink. You think Coco's got anything cold in the refrigerator—maybe a sandwich to go with it?"

"Sure. I'll go check."

He knew that her aunt would insist on putting the quick meal together, and Suzanna would get that much time to sit and do nothing. "Two sandwiches," he added, and kissed her.

"Right." She rose, stretching her back. "It's sad to think about those three children, lying in here at night knowing their mother wasn't going to come and tuck them in again. Speaking of which, I'd better tuck in my own before I come back."

"Take your time." He was already headfirst in another crate.

She started out, thinking wistfully of Bianca's babies. Little Sean, who'd barely have been toddling, Ethan, who would grow up to father her father, Colleen, who was even now downstairs surely finding fault with something Coco had done. How the woman had ever been a sweet little girl...

A little girl, Suzanna thought, stopping on the second-floor landing. The oldest girl who would have been five or six when her mother died. Suzanna detoured and knocked on her great-aunt's door.

"Come in, damn it. I'm not getting up."

"Aunt Colleen." She stepped, amused to see the old woman was engrossed in a romance novel. "I'm sorry to disturb you."

"Why? No one else is."

Suzanna bit the tip of her tongue. "I was just wondering, the summer...that last summer, were you still in the nursery with your brothers?"

"I wasn't a baby, no need for a nursery."

"So you had your own room," Suzanna prompted, struggling to contain the excitement. "Near the nursery?"

"At the other end of the east wing. There was the nursery, then Nanny's room, the children's bath, and the three rooms kept for children of guests. I had the corner room at the top of the stairs." She frowned down at her book. "The next summer, I moved into one of the guest rooms. I didn't want to sleep in the room my mother had decorated for me, knowing she wouldn't come back to it."

"I'm sorry. When Bianca told you that you were going away, did she come to your room?"

"Yes. She let me pick out a few of my favorite dresses, then she packed them herself."

"Then after—I suppose they were unpacked again."

"I never wore those dresses again. I never wanted to. Shoved the trunk under my bed."

"I see." So there was hope. "Thank you."

"Moth-eaten by now," Colleen grumbled as Suzanna went out again. She thought of her favorite white muslin with its blue satin sash and with a sigh got up to walk to the terrace.

Dusk was coming early, she thought. Storm brewing. She could smell it in the wind, see it in the bad-tempered clouds already blocking the sun.

Suzanna raced up the stairs again. The sandwiches would

have to wait. She pushed open the door of Colleen's old room. It too had been consigned to storage, but being smaller than the nursery wasn't as cramped. The wallpaper, perhaps the same that Bianca had picked for her daughter, was faded and spotted, but Suzanna could still see the delicate pattern of rosebuds and violets.

She didn't bother with the cases or boxes, but dragged or pushed them aside. She was looking for a traveling trunk, suitable for a young girl. What better place? she thought as she pushed aside a crate marked Winter Draperies. Fergus hadn't cared for his daughter. He would hardly have bothered to look through a trunk of dresses, particularly when that trunk had been shoved out of sight by a traumatized young girl.

It had no doubt been opened in later years. Perhaps someone—Suzanna's own mother?—had shaken out a dress or two, then finding them quaint but useless, had designated them to storage.

It could be anywhere, of course, she mused. But what better place to start than the source?

Her heart pounded dully as she stumbled across an old leather-strapped truck. Pulling it open, she found bolts of material carefully folded in tissue. But no little girl's dresses. And no emeralds.

Because the light was growing dim, she rose and started toward the door. She would get Holt, and a flashlight, before continuing. In the gloom, she rapped her shin sharply. Swearing, she looked down and saw the small trunk.

It had once been a glistening white, but now it was dull with age and dust. It had been shoved to the side, piled with other boxes and nearly hidden by them and a faded tapestry. Kneeling in the half-light, Suzanna uncovered it. She flexed her unsteady fingers then opened the lid.

There was a smell of lavender, sealed inside perhaps for

decades. She lifted the first dress, a frilly white muslin, going ivory with time and banded by a faded blue satin sash. Suzanna set it carefully aside and drew out another. There were leggings and ribbons, pretty bows and a lacy nightie. And there, at the bottom, beside a small stuffed bear, a box and a book.

Suzanna put a trembling hand to her lips, then slowly reached down to lift the book.

Her journal, she thought as tears misted her eyes. Bianca's journal. Hardly daring to breathe, she turned the first page.

Bar Harbor, June 12, 1912
I saw him on the cliffs, overlooking Frenchman Bay

Suzanna let out an unsteady breath and laid the book in her lap. This was not for her to read alone. It would wait for her family. Heart pounding, she reached down to take the box from the trunk. She knew before she opened it. She could feel the change in the room, the trembling of the air. As the first tear slid down her cheek, she opened the lid and uncovered Bianca's emeralds.

They pulsed like green suns, throbbing with life and passion. She lifted the necklace, the glorious three tiers, and felt the heat on her hands. Hidden eighty years before, in hope and desperation, they were now free. The gloom that filled the room was no match for them.

As she knelt, the necklace dripping from her fingers, she reached into the box and took out the matching earrings. Strange, she thought. She'd all but forgotten them. They were lovely, exquisite, but the necklace dominated. It was made to dominate.

Stunned, she stared down at the power in her hands. They weren't just gems, she realized. They were far from being simply beautiful stones. They were Bianca's passions and hopes and dreams. From the time she had placed them in the box until now, when they had been lifted out by her descendant, they had waited to see the light again.

"Oh, Bianca."

"A charming sight."

Her head jerked up at the voice. He stood in the doorway, hardly more than a shadow. When he stepped into the room, she saw the glint of the gun in his hand.

"Patience pays off," Livingston said. "I watched you and the cop go into the room down the hall. I've been losing quite a bit of sleep wandering these rooms at night."

As he came closer, she stared at him. He didn't look like the man she remembered. His coloring was wrong, even the shape of his face. She rose very slowly, clutching the book and earrings in one hand, the necklace in the other.

"You don't recognize me. But I know you. I know all of you. You're Suzanna, just one of the Calhouns who owes me quite a bit."

"I don't know what you're talking about."

"Three months of my time, and not a little trouble. Then there was the loss of Hawkins, of course. He wasn't much of a partner, but he was mine. Just as those are mine." He looked down at the necklace and his mouth watered. They dazzled him. More than he had dreamed, more than he had imagined. Everything he wanted. His fingers trembled lightly on the gun as he reached out. Suzanna jerked away. He lifted a brow. "Do you really think you can keep them from me? They're meant to be mine. And when they are, everything they are will be mine."

He stepped closer, and as she looked around for the best route of escape, his hand closed over her hair. "Some stones have power," he told her softly. "Tragedy seeps into them, making them stronger. Death and grief. It hones them. Hawkins didn't understand that, but he was a simple man."

And the one she was facing was a mad one. "The necklace belongs to the Calhouns. It always has. It always will."

He jerked her hair hard and fast. She would have yelped, but the gun was now pressed against the racing pulse in her throat. "It belongs to me. Because I've been clever enough, I've been determined enough to wait for it. The moment I read about it, I knew. Now tonight, it's done."

She wasn't certain what she would have done—given it to him, tried to reason. But at the moment, her little girl moved into the doorway. "Mom." Her voice trembled as she rubbed her eyes. "It's thundering. You're supposed to come get me when it thunders."

It happened fast. He turned, swinging the gun. With all her strength, Suzanna hurled herself at him, blocking his aim. "Run!" she screamed to Jenny. "Run down the hall to Holt." She shoved, and raced after her daughter. The decision had to be made the minute she hit the doorway. As she watched Jenny streak toward the right and—she hoped—safety, Suzanna plunged in the opposite direction.

He would follow her, not the child, she told herself. Because she still had the necklace. The next decision had to be made at the steps. To go down to her family and risk them. Or to go up, alone.

She was halfway up the stairs when she heard him pounding behind her. She jerked in shock as a bullet plowed into the plaster an inch from her shoulder.

Breathless, she streaked up, only now hearing the boom of thunder that had frightened Jenny and made her look for her mother. Her single thought was to put as much distance between the madman behind her and her child. Her feet clattered on the winding metal staircase that led to Bianca's tower.

His fingers darted through the open treads and snatched at her ankle. With a sound of terror and fury, she kicked out, dislodging them, then stumbled up the rest of the way. The door was shut. She nearly wept as she threw her weight against the thick wood. It gave, with painful slowness, then allowed her to fall inside. But before she could slam it closed, he was hurtling in.

She braced, certain it would be only seconds before she felt the bullet. He was panting, sweating, his eyes glazed. At the corner of his mouth, a muscle ticked and jerked. "Give it to me." The gun shook as he advanced on her. A flash of lightning had him looking wildly around the shadowy room. "Give it to me now."

He's afraid, she realized. Of this room. "You've been in here before."

He had, only once, and had run out again, terrified. There was something here, something that hated him. It crawled cold as ice along his skin. "Give me the necklace, or I'll just kill you and take it."

"This was her room," Suzanna murmured, keeping her eyes on his. "Bianca's room. She died when her husband threw her from that window."

Unable to resist, he looked at the glass, dark with gloom, then away again.

"She still comes here, to wait, and to watch the cliffs." She heard, as she had known she would, the sound of Holt racing up the steps. "She's here now. Take them." She held the emeralds out. "But she won't let you leave with them."

His face was bone white and sheened with sweat as he reached for the necklace. He gripped it, but rather than the heat Suzanna had felt, he felt only cold. And a terror.

"They're mine now." He shivered and stumbled.

"Suzanna," Holt said quietly from the doorway. "Move

away from him." His weapon was drawn, gripped in both hands. "Move away," he repeated. "Slow."

She took one step back, then two, but Livingston paid no attention to her. He was wiping his gun hand over his dry lips.

"It's over," Holt told him. "Drop the gun, kick it aside." But Livingston continued to stare at the necklace, breathing raggedly. "Drop it." Braced, Holt moved closer. "Get out, Suzanna."

"No, I'm not leaving you."

He didn't have time to swear at her. Though he was prepared to kill, he could see that the man was no longer concerned with his weapon, or with escape. Instead, Livingston merely stared down at the emeralds and trembled.

With his eyes trained on Livingston, Holt reached up to grasp the wrist of his gun hand. "It's over," he said again.

"It's mine." Wild with rage and fear, Livingston lunged. He fired once into the ceiling before Holt disarmed him. Even then he struggled, but the struggle was brief. With the next crash of thunder, he howled, striking out wildly even as the others raced into the room. Disoriented or terrified, stunned by Holt's blow to his jaw or no longer sane, he whirled.

There was the crash of breaking glass. Then a sound Suzanna would never forget. A man's horrified scream. Even as Holt leaped forward to try to save him, Livingston pinwheeled through the broken window and tumbled to the rain-swept rock below.

"My God." Suzanna pressed back against the wall, her hands over her mouth to stop her own screams. There were arms around her, a babble of voices.

Her family poured into the tower room. She bent to her children, pressing kisses on their cheeks. "It's all right," she soothed. "It's all right now. There's nothing to be afraid of."

She looked up at Holt. He stood facing her, the black space at his back, the glitter of emeralds at his feet. "Everything's all right now. I'm going to take you downstairs."

Holt pushed the gun back in its holster. "We'll take them down."

An hour later, when the children were soothed and sleeping, he took her by the arm and pulled her out on the terrace. All the fear and rage he'd felt since Jenny had run crying down the hallway came pouring out.

"What the hell did you think you were doing?"

"I had to keep him away from Jenny." She thought she was calm, but her hands began to shake. "I suddenly had an idea about the emeralds. It was so simple, really. And I found them. Then he was there—and Jenny. He had a gun, and God, oh God, I thought he would kill her."

"All right, all right," Holt said. Suzanna didn't choke back the tears this time, but clung to him as they shuddered out of her. "The kids are fine, Suzanna. Nobody's going to hurt them. Or you."

"I didn't know what else to do. I wasn't trying to be brave or stupid."

"You were both. I love you." He framed her face in his hands and kissed her. "Did he hurt you?"

"No." She sniffled a little and wiped her eyes. "He chased me up there, and then...he snapped. You saw how he was when you came in."

"Yeah." Two feet away from her, with a gun in his hand. Holt's fingers tightened on her shoulders. "Don't you ever scare me like that again."

"It's a deal." She rubbed her cheek against his, for comfort and for love. "It's really over now, isn't it?"

He kissed the top of her head. "It's just beginning."

Epilogue

It was late when the family gathered together in the parlor. The police had finally finished and left them alone. They were drawn together, a solid, united front beneath the portrait of Bianca.

Colleen sat, a dog at her feet, the emeralds in her lap. She had shed no tears when Suzanna had explained how and where she had found them, but took comfort in having that small, precious memory of her mother.

There was no talk of death.

Holt keep Suzanna close, his arm firm around her. The storm had passed, and the moon had risen. The parlor was washed with light. The only sound was Suzanna's soft, clear voice as she read from Bianca's journal.

She turned the last page and spoke of Bianca's thoughts as she'd prepared to hide the emeralds.

"'I didn't think of their monetary value as I took them out, held them in my hands and watched them gleam in the light of the lamp. They would be a legacy for my children, and their children, a symbol of freedom, and of hope. And with Christian, of love.

"'As dawn broke, I decided to put them, together with this journal, in a safe place until I joined Christian again.'"

Slowly, quietly Suzanna closed the book. "I think she's with him now. That they're with each other."

She smiled when Holt's fingers gripped hers. Looking around the room, she saw her sisters, the men they loved, her aunt smiling through tears, and Bianca's daughter, gazing up at the portrait that had been painted with unconquerable love.

"It was Bianca, more than the emeralds, who brought us all together. I like to think that by finding them, by bringing them back, we've helped them find each other."

Beyond the house, the moon glimmered on the cliffs far above where the sea churned and fought with the rocks. The wind whispered through the wild roses and warmed the lovers who walked there.

* * * * *